SECRECY

BELVA PLAIN

Thorndike Press • Chivers Press
Thorndike, Maine USA   Bath, England

This Large Print edition is published by Thorndike Press, USA and by Chivers Press, England.

Published in 1997 in the U.S. by arrangement with Delacorte Press, an imprint of Dell Publishing, a division of Bantam Doubleday Dell Publishing Group, Inc.

Published in 1998 in the U.K. by arrangement with Hodder and Stoughton Ltd.

U.S.   Hardcover   0-7862-1219-5 (Basic Series Edition)
U.S.   Softcover   0-7862-1220-9
U.K.   Hardcover   0-7540-1086-4 (Windsor Large Print)
U.K.   Softcover   0-7540-2062-2 (Paragon Large Print)

The text of this Large Print edition is unabridged.
Other aspects of the book may vary from the original edition.

Set in 16 pt. Plantin by Minnie B. Raven.

Printed in the United States on permanent paper.

British Library Cataloguing in Publication Data available

Library of Congress Cataloging in Publication Data
Plain, Belva.
    Secrecy / Belva Plain.
        p.   cm.
    ISBN 0-7862-1219-5 (lg. print : hc : alk. paper)
    ISBN 0-7862-1220-9 (lg. print : sc : alk. paper)
    1. Large type books.   I. Title.
    [PS3566.L254S43   1997b]
    813'.54—dc21   97-28019

SECRECY

PART ONE

1986

ONE

A door slammed so hard that the glass prisms on the hall light clashed in alarm. Someone very angry had either gone into a room or had left it. Then silence, thick and ominous, fell back. When the silence began to ring, Charlotte pulled the pillow around her ears.

They were arguing again. But they would get over it as they always did. After a while her mother, who was undoubtedly the one who had slammed the door, would quiet down. She wondered whether other people's parents lived like this.

"Childish," said Emmabrown, talking to her nephew the mailman at the front door. "Charlotte's fourteen, and she has more sense in her little finger than her mother has in her whole body."

Emmabrown — that being the name Charlotte herself had bestowed — was proud of her connection with the family; she had kept house for three generations of the Daweses, and liked to talk about their affairs. Dad was her favorite. On the telephone while Charlotte eavesdropped, she grumbled and boasted to her friends.

9

"I knew Bill and Cliff when those two boys were learning to talk. Bill was the smart one, good natured, too, a real pleasure. So then he goes to Europe one summer for some studies, Lord knows why you have to go there to study, but anyway he did, and comes home three months later married to this Elena, she just twenty and he twenty-two. Kids, they were. The family wasn't too happy about it, either, I can tell you. The one good thing was she's no gold digger. She's an orphan, left with a pile of money of her own. A real good-looker with a foreign accent — Italian — and a figure like a movie star. Pretty face too. Big eyes and big smile. You can see why he fell for her. She winds him around her little finger."

Did she really? Well, maybe. Dad didn't like to fight with people. Sometimes he didn't even answer back, which made Mama more angry. *Mama.* People called their mothers *Mom,* but she wanted to be called Mama, with the accent on the end. Silly. Stubborn. In her private thoughts Charlotte called her *Elena.*

It was cold, even under the quilt. She could feel the October wind coming through the walls. No, she thought then, it's not coming through the walls; the cold is inside me. It's because I'm scared, although I should be used to all this, shouldn't I?

Now there were voices in the hall, barely loud enough to be heard. Dad's voice rumbled.

"What do I do that you don't like?"

"Nothing."

"Nothing? You like everything I do? I take it you like everything about me, then?"

Laughter. "No. Oh, no."

Pause. "Oh, good God, Elena, will you open your mouth and say specifically what's wrong today? Specifically?"

"A lot of things. Nothing. I don't know."

"You really don't know anything, do you?"

"That's true. I don't know anything."

"Well, if you didn't spend all your days at the country club, you might know something. I joined for your sake, but I didn't think you were going to make a second home of the place."

"And what am I supposed to do with myself? Get elected to the Board of Education? And the Committee for the Environment? I'm not you, Bill. Those aren't my thing. I wouldn't fit."

That was true. She wouldn't fit. She not only looked different from most other girls' mothers with their sweaters and moccasins and Jeeps, but she was different. That's

11

probably why she had no friends among the PTA ladies; they didn't like her.

But their husbands do, Charlotte thought, thinking, too, how people would be surprised if they knew how much their children noticed: glances, little greetings on a Saturday morning at the post office or at the school play.

They had gone into their room now, which was just across the hall, yet she was still able to hear. They were assuming that she was asleep.

"Get busy with worthwhile things, Elena, and you'll be happier."

"I'll be happier when I get away from this town, this city, whatever you call it. Of all the places in America, I have to end up in New England in a dying factory town. Fifteen years in this town. 'A country town,' you said, and I imagined something with charm, something like Tuscany, with vineyards and old stone houses. Fifteen years in this place."

"You've been living pretty darn well in this place."

"The winter hasn't even begun and I'm already freezing."

Dad sighed. "Oh, what the hell do you want, Elena?"

"I want to go to Florida, to rent a place

12

for a few months."

"That's ridiculous. Charlotte has school."

"We can get tutors for her there. She'd learn more than she would here in school."

"Ridiculous!"

"We'll leave her here with Emmabrown. We could shorten our time to six weeks."

"You know all the trouble we've been having with the business. Anyway, I wouldn't leave her for six weeks, no matter what."

"All right, Bill, I may just go by myself."

"You do that."

Dad's anger had petered out, and he was tired. The door closed.

Maybe now I can sleep, Charlotte thought. Suddenly she remembered to put her hand on her heart and feel whether it was beating faster. It was. It always did, whenever they fought.

Even the night before Uncle Cliff's wedding, they had to fight. Even that day they had to spoil.

TWO

The chairs were set in rows, and there were flowers in tall holders where the bride and groom were to stand, so that it felt like being in church, or would have felt like it, if the two collies, Rob and Roy, hadn't been there too. Somehow, Charlotte had known that Uncle Cliff would not want a solemn atmosphere, nor would Claudia, whom he was marrying. They were not what Charlotte called "fancy" people.

They suited this house, where Dad had grown up and had lived until he married and had built a new house for Elena, a modern one where things were orderly and shining. Here there were unexpected nooks, back stairs, porches, dog beds, untidy flowering plants on the windowsills, and raincoats on the clothes tree in the hall.

"The best house in town," Emmabrown scoffed, "and he had to move out of it because she wanted something modern."

Emmabrown, in black silk, sat now in the front row next to Charlotte. Elena was on Charlotte's other side, while Dad, as best man, stood with the minister and Uncle Cliff, waiting for Claudia.

14

Elena's neighbor inquired, "Who's to be maid of honor?"

"No maid. Her son Ted."

"Her son? That's unusual."

"Claudia is unconventional. But she's very nice, and just right for Cliff."

"She's had a hard life, I hear."

"Oh, terribly. Her husband was shot to death at his office. She came here from Chicago to make a fresh start. Change of scene, you know."

Elena was in a satisfied mood this morning. She liked being at places when you dressed up and were admired. She liked big, sociable occasions. Her hands, with their beautiful rings, rested quietly on her dark green velvet skirt. Emmabrown was looking at the skirt, which ended several inches above Elena's knees.

"Posture," Elena whispered. "Do sit up straight, Charlotte. And when the ceremony is over, go into the guest bathroom and comb the back of your hair." She smiled. "I know I'm nagging you, but it's for your own good, so don't be angry at me, darling."

The smile and the *darling* gave Charlotte a soft feeling in her chest. Dad always told her she was soft, and she knew she was, soft like him. Affection sometimes brought tears to her eyes. Elena's little nagging

15

could be affectionate, so this morning she didn't mind it so much. She was even grateful for it.

Now somebody at the back of the room began the bridal march on the piano, and there on the arm of her tall, dark-haired son came Claudia, blond and a little overweight in baby blue. Her face is all upturned, Charlotte thought, a lovely face, with lips curved up at the corners; even her eyes seemed to tilt a bit in the corners, as though they could either laugh or cry at any moment.

Uncle Cliff looked very serious, the minister smiled, and Dad winked at Charlotte.

"Isn't he handsome," Charlotte whispered.

"Who is?" Elena whispered back.

"Ted, her son."

"I thought you meant your father."

She can't be still angry at him, Charlotte thought, or she wouldn't have said that.

Then all whispering and rustling stopped as the minister began. "Dearly Beloved . . ."

Charlotte was feeling awe, as when music went shivering through her body. She sought a word: *profound.* Deep. Yes, that was it. The serious words and the serious expressions on all the faces made her wonder whether everyone was feeling what she was feeling.

16

Were they remembering something? Or wanting something?

Elena was remembering. *So little,* he had said. *So light,* lifting her from her feet into the air, as though the contrast between her smallness and his own tall bulk was a marvel. Yet his size and strength had been an immediate attraction to her. *At home they call me Big Bill,* he had told her, laughing. Then there had been his calm good nature, so mature, so manly. Of course, there had also been the excitement, the adventure, of going with him to America.

She watched him now with his courteous stance and eyes directed toward the clergyman. His eyes were large, opalescent, and rather beautiful, giving an impression of vagueness or inattention, so that you were often surprised to find that he had been listening, observing, and had missed nothing. He was a man of great intelligence; of that there could be no doubt. And yet he bored her. So many things bored her.

". . . forsaking all others until death do you part?"

Yes, Bill thought, that's certainly how it was. And then great changes take place. He knew she was looking at him now, contemplating — what? So he kept himself turned toward the minister. Still, he could see her

17

in his mind's eye: exquisite, doll-like, with black curls thickly massed, a too-heavy frame for the delicate, witty face.

They would have to control their war of words, have to keep firm hold for Charlotte's sake. Moving his head just an unnoticeable part of an inch, she entered his vision, this ponytailed, awkward product of two opposites. Tall and large-boned like himself, she had nothing of her mother in her that anyone could recognize. Listening, rapt, she displayed all her gentleness upon her face. So fragile, he thought, so trusting, so innocent! And then he withdrew the last, for who was ever really innocent at fourteen? Nevertheless, she must be guarded, shielded from all unnecessary pain.

"I pronounce you man and wife. . . ."

It was over. Then would come the greeting and kissing, the customary humorless jokes, and the aimless mingling until it was time to move into the dining room for lunch. Charlotte had been at a wedding once before, so she knew how it would be, and knew, too, that since there was no one of her age here, she had best take care of herself.

As soon as she was past the receiving line, she made her way to the hors d'oeuvres table, where immediately she spotted some of

18

her favorites: shrimp, tiny hot dogs, and those delicious little mushroom things. There, from a lookout station between the bar and the food, she stood with her heaped plate in hand, observing the room. It was fun to watch people and speculate about them when they didn't know they were being watched. Not that her opinions would bother anyone! She was as much removed from the adults' world as if she were three years old. So she surveyed the moving scene, expecting no attention and receiving none except once when Patsy Jersey's mother congratulated her for being on the high honor roll. Mrs. Jersey was clearly a loner; shy and uncertain, she was a little brown hen on the edge of the crowd. Mr. Jersey had been talking to Elena for the last ten minutes, and they were laughing. Elena sparkled, with diamonds in her ears and on her wrists. Charlotte felt sorry for Mrs. Jersey.

All around her people came, clustered, and went away, leaving their remarks hanging in the air.

"Yes, it's nice to see Cliff married at last. It's time, though. He must be near forty."

". . . a lovely woman. She had that bookstore over in Ridgedale, you know. That's how he met her."

"The son's a good-looking kid, isn't he?"

"Oh, my goodness, he's probably the most popular boy in the school. Not much of a student, but a football star and the idol of the girls."

"Not very friendly, I thought."

"Oh, well, at seventeen or eighteen —"

"Goodness," Elena exclaimed, "you're really not eating all that before the luncheon, Charlotte?"

"I'm hungry, Mama."

"Yes, but before you know it, you'll be way overweight, and with your build you can't afford an extra ounce of fat. Again, dear, go in and redo your ponytail before we sit down to lunch. It's coming loose. Are you having a good time?"

"Not especially."

"Well, of course not, standing here all by yourself. You need to learn to mingle."

Mingle, said Charlotte in scorn and silence. In front of the mirror in the bathroom she glimpsed herself: dirty blond, with pale skin and light eyes, Dad's eyes, of no particular color. At least the braces were off her teeth, thank God. Otherwise, there was little to be said about her. Stuffed with food now, she wished she could go home.

She was seated, naturally, at the family table among a handful of middle-aged cousins and some of Uncle Cliff's close friends. Also quite naturally, they had put her next to Ted.

"You two are related now," Claudia said happily, "so you need to get acquainted."

You could tell how happy she was and that she wanted everybody else to be the same. Charlotte could not have said how she knew this. It was simply that she felt a warmth in Claudia; maybe it came from her voice or her gestures, which were unhurried and peaceful. But she ought to have known that Ted would have no interest in Charlotte.

With obvious reluctance he asked her what grade she was in.

"Ninth."

His bright eyes, black olives, swept over Charlotte and dismissed her. Yet, since he still had to say something more, he inquired who her homeroom teacher was. "I hope not Mr. Hudson. He stinks."

"I don't go to public school."

She shouldn't have said that. The words had come out as if she felt superior because of going to private school, and of course she hadn't meant that at all. Why did her words so often get tangled up this way? And she felt a hot flush on her cheeks.

"Where do you go?" he asked carelessly.

"The Lakewood School."

"Oh. All girls."

"Yes," she said.

He turned away to the man on his other side, who had begun a conversation about football. Naturally, that would be more interesting for him than anything Charlotte was able to talk about. Still, if she were beautiful, if she knew how to "mingle," as Elena had said, it might, in spite of her youth, be different.

So she sat silently, watching and listening as before. It was interesting how if you watched and listened carefully, things meant to be hidden became clear. You could tell when two people who were very polite to each other did not like each other.

"A wedding trip to Italy," Elena said in her bright voice. "How wonderful. You'll love it. I sometimes wonder how I ever could have left."

"I should imagine you left for your husband's sake," said a woman whom Charlotte recognized as the mother of one of the popular girls. Her mouth smiled at Elena while she reproved her.

Elena knew it too. Her shrug said: *Your opinions make no difference to me.* And she returned to her little flirtation with the man next to her.

Why was Dad not noticing? Perhaps he was but had too many other things to think about.

"After eighty years we have to close the plant," Uncle Cliff was remarking to someone. "And let me tell you, we feel the pain. But textiles are moving south, or else to Asia. You know what's happening."

Dad worried. When he caught Charlotte's glance, he smiled. But he worried.

Many things troubled Bill, even in the middle of a wedding feast. He wondered whether Charlotte had heard them quarreling last night. But even if she had not, she knew too much. You can't hide things when you're living next to each other in the same house. Even when you keep a surface calm, the current is felt, the undercurrent is palpable. How we suffer, some of us, and how our children suffer because of us!

His glance touched on Ted and moved to Claudia. Yes, he thought, regardless of her joy today, there is a shadow on her face. Ted is a problem for her. She may not even know it. She may not yet see, or perhaps never will see plainly, what I saw the first time I met him: the contemptuous swing of his walk, the sullen mouth, the narrow eyes, fast-shifting, never looking straight at your eyes. He is a fox. He can be cruel.

And then he thought: This is absurd. What am I, a mind-reader? It's only my mood that makes up such morbid fictions. . . . Elena and I will part. In spite of my best efforts, and I shall make them, it will happen, though I don't know when. And it will be so hard for Charlotte, my little Charlotte.

On the way home Bill remarked cheerfully, "It was a nice wedding, small and intimate. And I really do like Claudia."

"Yes, it was very pretty," Elena said. "If only Claudia knew how to dress!"

No one replied. The comment left an unpleasant sense of gloom, quite out of proportion to its importance.

After a while Bill said, "She's had to struggle for a living. I don't imagine she's had the time or the means to fuss much about clothes. Oh, look over there on the left — must be a dozen bluejays on that limb. I guess they plan to stay all winter."

Charlotte was familiar with this effort to keep a genial mood alive. Sometimes the effort seemed almost ridiculous, since it seldom worked. Elena laid her head back on the seat; her plump, glossy curls rested on her upturned collar; she had never ceased her animated talk all through the day, but now she was silent.

And soundlessly, Charlotte implored: Say something, answer him. Inside, near her stomach, or perhaps actually within her stomach, things quivered.

Bill cried out, "Do I scc snowflakes?"

The day had started out mild, but while they had been indoors, the sky had gone gray and cold. Hard, Charlotte thought, like an iron lid.

"They've been predicting an early winter," Bill resumed, "and I think I've noticed squirrels doing more scurrying for food than usual. Have you noticed, Charlotte?"

"No, but I'll watch out tomorrow."

"How I dread the winter." Elena sighed. "This miserable climate. Just getting out of bed in the morning — my flesh shrinks to think of it. Where are you going, Bill? I thought we were going straight home."

"I want to take a look at the plant first."

"What on earth for?"

"Sentimental reasons, I suppose."

From where the car stopped on the opposite bank of the river, the old Dawes Textile Building looked as if it had been long abandoned, although it had only been closed for the last two months. Already it was a relic, Bill thought ruefully, one of a string of old industries on countless East Coast rivers that the century had passed by. Of its many small-paned, old-fashioned windows a good number, tempting targets for stone-throwing boys, were already smashed. Soon rain and snow would rot the interior. Birds and rats would nest unless — unless a buyer should come along and rescue it. But there was a singular dearth of buyers for a place like this one, three floors high, eighty years old, four acres square with another thirty acres, mostly swampland, behind it. In front of it the river rolled toward the distant ocean. There was no sign of life in any direction. For a few moments they all sat staring into the faded afternoon.

Suddenly Elena said, "No one's ever going to buy this thing. Kingsley is a decaying town. In fact, it's decayed already. No one's built anything here since 1890 except for the mall out on the highway."

Bill corrected her. "That's not quite true."

"Well, you should have sold out five years ago to the conglomerate. Now you're stuck with it."

"You know very well why we didn't. We held on, tried to keep going to save our people's jobs."

"So now they're unemployed anyway. You're too soft, Bill. You always have been. A rugged six feet four, and soft inside. My God, when I remember the fuss you made about Mrs. Boland! And she survived, didn't she?"

He did not say that she had survived because Cliff and he had given her a nest egg large enough for her to live on the interest it paid. Instead, he said, "Mrs. B. was my father's secretary before she was mine. She was an old widow with an older widowed mother in a wheelchair, for God's sake. Of course we 'made a fuss,' as you call it." And then, giving way unwillingly to his impatience, he added, "Claudia would understand. She's been there herself."

"Oh, Claudia," Elena mocked.

Something broke in Charlotte. "Why don't you stop?" she cried. "You've been fighting over this business ever since I was in fifth grade."

Bill said instantly, "You're right. How about dropping the subject, going home, and getting something to eat? It's been a long time since lunch. We'll light a fire and maybe toast some marshmallows."

"That'll be nice," Elena agreed. She turned around and smiled at Charlotte. "People said lovely things about you, darling. About how smart you are in school and what a pleasant girl you are. I was really proud."

It was dark when they reached home.

Darkness in the fall felt different from the summer dark, which, gauzy and shot through with skylight, invited you to stay outside in it. Now it was thick and heavy here, pressing against the black windows as if it were trying to get in. Charlotte spread out her hands before the fire, not because she was cold, but because it was friendly.

She had been eating her way through sandwiches, apples, and marshmallows, when Elena exclaimed, "Where do you put all that food?"

"In my stomach," she answered.

"I can't believe it," Elena still exclaimed, although she often described herself as one who never gained an ounce and could afford to be greedy.

"Charlotte is growing," Bill said, putting a stop to the subject.

After that they talked, the two parents, quietly and sensibly as people should. Charlotte, reading a magazine, had no interest in what they were saying. It was just good that they were being nice together. Maybe this niceness would last for a long time, for two or three weeks, as it often did. Only once did she come to attention, when Elena said something about Florida and was stopped by Dad's look of warning: *Not now. Not in front of Charlotte,* it meant.

So the quiet talk resumed. Maybe, then, everything would be all right? And her butterflies would stop flickering? Or maybe she should simply get used to the way things were and not always be so scared that something was going to *happen*.

Cliff and Claudia were also having a tray before their fire, eating leftovers and drinking wine. The guests were gone, the caterers had made everything tidy again, and Ted had gone out with friends, leaving the newlywed couple alone in their home. Their relationship now, after two years, was at last official under one roof.

"I can't believe it's over," Claudia said.

"It's just beginning. We have to make an early start for the Boston airport tomorrow. Then, Rome, here we come."

Claudia laid her hand over Cliff's. "I almost hate to leave this house. You can't know how thrilled I am. You and this wonderful house — I'm in paradise."

"It's funny," he said, "I've lived all my life here, and although I know it's a pretty big place, I never felt that it was too big until you came along. I used to fill it up with business guests, or visiting relatives, and was glad to have the space. But after the day I walked into that bookstore and got to know you, this house became as empty as a strange hotel." He raised her hand and kissed it. "I'd never realized I was lonesome."

"Thirty-eight years and never married —"

He laughed. "Until I found the irresistible woman." And then, becoming suddenly grave, he said, "I want all your worries to be over. Now that you're rid of the store, I want you to stay home here and relax. Do nothing."

"I can't imagine 'doing nothing,' Cliff."

"You've got that little heart problem —"

"For which exercise and work are the best medicines."

"Well, cook some good meals, do some volunteering, and that's work enough. I order you."

She was not used to being cared for this way, and she felt a kind of astonishment that these things should be happening to her. "It's the first time —" She broke off. "This is so wonderful for Ted too. I hope you'll like him, Cliff, now that you'll be getting to know him. He's not easy to know, maybe because of not having had a father since he was four. A boy needs a father, even at eighteen." She heard herself being apologetic, yet could not help it. "Today must have been a difficult one for him. I'm sure he felt uncomfortable, although he didn't say so.

He's rather silent, anyway."

"Think nothing of it. As to being silent, I'm used to that. In case you haven't noticed, I'm the talkative one in my small family. Bill's the silent thinker."

"I like Bill. You can feel how solid he is. Dependable."

"And what do you think of her?"

"She's rather charming," Claudia responded. It behooved a new wife to be uncritical.

"Yes, but not my type."

"Is she Bill's type, do you think?"

"Honey, you're asking because you can see she isn't. She's a little flirt — a harmless one, I think. I hope."

"But he loves her?"

Cliff shrugged. "I told you, he's my silent brother. He certainly wouldn't tell me if he didn't love her."

"It's possible he doesn't know whether he does or not."

"You're pretty sharp, Mrs. Dawes. But what makes you say that?"

"The few times I've been with them, I've felt that he was trying somehow to please her and that they just weren't comfortable together."

"Not like you and me."

"No, not at all like you and me." She had

a long vision of evenings being comfortable together in this room, or under the trees on summer afternoons.

"The person who'll suffer from their discomfort will be Charlotte, naturally. She's a lovely child and she deserves better. I'm very fond of her." He paused. "Elena's going to Florida for a couple of months."

"Alone? That's odd, isn't it?"

"Well, I think so. But maybe it isn't."

She saw that Cliff was troubled, and that the subject ought to be dropped. "Let's go up," she said. "It's getting late."

Rob and Roy, as if they had understood, followed them up the stairs and started down the hall.

"Not that way," Cliff signaled. "That's Ted's room now, not mine. They'll sleep in the corner of our room. Here we are. All done over for you. Do you like it?"

The wide old bed was covered with a puffed quilt padded in sea-green and rose. The walls were painted in the same sea-green. A mound of shell-pink roses in an emerald bowl stood on a bedside table. And the air was fragrant. It was a room perfected for love, for sleeping side by side and for waking together on a new morning.

"Elena did the decorating. She left the walls bare because she knew you love paintings and you'll want to choose them for yourself."

"It's wonderful, Cliff. The color of the sea, like a grotto. I've never seen one, but I think it must be like this."

"You'll see a famous one in Capri. Now tell me, do you want to pretend you're a shy virgin bride and get undressed in the bathroom? Or shall I —"

"You shall. You shall right now."

No, she was hardly a shy virgin bride. Were there such anymore? Nevertheless, she had bought for this night the laciest lace that any virginal bride could want. What a pity, she thought, laughing at herself, that I'll not even get to put it on.

THREE

"Your father really could have come down this week," Elena said, applying sunblock to her nose.

"He couldn't. Some people were in town again to look at the plant and maybe buy it."

"Nobody's ever going to buy it. They might as well dynamite the place."

"That's silly."

"Well, of course it is. Dynamiting, I mean. But give up — give it to the town or something. Oh, well, come on in for a swim."

"I can't. I'm supposed to finish this whole book over vacation, and I'm going home the day after tomorrow."

"You haven't looked at it for the last ten minutes. What on earth have you been dreaming about?"

"I'm not dreaming."

"Gazing, then."

Elena wanted people to be as alert and busy as she was, even if busyness meant only applying makeup or talking on the telephone. You weren't supposed to sit and do nothing.

Charlotte answered patiently, her patience masking impatience, "I was looking at that boat."

"What about it? They're waiting their chance to slide into the lagoon."

"I was thinking how sinister it seems. It has a shark's pointed nose. And the cabin windows up front are like shark's eyes. I think maybe they run guns or drugs in it."

"You're a funny girl," Elena said. "Funny and lovable."

She sprang up. Other people seemed to struggle up from a beach chair, whereas she got onto her feet in one easy movement. Now she stretched out her arms as if to limber herself and yawned.

"This sun makes me sleepy. Okay, I'll be back soon."

Charlotte watched her. Other people watched her, too, for Elena was wearing a black string bikini and a red straw cartwheel hat, which she would leave at the water's edge. She had no objections to a tanned body, but always protected her face. No matter what Charlotte ever thought of her mother, even in those moments when she was filled with love for her, there was always a painful awareness of her mother's difference. And this went along with her own embarrassment over it. She certainly knew that teenagers like herself are often embarrassed by their parents. So was this normal of her or not? Her mind was always divided. A mother should just *be* there, the way one's bed is there, or one's shoes on the closet floor; you didn't have to *think* about them, did you?

Elena had already joined a group going into the water, or probably it was they who had joined her. Did she know everybody on this beach, and in the condominium, too, when they all sat around the pool in the late afternoon? It certainly seemed that way. The group was laughing now. Charlotte could even hear one man's loud whoop. Elena must have said something funny.

Actually, the week had been a success so far. All Charlotte's previous vacations had been in western or northern places, and this was the first time she had seen palm trees, the first time she had seen water as blue as this intense, vast blue. Elena had made friends with a family who were cruising on their own boat and had taken them out on it for a day. Yesterday they had been invited to somebody's enormous house for lunch; it had enormous lawns and white marble floors. Charlotte thought the house was too large and chilly to feel like anybody's home. But there had been two girls of her age there, and it had turned out to be a rather good day.

There was only one thing wrong with any of the days this week. That thing was Judd. He was always there.

Yet he might be a perfectly nice person, she argued now, and he probably was. It was indecent to dislike someone who had given you no reason. He was a friendly young man, very neat, and he had a beautiful convertible in which he drove them anywhere they wanted to go. Obviously, he liked Elena, and she was jolly with him. But that was hardly any reason to mind his presence; Elena was always especially jolly with men. She was candid about liking men. She always said, even to Dad, that men were easier to get along with. Well, maybe they are, Charlotte thought now. I haven't had experience, that's for sure.

"Look what's happened to the sky," Elena said, wrapping herself in a scarlet cover-up that matched the hat. "We're in for rain. It happens down here with no more than ten seconds' warning."

Clouds, massing and rolling, had turned the sky into a dull gray-brown ceiling. The day had gone sultry and heavy with heat.

"Let's go in. Judd's going to pick us up for lunch."

"Does he have to come along?" asked Charlotte. She hadn't intended to whine, yet the question came out that way.

Elena tossed her paraphernalia — sunglasses, lotions, sandals, magazines, purse, and collapsible umbrella — into a beach bag. "No, he doesn't have to," she said a trifle sharply. "But what's your objection?"

Charlotte shrugged. "I don't know. . . . Only, it might be fun not to have him along."

"That's not very kind. He's taking us out for real Maine lobster. Actually, it was his idea to do it for you because you said you liked real Maine lobster."

Rebuked, Charlotte gave no answer. They walked back across the road.

"Please don't let him see that he's not welcome, Charlotte."

She gave no answer to that either. As if she would be so disgusting as to hurt the man's feelings! *She's* the one who needs to be reminded, Charlotte thought. They had even had a tiny argument the other day when Elena was having a manicure. Charlotte, who had trailed along, had heard her talking to the manicurist about ranch mink versus wild mink, and it had seemed mean and boastful to speak about things that the other woman could not afford. Afterward, very gently, Charlotte had said so.

"Isn't that a little nervy of you to tell me what I should talk about?" Elena had responded.

"I don't mean to be nervy. I only felt sorry for her. I heard her talking about her children and how much things cost."

"Okay, you're like your father, and that's not all bad," Elena had said then, smiling to make up for her first irritation. "He takes note of every word a person says."

She thinks I'm odd, Charlotte thought suddenly. And perhaps I am, but at least Dad doesn't think I am.

"Let's hurry," Elena said. "I'm starved. Wear your white linen slacks. People dress a bit where we're going."

The two bedrooms were separated by a square hall, small enough to allow conversation between them.

"Judd's practically the first friend I made when I got here. Some people introduced me to his sister, and that's how I came to know him. They're very nice, both of them. It's a really nice crowd, very friendly. No airs. Lots of fun." Elena's voice rose. "But don't get any silly ideas about him, Charlotte."

"Of course not. Why would I?" You didn't get "ideas" about your own mother.

"I don't know. I just wanted to make everything clear. Judd's a great tennis partner. I should be flattered. He's not thirty yet, and goodness knows what he wants with me except that I play a good game too." Elena laughed. "Maybe he likes my little foreign accent."

Judd was waiting in his car. It certainly was a cool car, the kind you could dream of driving when you were seventeen.

"Hey, there, that's a cool outfit you're wearing," he said.

It took Charlotte an instant to realize that he meant her. "Thanks," she answered. "I like yours too."

Like her he wore white slacks and shirt. Unlike her he wore a sleeveless sweater striped in red and blue, along with two heavy gold chains.

The rain had not arrived yet, so the top was down. The car skimmed along the shore drive, and when Judd turned on the radio, he and Elena sang along with it. They were having a good time. He drove with one hand. The other arm rested on the seat behind Elena's back. In the parking lot at the restaurant, it occurred to Charlotte as she walked behind them that they looked alike. Judd was slender, and his thick black hair was curly. She wondered whether people

40

might assume that they were both her parents. Odd thought.

Judd was a talker, too, like Elena when she wanted to be. Their conversation wasn't interesting. It was all about people Charlotte didn't know, and about the things they owned, their cars and their houses, mostly.

Judd said, "I bet you'd give your eyeteeth for one of those big places on the shore drive."

"If I could live down here, that's what I'd have," Elena told him, "with a private beach across the road."

"Oh, ho," he cried, throwing his head back. "Why don't you?"

"Well, I just might," she answered, tossing her own head.

She seemed to be teasing him. Charlotte had never seen her behaving quite like this. There was a silence that now suddenly seemed interesting. Judd broke it by addressing Charlotte, to whom no attention had been paid since his first compliment.

"You don't mean to tell me you're going to leave all that on your plate?"

"It was delicious, but it was huge," she replied politely. "Too much for me."

Judd laughed. "Look at your mother. One hundred four pounds soaking wet, and she eats enough for two."

41

Why did he know her weight? It seemed too intimate a thing for him to know. Still, perhaps that's silly of me, Charlotte argued. Most likely I'm picking on him because I wish he wasn't here.

"Look at the rain," Elena said. "Let's go to the mall."

"What do you want to do there?" Judd demanded.

"Shop. What else is there to do on a rainy day?"

"I can think of things."

"Oh, sure," Elena said. "Let's go." And summoning the waiter, she paid the check.

That was strange, too, Charlotte thought. Wasn't he supposed to have invited us?

"Do I have to go to the mall?" she asked. "You could take me back so I can finish my book."

"You have a long plane ride home. You can finish it then. Besides, you've never seen a mall like this one."

That turned out to be true. This mall glittered like a Christmas tree. In shops filled with shoes, perfumes, tennis rackets, Italian silks and chocolates, and Irish linens, they looked and bought. Judd bought ties and a tennis-racket cover. Elena bought a scarf, a dark-brown lipstick, and a crystal elephant. It seemed to Charlotte, who was growing tired, that they were buying just for the sake of buying. And she tried to imagine Dad in this place.

"You could use a summer dress or two," Elena remarked. "Look there. The blue one would be lovely on you."

"Mama." The word was a protest. "Mama. When would I wear a dress like that in Kingsley? Nobody gives parties like that in the summer."

"Nobody does much there anytime, if you ask me. Okay, enough. Let's go back."

The return ride was quiet. Judd had the radio on, but nobody sang. A different mood had blown in on the wind. He stopped at the door, they got out and thanked him, and he drove away.

"See you tomorrow."

"Tomorrow on the beach."

"He's such fun," Elena said as they went inside. "Tell the truth, don't you agree?"

Why should I disagree? Charlotte asked herself. It's easier not to.

"Yes, he's fun," she said.

She woke early while Elena was still sleeping. She dressed and went outside. Apparently everyone in the community was still sleeping. She sat down in the garden area near a small pond surrounded by some vivid flowers whose name she did not know. There were goldfish in the pond, gliding and gleaming through light and shadow. The morning was still, without wind or motion. Only the goldfish moved.

On such a morning a person ought to feel happy. It was all so beautiful. What, then, was wrong with her? She felt — she felt superfluous. It was as if she did not belong here, even with her mother who loved her and had been disappointed when she refused the silly blue dress. She tried to analyze herself. At school from time to time they had visitors, psychologists, who came to explain to the girls about sex and popularity problems and family relationships. You went away from these talks wondering about other people and about yourself. What did it mean to be happy? Nobody could possibly be happy all the time. You had to have some times when you felt miserable. But how often? How often was too often? Would she feel very different if her parents didn't fight so much? After a whole week's vacation she was sitting here moping. That's what Emmabrown would call it. *Stop moping,* she would say, *and help me peel these apples.* But the way she said it, you wouldn't mind.

Now through an open window came the sound of voices. On the far side of the lawn a fat man went jogging down the path. The world was awake. She stood up to go inside and begin the day. It was queer that she should be looking forward to tomorrow and the end of her vacation.

"Mama," she called, looking in at the open bedroom door.

Then, hearing the rush of water in the bathtub, she went back through the living room to start breakfast — and came to a full stop. Judd's sweater and gold chains were lying on the sofa. Puzzled, she stood there staring at them.

But he was wearing them when he drove away last evening! And she recalled exactly how, going too fast, the car had swung around the circle. She recalled exactly the striped sweater and the blaring music.

He had come back here, then, very late. Charlotte herself had stayed up very late watching television.

"Aren't you going to bed soon?" Elena had kept asking.

She wanted to get me out of the way, Charlotte thought now, so he could return. He had stayed the night. And, in his hurry to get out before Charlotte should discover him, had forgotten the things tossed on the sofa. It was all quite clear.

Feeling sick to her stomach, she sat down.

She was still sitting there when Elena appeared in the doorway. Half-dressed, she had a pink dressing gown slung over her arm.

"Hey," she called, "you're the early bird this morning —"

Like arrows the two pairs of eyes shot to the little heap on the sofa, shot back to meet, and separated. Lightly, Elena dropped herself onto the sofa; lightly, she dropped the dressing gown on the little incriminating heap as if she had not even noticed it there.

"So, another lovely day for the beach. What time is it?"

"I don't know," Charlotte said.

"It can't be too late. Oh, well, no rush. Shall we have eggs this morning?"

"I don't care. Whatever you want."

This is absurd, Charlotte thought. Play-acting! She knows I know, but she hasn't figured out yet how to handle it. She must be stunned. She needs time to work out a strategy. It can't be the nicest feeling to have your daughter find you out.

Oh, Elena, why? she cried to herself in fierce and silent anger. And then perversely, along with the anger came pity, the pity one has for an animal caught in a trap.

"I'll get my clothes on," Elena said, "and

then we'll eat. It's been a long time since dinner."

She got up and, carelessly sweeping Judd's things under a trail of pink silk, disappeared into the bedroom. So, without words, it had apparently been agreed that each of them would pretend that nothing had been seen and nothing had happened. Everything must be normal.

Crazy, crazy . . . And yet, would it be better to battle it out, mother with daughter? What would be the result? Tears, transparent lies, and shame. Terrible questions and terrible answers, such as: *Does this mean that you are never coming home? And if not, what is to happen to me?* Why have you done this to us?

I need to get through this day, Charlotte thought. But he had just better not come back here. About that she was resolute. He had better not.

And he did not. And the day passed, somehow.

They stood together at the airport waiting for Charlotte to board. Elena felt naked, as in some horrid dream in which you discover that you have gone out with nothing on but your bathrobe and it's too late to go home for some clothes.

That so much pain should come from such trivia. A lightweight, insignificant fool like Judd. And I have broken her ignorant little heart. She looks dreadful, with dull eyes and dark blue rings beneath them, not pretty at all today, not the way a young girl should appear so that boys will turn and look at her with that quick curiosity they have.

What shall I say to her? Shall I explain that I'm really not the kind of woman who cheats on her husband in the afternoon, comes home with a cheerful face, eats dinner with him, and tolerates his bed? That's not me. I'm really not that kind of woman. What kind am I, then? And is this something that can be discussed with a girl of fourteen?

Charlotte had not asked her when she was coming home, or more significantly, whether she was. For the last few weeks when she talked to Bill, he had not asked her either. He was probably, as she was, waiting for their situation to resolve itself. And that made sense. Things always did get either better or worse. They seldom stayed the same. The thought of going back was deadening in a way. And yet the possibility of not going back was chilling in another way.

So now they stood together unspeaking, observing the crowds, the people greeting and parting. There was always so much emotion in airports.

All at once it was time for Charlotte to board. And all at once, impelled by some wave of despairing, painful love, they threw their arms around each other.

"Good-bye, Mama."

"Good-bye, darling. Take care of yourself."

In the passing of a moment Charlotte's ponytail and backpack moved out of sight.

FOUR

"She looks peaked," Emmabrown observed when, after dinner, Charlotte went upstairs to unpack her suitcase. "Seems to me she didn't have such a good time down there."

"She's probably just tired from the trip," Bill said, not quite believing it.

Emmabrown saw everything and was usually right. Besides, he had not been happy with the nuggets of information that, on the long ride from the airport, had dropped out of Charlotte's conversation. Or had he himself dug them out? Or had they simply revealed themselves in the ordinary course of conversation?

". . . the day we drove down Alligator Alley. I was hoping there would be alligators, but there weren't any, and Mama fell asleep."

"Fell asleep? Who was driving?"

"Judd. He's one of her friends. I told you."

"Oh, yes. I remember you mentioned the name."

Elena, too, had done her part to confuse him. During those telephone discussions about his coming to Florida or her coming home, she had, in one of her chatty moods,

50

run through a string of names, "delightful people, so natural, so casual." It was all casual, even her airy, light account of it was casual.

But was he perhaps foul-minded to think otherwise of Elena? She had never given him reason to have any serious suspicions. On the other hand, she might well be acting the fool.

She was a passionate woman, little changed after all their years together. Still, a nasty squabble had a way of pouring cold water on desire, and they had for a long time been having far too many of them.

If indeed there is anyone, he thought now, examining himself and with some astonishment concluding, I will not feel the rage and pain that I would have felt only a few years ago. I will not be torn with grief. I will have only a deep, deep regret.

The rustle of Charlotte's book was the only sound in the room. And looking toward the whispered sound, he realized that, like himself, she was not reading but had put the book away and was gazing out of the window into the looming night. Emmabrown had been right: the girl was "peaked." Something had most definitely gone wrong.

"What do you all talk about?" he inquired, knowing that the question was too vague to make sense, that it stemmed, too, from an inability to come to the point. Yet how could a man even approach such a point when speaking to his daughter about her mother?

"Just things," Charlotte said. "I don't know. Sports, mostly. Tennis and golf."

"Oh," he said. "And swimming, too, I suppose? I hope you got in a lot of swimming."

"Yes, every morning."

For a moment her glance fell fully upon Bill, and in that moment he saw again how very young she was, younger than most girls of her age. And at the same time he saw how old she was. There was a tired appeal from that glance; it seemed to be saying: *We both know that something is finally going to happen.*

"Go to bed," he said gently. "You've had a long day, and you must be exhausted."

"I'm going to Florida for a couple of days," Bill told his brother.

"Can't you wait until we negotiate this deal to the end? Frankly, I don't feel up to doing it alone."

Bill thought fondly that Cliff was quite correct; he wasn't up to it. Bill himself was the tougher negotiator. But Bill also saw that these negotiations were getting nowhere fast, and he said so again now.

"Property taxes will kill us if we don't do something with the place," Cliff complained.

"We'll have to lease it if we can't sell it. Take whatever we can get until maybe something better comes along. Maybe. Anyway, I need to see Elena."

Cliff, in spite of being the garrulous brother, refrained from asking what he must have been wanting to ask: *What, if anything, is going on between you?*

They were close brothers, yet they kept their private spaces, for they were of a family and a tradition in a region of the country that is known for the avoidance of too many intimacies. So it was with clear recognition of his own need to confide, perhaps even to receive encouragement, that Bill began.

"I'm worried about Charlotte. Her mother's been away too long, and she needs her mother. She's been spending too much time alone in her room. She's too quiet."

Charlotte was suffering, there could be no doubt of it. He wanted to ask her why, had indeed started to do so several times, but she had resisted, and seeing her distress, he had not pressed her. And now, to his dismay, Bill's eyes filled.

Considerately, Cliff looked away into the bustle of the coffee shop and waited until Bill spoke again.

53

"These times we're in, with all the stuff on TV and the world as it is . . . It's a frightening responsibility to rear a young girl."

Those grave, wide eyes of hers! The tenderness in her!

"They don't make many like her," said Emmabrown, "especially these days."

"Yes," he repeated now, having controlled the troublesome tears, "it's hard to rear a girl."

"Ah, well," Cliff said cheerfully, "you mustn't take it so hard. Curb your worrying. I've learned a lot from Claudia."

He hesitated. Bill had the impression that he was trying to make up his mind whether he should say something more or not. Then, leaning across the table, he lowered his voice almost to a whisper.

"That boy of hers is no one hundred percent pleasure, you know. I could lose plenty of sleep over him if I let myself. The fact is, Bill, and I'm ashamed to say it about my wife's fatherless son, but I don't like him. I had every intention of being a companion, a father, to him, but it's not working out all that well. He never looks me in the eye. Oh, he's perfectly polite and all that — Claudia's brought him up that way — but I have a strange feeling that he's taking stock of me, assessing my strength, my intelligence, or what? My financial worth, perhaps? As the kids say, it's weird."

The situation had gone suddenly into reverse. Cliff, who had begun by counseling Bill, now wore an anxious, puzzled frown, as if he were hoping for enlightenment from Bill.

"Lately I've had queer fleeting thoughts. Do you know I've caught him listening in unexpected places? I hate to say it, but I've even thought I wouldn't put it past him to listen outside our bedroom door."

"Good God! Have you told Claudia?"

"No, no, no! I can't hurt her like that. Anyway, she'd see it too differently. She believes in tolerance. You have to understand the adolescent's reaching toward independence, she says."

Cliff pondered for a minute or two while Bill, uncertain what to say, waited. And then Cliff's face turned sunny again. "You know, maybe she's right. After all, Ted does do well in school, he has many friends, and makes no trouble at home. So I'm probably exaggerating what I think I see. And you're probably doing the same with Charlotte."

Having relieved himself by his confession, he was back precisely where he had started, cheerfully confident about the business of parenthood and obviously unaware that he had been moving in a circle.

The foolishness of this irked Bill, so that he spoke a trifle sternly. "We're talking about two entirely different things." He stopped. He, too, was moving in a circle. What was the use of half an admission?

"It's a strange year," he said then. "You find a wife and I lose one."

"What do you mean? Because Elena's taking a vacation? She's flighty, that's all." Cliff's smile was kind. "You ought to be used to her. Now that the weather's warming, she'll be back."

"I don't think so," Bill said. "Not this time."

For a long week now, while Dad was away — a hundred-year-long week, it seemed — Charlotte had known what news he would bring back.

"Since your mother really wants to leave, it will be better for her," Dad had said.

His forehead had been wrinkled, and he had put his hand over hers. She had understood the meaning of the hand. It was to tell her not to be afraid, that the world was going to hold steady.

For a minute it had seemed as if the world had gone whirling, like a balloon taken by the wind beyond reach. And yet, had she not really expected this? And she saw again the red-and-blue-striped sweater, the gold chains on the sofa, in the early morning light.

Even now, alone in the room with her homework still unfinished on her desk, she was undecided over whether she ought to tell Dad about that morning or not. It was so ugly. It was so sad. Still, in the long run, it did not really matter; it was only a detail in the story that was coming to an end.

Dad, passing in the hall, looked and paused. "Are you working? Will I disturb you?"

"Come in. I'm not doing much."

"I know you aren't. But, honey, you can't let this derail you."

"I think I failed the math test today."

"You'll make it up. Charlotte, you have to. This is *your* life, not your mother's or mine."

"That's not quite true," she said, reproaching him.

"Of course it's not altogether true, but mostly it is." He sat on the edge of the bed and continued. "I see you had a letter from Mama in the mail."

"Yes. Do you want to read it?"

"No, it's your letter."

"It's very sad."

"Of course it is."

On the telephone, too, Elena had cried. But she had no right to cry. It was her fault.

"Was it because of that man Judd?" Charlotte blurted now.

Dad shook his head. He felt bad, but because he was a man, he probably thought he shouldn't show it that much.

"I'm keeping you from your work," he said, standing up.

"I don't feel like doing any. She says I should come back to Florida when school's over in June. And I don't want to go. Do I have to?"

"I can't answer now. All these things need to be ironed out."

"She said she might like to live in Italy again. Would I have to go there too?" Panic ran through Charlotte like a shaking chill.

"Oh, honey, if that happens . . . If you don't want to go, I'll fight it. Besides, I think . . . I can't promise, but I think anybody who, I mean, the people who decide these things will know that you're fourteen, old enough to know and say what you want."

When he moved toward the door, she saw his pain. He wanted to get out of the room. And the sight of her father's pain, of his love for her and the enormity of what was happening, was suddenly too hard to control. As soon as the door closed behind him, she put her head down on the desk and cried.

She hated Elena. Hated her! And yet, the only reason that she was unable to cry to Emmabrown, when she needed so badly to cry to someone and had always gone to her with her troubles, was that Emmabrown would surely say nasty things about Elena.

Then she sat up. Other people's parents separated. Other people didn't fall apart over it, so why should Charlotte Dawes? She would stiffen her back and her resolve.

Yet the floor of the room, the very ground beneath the house, had caved in, and she was falling.

Claudia told herself that she would like to do something for "that child." It was a pity to see her caught as she was in anxious suspense, while all these protracted decisions were being made and unmade. The sins that parents perpetrate upon their children! It was certainly, in this case at least, without intent, especially on Bill's part. Charlotte meant the world to him; Claudia had observed that the very first time they had met. Cliff said Bill should have had a big family, but there had been none after

Charlotte. She wondered whether that had been Elena's decision. Claudia was not a person to sit in judgment of others — she had seen enough of the way life can toss people around to cast much blame — but the truth was that Elena had not made a particularly good impression on her. The first impression had resulted from a contemptuous remark of hers, disparaging another woman for being "the type who baked cookies." Of course, it was fashionable in some circles nowadays to talk that way, Claudia thought. The dickens with them. Claudia enjoyed baking cookies.

So she drove over one rainy Saturday and invited Charlotte to come to lunch.

"Thank you, but I have homework to do," Charlotte said.

Bill gave Claudia a glance whose meaning was clear, so she responded firmly, "You needn't glue yourself to homework all day. Come for a while, and whenever you feel like going home, I'll take you."

Claudia believed in the direct approach. So they had not yet arrived at her house, when she said, "You need to get this trouble out of your system, Charlotte. It's not good to close things up inside. I know, I've been there. So my advice is: talk to somebody, preferably to a woman. There must be someone you believe in." And when Charlotte did not reply, she suggested, "Emmabrown, perhaps? You've grown up with her."

"I would, except she doesn't like my mother, and I don't want to hear bad things about my mother."

There was a sorrowful dignity in the girl's words, and Claudia felt a sudden lump in her throat.

"Of course you don't want to," she said. "And anyway, there's no sense now in casting blame."

"No."

"Sometimes, you see, although people marry with the best intentions, it doesn't work out. Unfortunately, it's not so simple to end it. But that's their problem, Charlotte. And there's nothing anyone else can do about it."

"I know."

The tone was resigned. Claudia glanced at the girl's head, which was turned away into a three-quarter profile, a position almost demure, as in an old engraving. She would be beautiful someday, not in any popular or fashionable sense, but profoundly so, with Bill's strong features tempered toward the feminine.

I must not urge her, Claudia thought suddenly, changing her mind. She has probably

61

heard enough pep talks. Let her rest.

"How about doing some baking together?" she asked briskly. Keep it natural, not too emotional. "I'm a very good baker, even if I do say so myself. I thought I'd do lemon tarts today. They're Ted's favorites, and Cliff likes them too. We'll make enough for you to take some home."

I've never had a companion in the kitchen, she thought sometime later, while Charlotte was beating egg whites. That's the joy in having a girl. Of course, Ted is a joy in his own way. But boys grow away from you so fast. On weekends I hardly ever see him. And boys never tell you where they're going, or what they're doing.

Already after these few hours Charlotte had begun to relax and confide.

"I think I'd like to talk to you," she said shyly.

"Would you? I'm glad."

"Sometimes I feel guilty because I feel closer to Dad. It's not that Mama was ever anything but good to me. She's always thinking about me or buying presents. She has lots of money, you see."

The naïveté of this remark was touching. "Lots of money," the magic salve, the solvent and excuse. Cliff said Elena mothered in fits and starts, between indifference and doting, between pampering and neglect.

"But it's Mama who wants to — to go away. It's Mama who has done — do you know about it? I hope you do, because then I won't have to say it."

"You don't have to say it."

"Dad said she wants me to live with her and go to school in Florida and come back here for vacations. I don't want to, Claudia — Aunt Claudia."

"That's all right. Call me just Claudia. It makes me feel young."

Oh, this nice, nice child! And the mother, running around like a damned fool with God knows whom! No wonder Bill was almost ill from smothering his rage.

"I wish they'd make up their minds. Dad says I can tell the judge, if it should come to court, where I want to live. But he can't promise that I'll get what I want. Do you think that's fair, Claudia?"

"No, I don't." She felt the words snap out of her mouth. *Fair!* The whole thing was outrageous, a heap of coals dumped on this guiltless young head. And with sudden tenderness she said, "How about some lunch? You can mix the salad, and I'll make a cheese omelette."

She had made some changes in the house: new curtains in the downstairs rooms and an entire wall of books in the living room. It was pleasant after lunch to display these changes.

"I love your curtains," Charlotte said. "They're Irish lace, aren't they?" And perhaps because Claudia had looked surprised, she added, "Mama knows about things like that, and I guess I learned a little from her."

"Your mother has beautiful taste," Claudia said, satisfied to have something good to say about Elena.

"And all these books. Oh, *David Copperfield*, my favorite. I thought we had a big collection, mostly Dad's, but you have ten times as many."

"Well, not quite. I owned a bookstore, you see, and I made sure to take a pile of books with me when I sold it."

Charlotte went around the room examining coffee-table art books, a landscape of the Maine coast, a small marble cat, and finally a collection of photographs.

"My parents," Claudia said, identifying one after the other. "My college class, my sister, and, of course, there's Ted."

"He's handsome, Claudia."

Claudia was used to hearing that. How the girls ran after him! Even their mothers sometimes told her about them. But there was a good deal more to Ted than his looks. And hearing herself prattle like any fatuous mother, yet unable to stop, she said, "Ted's not merely a handsome football hero, Charlotte. He may not be the best student in most things, but when it comes to math, he's almost a whiz. I don't know yet what he'll do with it, but something remarkable, I'm sure. Cliff thinks so too."

There was no doubt that Ted was going to amount to something. Yes, he could be a bit headstrong sometimes, like a colt or any other young male creature, but what did you expect? He *was* a young male creature.

And Claudia, feeling an inward smile as any mother would, hoped that her son might get through life with as few obstacles as possible in his way. A good, intelligent, and kindly wife, she wished for him, as mentally she raced into the future. Someone, perhaps, like this young Charlotte, who was now surveying the books again.

"This is so interesting," Charlotte said, taking a book from a shelf. "I was thinking, in fact I have thought, I might like to be an architect. I love to look at houses. But then, I'm sure you have to know a lot of math, and it's not my best subject. I'm not like Ted."

"If that's what you really want, you'll master the math. It might be hard, but nothing worth fighting for is easy," Claudia said stoutly. "You want to borrow the book, don't you?"

Charlotte nodded and smiled. It was her first wholehearted smile of the day. "You make me feel cheerful, Claudia," she said.

They had progressed. And Claudia felt as if she had won the first round in a tournament.

FIVE

One Saturday morning Charlotte decided to take the long walk over to Claudia's house. A month had passed since the day of the lemon tarts, and she had been there several times since. It pleased her to know that Claudia wanted her company.

"Because she has no daughter," said Emmabrown, who, Charlotte guessed, would have liked to add, though she did not, "and because you have no mother."

Rob and Roy came rushing and barking to the door, which was opened by Ted. Startled and absurdly flustered, Charlotte bent to stroke the dogs.

"They know you," said Ted.

"Yes, I've been visiting your mother." Still flustered, she displayed a book. "I've come to return this. Is she here?"

"No, they've gone to Boston for a couple of days."

"Well, then, I'll just leave this for her."

"Why don't you come in, anyway?"

He stood surveying her as if he had never seen her before. Actually, he had not seen her very often. She had put on the pink skirt and top that had come in Elena's latest package from Florida. For no reason at all she had simply felt like dressing up. And now she was glad she had.

"Come on in," he repeated. "I'm just having a sandwich. Want one?"

The fact was that Charlotte had taken lunch for granted, as Claudia expected her to do.

"I wouldn't mind," she said.

"Make a sandwich for yourself. There's bread and there's sliced turkey. Coleslaw, potato salad. My mother left enough for an army."

He had a rough way of talking, sort of slapdash and careless, that was interesting. And she thought how ridiculous it was to have no brother, to go to a school for girls, and not even know how to talk to a boy or what to expect from him.

He wasn't a boy, though. He stood ten inches above her. He was a senior, old enough to vote or be in the army. No doubt, barging in like this, she was being a nuisance to him.

She made a sandwich and sat down at the kitchen table, wondering how to begin a conversation, since he had not begun one.

"Have a beer," he said, shoving a glass and another bottle across the table.

"I've never had beer," she said.

"Well, there's always a first time. Here, I'll open it for you."

She sipped and shuddered. It was awful, sour enough to make you want to spit it out.

Ted was amused. "Takes getting used to, like olives."

"Oh, I like olives."

"Good, I'll get some. And a Coke."

When he had set these out, there came a silence, made deeper by the small clicks and clinks of plates and forks. The dogs scratched and thumped. Ted's chair squeaked when he tipped back on it. Elena would say he was hard on furniture, Charlotte thought. But he was so big. He was powerful and manly. That was the word: *manly*, and much handsomer than some of the men on television or in the movies. He made her self-conscious. It was stupid for two people to sit there chewing and not saying anything.

"You're a cute kid," Ted said abruptly. "In another couple of years you'll be really cute. You've got a nice shape."

When your breasts are bigger, he meant. They were already big enough for him to notice. And she felt confusion, not knowing how to respond to the compliment.

"So, Charlotte, tell me about yourself."

What was there to say? There was nothing.

"There isn't much to tell," she said.

Elena would say: *You have to sparkle, be alive, be interesting. You can't just sit there!*

"There must be. Anyway, I already know a few things about you. C.D. talks about you a lot."

"C.D.?"

"Your uncle."

"Why do you call him C.D.?"

"Clifford Dawes, of course. I don't like the sound of *uncle* because he isn't my uncle. And he's surely not my father. So you see . . ." Ted shrugged.

She thought he looked somber. A thrill of sympathy, first hot, then cold, seemed to shoot through her veins. His father was dead, while her mother was —

"C.D. says you're very smart and you're an expert swimmer. True?"

"I don't know that I'm so smart, but I am a pretty good swimmer."

"That's great. Maybe you and I can go out to the lake this summer. I'll bet you look great in a swimsuit."

She was astonished. If she were to tell anyone at school that Ted Marple — Ted Marple! — had invited her to go to the lake, they might not even believe it. She would certainly tell them, though, and no later than next Monday. Tell them all, too, not only

70

her friends, but even snobs like Addie Thompson, who thought she was God's gift to boys. With this thought enlivening her the words began to flow.

"I know things about you too. I mean, everybody who reads the paper knows about you, about the Thanksgiving game with Franklin High and stuff like that. But I know other things. Your mother says you're the best math student in the senior class."

"Oh, mothers. They boast too much."

But she saw that he was pleased, so she continued. "Between that and football, you'll get into any college you want, I guess."

"You're pretty young to know about colleges."

"No, I think about it all the time. I want to be an architect."

"You can't know that already."

"Of course I can."

"Ah, you're a baby."

For an instant Charlotte felt a rise of anger; then she saw that he was teasing, and they both laughed.

"A pretty baby. Listen, pretty baby, I'd like to stay here talking to you, but I have to go now. Meeting some friends downtown." Ted looked at his watch. "Geez, I'm late. I'm supposed to give the dogs a walk, but too bad, I can't."

The dogs, alert to the word *walk*, had gotten up and gone to the door. "Poor fellows," Charlotte said.

"Tell you what, Charlotte. How about you and me taking them for a hike tomorrow afternoon? I'll pick you up at your house. Is it a date?"

"A date," she said happily.

Ted picked up her ponytail as if he were weighing it. "I'll bet you look beautiful with all that hair spread out loose. Thick and blond. Not bad. Not bad at all."

She was flushed and thrilled. "It's dirty blond," she said.

"Don't say that. You need to learn how to accept a compliment. Come on, I'll drive you home."

Dad asked, "Where were you? Whose car was that?"

"Ted's."

"How did that happen?"

"I went to see Claudia, but she wasn't home, so I had lunch with him."

"Just you and Ted? You didn't know they were away for the weekend?"

"Of course I didn't know. But what's the difference?"

Dad frowned. "I don't like the idea of your

being alone in the house with him — or any boy."

"Daddy! That's the silliest thing I ever heard. You sound like Queen Victoria. Do you think that all a boy wants is sex? That you can't be friends with a boy, for heaven's sake?"

"People can be too old for you," Dad grumbled.

"Ted's not too old. And he's really nice. You don't even know him."

"Well, all the same, I don't want . . ." He raised the newspaper so that his face was hidden.

He doesn't know what else to say, Charlotte thought. What he's already said is stupid, and he knows it is.

Around the paper's edge Bill peered at Charlotte, thinking, Aging comes on so slowly that you don't notice it. Two years ago she had her first bra and braces on her teeth. She and her friends went charging through the house like wild ponies. Now, with a book on her lap, her pink skirt smooth, and charm bracelet dangling, she has a woman's posture.

Yet she still had the face of a child, a face that made his heart ache. They were pulling her apart, he and Elena! At the most critical period of adolescence, when she most needed them, they were doing this to her. He worried so. . . . Elena didn't see their child as he saw her. Elena, to begin with, didn't feel with the intensity that was almost palpable in Charlotte. Elena, in that fragile-seeming body, had the toughness of one of those thin weeds that take all a man's strength to uproot. Hardly a flattering comparison!

Charlotte, not reading now, dreamed with eyes unfocused and a tiny smile. Most probably she was dreaming of the ultimate romance, the wine-and-roses thing. She was in a hurry to grow up. And he wanted to warn her: *Men don't think like that, my dear. In spite of all the unisex talk these days, the boys are different, my dear, they really are. Believe me. Take care of yourself.*

The flowery spring had finally come north of Boston to stay. Cliff's house was on the fringe of town, almost in sight of farms and open country. With the two dogs at heel Charlotte and Ted walked out in the direction of the lake.

Ted strode along with his hands in his pockets. Every now and then he picked up a small stone and hurled it ahead. When he leaned back to throw with his right arm, his left foot came up. She must be careful not to be caught watching him. It would be terribly embarrassing. He would think she was falling in love with him or something.

Still, maybe she was. The thought was astonishing. Was it possible that such a thing could happen so fast? You read about it in junky novels — but they were just junky novels. Yet what about the classics? *Romeo and Juliet?* And surely there were dozens of others, although she couldn't remember offhand which ones they were.

A car approached and, passing, slowed enough for a girl to wave from the rear window. Addie! It was exactly what Charlotte had dreamed about and never expected to see. Addie would spread it all over the school: *Charlotte Dawes was out walking with Ted Marple on Sunday.*

For a long time she had not been exhilarated or energetic, but now she broke into a run, so fast that the breeze lifted her hair from her shoulders.

"Hey! Where you all going?" cried Ted, catching up.

"I often run with the dogs. I almost feel as if Rob and Roy belong to me. I've grown up with them."

"Why don't you have a dog of your own?"

"I always wanted one."

"So why didn't you have one? Don't your

folks always give you everything you want?"

"Well, mostly yes, but my mother doesn't like dogs in the house. They shed and throw up and make a mess, she thinks."

"She sounds like a crank. Oh, I'm sorry, I didn't mean to hurt your feelings." Ted's rueful smile asked her to forgive him. "I shouldn't have said that."

She reassured him, saying quickly, "That's all right. It's partly true. Sometimes she is a nag."

"Are they really getting a divorce?"

"I guess. Although it does seem as if they can't even agree on that much."

"It's a bad break for you."

They broke stride to lean against a stone wall. Beyond it a herd of Holsteins went moving with heads down through a long pasture.

"They're looking for fresh grass, but it's too early," Charlotte said. "They'll still be eating hay for another couple of weeks."

Ted shrugged. "I never gave it any thought. Don't know much about animals."

"My dad knows a lot. He does stuff for wildlife and the environment. Uncle Cliff does too."

"Yeah, C.D.'s been writing something for the Wildlife Commission. Funny business for a couple of textile manufacturers."

"Oh, no," Charlotte said earnestly. "Not really. They got the business from their grandfather, and so they kept it. But I think they would really have liked to be explorers, or maybe even farmers. Oh, look, on the other side of the road, there's a mare with a new colt. Isn't he darling? Let's go see."

Ted was looking at her. He was almost staring. She knew he was admiring her hair, which she had kept loose today, letting it ripple into two deep curves around her face. She had put on some of Elena's perfume. And again that little thrill went through her.

"I suppose," he said, "your father's home with the Sunday paper today."

"No, he left early to meet some people who may lease the plant. They can't seem to sell it."

He was still looking at her, or rather, looking down to her, with such an odd expression, partly smiling and partly analyzing, as though he found her fascinating. Could that be possible?

And confused now, she rattled on, "Dad doesn't even like these people all that much. It's a recycling company that'll use the place to store rubbish. After buildings are torn down, for instance, the rubbish has to be put somewhere, so that's what their business is. And it's not what Dad wanted at all. But he needs the money. It's very hard on him. I'm sorry for him with all his worries."

Her voice trailed, for now Ted had looked away. He picked up a stone and sent it skimming down the road. Suddenly she was boring him, and no wonder. Laughter is what people want, Elena said. Be entertaining.

"Life's a bummer for some people," Ted said.

"But not for you," she said brightly. "I think you must have a great life."

"Nah, not always. My father was shot, sitting right in his office, he was shot. The case came to trial and the jury acquitted the killer. Can you imagine that? I was four. My mom was advised to get out of town. I still don't understand why, but anyway, we came here. She had some old relative here, so she knew somebody at least. Then he died, and she opened the bookstore. It wasn't easy, I can tell you."

"But now everything's fine for you," Charlotte said eagerly, wanting him to be comforted.

"Yeah. What are we doing here, gabbing about all this stuff? You're too serious for your own good. How about we lighten up? How about going back to my place. I'll have a beer, and you'll have a Coke. We've walked far enough."

"Sure," said Charlotte. "I'd like that."

When you entered the house, you immediately felt vacancy. There was no Claudia in the kitchen and no sound of the radio that she kept tuned to music. There were dirty dishes in the sink and newspapers scattered on the floor.

Ted grinned. "Place is a mess, isn't it? I'll have to clean it up tonight before they get home. Hey, here's a chocolate cake in the cake box. Want some?"

"Sure. Thanks."

"We'll have it in there in style," Ted said, pointing toward the living room.

"Where's your beer?"

"Beer and chocolate cake don't mix, little girl. I'm having wine. Why don't you try some? Coke and chocolate cake don't mix that well either."

"I never had wine. Aren't you supposed to be eighteen? That's what Dad said."

"Excuse me, but your dad sounds like a cop or a lawyer. That talk's all garbage. The French give wine to their kids, for God's sake."

In the living room Ted put two plates, two goblets, and a bottle of red wine on the coffee table. They sat down together on the sofa. Ted poured the wine.

"Taste it. It'll make you feel good."

It was faintly tart and faintly sweet, silky and cool. It seemed to go with the room, which was as green and white as the spring outdoors. Leaning back on the cushions, Charlotte had a sense of luxury, as in those advertisements where beautiful women recline in rooms like this one, filled with paintings, flowers, and books. Her charm bracelet tinkled, and she smiled.

"You see, it does make you feel good," Ted said. "Have some more."

"I already had half a glassful."

"So? What's a half? You can certainly drink another half. That's nothing at all." He laughed. "Have another piece of cake to wash it down."

"Your mother's a great cook. I love coming here for lunch. I mean — that sounds dumb, doesn't it? I love coming here because she's so sweet. I love the way she talks to me. Like equals, you know. Once — we were studying opera in school — she put on a record of *Tosca* and explained it so I almost didn't have to do the reading. Do you know the story of *Tosca*? It starts in the cathedral when this man is escaping. . . ."

It was wonderful the way the words came pouring so smoothly now. She wasn't the least bit self-conscious anymore with Ted. He sat there listening and watching her so respectfully, so closely. . . . It was lovely.

Once he reached over to refill her glass, but when she objected, he said, "You're imagining things. This is the half you didn't have the first time. Do you think I want to get you drunk?"

She giggled. Of course he didn't. He was Claudia's son and, by now, practically Uncle Cliff's son too.

"Let's have some music," he said abruptly. "Some dance music."

She got to her feet. Dancing in the afternoon! Yes, it was all lovely.

But when he took her in his arms, guiding her into the slow rhythm of the music, she said, "Not this kind of dancing. I don't know how to do this old-fashioned stuff."

"You'd better learn, because it's coming back in style. It's really nice, you'll see. Just follow my steps."

His firm hold tightened until there was no space at all between their bodies. Her head was pressed against his chest so that she felt him breathing. The music was soft and yearning, a little bit happy and also a little bit sad. Her eyes filled with tears.

"You're so sweet," Ted murmured. "I never thought when I first saw you — I thought you were only a little kid. But when I looked again, I saw something else. You're very adult for your age."

As they moved around the room, the walls began to spin slowly, as when a merry-go-round starts rolling. Her legs felt heavy, but it wouldn't be right for her to break up the dance, so she clung to him to keep from falling.

"So sweet," he murmured again. "Tender and sweet. And here I am in this beautiful house with a beautiful girl. Lucky me. I never thought I'd be so lucky. I haven't had the easiest life, Charlotte."

"Oh, I know, I heard," she whispered back.

All the happiness was melting into sadness. Life was hard. Poor Ted, he had had his troubles too. They had killed his father. And poor me. Poor Dad. Elena too. The world was so sad, so beautiful and sad. A little sob stuck in Charlotte's throat.

"Can't dance on this carpet. Let's sit down," Ted urged, and kissed the top of her head.

"Yes, let's. I feel a little dizzy," she said.

Back on the sofa he put his arm around her. "Lay your head on my shoulder. You'll be all right in a minute."

"Dizzy," she said again, "and sleepy too. It must be the wine."

"No, no. Those few sips wouldn't do that

to you. It was dancing in circles that did it. Lie back."

He was so gentle. His firm fingers began to stroke her shoulders. When he slid his arm around and scratched her back, it felt as good as the Chinese back-scratcher she had won long ago at a fair. She told him so, and giggled.

"You're like a cat," he said. "I had a cat once that would lie there all day and purr if you rubbed its back."

Gradually, his fingers had slid down along her leg. When they reached her feet, he took off her shoes and massaged her soles. She floated; sunlight dazzled through the venetian blinds, and she closed her eyes against the glare.

"I'm like that cat you had," she murmured. "I'm falling asleep."

"Good. That's good."

So she lay — she could not have said for how long — until suddenly, with no warning at all, he lunged. His enormous, crushing weight pushed her flat on the sofa. His wet, crushing mouth clamped on hers.

"What are you doing?" she cried, struggling to raise herself.

Twisting beneath him, she pushed his face away. She did not understand; a second ago she had been sleepy and warm while he

83

stroked her so gently, so gently. . . . What was he doing? What did he want?

In her squirming struggle to free herself, she saw him withdraw far enough to undo his clothes. And glimpsing then his astonishing, terrifying flesh, she screamed. The scream tore her throat.

"No! No! No!"

Again he thrust her back. His hand covered her mouth, while his other hand probed her body, rolled her skirt roughly up around her neck, and pulled her underclothes down.

"What are you doing?" she said, and when he didn't answer, she pleaded, "Don't, don't." Then she called out, "Oh, God, somebody help me, please."

Sweating and breathing out the sour stench of wine, he moved upon her. She was stifled. Her fists were impotent and her teeth, with which she would have torn him, could only graze his chest, which was hard as a board. There was nothing there for teeth or hands to seize. He was going to kill her. Claudia's son was going to kill her. He was a maniac, the nice, quiet murderer you read about. He was going to strangle her. And with all her strength she fought. Her shrieks pierced her ears. Surely somebody, somewhere, would hear!

But there was no one, and her strength

was going. Her voice was dying into a whimper. Her heart was going to stop. There was no one to help her, no one at all.

Suddenly, as abruptly as it had begun, it ended, and he released her. For an instant, before he could turn his back to rearrange his clothes, she saw again that shocking, terrible flesh. It was hideous. It sickened her stomach. And she pulled down her skirt so that he might not look at her. She wanted to kill him. And because she knew she had no way to hurt him, she could do nothing but sob. The sobs raged in her chest and ripped her apart.

Shaking, she lay there in her rumpled skirt. Turned facedown, she cried into the pillow and beat the armrest as she had wanted to beat Ted. Finding one of her shoes, she hurled it across the room. The sound of her weeping was turning into a peal of hysterical laughter. And she heard it from far away, as though in a distant room someone was losing control of her mind, heard it and was unable to stop it.

"You've got to quit this," Ted said. His voice was very quiet. "You're making yourself sick."

She whirled about. "What did you do to me? What did you do?"

"Nothing, Charlotte. Here you are, all in

one piece. There's nothing wrong with you."

"There is! You hurt me. You ought to — to go to jail, you rotten, rotten bastard. You hurt me."

She cried and cried. Her nose ran. He gave her a tissue and stood watching her.

"You've got it all wrong," he said after a while. "Nothing happened at all, Charlotte, I didn't hurt you. And don't go home and shoot your mouth off."

A tremendous exhaustion drained her. After a while she was too weak even to cry anymore. She lay quite still with her eyes closed, listening to Ted's footsteps strike the floor between the scatter rugs as he paced. When she opened her eyes, she saw the cake and the wineglasses on the table. She felt cold and closed her eyes again.

He was standing over her; without looking she felt his presence.

"You're all right," he repeated. "Remember, nothing happened."

"I have to go home," she said, wiping her nose.

"You can't go, crying like that."

"I'm not crying anymore." Then the thought struck her that perhaps he wasn't going to let her out of the house, and she screamed again. "I have to go home."

"Fine. No problem. Just wash your face

and comb your hair, and I'll take you."

On the brief ride to her house, neither of them spoke until the car stopped and Ted said, "I think you'd better not come again."

His tone was flat, but she understood his meaning. He was afraid of her now; he was in terror. In any case she had no intention of going near that house again, ever.

She walked in softly on tiptoe. At the end of the hall the door was open, revealing her father on the porch. She wanted only to hide in her room, but had barely set foot on the stairs before he heard her and called out.

"Where in heaven's name have you been? Come in here, I want to talk to you."

"I'm sick," she mumbled, forestalling the question he would surely put when he saw her.

He rose from his chair, confronting her in the full blaze of afternoon light, and demanded, "What is wrong with you?"

"I feel like throwing up. I must have eaten something."

" 'Must have'! What do you mean? You know what you ate. Where were you? It's after five. I've been home since half past two. I called all your friends where I thought you might have gone, and then I had to give up. Where were you, I asked?"

"Ted and I took the dogs for a walk," she said, looking down at her shoes.

"Ted. I told you yesterday that I didn't want you there. I don't like him. I have an uneasy feeling about him, Charlotte, and maybe that sounds crazy to you, and maybe I'm all wrong, but dammit, I'm your father, and I have a right to sound crazy. And I have a right to know why you went there when I told you not to."

She had never seen her father so angry. Even during those overheard arguments with Elena, it had been she who had the hot temper, never he. And she waited in silence for him to finish.

"What does he want with a kid like you? He's not right for you, he's not honest, it's written on his face. I don't like this, Charlotte, I told you I didn't and I'm telling you again. If you have any more dates with him, you'll be in real trouble with me. Real trouble. And it seems to me that we've got enough troubles under this roof already."

She trembled. A chill ran through her again; nausea filled her throat, and in a whisper she pleaded, "Dad, I have to go to the bathroom. I'm sick."

She lay flat on her back, flung out, her body sore and bruised, until the nausea passed. If only she had someone to talk to.

It had to be a woman, and there was none. Emmabrown would only scold like a fury. Claudia, who would not scold, was obviously out of the question, and Elena was far away. Maybe, though, she would be coming home soon. If only she would come home soon!

Two cold tears slid to her temples and lost themselves in the tangle of her hair. She felt terribly alone, lost in a strange place with no one to help her.

Presently the door opened, and her father came in, looking anxious. "Are you feeling better? Get up, honey." And when she nodded, "I know I yelled. But it wasn't really yelling. It was just being emphatic. You had me terribly scared. I didn't know what might have happened to you."

She got up and redid her hair in the familiar ponytail.

"Now you look like yourself," Dad said, coaxing her, wanting her to smile and assure him that everything was all right again.

How could everything be all right? Over and over, all that week and beyond, she relived the terror and humiliation of that afternoon. She sat in class and she lay in bed, reliving the scene on the sofa in Claudia's living room. She was outraged. And in a strange way she was angry, too, at Elena. . . .

"Do you want to fly to Florida over Memorial weekend?" Dad asked one evening. He hesitated; the words came hard to him. "Your mother wants to talk to you about herself and me, about your feelings."

"She can come here."

"She thinks it would be good for the two of you to be alone."

But Mama should be here, at home, in this house. She should have been here before this thing happened; then probably it wouldn't have happened.

"I'm not going," Charlotte said. "You can tell her."

There was a silence.

There were many silences now. Dad at mealtimes, becoming aware of one, would turn from the distance into which he had absently been gazing to ask Charlotte what had happened in school that day. She knew that he was doing it for her sake. His mind was filled with his own worries: down by the river, the vacant building that was draining his pocketbook, and most of all the vacant chair at the opposite end of the table.

What if he knew what had happened to her. He must never know. . . . Her hand shook, spilling half a glass of milk.

SIX

"We signed a lease today," Cliff told Claudia one evening after dinner.

"Well, that should be a relief," she said.

"I don't know. I hoped so much that we could sell the place and get it off our hands. Bill worked hard over two deals that looked promising, but no use. This last one almost went through, but then their engineers told them we were too close to the river. One big flood, they said, and we'd slide right into it. Good Lord, the building's been standing since 1910, and the river's never flooded yet. It was probably just an excuse to back out because they weren't able to come up with the money."

"Who are these tenants?" Claudia asked, seeing that he was to some extent troubled and needed to talk.

"They're a big company that does waste disposal — stuff left after demolitions, for instance. They say it's a clean recycling process. I hope so." Cliff frowned. "Bill has some idea in the back of his head that this firm isn't exactly first class, but we've had no other offers in two years. We have no choice."

"Why, what does he think?"

"Thinks maybe they're a front for somebody, or might have some mob connections in the Midwest. I don't know. But Bill tends to be suspicious. Our lawyers told us to go ahead, so I'm not going to worry. And the income's mighty welcome. We're not used to penny-pinching, either of us."

Claudia smiled at these brothers' definition of *penny-pinching*. Still, after a lifetime of comfortable living and famously generous giving, it must be very painful to retrench.

"What are you men going to do with all your time now?" she asked.

"Bill's going to stay with the Environmental Commission. They want to make him director, he says. That'll mean a salary and I can keep teaching a couple of courses at the business college. We'll manage. I'll still be able to spend enough time on my book too. The history of textiles is really the history of civilization, you know."

"I have to get you a better desk lamp," she said, "a three-way with a green shade."

She wondered how long it would take her to become used to all this comfortable domesticity. Perhaps she never would. It was just as well, though, not to take any good things for granted; in this uncertain world they were rather to be savored, every single day to be treasured, every hour like this one, the two of them in peace on the cool side porch with their after-dinner coffee in a beautiful pewter pot.

"Where's Ted gone? He rushed out of the house as if a bee had stung him."

"You're not used to boys, darling. Don't you remember that when you were his age you only wanted to get out with your friends?"

"I think I spent more time at home than he does. But maybe I don't remember exactly."

Claudia was disappointed. She had wanted to be assured that, yes, that's how all boys — all young men — were. She had hoped, too, that Cliff and Ted would form a bond; pictures of them going off together with fishing rods and a box lunch went floating through her imagination. But nothing of the sort had happened. It certainly wasn't Cliff's fault. In his quiet way he was the friendliest, the most approachable, of men.

Abruptly, she thought of something else and, frowning a little, wondered aloud: "It's strange that Charlotte hasn't come here lately. It must be three weeks now. I've asked her, but she always has an excuse. And I thought we were getting along just fine."

"The poor kid's all upset. Bill's sick over

it. It has nothing to do with you."

Claudia shook her head. "People make so much trouble for themselves. That Elena —"

Someone was coming up the gravel walk. At the foot of the steps he stopped and, in a polite voice, introduced himself.

"Hugh Bowman. I don't like to intrude, but there's a personal matter I need to talk about. It's quite serious."

"Come in. Sit down," Cliff said at once.

"Thank you." Mr. Bowman sat erectly, a rather formal, proper man whose words were therefore all the more astonishing. "It's about your son, Ted." And as Claudia started, "No, there's been no accident, he's not hurt. But he ought to be hurt. A good many other men in my position would take care of that."

Claudia gasped. "What is it? What has he done?"

"He has behaved disgracefully to my daughter. Insultingly. It happened on the way back from the movies last night. I don't care to go into details. She arrived home with her dress torn." Bowman's voice was quiet, but his face was flushed. "Fortunately, Joan's all right. She had a handbag with metal trim. It cut his cheek."

This morning at breakfast Ted had told

them, making a joke of it, that he had walked right into a screen door.

Humiliated, as if she herself had been caught shoplifting or breaking china in a store, Claudia appealed with frightened eyes from one man to the other.

"I don't understand. . . . Ted never . . ." Her voice broke.

Cliff got up immediately to stand beside her with his hand on her shoulder. "This is a terrible shock to my wife," he began, when Bowman interrupted.

"I understand. Believe me, I didn't come here to start any trouble, to go to the school authorities or do anything. We, my wife and I, don't want anything like that. This is awful for you. We only want to tell you so that you can take control of your son before something worse happens. That's all." He paused, not looking at Cliff and Claudia, but out into the trees. "I'm sure you'll know what to do, Mr. Dawes. I'm just sorry about the whole thing."

"Ted's my son," Claudia said, "not Cliff's."

"I know. The Daweses are well known in Kingsley." Bowman stepped down from the porch, repeating, "I'm sorry to have upset you like this. But I'm sure you understand that I had to."

"Of course," Cliff said. He had both hands on Claudia's trembling shoulders. "I'll send him to your house to apologize first thing in the morning, or even tonight."

"No, please don't. I wouldn't want Joan to go through that. The only thing you can do is teach him. . . ."

"Oh, I assure you I'll teach him," Cliff said grimly.

They watched Bowman go down the walk. They were both speechless. Then Cliff said, "He was remarkably decent about it. Not everyone would be that reasonable."

She felt so ashamed before her husband. They were hardly married a year, and Cliff's face had turned red in front of a stranger because of her son. What in God's name had come over Ted?

"I don't know what to say," she murmured, beginning to cry. In ten minutes or less a world totters.

"Don't," Cliff said with his arm around her. "We'll get to the bottom of it. I'm not going to sleep without seeing Ted. I'm his father now and I'll take care of things. Just try to relax."

It was not very long before Ted came up the walk. There must have been some revealing expression on their faces or in their stance, because he stopped in surprise.

"What's the matter? Has anything happened?"

"Plenty, it seems," Cliff said.

Claudia had been about to speak first, but when Cliff began, it occurred to her that it was better that way; Cliff would act the father's part and be the father that Ted had never had.

"We had a visit from Mr. Bowman. You were out last night with his daughter, Joan."

"I know I was. What's the beef?"

"The beef? I believe you can imagine what it was."

"No," said Ted. Nonchalant, with his sweater slung over one shoulder, he stood propped against a post. "No, I can't."

"Joan Bowman hit you. She must have had a reason. That's quite a cut you have on your face."

"She's a little b— a nasty little cat. I didn't do a thing to her."

Claudia, going weak in the knees, had to sit down. What she could see of Cliff's face in the dusk was cold and stern. She had never seen him like that.

"Don't lie, Ted, the way you lied about the screen door. What happened?"

"Nothing. I swear it. This is a big fuss about nothing. You've got to believe me."

He was pleading. "All right, here's the truth. I tried a little kiss, that's all. Okay, probably I shouldn't have. But there's nothing abnormal about that, is there, for Pete's sake?" He was righteously indignant. "Another girl would have said either yes or no, and that would have been the end of it. This girl" — he shook his head — "this girl's a creep. And that's the whole truth."

Cliff considered for a moment. "I hope so," he said then. "It had better be the truth, Ted. We don't want any more complaints like this. It's not fair to your mother, and it's not good for your reputation. So keep your hands to yourself. That's all I have to say."

Cliff turned about and went into the house. Claudia followed, carrying the coffee tray. Ted went straight upstairs. She had hoped that the two of them might shake hands, might end on a note of understanding. After all, the boy had probably intended nothing but some harmless fumbling; Ted would never be violent!

Cliff sat down at the kitchen table and poured a cup of coffee. He looked as he had sounded, grim.

"Don't you believe him?" she asked, begging.

"You're all unnerved," he said. Then he

smiled at her. "I believe him. Come sit down."

No, she thought, smiling back, you're saying this to comfort me. You don't believe him.

And her heart was heavy.

SEVEN

"I want to tell you something in strictest confidence," Dad said seriously. "They had a bit of trouble with Ted recently. Some girl's father went to the house to complain about him. He — did things, or tried to, and the girl cut his face."

Charlotte felt a rush of blood into her neck. "What happened to him?" she asked.

"He was lucky. The people could have reported him, but they didn't. Remember how I told you I had queer doubts about Ted? And secretly, Uncle Cliff did, too, although neither of us expected anything like this. I'll tell you, the person I feel sorry for is Claudia, poor woman. Well, I don't mean to frighten you. He's no ax murderer, after all. Just don't spend any time with him again. But I guess I don't have to repeat that, do I?"

"No," Charlotte said. "No."

Her father had a quizzical expression, with his head tilted to one side, as if to examine her from another angle. "Wouldn't you be better off," he asked, "if you talked to me about your feelings? Of course I know that you're troubled about your mother and me, and I don't want to pressure you, but sometimes it helps to talk things out."

"I'm fine, I really am, Dad," she said quickly.

Of course, he did *not* know what was troubling her. She was not even sure herself. Panic struck at the thought of what it might be. More than a month had passed, and now the second month was approaching. She kept returning to the calendar on which she marked the monthly date, as Elena had instructed her the very first time. Elena had also explained that at her age, the count might fluctuate. . . . It was incredible that a girl, who only a few weeks ago would have been sure of her answer to any question about sex, could now be in a state of ignorant confusion.

Mentally she went over that scene. Had he or hadn't he? It was all different from the way they described it in books. And there was so much written about people who had to try for years; there was all that stuff about fertility clinics. . . . She knew nothing.

Panic had struck on each of the few times that Claudia had telephoned. Shuddering, she had seen it all again, the table, the chocolate on the plate, and the wine. Claudia was probably using the telephone at the desk across from that green sofa. . . .

And she had trembled while refusing, so calmly, so politely, the invitations: "I'm sorry, I can't. I have to study for finals."

Ever since Dad had told of Ted's trouble, though, Claudia had not called again. Was there, could there be, any connection?

And shortly, too, after that conversation with Dad, she had begun to feel a sharp pain in her side. Was there, could there be, any connection?

She thought of going to the school nurse, and almost instantly thought not. You had to know well whom you could trust. You never knew about people. Even your own mother could fool you.

Yet she had to do something.

In midafternoon on the last day of school, as she started to walk toward the school bus, Charlotte's feet turned her around. Without conscious plan or will her feet took her up the street toward the public bus. It was only after she had sat and the bus had left Kingsley behind it that she knew what she was doing.

Loudontown was the next stop. But it was too near. Next on the schedule was Arkville, nine miles farther on. There on one of the main streets she would find someone who could assure her that there was nothing to worry about. And she imagined the young woman, or perhaps an old man, no matter who, dismissing her lightly: *For goodness' sake, there's nothing at all the matter with you! Perfectly normal. The pain? A little muscle ache. Nothing. Forget it.*

Yes, that's how it would be. A sudden calmness came over her. The bus rolled along the familiar road past farms, a church, and a gas station at an intersection. Kids were walking home from school. A woman on the seat ahead was carrying a squirming baby. A man had a basket of oranges on his knees. It was all ordinary.

"I'm not afraid," she whispered.

The man with the oranges turned to stare at her, so it must have been a loud whisper. And panic struck back.

In Arkville she got off at the bus station and walked down Main Street looking for a doctor's office. There were shops, a department store, and banks with people hurrying in and out, a bustle of strangers among whom she now felt a fearful strangeness. As she was passing a medical office building, this fear overcame her. The building challenged her with its cold aloofness, and she was unable to open its door. It took all her strength to keep from running back to the bus station.

"I must," she said, so kept on walking.

And, rounding a corner into a quiet side street, came upon a frame house with a doctor's shingle: IMMEDIATE HEALTH CARE, WALK-IN FACILITY. Two tubs filled with begonias stood beside the door. They looked friendly.

"I must," she said again, and went in.

The doctor was perhaps old, or perhaps young, somewhat like Dad. Setting her schoolbag on the chair beside her, she sat down and answered his questions in as general a fashion as she possibly could, telling him nothing about Ted or even giving him her own right name.

"This pain I have," she said, "was pretty bad yesterday. I'm thinking it might be appendicitis."

"We'll see. I'll have to examine you."

Well, she had come this far and would have to go on till the end. And she felt a kind of pride in her own control as she followed the nurse into the examining room. On the table with her eyes squeezed shut, she kept saying inwardly, *I'm not here. This isn't me. I'm not here,* until it was over. She gave a specimen. She got dressed. *Scared. Must not give way. Must not.*

"The doctor will see you in a little while," said the nurse. "Would you like a cold drink while you wait?"

It seemed to Charlotte as she accepted the drink that the woman had shown a special kindness of face and voice, an unusual kindness, as though she was actually interested in Charlotte, or as though she was curious about her. This was odd. Yet she was aware that lately she had often felt as if people were looking at her with an odd expression.

After a while she was summoned to the doctor. He, too, from the other side of his desk, was looking at her with a marked expression on his face. She understood at once that he was going to say something important. When, very quietly, he began, "Betsy —" she knew what he was going to say.

"Betsy, there are things that you haven't told me. Perhaps you haven't told anyone. But they can't be hidden any longer. I think you know that. I think you must have suspected when you came here that you are pregnant."

She lowered her head, receiving the blow. So the charms she had said, all the superstitious promises to herself — *If it isn't true, I will never complain about anything for the rest of my life, I will get straight A's, I will not stuff on sweets, I will give half my allowance to charity* — had meant nothing. Stupid magic, they were, as she had known all along.

"I won't ask you any questions. It's not my business to do that. But I must speak to your parents."

Proud of being able to withstand the blow, Charlotte looked up and spoke steadily. "I'd rather you didn't. I'd rather tell them myself."

He was studying her. "There are things to be discussed. How do I know you'll tell them?"

"I'll tell them. I have to."

"You are very young. I don't want you to do anything foolish to yourself."

What did he mean? A secret abortion? Suicide?

"I won't. I promise I won't."

"But I don't know you, Betsy." He smiled. "Would you accept a promise from a stranger?"

"No. But I can't let a stranger tell me what to do either."

Things — the doctor's pale face, the pattern on the curtains, the white glare of the lightbulb — went whirling. She had to get home, to her room and her bed.

"Are you all right, Betsy?"

"Yes, but I have to get home. I want to pay you."

"Never mind that. I haven't done anything."

106

"Your time," she said, conscious of dignity in the face of what he must see as her pitiful shame. "I took your time."

The doctor got up, opened the door for her, saying gently, "We won't argue about it." And as she still waited, stubborn in her intent, he said quickly, "Send me whatever you think it's worth. Go. Get home as fast as you can. Take care of yourself, Betsy. Here, don't forget your book bag."

She fled. Outdoors, the sun shot wavering stripes of light on all the moving metal in the streets. The late afternoon was coppery, the glare sickening, so that once she stumbled over a curb and was saved by an old man's arm.

"Watch yourself, girlie."

Out of the glare, on the bus, she turned cold. Cold sweat wet her palms and her forehead. That pain, that cramp, was gnawing at her stomach, or near her stomach. From all she had read and heard, the calm of which in the doctor's office she had been proud was really the calm of shock. She had not yet absorbed the facts, the truth.

The bus jolted back toward Kingsley, past the farms, the service station at the intersection and the vacant schoolyard, back toward home and the facts. Now, the truth.

"Charlotte wasn't on the bus," Emmabrown announced when Bill came home.

"She probably went to a friend's house."

"She should have phoned, then."

Emmabrown, he reflected, is a mother. She worries too much, but she's a mother.

He answered easily. "Oh, well. Kids. There's the phone. There she is now."

A man's voice inquired for Mr. Dawes. "This is Dr. Welsh in Arkville. Do you have a daughter named Charlotte?"

"Yes. What's wrong?"

"Don't be alarmed. There's been no accident or anything, but I need to talk to you."

Bill's hands were shaking. Nevertheless, there had been no accident. . . . He sat down.

"She left my office a few minutes ago, said she was going home. She'd given me the wrong name, and when I heard her story, I suspected she had, so I asked my nurse to get the right name out of her schoolbag."

There came a long pause. Bill, waiting silently, urged: *Say it, for God's sake, say it.*

"This is pretty startling news to be telling a father about his young daughter, but I might as well get it over with. She's pregnant, Mr. Dawes."

Charlotte? Charlotte?

"Are you there, Mr. Dawes?"

He was outside himself, observing and remembering in a lurid flash the day long years ago when they had come in to the family sitting at dinner to say that his sister had been in an accident; he saw the faces, his mother's face with eyes stretched open, mouth open, not quite believing.

And now he, not accepting yet understanding that he must, fumbled for words. "Is she all right, I mean, is she coming home, I mean —"

"I think she's all right. I didn't get the impression that she was going to harm herself. Still" — there was a very faint doubt in the man's voice — "still, she's in a state of shock. She wouldn't tell me anything. Said she'd tell her parents herself."

"My God! She never — she's always at home — I don't see how —"

"It seems she's between the first and second month."

Bill floundered. Who? When? How? In that all-girls' school, they were so isolated, so supervised. Who, then? his brain insisted. That fellow Ted? God, no. Can't be. Can't.

"But she also complained of some fairly severe pain that she thought might be appendicitis. It might be, but I rather think not. I rather think there's another problem.

She ought to see a gynecologist right away, Mr. Dawes. Right away. I'm in family medicine, but I can recommend —"

"No. I — her mother and I will have to talk — I appreciate —" The proper words weren't coming, he couldn't think. "Do I owe you anything?"

The doctor's voice was very gentle. "Not at all. I have two daughters, so I can imagine — well, there's nothing much to say. Just that, well, Charlotte has what I'd call elegance. She'll get through this. You will too."

"Thank you. Thank you for your kindness. Thank you."

He put the phone down and groaned. Get through it? How? *Charlotte has elegance. . . .*

He was still sitting there, bowed, near to tears and as close to being beaten as in all his life he had ever been, when he heard Charlotte coming in at the kitchen door. He heard her rushing upstairs, quite obviously in avoidance of him. Let her go. Neither one of them was ready yet to talk.

At least she had come home. Thank God. Thank God.

Prone and rigid, she lay on the bed, afraid to reveal by the faintest rustle of movement that she was there. Eventually, though, her father would come looking for her. But for a while yet the room was a safe haven. If only she might shut herself away in it, just rest there, sleep there, even die in it.

So he really had done this to her, the filthy creep, the rattlesnake. Her fists and her teeth alike were clenched. If she could get her hands on him, she would claw his eyes out.

And I so stupid . . . She wept, covering the sound with the sheet. How to explain it? No one would understand or believe any explanation. You would have to have been there, to see with your own eyes how it had happened. How was she going to get through this? She supposed she would, but she had no idea how.

The bed shook with her stifled weeping, until at last her final sob expired in a long, spent sigh. She got up and went to the bathroom for a drink of water. From the full-length mirror an ugly face with swollen eyes and dry, puffed lips stared out. It was incredible that a person's face could turn into anything so queer and strange.

I suppose, she told it, someday I will look back at all this and wonder how I got through. I suppose I will get through, but I don't know how.

And the pain came shooting, subsiding, and shooting back. She lay down again on the bed, counting time between the throes of that small, hot pain.

The sun, moving west, had left dusk at the far end of the room, dusk creeping toward her across the ceiling. Somebody would be coming soon, most probably Dad, since Emmabrown would be going home. And like one floating, willing to go wherever the current should direct, she waited.

Presently, she heard the heavy footsteps in the hall and the knock at the door.

"Come in," she said.

The moment she saw him, she sensed that something was wrong. He came in and sat down on the edge of the bed. And his hand found hers and held it. For a while neither spoke.

"That doctor telephoned," he said, looking over her toward the darkening window.

"How did he —" she began.

"From your book bag." He was still not looking at her. "Was it Ted?"

"Yes."

"Aaahhh." The sound was so harsh, so terrible, that she flinched. Now would come the reproaches and the blame. Now.

But instead, his hand tightened on hers, while the other hand went to her forehead to stroke her tumbled hair.

"I've spoken to Mama," he said quietly. "She will be here tomorrow."

And he sat there beside her, not speaking, just smoothing and smoothing her hair.

This could be the first circle of hell, Bill thought. His brother was as flushed as if his blood pressure had doubled, while Claudia, except for her reddened eyes, was ghastly. Elena, unable to be still, kept rising and sitting, moving from one chair to the next, clacking her heels as she walked the bare floor between the rugs. She had objected violently to the presence of Claudia and Cliff, but Bill had overruled her.

"They're frantic. They, especially Claudia, are as much involved in this madness as we are."

A furious small figure, Elena stood now in the window's bay, sparking and about to explode again in a tearful rage for the third time today.

"It's an outrage. You can't let an innocent child out of your sight for five minutes with-out — without —"

Bill gave her an expressive look. A fine one to talk, she was. Five minutes. More like months, wasn't it?

"If Ted did this —" cried Claudia, "my God, what can I say? I am so ashamed!"

" 'If' he did this?" Elena screamed. "What do you mean 'if'? My little girl upstairs, my poor, sick, terrified baby, who's been in her bed since yesterday afternoon, isn't hallucinating, you know. She isn't lying either. Does she look like a party girl or the town tramp? She doesn't even know any boys! How do you people think this happened to her? How does your son think it happened?"

"What Ted thinks doesn't matter," Bill interjected.

Claudia said weakly, "We called him in right after you gave us the news this morning, and he was absolutely shocked."

"I can imagine," Bill said. "Look. Charlotte described the entire thing. You had baked a chocolate cake. He gave her wine, red wine, she said. He —" The words choked him.

Claudia's head went down on her clasped hands, and Cliff moved closer to her.

"I think Ted should come here and face you," Cliff said. "I can call him at his friend's house right now."

"Yes," agreed Elena, "you do that. Bring him here so I can get my hands on him. I want to kill him the way you kill a wild rat."

Bill shook his head. "No. I can't look at him. No. To sit in the same room with him would be unbearable. He would defile this house. No," he repeated.

"What is to be done, then," Cliff said

reasonably, "is what we really should be discussing. Obviously, the first thing is to take care of Charlotte —"

"We'll take care of her," Elena said fiercely.

"Of course," Cliff said. "But I am talking about the other side." And then, ignoring Elena, he asked painfully, "Do you want to bring charges against Ted, Bill?"

When Claudia gasped, he put his arm around her again, saying still in that painfully reasonable manner, "We have to face reality. If Ted is guilty, and it certainly seems that he is, why, then . . ." He did not finish.

Claudia raised a tortured face from her hands. "What do you mean? What will happen?"

"He's over eighteen, adult enough to vote and to serve in the army. Adult enough to take his punishment. All this is not your responsibility, Claudia, although knowing you as I do, I know you feel that it is."

Claudia sprang up. "All I want, all I ask, is to see Charlotte. I want to tell her — I don't know what. I just want to see her. We were — for a little while we were friends."

"Absolutely not!" Elena objected. "She's in no condition to see you."

"I'm afraid Elena's right," Bill said. "But as to the other business about pressing charges, I don't see what good is to be gained by hauling Ted into court. I think you should immediately take him for some serious counseling. Nip this in the bud before something else happens."

"I can't believe what I'm hearing," Elena cried. "He's to get away with this? No punishment? Are you out of your mind?"

"I don't think I am. Consider what it would mean to Charlotte to be questioned, first by the police and then by lawyers. The courts would require Ted to have a defense. And do you think that the news, that Charlotte's name, wouldn't leak out? It's all a huge bag of worms. No, this has to be kept quiet. It has to," Bill declared.

For a moment no one spoke. The weight of accumulated fears was smothering them all.

"He'll be going away to college in the fall," Cliff said, meaning, Bill now understood as his eyes met his brother's, *I will keep him out of sight. Don't you worry.*

"No," Bill answered, "that's not enough. I want him away from here right now. No waiting for college."

"Whatever you think best," Claudia said hastily. "Oh, my God, I think I'm dreaming this horror."

"Where can we send him?" Cliff asked.

"Some summer program. A lot of schools have them."

"Try a reform school," Elena said.

"Take any school you can find," Bill said. "The farther away the better."

Cliff, looking sad and solemn, gave assurance. "Will do."

They were moving toward the front door, when Bill, equally sad and solemn, added, "This calamity must not spoil our relationship. Each of us has a problem to deal with, and we need to support, not confront, each other."

When he had closed the door behind them, Elena turned upon him. "What's wrong with you? You seem to think more of your brother and that monster, than you do of your own daughter. And that woman, the monster's mother —"

"She was crushed," Bill said. "Didn't you see? What do you want of her?"

"Crushed. She deserves to be."

"That's cruel and absurd, Elena, and you know it."

" 'If he did it,' she says. Her precious boy! Claudia is a fool. She's out of her mind. She ought to be locked up someplace."

Bill's thoughts were not on Claudia; he flung them out now at Elena. "If you had been home where a mother should be, this wouldn't have happened."

"And if I had been, could I have watched her for every second?"

He did not reply. Maybe he himself should have been more alert. It was on a Sunday, Charlotte had said, so very likely it was the Sunday when he had met with that Midwest group that was leasing the plant. Well, business had to go on if you wanted to pay your bills and eat, didn't it? he demanded angrily. But I didn't like him. I should have been more firm with Charlotte, should have said: *I forbid you under pain of* — of what? That was not his style. He had always been gentle with his gentle child, a sheltered child, perhaps too sheltered. And maybe she hadn't been taught well enough. The wine . . . She hadn't known how fast it can work. His mind ran from one thought to another. Her flighty mother. Flighty? Impossible. That man in Florida. Damn. Talk about life's injustice. That poor child upstairs. What are we going to do?

Elena was in the hall, walking up and down, her idiotic heels hammering the floor.

"How about sitting down, or taking those shoes off?" he heard himself barking. "You're splitting my head open."

Then he was ashamed. She was, after all,

Charlotte's mother, and she was distraught.

"I'm sorry, Elena. But my brain, what's left of it, is going in circles. What are we going to do?"

"What do you mean? We're going to take her to a doctor, and nobody around here either. We're going to Boston."

Yes, of course. Nobody here must ever know, he thought again. Boston's a good idea. And he said, "I'll find out tomorrow morning who's the best. What I'm thinking is, what's the best path after we see the doctor?"

"Path? An abortion, what else?"

"I don't like it, Elena. I hate it."

She was staring at him with total incredulity. "*You* hate it? What about Charlotte? You surely don't expect her to go through a birth, do you?"

His mind was split. Between the split lay the vacancy of denial. Charlotte, at fourteen. A baby. And that wretch the father. And yet, an abortion —

"Well, answer me, Bill. Do you know what it would do to her life, having a baby to care for at her age? And she certainly" — this was said with a sneer — "certainly couldn't go on living in Kingsley. A Dawes girl in Kingsley, of all places."

"What would an abortion do to her life?

She would never forgive herself."

"Maybe. But she showed us both an hour ago that she's terrified of having a baby."

"We could all travel to Europe and give it up there for adoption."

"For God's sake, Charlotte was raped! Don't you understand what that means? Can't you conceive of the humiliation? She would lose her mind, growing that thing for nine months, the spawn of a thug. Might as well hatch a rattlesnake in her belly."

Bill winced. "But it's not a rattlesnake, it's a human child, and it's not responsible for its father."

"Listen to me. Are you forgetting that there may be something else wrong with her? What did that doctor say? Oh, why didn't she call and tell me what had happened to her!" Elena pounded her fist into her palm. "I can understand that she might have been afraid to tell you, but she should have told me."

"Charlotte has never been afraid to tell me anything."

"Oh, of course. Don't you think I know she prefers you? But do you have to rub it in?"

Here we go again, he thought. Even now in the midst of all this. Or perhaps especially now? Anyway, here we go again.

"We had to stop on the drive down to Boston," Elena said. "She had new pains, very sharp. It felt like tearing, she said, and she began to bleed. Did she tell you?"

"It was evident," the doctor replied.

He has a dry manner, Bill thought, a surgeon's, not a bedsider's manner. Analyze, decide, and cut. I knew before the three of us had walked into his office that it would come to surgery.

Charlotte had been so sick in the car. And Elena had never stopped talking the whole time. It was partly to keep cheer afloat and partly her nervous way. As for himself, having spoken his brief piece, he was now a silent listener, benumbed and dull, sterile as this office. Silent Bill, he thought. That's what Cliff calls me.

"She fainted just now after I examined her. She's lying down. We have a problem, Mr. and Mrs. Dawes. The one I suspected."

"We." They say that, but it's not theirs, it's ours, here in my heart. Ponytail, riding her bike —

". . . this is a ruptured tubal pregnancy. I've arranged to have her admitted immediately."

Hospital, Bill thought. It's in his hands. Charlotte's body. Her life? The wall is covered with writings in black frames, very serious writings, some in Latin. Citations too: *In honor of your participation* . . . He turned around, craning toward more of the same on the other wall, but through the blurring in his eyes it was too hard to read them.

Must collect myself. "It's definite, then? I mean, excuse me, there's no doubt in your mind, doctor?"

Stupid question. He said "immediately," didn't he?

"No doubt, Mr. Dawes. Charlotte has exquisite pain upon abdominal palpation, pain radiating to her shoulders and the side of her neck."

Exquisite pain. Queer language these doctors use. Exquisite paintings or workmanship, you say, not pain.

"It is an acute emergency, so that solves your argument about abortion. No more moral dilemma between the two of you." The doctor stood up. "You can take her now. It's only six blocks to the hospital. I'll be over there shortly."

Everyone stood up. How long have we been here? Bill wondered. All day or five minutes?

Through tears Elena asked, "Is it, I mean, can she, do people die? I heard, ectopic pregnancy, sometimes they —"

"Mortality rates have fallen dramatically."

The doctor pats her shoulder near where the curls touch her crisp collar. Even he, formal, desiccated, and grave, cannot resist.

"In fact, they have fallen almost to nothing. Notice I said 'almost.' "

We notice. We go out.

At first there was the dim sound of voices in the distance, far at the end of the hall, or in another room. Then the sound neared and, clarifying, broke into separate voices, Elena's answered by another woman's. Charlotte opened her eyes and saw them in a gloss of white, a uniform, bedcovers, white sky at a window, all light and white except for dark dots on her mother's dress.

Reality came swimming in a great, thankful tide: So I didn't die after all. I really thought I would. So it's over. All the way down in the car they fought while they thought I was asleep. I didn't kill it. Even though I didn't want it, I wouldn't want to think I had killed it. But I would have hated having it. He was so disgusting. I hope he suffers. I hope he dies. What he did to me . . . I'm so tired.

When she woke again, a lamp was lit. She had no idea of the time except that it was dark and felt late. She sensed that her parents were in the room.

"Is it night?" she asked.

"No, darling," Elena answered. "It's evening. How do you feel?"

"All right, I guess."

She felt kisses on her forehead, first Elena's, fragrant with perfume, and then Dad's.

There were a lot of tubes, a tall thing like a lamppost standing beside the bed, and something else clasped on her wrist, all puzzling, all fastened to her. "What's this? What's all this?"

"Intravenous, to feed you. It's only temporary. Don't pull." Dad held her hand, his hand and his voice comforting. "Don't worry. You'll be fine. You are fine now."

"I'm so sleepy."

"Of course you are," Dad said. "You're supposed to be."

"Can you stay awake for a second more?" asked Elena. "Can you see these? I bought two new nightgowns so you won't have to wear a horrible hospital thing. Look, aren't they pretty?"

Her voice pleaded: *See how I love you, I think of you, don't be angry about anything.*

About me and Judd, she meant. Emmabrown said this wouldn't have happened if Elena had been around. I don't know. There is too much to think about.

"Look at this yellow one with pansies. Do you like it?"

"Yes, Mama. Thank you."

"We'll be going home soon. You have to stay here a few days then get some rest, and we'll go home. You'll be back with your friends."

Friends. None of my friends knows what I know now.

"We'll have a wonderful summer," Dad said. "You'll see. We'll forget all this."

Forget. They won't. They won't want to mention it because it's too nasty, but whenever they look at me, they'll think of it. Always. Forever.

And Charlotte, seeing them both — poor father and poor mother — on either side of her bed, was deeply sad.

Bill, as the evening drew on, was the only one awake. Elena had slumped in the single easy chair. He had the queerest sensation even as he observed her in detail — the head resting on the chairback, the mouth slightly open, the long fingers splayed on the chair arm — that she was ephemeral. He had never really held her, nor really known her in any depth. Perhaps there was no depth to be known? And he wondered now, after what had occurred to their child, how they would fare together.

But, "sufficient unto the day," et cetera. Charlotte, at least, had survived.

"We used a conservative surgical approach," the doctor had explained there in the waiting room, the torture chamber. "Years ago we always had to remove the tube, but now we are able to preserve it, so when her day comes, she will have children as easily as if this had never happened."

Children! That's the least of my worries right now, Bill thought. I'm just glad she's alive. Let her get back to school and be her age. Let God help her to wipe this awful thing out of her mind — if that's possible, which I don't think it is.

He raised his eyes to look around the periphery of the room, from Charlotte lying in peaceful sleep to the door ajar, through which, as if in a haze, he could see people passing in the hall. And he was sure that none of them, seeing him here, a quiet ordinary man in a gray suit, could possibly guess what was going on within him.

My pounding heart, he thought. I am almost forty years old, and have just now arrived at the knowledge of evil.

EIGHT

The gloom was palpable. When Claudia had finished the supper dishes, she went to the kitchen door and looked out into the sultry evening. There was no movement of bird or leaf; only the buzz and hum of a myriad hidden insects gave sign of life. For a while she stood there, gazing without thought into this vacancy, then, turning, went inside to the same vacant silence.

On the table Ted's place was still laid. Sulking in his room, he refused to eat with them. She considered the wisdom of bringing a tray to him; he was, after all, her child and he must be hungry. All day he had been upstairs alone, or not entirely alone, since she had heard him using the telephone. She wondered how, with the weight that must be upon him now, he managed to be so jovial with his friends. Surely he must be tormented by the thought of that poor child in the hospital. On the other hand he kept denying any guilt, which was absurd.

Of course he had done it to her. Even the counselor to whom Cliff had had to drag him did not believe his denial. Not that it mattered, because Ted had refused to go back a second time. So they were now at an impasse. What was to be done? Was it in some way her fault that he had done this thing, that he had committed this crime, that he had turned out this way?

What was wrong with him? She was conflicted. It was hard to admit that there was anything "wrong" with your own child. He was hers, and she loved him. But then there was Charlotte. . . . A girl like her, no girl, should have to undergo what she was undergoing. So sweet, she was, so trustful, with those fine, candid eyes.

I am sick, Claudia said to herself. I am really sick.

And she went to the room where Cliff would be sitting with his dogs beside him and an unread book or newspaper on his lap. Cliff was in no mood for reading.

No, she would not carry his dinner up to Ted. Cliff, good-natured, goodwilled Cliff, would most definitely object, and he would be right.

He looked up, smiling. "Come join me. This is fascinating. Remember when they found that prehistoric man frozen in an Italian glacier a few years ago? There were remnants of some sort of fabric. I wonder —"

Claudia said, "You're not fooling me, Cliff, but thanks for trying. You've got the book upside down."

He shrugged. "Okay, I'm not concentrating very well. My mind is in Boston."

"Cliff, I can't tell you how I —" she began, when he stopped her.

"Don't say it again. Don't you think I understand how you feel? Claudia dearest, this has nothing to do with you. Your son is a separate entity. I've said it before and I'll say it again. You are not responsible for his sins."

In spite of all her resolve her eyes filled. "Shall we turn the news on?" she asked. "I don't think there is anything much, but it's something to do, unless you want to take a walk."

"It's too hot," Cliff said.

What he might more truly have said was: *I'm too tired. I haven't the energy.*

On the screen the talking heads talked and made their earnest gestures. She barely saw them. Instead, her eyes went wandering around the room, from the comfortable abundance of books upon the shelves to the wilting roses, to the wedding portrait on the mantel. Only months ago she had entered this house and taken her place, filled with promise of long, long years of love and peace. She ought to have known better. Her own life should have taught her that you can have no inkling today of what tomorrow may bring.

Presently, Ted's footsteps were heard upon the stairs, and she called to him.

"Ted. Your dinner's on the stove."

"I don't want any. I'm going out."

"Come in here, please."

In plain shirt and jeans, a well-washed, well-dressed young man wearing, too, a severe expression, he stood at the door, inquiring, "What do you want?"

"I want to know where you're going," Claudia replied.

"Out. Out with friends."

"But where? With whom?"

"I don't know. I'm not in kindergarten, Ma."

She hated the way he snapped the words. He hadn't ever done that before. It was only during these last few days that his nerves seemed to have given way like this.

Cliff said quietly, "We know you're not, Ted. But your mother's anxious. It's a simple enough thing for you to understand that and give her an answer."

"Yes, I could tell her," Ted said. He spoke not rudely, but stubbornly. "But it's all about that girl, isn't it? Must my friends be under suspicion too? You're making me miserable. This whole thing is crazy. All on account of a crazy kid."

"What about Mr. Bowman's daughter? No, Ted, your stories don't wash." Cliff's voice rose. "And Charlotte, my niece —" Becoming emotional, he stopped.

"Can you prove she wasn't fooling around with somebody else? No, you couldn't prove it in a court of law. Just because she's your niece, you're trying to pin it on me. Okay, I'm going to Bud's house. Are you satisfied?"

"Ted!" cried Claudia, starting from her chair. "You shock me. I want you to apologize."

"No, Ma." Ted was aggrieved. "You should all apologize to me. You're not being fair."

And he went out, clattering the screen door behind him.

Once more, as in moments of acute awareness during these last dreadful days, Claudia felt the heat of an intolerable shame. It's no use Cliff's telling me that Ted is a "separate entity," she thought. I still feel lower than a worm. And they are all — well, except for Elena, although God knows I can't blame her — so civilized in understanding me. Bill understanding *me* in the face of what my son has done to his daughter!

"Let's put some music on," Cliff said.

131

"There's always comfort in it. I remember after my sister was killed in the accident, Mother used to listen to Bach." He bent down and kissed Claudia's head. "Not that anyone is dead here. Darling, it's all awful, but I won't let it crush you."

In a kind of quietude they were listening to a glorious violin when the dogs barked and the doorbell rang.

"I'll get it," Cliff said.

From the front door came the boom of male voices. A few seconds later Cliff returned with two policemen. Claudia got up and switched off the music.

"These officers want to see Ted," Cliff said.

She stared at him, and saw that he was shaken.

"What is it?" she cried. "He just left. Ted —"

He put his hand on her arm, saying firmly, "Hold it. Nothing's happened to him. Where did he say he was going?"

"Bud's house."

"I'll go get him. Perhaps — it would be easier for my wife if you'd wait outside?"

"No problem. We'll stand out front."

"You don't have to worry, Officer. I'll be right back with him."

"That's okay, Mr. Dawes. We know you."

Alone in the room, Claudia stared at the wall. My God, my God, what has he done? A speeding ticket? They don't send police to your house for that. Maybe they do. I don't know. I've never had a ticket. What else could it be?

The blood throbbed in her ears. Could that nice Mr. Bowman have changed his mind after all? But he only said Ted had insulted his daughter, not that he had harmed her. Or could Bill have reported anything? No, not Bill. For Charlotte's sake alone he wouldn't do it. He had clearly said so. Then perhaps Elena?

She went to the window. They were all coming up the walk, Cliff and Ted with the police behind them. She ran toward the door and met them in the front hall.

The older officer thrust a paper at Ted. "You're Theodore Marple?" And when Ted, with wide eyes and blanched face, nodded, "Read this. It's a warrant for your arrest."

Ted gasped. "For what? I haven't done —" He clutched the doorknob behind him.

Words raced through Claudia's brain: He knows. He knows what they're here for.

"Read it. Two complaints to the district attorney charging rape, kidnapping, and endangering the morals of a minor on June seventeenth last."

"I never —" Ted stopped.

And words raced through Claudia's head: He is paralyzed with fear.

"Sit down, Claudia. My wife has a heart condition, Officer. This is the last thing she needs."

"There has to be some mistake." She was babbling. A fool, denying, when all the time the truth was so clear. And they were paying no attention to her, anyway.

". . . these are your rights," the man was saying. "You need answer no questions without the presence of your attorney. There will be a hearing before the court tomorrow morning. In the meantime you will come with us."

"May he go upstairs and get some clothes?" asked Cliff.

"No, sorry. Let someone else go for them."

"I'll go," Cliff said promptly. "Stay still, Claudia."

Ted turned to her, his eyes, now emptied of bravado, calling: Help me.

I can't, hers answered. I am drowning, hanging on by my fingernails, and there is nothing I can do.

When Cliff came back with a small bundle, which he tried to hand to Ted, one of the officers took it from him. The other brought handcuffs out of his pocket.

Cliff asked softly, "Are those necessary? I'm sure Ted won't make any trouble. He'll go quietly."

The younger man, who had not spoken, looked pitying. Perhaps he had a boy of his own. The other one fastened the handcuffs.

"Sorry, Mr. Dawes," he apologized, "but I have to. Come on, son."

Claudia watched them go down the walk, Ted tall and narrow between the other two, who were tall and broad, authority in dark blue coats and brass buttons. Well, we have to have authority. But she had never dreamed her child would come up against it.

"Cliff, you don't think Bill reported this after all?"

"He said he wouldn't."

"Leave the door open until they drive out of sight."

"No, get up. Lock the back door. I'm calling Miller to meet us at the station house." Cliff paused. "Miller's been our lawyer from the year one. Wills and trusts and business. I don't imagine he handles many cases like this. Still, we'll see. Try to take it easy if you can. Leave it to me."

She had not moved from the hard little chair when, a minute later, he returned.

"Miller's out. I left a message. Where are the car keys? Let's go."

"Where are they putting — I mean — where will he sleep?" she asked when they were in the car. At the same time she knew the answer. "Tell me the truth, Cliff."

He turned to look at her. "Of course you know where. Listen to me. A jail cell is hardly pretty, but it won't be as if he were convicted and sent to prison. It's just a holding operation until bail is set. Darling, they're not going to hurt him. This isn't Nazi Germany. Believe me."

They drove on, passing the mall where people were doing normal things like buying sneakers for their children. Then, as they neared the old heart of the city, they passed the Dawes mill, where a line of laden trucks waited for morning to discharge their ugly waste. Cliff's quick glance at it did not escape her; he has too much on his mind, she mourned, and now I bring him this.

"Don't cry when you walk in there," he warned her. "Don't let him see you do that."

"I won't," she assured him, sitting up straighter. And she reminded herself of the old adages with which she had been brought up: *Head over heart. Stiff upper lip. Be a man.*

Nowadays you also said: *Be a woman.*

Public buildings, courthouses, town halls, and police departments all had the same smell of cleaning fluid, the same sound of rapid feet striking hard floor, and the same brown varnished benches. Cliff motioned her to sit on one and wait.

"Wait there and count sheep while I find out what's going on."

She scolded herself. I shouldn't let him take charge for me. I've never had a man share my responsibilities. I've done everything alone, and I've done pretty well. But right now, although the spirit's willing, the flesh is weak. My legs don't want to hold up. What are they going to do to Ted? Kidnapping, rape, endangering the morals . . . Oh, why, Ted? Why?

Cliff was returning. She recognized his fast, determined walk from down the corridor. Everything echoed in this cold, hollow place, empty now at the end of the day.

"I saw him. They're doing stuff, filling out papers and taking his fingerprints. He's scared out of his wits, but he's holding up. I called Miller. He says there's nothing he can do tonight. He'll meet us at court before it convenes in the morning."

"Did he say —"

"He said nothing. He has to find out what's going on first. He's very competent. We're in good hands, I promise. I suppose you'll want to see Ted now?"

A policeman, the one who had shown that glimmer of pity, led them to a cement-walled room in which there were a few cells. The bars, the small window high up near the ceiling, were all familiar from movies and television; even the drunk bawling nonsense was a familiar stock figure. Only Ted was not.

He was sitting on the edge of a cot that stood against the wall. When he saw them, he got up and came to the bars. He looked dazed. They were all dazed. There seemed to be nothing to say.

She wanted to put her hands between the bars to touch him, but he was not quite near enough. Besides, if she were to touch him, she knew she would break into tears, and she had promised not to.

"It'll be all right," she whispered, "Cliff has a good lawyer. Can you sleep tonight? Have you got your things?" Then she saw the bundle on the cot, the pathetic little bundle. "Is there anything you need?"

"No," he said. "Thanks." The syllables emerged like a sob from a tight throat.

She wanted to say: *Oh, Ted, I'm so sad.*

*What have you done with your life? How can
I help you?* But of course she did not, and
gave him a smile intended to be encouraging.

"Good night, as good as possible. We'll
see you in the morning. And — oh, Ted,
we're going to do everything we can for
you."

"Thanks, Ma. Thanks, Cliff. I'm sorry.
I'm really sorry."

Cliff, on the way home, was unusually
silent.

"It's very bad, isn't it?" Claudia ventured
to say.

"We'll learn more from Miller tomorrow."

"Kidnapping. I don't understand 'kidnapping,' do you?"

"No."

"I know I should be thinking of his — his
crimes, of those young girls, whatever he did
to them. You certainly know I think every
minute of Charlotte. But I can't get out of
my mind why he has done all this. He was
never cruel."

"I can't answer, Claudia."

"What do you think will happen to him?"

"I can't answer that either."

"College is out of the question now.
They'll revoke their acceptance."

Cliff did not deny it. They went into the house, where Ted's place was still set on the table.

"I guess I'll take a hot bath and go to bed," she said. "It's funny, I'm freezing and it's still warm outside."

"I'm calling Dr. Billings. I want him to have the drugstore deliver some sleeping pills. You'll need a good night's rest."

"I never needed pills," she protested. "And I've had plenty of troubles."

"Not like this one."

"Well, if you must, at least please don't tell Billings why."

"I won't, but we have to face it, Claudia, it will be in the newspaper soon enough."

Later, lying in bed after Cliff had seen her take the pill, she heard him grumbling in the bathroom.

"Damn bastard. What does he think he is, the neighborhood stud? A mad bull. They ought to pen him up and throw the key away."

When he got into the bed, she pretended she had not overheard. He was entitled to his rage. Indeed, her anguish over her son had its own admixture of rage.

"Feeling sleepy yet?" he asked.

"A little."

"Come here."

And he took her, drowsy now, into his arms.

Mr. Miller was the classic lawyer from the top rank, with a well-tailored suit, conservative tie, and attractive, silvering hair. His manner, although pleasant, was *Waste no words.* They met in the courthouse lobby.

"I spoke to the DA," he said. "Frankly, it doesn't look too good. There are two girls involved, one the daughter of Monroe Dieter, the other the daughter of Frederick Callahan."

"Frederick Callahan," Cliff said. "He's a vice-president at my bank."

"I know. I know him well. His daughter got a fist in her face when she resisted. They have the medical report. It seems he was taking her home from a party but drove out toward the lake instead, where he attacked her. So that's not only rape, but also kidnapping. With the other girl it was rape alone. There are witnesses who heard her screaming."

Claudia whispered, "What do you expect? What's next?"

"We're going in to the hearing in a minute. The DA or his assistant will seek an indictment, meaning that the evidence will be presented to a grand jury, and they will either vote or not vote a bill of indictment. In this case, you can be sure, they will vote one. The case will then go to trial."

"What will happen if he loses at the trial?" she asked, still whispering.

"If he's convicted? Oh, let's not jump that far ahead," Miller said gently.

"Please, Mr. Miller. It's easier for me to know what to expect, even the worst. What's the worst?"

"A pretty stiff sentence."

"I see. How long does it take before the indictment is handed down?"

"I can't be exact, but in this county, let's say about three weeks at the earliest." Miller looked at his watch. "All right, it's time to go in."

Courtrooms, too, are identical all over the country, Claudia supposed. The one in Illinois where men had gone on trial for the killing of Ted's father had looked just like this one, although a bit larger. But otherwise it had been the same, with the flag and the judge in his black robes sitting high at his bench, with the shuffling of papers as the previous case ended, and a hot breeze flapping the green window shades. These buildings had been made long before air-conditioning had even been thought of.

Except for the district attorney and Mr.

Miller, the room had emptied when Claudia and Cliff took their seats. The judge entered, then Ted between two attendants. He looked so pale! He was in the row in front of Claudia, a little over to the side, so that her eyes rested on the back of his head. Such beautiful hair he had, like thick black silk! Many a girl might wish she had such hair. She wondered whether Cliff had remembered to pack a toothbrush and a comb yesterday.

She felt faint. Her palms were sweating. Low blood sugar, it was. Cliff had warned her not to go without breakfast, but she had not been able to swallow food; she had been in a hurry to get here. Now she was in a hurry to get out.

The proceedings moved ahead. She barely heard them, closing her eyes as she fought to control sickness. When she opened them after a surprisingly short time, the district attorney and Miller were conferring with the judge at the bench.

"A particularly nasty, violent rape. No date rape, Your Honor," she heard, and then heard only murmurs again.

Presently the two men returned to their seats, and the judge addressed the court, his face turned toward Cliff and Claudia.

"The question here has nothing to do with

innocence or guilt. It has only to do with whether the defendant is liable to flee. In a charge this serious the court will take no chances and will require bail. In view of the fact that there are two separate plaintiffs, bail will be set at four hundred thousand dollars. The defendant will then be released in the custody of his parents."

Miller rose. "I should like to confer with my clients, Your Honor." He sat down again and, with a somewhat dubious expression, regarded Cliff. "Well?"

"A hefty sum," said Cliff, exhaling an almost inaudible whistle.

"Yes. Can you do it?"

"I'll have to. What choice is there?"

Claudia stared down at a large splinter where some unknown piece of metal had gouged the floor. She was burning within. Live coals in the stomach. What choice was there? Plain enough: Let him sit in jail until the trial.

No one spoke for a few moments until Cliff said, "It's been a long time, before the mill shut down, since I've been what most people would call very well off. I'll have to borrow, put my house up as collateral. It's worth a deal more than four hundred."

His beloved house, the family home. And all the rotten publicity. Cliff's good name.

On account of Ted. My contribution to our marriage, she thought in her bitter shame. Did he, this minute, have any regrets? She couldn't look at him.

"It's a good thing we have business with two banks. I'd hate to have to ask Callahan's bank for a loan, even with good collateral. I'd hate to come face to face with him at all right now."

"How soon do you think you'll get it?" asked Miller.

"I can take care of it today."

"Okay," Miller said. "Why don't you go outside, Mrs. Dawes? You look as if you need some air."

"Yes, go," Cliff urged. "I'll be there as soon as we get the paperwork done."

Claudia did not protest. Leaving the courtroom, she passed close to Ted. In custody, she thought, Ted's in custody. Though he said nothing, his eyes implored her. And she gave him a smile with a "thumbs up," lifting her head high as she went out.

Cliff brought her home and left again for the bank. Alone, she walked through the house just looking at things, from the dining room with its 1910 family portrait above the mantel, through the broad hall into the sunroom, where flowering plants kept summer alive through the dark winter. This house had never had a mortgage. And she stood in the sunny hallway again, wringing her hands. Odd, she thought as she became aware that she was doing so, it's not only in Victorian novels, but true, that people in despair do wring their hands.

After a while, though, she spoke aloud to herself. "This won't do. No, Claudia, it won't do at all."

The remedy, the oldest remedy known to women, had always been work. For some time she had been reminding herself that the pantry cabinets, stored with fancy old china and cut glass seldom used, could stand a good cleaning. Very well, there was no better moment than the present to begin.

She was in the midst of this chore, surrounded by bric-a-brac, when Cliff came home. She looked at him, asking a silent question. Speech right now was not only difficult but apparently, for both of them, unnecessary, because his answer, though soft, was brief.

"It'll be taken care of."

Her response was a nod. How explain her gratitude or her pain? Surely, knowing her as he did, he knew that too.

"It's cooling off," he said. "What about having supper out under the trees?"

So with scant appetite they ate and talked

a little about daily things, whether they should take Rob to a different veterinarian, or whether they needed a new fence in back. Later they listened to the news, heard some music, and went to bed.

"Do you want a sleeping pill?" asked Cliff.

"No pills."

I must get through this by my own strength. There's a long road ahead.

NINE

Having said nothing for the last half hour, Mama complained, "I'm trying to figure out why you're taking all these blacktop byways instead of the interstate. We'll never get home at this rate."

"Because," Dad said, "I like to watch summer marching up north of Boston. You don't see anything on an interstate. Besides, what's the hurry?"

North of Boston. Last semester they had had to memorize a poem of Robert Frost's.

The mountain held the town as in a
* shadow.*
I saw so much before I slept there once. . . .

Charlotte had selected that one because of the mountain, which she could see from her window; far off and dark blue, it merged into clouds so that sometimes you were not sure whether you were really seeing it at all.

But now I don't want to go back there, Charlotte thought. I have to get away. My friends will ask where I've been. I don't want to talk to them. I look awful, skinny and scrawny. Emmabrown will hug me and cry and want to know what they did to me in Boston. I'll cover my eyes if Dad drives past Claudia's house. If only there were some cleaning cloth or dust mop that could just wipe things out of my head, things that keep cropping up when I don't want them to! Elena, giggling with Judd in Florida. His striped shirt. Elena and Dad at night, doors slamming and the chandelier tinkling in the hall.

Listen, Charlotte, you'd better pull yourself together or they'll take you to a shrink, at least they'll try to. But you won't go. You only need to get away where nobody knows you, and you'll be all right. Yes, you will, Charlotte.

"Look," Dad said. "There's a real country school. I wonder whether it's still in use. Probably not. Can't have more than three rooms with a stove in each. McGuffey's readers. Well, at least they learned grammar then, which is more than they do today."

A country school would be nice. It wouldn't be like this one, with a cow pasture across the road, although I would like that. But I could go to a boarding school. Long ago and far away. Isn't that somebody's poem? At least it would be far away.

"Have you heard anything from your

149

brother about what's going on?" Elena asked. "You never tell me."

"We've had other things on our minds, haven't we? Besides, I hate the subject."

"We can't dodge it. No, don't look warnings at me. Charlotte certainly wants to know what's happening."

Dad looked back at her through the rearview mirror. His forehead had worry wrinkles.

"Do you, Charlotte?"

She did, and also she didn't. "I suppose I do," she said.

"Well, I'll make it short and simple. Ted's been arrested on two rape charges. Rape and kidnapping. He drove a girl out to the lake against her will. He broke her nose."

Little fingers of alarm ran down Charlotte's back. "How did they find out? I mean, does everybody know?"

"You needn't be afraid. We haven't made any complaint, so no one will know about you. These girls' parents went to the police. That's different. It's in all the newspapers."

"Who are the girls?"

"Their names are withheld. That's not to say their names won't leak out when they have to testify."

"What will happen to Ted?"

"I imagine he'll serve time."

"They should take him out and shoot him," Elena said.

Dad sighed. "Everything's a mess. Cliff had to make enormous bail. And Claudia — well, you can imagine how she must be."

A memory of lemon tarts flashed. I still have some of the books that she lent me, Charlotte thought.

"I'm sorry for her," she said.

"Sorry!" cried Elena. "The woman's a fool. If they put that monster away for the rest of his life, which they won't do, she'll be well rid of him."

Bill reproved her. "He's a heartbreaking blow to a mother. Don't you see that? And Claudia is far from being a fool."

"Oh, you two! You and Charlotte. Two softies if there ever were any."

No one answered. The car meandered through a long green aisle, around curves, up little hills and down. All you could hear was the soft throb of the engine.

Imagine having to go to court and tell, thought Charlotte. I would die.

"We'll be in Roseville soon," Elena said. "Let's stop for lunch."

"Are you hungry, Charlotte?" Dad inquired.

"It doesn't matter whether she is or not," Elena interrupted. "She needs building up.

She needs to eat."

"Meaning that, as usual, you are starved," Dad said, not unkindly. "Okay, we'll find a diner when we go through town."

"No diner, Bill, please. You know I hate the smell of frying grease. Let's go to a decent place. Roseville must have one. There!" Elena said a few minutes later. "The old Colonial Inn. That looks nice."

"Tearoom," Bill grumbled. "Little doilies, sweet salads, and a spinning wheel in the corner. Oh, and a warming pan used by Washington — no, he didn't get up this far north. Used by somebody, anyway, by Daniel Webster, maybe."

Elena laughed. But it wasn't funny. Couldn't they ever agree about anything? Even about where to eat lunch?

"Put your sweater on," Elena commanded. "It's chilly, Charlotte."

"Mama, it's warm. It's hot."

"Don't take any chances. Listen to me. You haven't got your strength back yet."

That was true. She did not have all her strength, and since it was easier not to argue, she put on the sweater. Besides, Mama meant well.

"It's not so bad. Even rather nice," Bill observed of the clean, bright room with the ubiquitous blackened fireplace and iron pots, ferns in hanging baskets, and middle-aged ladies wearing floral prints. He was being, as usual, conciliatory.

Elena's comment followed. "It's dreary, like all these towns."

Beyond the window where they were sitting, traffic was slow on the wide main street. People ambled under a typical arch of elms.

"It's remarkable," Bill said, making conversation. "The elm blight seems to have escaped this town. What a difference trees make! We don't prize them enough."

Elena played with her chicken salad. For someone known to have a huge appetite, she was not doing very well. She sighed, so audibly that a woman at the near table, which was very near, turned to look. Perhaps, too, Charlotte thought, she is looking at Mama's fashionable scarlet linen dress, a type not usually worn in Roseville.

"It's been a nightmare," Elena said. "This whole year, finishing up with the hospital, the horror of it. A nightmare."

"Nightmares end when you wake up," Bill said.

"Oh, I'm awake. That's how I know I have to get away for a while."

Calmly, Bill asked where she wanted to go this time. And Charlotte, suspending a fork midway to her mouth, waited for the answer.

Please, not Florida again!

"I want to go back to Italy. I haven't been there in years. I've been thinking — during all those miserable hours in the hospital there was plenty of time to think — that it would be wonderful for Charlotte to have a year at school abroad. We could have the rest of the summer to travel first. Wouldn't that be wonderful?"

"You know very well that I can't take any time away now," Bill said firmly. "There's too much going on."

"About Ted, you mean? I should think you'd be glad to get away from that mess. What they do with him is no concern of yours."

"Yes, about Ted, but also our business. I'm worried about the new tenants. They're our livelihood."

"Well, Charlotte and I can go."

This was simply a replay of the Florida affair. "No," Charlotte said flatly.

Elena raised her eyebrows. "So emphatic? Why not?"

You ask, Charlotte said to herself, but you know why not: Italy, and parties, and another Judd.

"Because I won't go without Dad," she replied, which was also true.

"You do hurt me, Charlotte. I am, after

all, your mother. Sometimes you seem to forget that."

"I don't mean to hurt you, Mama. But I don't want to go. What I want is boarding school, someplace out in the country." The idea was taking firmer shape as she spoke. "I want to start right away. Some schools have summer sessions."

"What do you think?" Elena asked Bill.

"Whatever Charlotte feels will be good for her. She's been through enough, and she knows best how she feels."

"You see," Elena said, "your father won't mind if you go to Italy with me."

"But I don't want to go there," Charlotte said.

Elena shrugged. "Well, I tried, that's all I can say. I, however, am definitely going to go."

There was a soreness in Charlotte's chest, a grieving that comes when, in a book or at the movies, men go off to war, a child dies, or even — even when a beloved old dog is abandoned. It's parting, she thought, a breaking apart. That's what it is.

"You won't come back," she said very low.

"I never said I wouldn't," Elena cried sharply. "I didn't say that."

"But I know," replied Charlotte.

A heavy atmosphere engulfed them all. When they rose from the table, it followed them into the car. The engulfing sweetness of the last two weeks' truce, when the parents on either side of Charlotte's bed were united in their love for her and all their words were soft, had vanished.

No one made any effort now to bring it back; even Dad stopped making conversation. In a semidoze Charlotte lay on the backseat watching the treetops fly by. When at last he broke the silence and she sat up, they were on the river road, nearing home.

"They've already got trucks dumping," he said, as if to himself. "I had no idea they'd get started so soon."

The desolate huddle of the barren building reminded her of the state penitentiary, and gloom overcame her. She hated Kingsley. She was going to leave it and never, never come back.

When Cliff and I were kids, Bill asked himself, who could have imagined where we would be today? We had the world in a jug, as the old folks used to say. We'd ride downtown with our father and visit the mill; it was the heart of Kingsley; our father was the respected king of the town, and we were the young princes.

156

In the days since their return from Boston he had fallen into the habit of taking an after-dinner walk, alone with his turbulent thoughts. Elena watched television, and Charlotte, postoperative but recovering, went early to bed. Sometimes he met Cliff walking. Each of them, needing now some brief escape from stress, seemed to find it in the dark and quiet summer evening. They understood each other perfectly, Cliff knowing that Elena did not want him in their house and Bill aware that an encounter with Ted at the other house would be a disaster.

"He hides in his room," Cliff had told him, "and won't come out. Claudia brings his meals up to him. He's terrified, and well he should be. I love her, and that's the problem. If I didn't, I'd have booted him out, let him rot in jail until the trial date, let him take his punishment. Now I've loaded myself with debt because of him."

Sorrowfully, Bill thought, My brother married a pack of trouble, and he said, "Some people are no good. That's it, plain and simple. No matter what you do for them, they're just no good. Bad seed. Not from Claudia," he added quickly.

Cliff always wanted to hear about Charlotte, but there was nothing new to tell him. She was remote, depressed, and determined

157

to go away. At night, going home from his walk, he would look up at her window where the light was still on. She read late, and she read serious books, much poetry. Also, she had read some newspaper articles and editorials about Ted. . . . Bill would miss her terribly when she was gone. She was still here under his roof, and yet he already felt the bone-ache and soreness of loss.

The summer was sliding away into August before applications were made and accepted and arrangements became final; Charlotte was to leave at the end of the month. The school was two hundred miles distant. It might just as well, Bill thought, be in the antipodes. No more walks together, no more chatter at the dinner table. She was going away among strangers with the weight of her heavy secret upon her.

He wondered that Elena could be so accepting. Brisk and cheerful, she had everything prepared for Charlotte. The proper clothes in abundance, the required booklist fulfilled, even writing paper and stamps, all were neatly packed in new luggage. A picnic lunch for the journey was ready in a basket, Emmabrown having made Charlotte's favorites, fried chicken and apple pie.

Emmabrown is teary, Elena is efficient as she has always been, while I am just clumsy,

Bill thought. I am bumbling my way through this departure.

On the ride he kept watching Charlotte. Without a doubt she was scared; everyone going away to school was scared. He tried in his usual way to lighten the atmosphere simply by breaking the silences, to remark that the days were noticeably shortening or to observe that the cicadas were unusually shrill this year and he had heard somewhere that it meant an early fall.

"Though that's probably just another superstition," he added.

Elena chose a picnic stop on the top of a hill looking northward into ever-rising mountains. She, too, made conversation; hers was all forward looking.

"You must polish your conversational French. So many people can read Molière and still not be able to go into a shop and ask for something. You'll find what fun it is to travel and be at ease in another language."

When Elena was really nervous, she had a slight stammer. He remembered how charming that had seemed the first time he heard it. Now it filled him with pity. Like him — and yet how unlike him — she was suffering. And for an instant he became an outsider, passing the little group at their country picnic, surrounded by wild lilies and

Queen Anne's lace, a pair of nice-looking parents with their wholesome daughter, enjoying a family hour together. This outsider would not see how sadly disconnected they were.

And yet, through Charlotte, they *were* connected, for all time.

"How much farther do we have to go?" asked Charlotte.

"We should be there by two," Bill said.

She seemed relieved. Probably, she was feeling the way you do when waiting your turn at the dentist's; you are in a hurry to get it over with. He knew that although she had wanted, had even insisted on, this great change, the last minutes would be very hard and should be made as short as they could make them.

Indeed, all went so quickly that afterward he had no clear recollection of very much except for a swirl of cars, luggage, parents, and noisy girls, a great bustle against a background of red brick, white columns, and old trees. There were a few well-controlled tears, some hugs and admonitions, these on Elena's part.

"School food is starchy, so eat plenty of vegetables and don't get fat. And call collect twice a week."

They hugged again, walked toward the

car, looked back, and waved. Then they got into the car and drove away. Bill's head swam. Those girls, those other girls, had seemed, in spite of their height and their makeup, so childlike! And to his mind's eye came again the picture of Charlotte being wheeled to the operating room. He wanted to punch the dashboard. He wanted to weep.

When, late in the day, they reached home, it was raining hard. The house was enveloped in the sound of it as they ate the supper that Emmabrown had left for them.

"Cold autumn here already," Elena said mournfully. "Listen to it."

Here are two people in the room, Bill thought, one hearing the dismal rain, while the other hears its peaceful rhythm.

"We don't understand each other," he said, feeling a vast tiredness. "I guess we never did."

He wished they could talk openly. But, given that they had not understood each other, how could they talk openly? He wanted to ask about that man in Florida. She would only deny the whole business, though, and he would be made to seem a fool. Then suddenly the words slipped out of his mouth.

"I've been wondering about that man in Florida. Do you want to say anything about him?"

"Oh, he! A lightweight, a fun person, that's all. I've already told you that, and there's nothing else to say now."

"So there really is no 'other man'?"

"No, none at all."

"You simply want a divorce."

"Did I say so? Why, do you?"

Halfhearted, not sure that he was in the right, he replied uncertainly, "I believe that marriage is worth saving."

"Any marriage?"

"Where there are children," he began, "Charlotte —"

"Charlotte's gone to boarding school."

He felt his temper rising. It was almost as though, with this parrying, this game of words, she was flirting with their tragedy.

"All the same," he said, "she needs to know there's a mother at home."

"A father will do just as well while I'm away, or better. She always loved you more than me."

"She loves you, Elena."

"Well, perhaps she does. But she doesn't like me. There's a difference."

"Then maybe you should make changes in yourself."

"I can't. People don't change. I am what I am."

Her complacent acceptance of her own faults infuriated him. Because of this fool — oh, me too — but mostly because of her, this awful thing befell our child. God alone knew what Charlotte's needs had been. Bitch, he thought, you foolish bitch.

"I saw your lips move. You said *bitch*."

"And so I did," he replied.

"Don't hate me, Bill. Don't fight with me."

Elena got up and walked through the hall into the living room, her heels pounding the bare floor as usual, and pounding in his ears as well.

He smothered his anger and followed her, saying quietly, "I'm not going to fight. The last thing you and I need is a battle. It's the last thing Charlotte needs too."

Her face was pale and shadowed. For a second she put her fingers to her lips, and he saw light glinting on the ring, the diamond, modest enough, that in the delight of a passionate first love, he had given to her. When she put her hand down and opened her lips as if to speak, she said nothing. Then suddenly, and again, he felt the warmth of forgivingness. She was what she was, and she had not asked to be what she was. There was no use in blaming her.

He often had these abrupt reversions from outrage to compassion. Maybe I need a shrink, he thought bitterly.

"So you are going?" he asked.

"Yes. Don't look like that, Bill. I'm not abandoning you, for heaven's sake. I never said anything about divorce. I'll be back."

He supposed that she really believed what she was saying, but he knew different. They had at long last come to the end. And very likely or maybe surely it was better so, after the way they had been living. Yet it hadn't been entirely bad. He didn't really know. From generation to generation, he thought, we move in a sort of twilight. We think we see, but there is so much hidden, so much.

"When do you want to go?" he asked.

She gave him a tentative smile, replying with a question. "Next Tuesday? Will that be all right?"

"Yes, Tuesday," he said gently. "I'll drive you to Boston to the airport."

TEN

They were at breakfast when Mr. Miller telephoned with the news. "I heard yesterday, very late, but I thought Claudia might gain a night of slightly better sleep if I waited till morning. Here it is: The grand jury voted to indict."

Miller's voice was loud enough for Claudia, on the other side of the table, to hear him. Laying down her spoon, she grasped the table's edge and stared at Cliff.

"Will you be taking it to trial?" Cliff asked.

"Not I. Criminal defense is not in my line, as you know. The firm has a very bright young litigator who'll be your best bet, the best in town. His name is Kevin Raleigh, and he'll see Ted at three-thirty this afternoon."

Criminal defense. All the tense and terrible courtroom scenes that Claudia had ever seen on television were melded into one picture. In a hellish circle with Ted at bay in the center were scornful faces and accusing fingers, pointing at him. For a few seconds the picture blazed; then she pushed the table away and started toward the stairs.

Cliff cried, "Where're you going?"

"To tell him."

"No, wait. We'll do it together. This is killing Claudia," he said into the telephone. "He's killing his mother. Let me phone you later."

From the foot of the stairs he called, "Ted? Come down here, please."

"He's still sleeping."

"I'll get him," Cliff said somberly. "He can't sleep this business away. He'd better pull himself together."

Ted had been escaping reality through sleep. At night he went out and prowled, but Claudia had no idea where. No friends called. Obviously, the horrendous publicity had warned them away. She had tried to talk to him, but he had refused to listen, even though he must see that she only wanted to give him hope, to explain that people can take harsh punishments and still change, can begin a new life, that it was hard but not impossible. All this went through her head.

In his bathrobe, barefoot, Ted followed Cliff down the stairs. And again the sight of him came as a shock; defeat and defiance, in contradiction of each other, were written on his face and in his very posture.

"Sit down," commanded Cliff. "I want you to eat a decent breakfast. Make some bacon and eggs, Claudia. Make plenty. He can't be allowed to deteriorate. He'll be needing his strength."

"Have you —"

"Yes, I've told him."

It was a relief to be out of the room and to busy her hands in the kitchen. Delaying her return, she made a batch of pancakes and squeezed a whole pitcherful of fresh orange juice. Cliff can do more for Ted than I can, she admitted.

When she returned with breakfast, Cliff was saying, "You'll be having one of the best lawyers in the state. Try to relax, Ted. Try to feel confident. I know it must be damn hard," he added kindly. "By the way, it would be a good idea to wear a suit and tie and shave that three days' growth." And turning to Claudia he added, "I'll take him. Let this be my job."

Unresponding, Ted slumped in the chair. He had a habit now of cracking his knuckles, a new and repulsive habit that made Claudia wince. Before her eyes he was falling apart.

"Suppose you eat your breakfast while I finish mine, Ted, and you finish yours, Claudia. You need your strength too."

"Oh, I can live off my fat," she replied, making a weak attempt at good humor, which failed as she might have expected it to.

Quickly and in silence the meal was completed. "I'll drive you downtown this afternoon," Cliff said as they left the table. "But don't worry, I'm not going in with you. This is your private business. I do want to urge one thing, though. You must tell Raleigh the whole truth, the whole truth, Ted, if you want him to help you."

"I tell the truth," Ted shouted, his eyes darting at Cliff.

"No, Ted, you don't. The accounts you gave to your mother and me are not the same as the ones presented to the grand jury."

"Why do you believe them and not me?"

"There's evidence, Ted, you know there is, you've been told. It's childish of you to keep up your denials in the face of evidence." Pausing, Cliff seemed to be holding something back. Then he said quietly, "You lied about Charlotte, and God knows, she had proof enough."

"You still won't believe that it could have been someone else, will you?"

"I can't bear this," Claudia said, close to tears. "It's indecent, Ted, I don't recognize you."

"You see why I don't come down here,

why I stay in my room? There's no talking to you, either one of you. I'm going back up to my room."

Cliff called after him, ignoring the outburst, "Be dressed and ready at three."

"I need another cup of coffee," Claudia said. "I need the caffeine to keep me going." And she sat for a moment musing, with the comforting hot cup between her hands. "Cliff, is there any chance of showing some psychological problem, maybe getting a doctor, I mean, so that he'd go to a hospital instead of —"

Cliff shook his head. "I've asked Miller and I've asked around. The answer is no. These boys who go in for date rape with injuries, and that's what this is — of a particularly nasty sort too — go to prison. Frankly, although I'm deeply sorry for Ted, as I'm sorry for any human being, even a criminal, who has messed up the only life he'll ever have, I believe he deserves to be punished. He's a wise-guy football hero. He thinks he's God's gift to the girls, especially, I'm sure, after he's had a few beers."

"You spoke about the lawyer's helping him. I'm sorry if I sound stupid — I don't think very clearly these days — but what can he do? Not that Ted shouldn't be punished. I know that too."

"They'll try for a shorter prison term, Claudia."

She saw in Cliff's eyes that he was suffering because of her suffering. So she said resolutely, "You need a nap. I insist. Go upstairs, or go lie in the hammock and rest. You can be ready for Ted by three."

Claudia was in the kitchen mixing the salad when Cliff and Ted came home. The moment Ted walked in, she saw that he had been crying. But not wanting to embarrass him, she pretended not to notice and spoke cheerfully.

"Dinner'll be ready in a second. Let's eat, and afterward you can tell us about Mr. Raleigh."

Ted gave her a long look. "Just like that. Let's eat. There's nothing unusual going on. We're just a happy family. So let's eat."

Stricken, she dropped the spoon. No matter what she said these days, it turned out to be wrong. She was clumsy.

"Ted, I didn't mean . . . I'm sorry, I only meant . . . All right, tell me now. How was it?"

"How do you think it was? It was bad."

"Here. Sit down. Tell me."

When automatically she looked at Cliff, he nodded slightly in confirmation; then,

170

clearly much distressed, he went to the cupboard and filled two bowls with kibble for the dogs.

"Sit down, Ted," she repeated.

"No. He can't do anything, your first-class lawyer. He can't get me off."

"But you can't expect to get off, Ted. It's a question now of how much you'll have to —"

"They claim I broke her nose. I didn't mean to if I did. A little rough sex —" He broke off, and she saw that he was too overwrought to say more. "I'm going up. Leave me alone."

"I'm so helpless," Claudia cried when he had gone, "so scared, so worried about him."

"And I'm worried about you," Cliff replied.

"Did he tell you anything on the way home? His eyes were red. He was crying, wasn't he?"

"Sobbing. He's terribly afraid. Frantic and furious. He can't face the thought of a prison sentence, which is understandable, God knows."

"Yes. God knows."

Later that evening she knocked on Ted's door to tell him that she had brought something to eat.

Without opening the door he answered, "I don't want it."

Nevertheless, she left the tray on the floor. In the morning when she found the tray still there, untouched, she called to him, pleading.

"Don't be foolish, Ted. You can't starve yourself because of this trouble. You have to get through it. You've a long life ahead."

"Go away," he answered.

"I'm going to take this tray and bring back a hot breakfast for you. Don't do this to me, Ted. You're treating me badly. If you don't care about yourself, think about me. You were never like this to me before."

"Leave me alone," he said.

Weary, filled with despair, she left a breakfast outside his door and went away. Cliff had a day filled with errands downtown. Too restless even to read the morning newspaper, she stood at the window looking out at the sunshine. Two squirrels chased each other across the lawn and up a maple tree. A few yellowing leaves floated to the ground. The house at her back, in contrast, held not brightness, but a threatening gloom; in its silence the mantel clock's tick-tock was ominous. She had an impulse to flee from it, to fling open the door and run outside, yet she did not.

After a while she went to the kitchen, reflecting that she had done more intensive cooking since this trouble than she had done for months before. She had almost stocked the freezer full with durable items, casseroles, soups, and pie crusts, and now she was about to add more. Somehow when her hands were busy, her mind knew a little relief.

She was rolling out dough when she heard Ted come down the stairs. Neatly dressed, he looked like his old self.

"I'm going downtown for a while," he said before she could frame a question.

Hope flashed through Claudia. Perhaps he was reconsidering, accepting the reality of punishment, dreadful as it was, and seeing beyond it. She had tried so hard to make him see!

"Enjoy yourself," she said. "It's a beautiful day."

The afternoon was late, Cliff had returned, and she was just about finished with her work, when Ted came home.

"Hey, look at all this!" he exclaimed. "You've been cooking up a storm."

She was astonished. Here stood the old Ted, the boy with the easy nonchalance!

"Why, yes," she said, "so I have. A beef stew, that's for tonight, hot out of the oven,

173

and a peach pie. The rest goes into the freezer."

"When do we eat? I'm starved."

"I'll bet you are. We can eat right now. Go call Cliff. He's reading someplace."

Across the table Claudia met Cliff's questioning glances, which were as surprised as her own. Ted said little, but what he did say was entirely agreeable and calm; he had seen a movie that afternoon and bought a pair of shoes.

"Well, this is nice," Cliff said. "Nice to be eating together again."

She wondered ruefully whether in the circumstances he could possibly mean what he was saying, but nevertheless, she was thankful for his effort to mend and heal, and she waited for Ted's response.

It came promptly. "Especially with peach pie like this. It's the best ever. I could eat a third piece."

After dinner he kissed Claudia and went to his room to lie down, "because that's what dogs do," he said with a grin. "Haven't you noticed? When their stomachs are full, they rest. This was great food, Mom."

"What do you make of this?" asked Claudia. "I think I'm dreaming it."

Cliff said thoughtfully, "He's probably, at great pains, worked things through and had some sort of an epiphany. He's decided to take his medicine and — well, the word *reform* can be misused, but it's certainly possible that he realizes finally and fully what he's done and is now off in the right direction. Or maybe he went back and talked to that counselor today. That's possible too. Who knows? We'll get through this yet, Claudia. Mark my words. Come on, let's take a walk."

They took a long walk on the familiar route toward the lake, past cornfields now cut to stubble, past laden apple orchards and a farmer's stand with zinnias and dahlias for sale, where they bought a bouquet wrapped in green tissue paper.

"I'm beginning to feel a little like myself again," Claudia said on the way back. "It's not that I'm a Pollyanna because, of course, I know there's a bad time ahead. Still, if Ted can get through it, he can be a better person. Fundamentally, he's honorable and decent." She grasped Cliff's arm, forcing him to look down at her. "You've been such a help to him, and a godsend to me. I can't even begin to thank you."

"No thanks between lovers," he said.

They went early to bed and slept better than they had in a long time. It had been a better day.

★ ★ ★

Cliff was always first up in the morning to let the dogs out. When Claudia followed a few minutes later, she was surprised to see Ted's bedroom door open. She looked in. The room was vacant.

"Ted!" she called.

There was no answer. She ran downstairs where Cliff was watching the early news on television.

"Is Ted here?"

"No. Isn't he in his room?"

"No. That's odd. Where can he be?"

"Out, obviously. Nothing odd about it."

"So early?" she said, vaguely alarmed.

There had been a strange feeling about his room. Not able to remember exactly what the strangeness was, she went back upstairs, and this time saw at once what was strange: The doors on each of the two closets were wide open.

Now her alarm took shape. She ran her eyes over the clothes rod. Half Ted's clothes were missing. There were marks of haste, empty hangers left lying on the floor and shoes, old scuffed ones, overturned. His new suitcase, along with his backpack, bought months ago for a promised family trip, were gone from the top shelf. In panic now, she surveyed the room. Drawers in the high chest were open, some emptied. The clock was missing from the night table.

Half hysterically, she ran to the head of the stairs and shouted, "Cliff, Cliff! Ted's gone!"

He came bounding up, crying, "What? What?"

"Gone! Come look."

In the glare of morning light the room lay unmistakably abandoned. Claudia began to weep. Cliff sat down on the disheveled bed.

"The bastard!" he said. "What's he doing to you?" He got up. "Maybe there's a note. Have you looked?"

There was nothing.

"Look in the leather box. He keeps money in it."

"No money. It's empty."

A light flared in her memory. "His passport. He got it for our vacation. He kept it in that box."

"It's not here."

Abruptly, as incredible fear took their place, her tears ceased. Ted was out on bail, in custody of his parents. They were responsible. He was not supposed to leave Kingsley unless he was with them, and certainly not allowed to leave the country, even with them.

Shivering, she whispered a futile question.

"Where can he possibly have gone?"

Cliff did not answer her. He gave a low whistle instead. "Jumped bail. God almighty, he's jumped bail."

"We must call Bill," she said, still whispering.

"Bill took Elena to Boston. He'll be back late tomorrow. Anyway, he's no lawyer. I need Miller. No, the new one. What's his name? I can't think."

"Raleigh. You'd better call him. Unless — are we being too hasty? Ted might be —"

"Might be what? After sneaking out with his luggage and a passport, you don't think he's gone down the road to visit Bud, do you?"

She thought her heart would faint in her chest. "He has no money," she said.

"He must have. I'll find Raleigh's number at home. Must let Miller know too."

Was it only last evening that she had told Cliff how fundamentally honorable her son was?

While Cliff was telephoning, she stayed in Ted's room, unable to move. The room was so innocent! You would have expected it to reveal something more about its occupant than was revealed by a display of athletic trophies and a row of textbooks, these artifacts of an ordinary high school life. But she was being naive, and she knew it.

Presently the doorbell rang, and she heard Cliff talking. Apparently Mr. Raleigh had wasted no time in getting here. Pausing before the hall mirror, she saw a frightened, flushed face suddenly become old. She wished she had done her hair; it would have restored a trifle of the dignity that in the last few minutes she had lost. It is my son who has done this, she said. My son. Then she went in to where the men were.

Mr. Raleigh was young, with a keen expression and a smudge of shaving cream on his earlobe. He had been sufficiently alarmed by the news to dress and rush over here in fifteen minutes. In fact, he was already on his way out again.

"We'll have to see what the day brings," he said. "It certainly doesn't look as if Ted plans to come back. However — well, there'll have to be notification, which I shall take care of right away. The police will have to question you people, so you'd better stay home. And you'll also need to be considering the financial aspect. You understand, Mr. Dawes."

" 'Cliff.' Make it 'Cliff' and 'Claudia.' It looks as if we'll be in frequent contact from now on," Cliff said grimly.

"Okay, I'm Kevin. I'll be in touch."

The financial aspect. Oh, yes, Claudia thought. Four hundred thousand dollars or forfeit this house. My son. Oh, God. What have I done to Cliff — and to Bill?

"I know very well what you're thinking," Cliff said when they were alone. He put his arms around her bent shoulders. "But I order you to stop thinking it. Let's have breakfast and keep ourselves steady until they come."

It was not long before they came, two men in blue, a lieutenant and a captain. There must be a reason, she thought irrelevantly, why they come in pairs. There were two the day they took him away. The younger one, the one who had pitied Ted, had red hair. Her mind was wandering. She forced it back to reality.

Cliff counted on his fingers. "The Maxwell boy, Bud, the Lewis family on Hay Street, the McCloud twins — that's about eight. I can't think of any more friends."

"He had so many, he was very popular, you see," Claudia interposed, "— that is, until all this happened. He hasn't seen any of them since."

"We'll check those, anyway," the captain said. "We've already got people checking the bus station. Unless some friend took him in a car, the bus is the only way he could have gotten out of town."

"It must have been the middle of the night when he left," Cliff said.

"There's a midnight bus out of town, and another at six A.M. to Arkville, Lorimer, all the way downriver to connect with the interstate lines."

The men exchanged possibilities, Cliff asking whether it was possible in this time of electronic miracles for a person simply to vanish forever.

"Very difficult — almost impossible, you might say," the captain replied, "and yet it happens sometimes. Take your terrorist who has five passports. With money you can buy a stolen passport and have it altered. Or with bribe money you can sign on to a cargo freighter without any passport. You can disappear for years in some of the craziest places."

"Really disappear," Claudia echoed.

"But as I said, not often, Mrs. Dawes. Remember how they found some guy in Indonesia? He'd been missing for six years. It was in the papers. Eventually they turn up."

She thought of something. "Do you need some pictures? I can get copies made right away."

The captain smiled. "Not necessary. We have everything."

"Of course." They had mug shots and fingerprints. They had everything.

And at that moment the captain said, "Yes, I guess we have everything." On the front step he hesitated, adding, "This is mighty hard on you folks. You won't remember, Mr. Dawes, but my father worked for you in the mill until he got his pension, and a mighty good one it was too. The Dawes mill always treated everybody right. You don't deserve this trouble."

"Thank you," Cliff said. "My wife doesn't deserve it either."

"Well, we don't always get what we deserve, that's for sure."

The officers had barely been gone a minute, when the dogs barked again and Claudia went to look out.

"Somebody else is coming. Go see."

"The newspapers," Cliff reported. "I recognize Haynes from the daily press. Next they'll be coming from Kingsley and the county weeklies. Go inside, Claudia, I'll handle them."

It's not enough to suffer, but the whole inquisitive, morbid world has to gape and gawk at your suffering, she thought with a bitterness that was totally unlike her.

On the second day Claudia received a telephone call from an official at the bank, asking whether she had authorized a withdrawal of six thousand dollars from the account held jointly by her and her son.

She almost shouted, "Why, no! Certainly not. That's his college money. What are you telling me?"

"The day before yesterday, on Wednesday, Ted Marple came in here with a withdrawal slip signed by himself and you."

"I never signed anything at all."

"I'm not saying you did, but the signature certainly looked like yours. Still, the minute the transaction came to my attention, I wondered about it. Maybe I had no business to, but — excuse me — in view of the circumstances —"

She interrupted. "It's all right, you can speak plainly. You wondered about it. But why," she cried, "didn't this come to somebody's attention when he was making the withdrawal?"

"The teller is new on the job, for one thing, and the signature was perfect. I'm terribly sorry, Mrs. Dawes. You don't deserve this."

She hung up. This seemed to be the universal commiseration: *You don't deserve this.*

"He forged your name?" Cliff asked.

"Yes. Add that to his other crimes. Oh,

he's clever, my son. Went to the movies downtown and bought shoes. Nothing about a little side trip to the bank. Planned it for the very last minute so if it should be discovered, he would be safely away. Very clever."

Silvery sunlight crept across the floor. Only a year ago she had been secure, standing in the same sunlight in this very room, planning her wedding.

Then the police came back, only one of them this time, the lieutenant of the previous day. In a curious way he reminded Claudia of the lawyers, Miller and Raleigh; there were no physical resemblances among the three, yet they all possessed a very marked quality of alertness, of sharp memory and attention to detail. No chance word would get by them unnoticed.

This man's name was Casper. Without hesitation, remembering the way, he led them into the sunroom, took out a notepad, and began.

"Our check of the bus stations came out zero. At this time of year the buses are loaded with eighteen-year-old boys carrying suitcases on their way back to college."

Cliff asked, "Even at midnight? I should think anyone using a bus at that time would probably work a shift at the hospital."

"You're right. But he could have waited somewhere, hidden, until the morning crowds arrived at the bus station, so he wouldn't be noticed. This kid is clever, clever enough to have forged his mother's name so skillfully."

So that was how the bank had known! And that man had wanted her to believe it had been his own quick thinking. It was almost amusing.

Surprise must have shown on Claudia's face, because Casper said, "Yes, we checked all the banks. A person planning a getaway needs money. What we'd like to know now is whether you have any relatives who might — I hate to say it — but might hide him? Help him? In other words, is there anyone anywhere in the country that you can think of?"

She made a helpless gesture. "The closest relative I have is a cousin in Colorado whom I haven't seen in at least fifteen years, ever since I came east. I doubt Ted even knows his name. My grandmother had a sister in California. She's in her nineties now, about ninety-two, I guess, and she's in a nursing home. We exchange Christmas and birthday cards. That's about it."

"Any close friends Ted might know?"

"All my friends are either in Kingsley or close by."

"Anybody outside of the country?"

"Not a soul."

Casper made ready to leave. "A case like this is a challenge," he said. "It may take a lot of time, but we'll find him, I'm convinced."

Cliff observed, "At least he hasn't had much of a head start."

"With transportation what it is these days, you can go around the world in forty-eight hours. But we'll find him. We've got to. Those girls — they're in school with my Maureen. Their parents are on my tail too. It's been horrible for them."

Although she had surely given painful thought to the girls and to their parents before this, Claudia was now instantly transposed into their persons; she *became* the terrified girl attacked on a country road at night; she *became* the parent who, agonized beyond words, needed vengeance. This sheer reality was unbearable.

"Well, I'll be going along," said Casper. "If you hear anything or have any ideas, you have my number. And of course, I'll do the same."

"Something tells me we'll be seeing a lot of Casper," Claudia told Cliff.

"No doubt. You must be awfully tired. Go lie down."

Whenever he had that anxious look, she knew he was worried about her heart.

"I'm fine," she insisted.

"You might even fall asleep."

"I'm fine, Cliff. I don't need to."

"Look out the window. Here's another reporter — with a camera too."

"Oh, God," she said, and fled upstairs.

In the evening Bill came. For obvious reasons he did not seem too happy; no matter how difficult a marriage has been, Claudia thought with pity, the ending of it, the memory of its original sweetness, must be a cruel hurt. For Bill knew, as they all knew, that Elena was not going to come back.

"You look worn out," Cliff said.

"I just got back. The round trip to Boston wore me out."

After hearing Cliff's account of events Bill looked even more gray and exhausted.

"If they don't find him right off," he said, "you'll have to come up with the bond money. We need to talk, Cliff."

Claudia stood up, offering to leave them to themselves. "You'll want to be private," she said.

Simultaneously, they objected, "Not at all.

Sit down. You're part of this."

Indeed she was. And not only part of the catastrophe, but central to it. And she, who was unused to feeling humble, who had always borne herself with confidence and pride, now sat down humbly to listen.

"I can sell the house and still have something to spare," Cliff said.

"Sell this house!" Bill cried. "I won't hear of it. It's — it's the family's house."

"I know. But I have to face facts. We don't have the mill running anymore, Bill, we don't have the cash flow or the borrowing capacity, and I don't have a fortune lying around. If they don't find him by the end of this week, which is almost here, I'm in big trouble."

Cliff stood, walked to the window, looked out, and returned, jingling keys in his pocket. It crossed Claudia's mind that she had never seen him do that; he was not given to nervous habits.

"And if they do find him," he continued, "there will be some very hefty legal fees before we're through."

"You can't sell this house," Bill repeated.

They were in the den, where Cliff had lighted a fire, the first of the season. All the connotations of fire were spelled out in its leap and crackle: heat, light, cheer, family, home. Old, old home. Never having had such a one, Claudia was nevertheless able, perhaps even more deeply able, to comprehend its meaning. These two men and their parents before them had been born here, had seen the trees grow, had selected the books on the shelves. . . .

"No," Bill said for the third time.

Speech, as always, was coming hard to him. When he spoke, you had to pay attention, hearing behind his words what was left unsaid. It was all too much for him, Charlotte's tragedy, Elena's departure, and now this trouble. His world was undone.

"I've thought and thought, and this is my conclusion. It's this way," Cliff explained. "I could maybe find someplace to borrow the four hundred against the income from the lease on the mill. But there's no guarantee that I could, and even if I could, the interest would be ruinous. I'd be loaded with debt that would take half the rest of my life to get rid of."

"And where will you live if you sell the house?" Bill demanded, his voice rising with the flush that had risen to his forehead.

Cliff shrugged. "I'd get a smaller place somewhere, that's all."

"You would, would you? After you paid up the bail bond, then capital gains on what was left from the sale of the house, how much do you think you'd have? You're not making any sense, dammit!"

"Then you figure it out, Bill. You were always better at numbers than I am. Calm down. Look at yourself and figure it out."

"I have figured it. Anyway, it might take months to sell the house. For God Almighty's sake, what makes you think that they'll wait for that? They'll be grabbing the place by the end of this week."

Cliff got up to poke the fire, which did not need poking. And Claudia knew he was hiding his wet eyes. She felt, as she sat with her nervous, helpless hands in her lap, like one of those guilty women who, after a war, are paraded with shaven heads as punishment for having consorted with the enemy.

"I don't know what to do," Cliff murmured. "And you're not helping. I've never seen you so upset. I'll just have to think about it myself."

"Don't think too hard. Listen to me, I'll calm down. Let me do the thinking. Between us we can come up with the four hundred. We can sell some stocks. And that's that. If they find him in time for the trial, we'll get our money back. And if they don't find him, we'll survive."

"It kills me to take from you. You've got

your own troubles."

"My expenses will be somewhat lower from now on." Bill's half smile was sardonic. "No more country club. The monthly bill from there could have supported a family, one with far lower expectations, of course. Seriously, Cliff, we can work this out. We have the income from the lease. The governor's asked me to stay on the state commission for environmental studies, and I'll have a small salary from it. So you can sit down to work on your book and get rich."

"Oh, sure. A history of textiles, bound for the top of the best-seller list."

"Well, if it doesn't, maybe I'll move in here with you and pay rent. You've got plenty of spare rooms."

Cliff managed to smile, and Bill clapped him on the back, saying with a hearty manner that was more typical of Cliff than of himself, "Come on, kid. We'll drive downtown tomorrow morning, go to the brokers, pool our stuff, and survive this mess. Claudia, I don't mind telling you I'm hungry. I drove back from Boston nonstop. Have you got anything to eat?"

This was the old Bill, taking charge. He was trying to pull himself together, Claudia saw, trying to hide his agitation. And she stood up at once. I may not be able to undo the damage that's come to their lives because of me, but at least I can feed them well, she thought ruefully.

Oh, Ted, wherever you are, I would give ten years of my life if you would only come back now. Come quickly. Don't you know what you've done? Can it be possible that you don't even care?

ELEVEN

Seven girls piled on the bed and the floor of Charlotte's tiny room on the top floor of Margate Hall. It was one of only two such dormer rooms that were too small for more than one occupant, and that was precisely the reason why Charlotte had chosen it. There was a certain uncomplicated peace in the economy of bed, desk, and chair, with just enough space, and no more, to move among them. There was, however, a broad window seat on which valued possessions like stuffed animals could lie, or where Charlotte herself could sit and look out through the trees to the hills. This spring a sparrow had built a nest on the window's ledge and was now sitting on her eggs; the presence of the little brown bird was, in an indefinable way, a comfort.

It was not often that visitors mounted the stairs to this quiet part of the house; the noisy social life of the school went on below, and Charlotte existed far from the center of that life, anyway. In fact, as she well knew, she would have been, if not for a single factor, a reserved and bookish nerd. That factor was her exceptional skill at swimming and diving, which she owed to both of her parents. As the best swimmer on the team she had already won medals for her new school, and was therefore treated with respect.

I was never in my life a nerd, she thought, but I have changed.

Today the crowd was here because another large package had arrived from Elena in Italy. "An embarrassment of riches," Charlotte thought, having somewhere read or heard the expression. There was always more food than she could eat: *biscotti* and cheeses sent by extravagant overnight air express, and, always, her favorite chocolates or marzipan, which, after she had secreted enough for herself, were to be shared out with the first comers.

And there were always gifts, from handmade sweaters to leather-bound books of poetry, so many gifts that the closet was crammed with them. Today's present was a blue velvet housecoat, a lovely garment, absurdly out of place in a school dormitory.

"Your mother must be rich," someone remarked.

"I don't know."

"You must know!"

"Well, I guess she is."

Unlike the others, most of whose parents

were divorced, Charlotte did not want to talk about her parents. But they pinned her down, forcing her into their own frank discussions.

"What about your father? Is he rich too?"

"He used to be, I think, until his business went bad. But he takes care of me," Charlotte said, defending Dad.

Another girl said somewhat sadly, "It's good your mother has money. It's awful when you live with your mother and all she does is complain that your father doesn't give her enough. My mother's so scornful about Dad. She says he's a loser who couldn't fight his way out of a paper bag. Sometimes I hate her. I wish she'd shut up."

Complaint, as in a fugue, passed from one voice to another.

"Sometimes I hate my father. He's always asking me what Mom's doing, what she's buying, and whether she goes out with anybody. She plays around, but I don't tell him. Why should I? He's doing it himself."

"I always know when some guy's been staying all night, even though he doesn't stay when I'm home for vacation. It's disgusting."

Disgusting, like Elena and Judd. I remember.

"You're lucky your mother's in Italy,

Charlotte. At least with the ocean between them they can't fight."

For a few moments no one spoke. The atmosphere was suddenly dejected. They are probably all like me, thought Charlotte, imagining a home where people live together without anger.

"But Charlotte's parents aren't divorced," somebody said.

"Are they going to be, Charlotte?"

"I don't know. She left last summer, and nothing's happened. I wish they'd make up their minds."

"Maybe it's better never to get married. Just have sex."

Everyone laughed, and another girl remarked, "Don't laugh. My sister, who's eleven, was asking me things you wouldn't believe. She'll probably be doing it soon. She'll have plenty of opportunity. Mom's never home. She's out every night with her boyfriend."

"A kid like that is liable to be raped."

"Did you read about that guy who raped those girls and ran away? They think he's in Europe. Isn't he from your town, from Kingsley, Charlotte? Did you know him?"

"No," said Charlotte, "I only read about him."

"A guy like that is a creep. I wonder

whether those girls got pregnant. They probably had it taken care of right away, though."

"There was a girl at my old school who got raped and then had an abortion. She had a fight with her parents and then tried to drown herself in the bathtub."

"Oh, God, rape. It makes you sick to think about it."

"I guess it really changes you. I mean, you would never forget it."

They talk, Charlotte thought, but they don't know anything. They don't know. You wake up in the middle of your nightmare. His nasty, scrabbling hands . . . His breath in your face . . . But you have to try to forget it. You have to. . . .

When they had all left, she closed her door and took the box of marzipan from where she had hidden it under her sweaters. Always a quick study, especially in math, she had finished her assignments and now had nothing to do except perhaps take her sketch pad and draw plans for the house that she liked to imagine, a little white house with a garden and space for two or three loving, big dogs. So, with the pad and box on her lap, she sat down on the window seat looking out.

The long spring evening was not yet over, and the watery light that comes after rain laid a green mist upon the hills. The sparrow had come to rest for the night, drowsing over her eggs. She knows I won't hurt her; she's quite at rest, Charlotte thought. And she sat there very still until she had finished the whole box of marzipan and it was too dark to see.

"Is Charlotte happy in school?" asked Claudia. "You never say, and I've hesitated to ask."

"It's hard to answer that," Bill replied. "Teenagers don't tell you much."

Then he realized that to Claudia, of all people, he should not have made such a remark about the foibles of teenagers. But his mind was filled with the burden of Charlotte's unhappiness, and he had simply not been thinking.

He had fallen into the habit of visiting Cliff's house once or twice every week, since his own house had emptied out. For a while he had considered the wisdom of moving, but Cliff had convinced him that in his heart he really did not want to move.

"You've had to face too many changes as it is," he had told him.

Indeed that was true, Bill reflected on the short drive home. And as bad as changes could be, uncertainties could be even worse. Well, he thought, at least one uncertainty has been removed: Elena has fallen in love.

Her letter crackled in his pocket. By now he must have read it a dozen times. After putting the car in the garage, he sat down at the kitchen table and read it again.

. . . Mario is a doctor, about my age, both of us old enough to know what we want. . . . You and I were too young to know, Bill. Don't grieve over this.

Grieve! he thought savagely. I grieve for no one but Charlotte.

. . . we shall live in Rome. I am hoping that Charlotte will come often, and that you will come with her sometimes, too, Bill. There is no reason why we cannot be amicable toward each other. . . . I understand perfectly well that Charlotte wants to remain with you, so there is no quarrel over that. Anyway, if we were to fight this out in court, you would probably get custody, since I am the adulteress. . . . I leave it to you to tell Charlotte in person. Then after you have done so, please let me know, and I will telephone to her.

So that was that. He gave a short laugh. Perhaps Dr. Mario would have better luck with her. Then he went upstairs to bed. Tomorrow was Saturday, and he must make an early start for Margate Hall.

On the path between the parking lot and

the entrance, he met the headmistress. Expecting a brief greeting, he was surprised when she stopped him.

"I've been wanting to talk to you about Charlotte," she said. "I understand you're taking her out to lunch, so this can't be the time. I really would like to make an appointment with you very soon."

"Of course," Bill said in some alarm. "But is anything wrong?"

"Well, no, and yes. That's a queer answer, I know. Charlotte is a fine, bright girl, a good student, and we have loved having her here. But I feel I should tell you that this may not be the best place for her. She cries at night. She denies it, but we see her red eyes. I've tried to gain her confidence, and it hasn't worked. Charlotte is very proud."

"Are you saying that you don't want her to come back next year?"

"I'm not saying anything at all like that. I would hope that we could help her to get past whatever is troubling her, so that she may come to love our school. She has all the potential. So whenever it's convenient for you, Mr. Dawes, or on the other hand should you not wish to meet with me at all, please let me know."

He did not commit himself to a choice, and while he hesitated, the brisk voice added, "Incidentally, congratulations on your good work at the state environmental commission. All of us who care about the world we're to leave to our children are pinning our hopes on people like you."

They parted, and Bill, walking on toward the wing where Charlotte was to meet him, made a quick decision; there would be no conference because he knew all too well what Charlotte's trouble was and had no intention of discussing it with anyone again.

He had already met with as many as five professional advisors, had described his child's situation with complete honesty, and had received a unanimous opinion: You cannot drag a person into therapy. Well, he knew that. He had often implored Charlotte to go, to no avail. He could, for the present anyway, do no more. . . .

They sat opposite each other in a country restaurant near the school.

The first thing he noticed about her now was that she had gained weight. The next thing was a surprising, very faint reminder of Elena, a strong definition of the lips that he had never observed before, a lovely parted bow between which shone a row of flawless teeth.

It occurred to Bill that nowhere else does

one have a better opportunity to scrutinize another human being than when confronting him across a table. Now, clearly, he saw the woman that his daughter would soon become; although just past her fifteenth birthday, she appeared to be much older; she had simply missed the normal years of adolescence.

He saw, too, that she was still resisting his efforts to touch upon her feelings. Their conversation now, like her letters and phone calls, was one that she might have been holding with a stranger.

"I haven't been able to do any real diving because the pool here isn't deep enough," she said.

And he responded, "Well, you can make up for that when you're back at the lake this summer. I was thinking maybe it would be fun to buy a canoe and try the river. I've never learned very well how to handle a canoe. What do you think?"

"I don't know. Maybe."

He was beginning to feel impatience, while he knew that he had no right to feel it. His daughter's awkward conversation, her silences, and her very posture told him only too poignantly of her need. But all his offers of help were rebuffed. For almost an hour now he had been sitting here in frustration, trying to create a mood between them that would allow him to speak out, but he had gotten nowhere. Suddenly, when she moved, he saw at the parting of her cardigan a large safety pin. She caught his glance, her face reddened, and clutching the sweater closer, she made an excuse.

"I seem to have gotten fat. My skirts don't fit anymore."

"Well, I wouldn't call you fat, exactly. But you do seem heavier."

A moment later the waitress brought a dessert menu that Charlotte carefully studied before deciding on a fudge sundae.

"With whipped cream, miss?"

"Yes, and some chopped nuts, too, please."

"Do you think you should?" Bill asked. "Why not have a melon or some yogurt?"

"Perhaps I'd better not have anything," Charlotte retorted.

"Perhaps so." Bill was angry, and yet again he was aware that he should not be. She was making it so hard for him. . . . "There's no need to be angry, Charlotte," he said. "I only made the suggestion because you said your skirts don't fit."

"You sounded like Elena."

To his dismay her eyes filled. And he looked away so as not to embarrass her, saying gently, "We're both playing a game. You don't want to tell me, and I'm afraid — or have been afraid — to ask you what's going on with you. But now I'm going to ask."

"I just seem to want to eat all the time, sweet things, candy and cake," she mumbled. "I don't know what's the matter with me."

"There's nothing unusual about it. Those are comfort foods, comfort and escape."

"Doesn't that explain everything, then?"

Two large, glossy tears rolled down Charlotte's cheeks. The explanation, the diagnosis, was clear enough, but where and what was the cure? And now there was this news about Elena that he had come here to give her, and who could predict how she would take that? We cheated her, Bill told himself. With all that quarreling over the years, what sort of a foundation did we build? And he remembered, as he often did, his own parents, how they had stood together in the face of his sister's awful death; surely they must have had other crises, too, but their children had always been protected. Damn Elena. It wasn't that he wanted to absolve himself of all the blame. That would be untrue and cheap. And yet . . .

Charlotte was fumbling for a handkerchief, and he gave her his own.

"Go out and wait in the car while I pay the check," he said, understanding her embarrassment at showing wet eyes in a public place.

In its way this tense control of hers was as painful to him as her most terrible, bitter sobs could be. He was overwhelmed by his own helplessness. Maybe a mother would not feel as helpless as he did. And heavy with dread of the message he had to bring, he walked toward the car.

"I feel like a bull in a china shop," he began. "I have something to tell you, and I'm so afraid it will hurt you too much. It's about Mama. She is going to stay in Italy, to live there."

"Why? Has she found a man again?"

The easier way would be to postpone, to let the truth out gradually. But Charlotte was well aware, or she would not have asked the harsh question. So he simply said, "Yes, she's going to be married as soon as we can be divorced."

It was hot in the parking lot, even there in the shade. Yet at the moment he had not the energy to start the engine and drive away. He put his hand over Charlotte's, which lay on the seat between them.

"Do you want to cry now?" he asked. "It's

205

better to do it now in front of me than to hold it back and do it alone at night."

"No, I'm all right. I'm not as sad as I thought I would be. I knew it would happen someday, although it's been a long time coming."

"Do you want to live there with her, Charlotte?"

"Dad, I've already said no."

"But surely you will miss her. Don't you miss her now as it is?"

"In some ways of course I do. But not enough to go there and be with her."

He could not help, in spite of himself, but feel a little vindicated, a little satisfied. "I want so much to see your smiles again," he said.

"Do you know what I thought your bad news was? I thought you were going to tell me that Ted had come back."

"No, but it would make no difference to you if he had. Believe me, you will never need to see him."

"Oh, God, I should have sensed he was rotten. And you told me to stay away from him, you told me."

"You're not the first person who failed to listen to a parent, darling, and you won't be the last."

"I'm so furious at myself."

"Be furious at him, not at yourself. Promise?"

She gave him a pale smile. And he felt that he had begun to penetrate the chill and lonely place into which she had withdrawn herself all this past year.

"I wish you would see someone," he said next. "Someone to help you."

Then immediately, as she drew away, he realized that he had again said the wrong thing and that he had lost her.

"A shrink? But I've told you a hundred times that I will not. I will never, never, as long as I live, tell anybody anything about myself. Please, Dad, don't ask me again."

"Okay, Charlotte. Okay, I won't."

Once more, when they reached the school, Bill took her hand and kissed her cheek.

"It wasn't such a bad day, was it?" he asked, pleading. "I mean, we've gotten through it all right, wouldn't you say?"

She nodded, giving him that same pale smile. As she was getting out of the car, he had a glimpse of the safety pin. Somehow it seemed to symbolize her cruel impairment, and with a laden heart he watched her walk away.

TWELVE

There was no way Bill could have refused his brother's tremulous appeal, much as he wanted to.

"I wish you'd be here," Cliff had said. "They're coming over this evening. You can imagine Claudia's state of mind. And mine's not much better."

"Who are they?"

"They live over near Arkville. Prescott, Peter Prescott. They didn't tell us anything more on the telephone except that they had just gotten home from Europe, and that they had seen Ted. By God, I'd like you to listen to them, Bill."

There was, Bill reflected now, no mistaking the Prescotts for anything but a pair of solid citizens. He was an accountant, and she was a sensibly spoken, sensible-appearing housewife. There was nothing fanciful about them; in short, they were not the kind of people who were apt to report encounters with little green creatures from outer space. They were quite positive. They had even brought a couple of photographs.

Claudia was holding these toward the light. Her face had no expression. She

208

looked totally numb, and in fact, her body was numb.

They were all watching her. Her thoughts were contradictory and distorted, some of them already embracing Ted at the airport with such thankful relief and others in terror of the courts and prisons that awaited his return.

She bent over the pictures. In one Ted was dressed in what looked like a white uniform of some sort; a table with various heads and shoulders hid the lower half of his body. The other was a three-quarter view with a door in the background. And in each the face was unmistakably Ted's.

"Yes," she said, "yes, it is."

There was a long silence. And the part of the mind that can, even in the worst, most painful situations, detach itself from the pain and see objectively, said to her, We are all feeling the drama of this. We are players in an extraordinary tragedy.

"Tell me about it, please," she cried.

Mr. Prescott began. "As we said, it was in Vichy at the spa. We had lunch there a few times. There was this young man, a waiter, whom we both noticed. It was strange that, almost at the same moment, Carol and I were sure we knew him or knew who he was. Of course, we realized later it was because of all the pictures in our local papers. And we heard him speaking English, American English. We didn't quite know what to do, how to handle it so as not to tip him off. So we asked somebody for his name. It was Timothy Matz."

"Maits?" asked Cliff.

"No, Matz. The suspicious thing is his avoidance of us. Hearing him speaking English, we tried to be friendly, although only in passing because he never served our table. We were sure he was deliberately staying away."

"I think," Mrs. Prescott added, "that he may have seen me with the camera. And I think he was worried about me because the last time we were there, when we were on our way out, he had a rather frightened expression."

"I don't know whether this is good news or bad news for you," Mr. Prescott said gently.

"I don't know either," Cliff said, "except that at least Ted's alive, and where there's life, there's hope. But what comes next is that tomorrow morning we have to tell the police and our lawyer."

"It's all right to hope," Bill agreed, "but not to overdo it. We must be prepared to be disappointed sometimes. Then it won't hurt so much," he added kindly, "believe me."

Claudia held the pictures up to the light again. Yes, there he was, a trifle thinner, perhaps, or perhaps not, but the face was his, his the dark deep eyes, the cheekbones, the narrow jaw . . . Ted.

There were so many questions. . . . *What are you doing in France? How did you get there? Are you well? Are you behaving yourself? Will you ever forgive me for reporting you? Will you understand that I must do it? That you must take your punishment?*

"I'd like to keep these if I may," she said.

"Of course. We had copies made, enough for you and for the authorities."

Cliff warned the couple, "The police will be calling on you too."

Mr. Prescott said, "No problem," and rose to leave.

His wife took Claudia's hand. The pressure and the glance into Claudia's eyes were more expressive of understanding than any words could have been. *I, too, have children,* they told her.

"Decent people," Cliff remarked later. "They weren't getting any thrill of excitement out of this the way a lot of people would. Are you all right, Claudia?"

She knew what he meant. Where her health was concerned, Cliff was an incurable worrier. Regardless of the fact that the doctor had cut back on her heart medication and was most encouraging, he still worried.

Right now her heart was beginning to hammer at her ribs, to race so fast that she herself was frightened. Then she thought, For heaven's sake, it's only nerves, and why not?

"Just nervous," she said lightly, "and who wouldn't be on a day like this?"

She got up and went to the kitchen. A cup of herb tea might be soothing. After that, in a safe bed next to Cliff would come sleep and a few hours of deliverance until the morning.

The sky on this midafternoon in the middle of summer was empty, its pure blue absolute, without cloud or motion. The day, like all the days during these last three weeks, was empty. Beyond a few ordinary chores there was little to do but think. A thousand times Claudia had examined all the possibilities and probabilities involved in the discovery of Ted, and now her thoughts had run dry.

She drove slowly home from the supermarket. This would be a good time to walk or go for a swim or sit under a tree with a friend and talk, but she had neither physical nor emotional energy for any of these; she was in a lethargy, just sufficiently alert to control the car.

It was the sight of Charlotte, walking alone on the side of the road, that aroused her. Not having seen the girl in over a year, Claudia's impulse was to stop the car and call out. Her second impulse was to drive on. Cliff had reported, and indeed Bill himself had confirmed, that Charlotte did not want a meeting.

"It's not that she's angry at you, far from it," he had tried to explain. "It's only that the connection, the memory . . ." He had faltered to a stop.

Well, she could certainly understand that. It would not be an easy meeting for me, either, she thought, making a sudden painful connection to that time when, first left alone with a child to support, she had dreaded the sight of a tradesman to whom she owed money. Now she owed Charlotte a great deal more than money; hers was a debt that could never be repaid.

It was this thought that changed her mind so that she stopped the car and waited for Charlotte to catch up.

They were both startled and unsure what to say. She's grown fat, Claudia thought irrelevantly. And she said the first thing that came into her head, which was the natural query, "Where are you going? Want a lift?"

"No, thanks. I'm just taking a walk."

"Will you come back home with me for a while?"

"No, thanks."

Clearly, Charlotte wanted to get away. Good manners alone constrained her. Claudia, however, was suddenly determined not to let her get away.

"You feel strange with me," she said, "and no wonder. I can't blame you. But we were friends once. At least I thought we were."

Charlotte nodded.

"I know it's asking a great deal," Claudia persisted, "but can't you try to separate me from — from what was done to you? Can you try to remember some of the things we did together, the lemon tarts and the books?"

In a gesture of dismay Charlotte's hand flew to her cheek. "The book on ancient architecture, that big book of photographs — I never returned it."

"I never missed it."

"I'm terribly sorry."

"You may keep it, Charlotte."

"No, I'll ask Dad to take it to you."

"Will you perhaps come with Dad?"

214

"I can't — you see, it's really your house, not you, that —"

The house. Yes, of course. It probably happened in the living room on the sofa. She will see that room forever, imprinted like the room in the hospital. We all have them, only for most of us they are not as horrible as hers, these images printed in black on white or carved in stone.

"What if I came to see you sometime at your house? I can bring Rob and Roy, if you want me to. You must have missed them."

Charlotte was looking away down the road, obviously wanting to be released. "I don't know," she answered.

At that Claudia put the car into gear. "Well, anytime," she said, and drove off thinking, I can only try.

The doorbell rang while she was sorting the groceries. She opened it to admit Casper from the police department.

He said at once, "Don't be alarmed, there's no bad news, or good news, either, depending on how you want to look at it."

They sat down and he began, "Here it is in a nutshell. The report just came in. The young man is not Ted."

A sigh, heavy as a groan, rose and fell in Claudia's chest; whether it came out of a vast relief or from dashed hopes, she could not have told.

"No, definitely not. The French police traced him from the restaurant where he was known as Timothy Matz, the name he gave those people, the Prescotts. They traced him to the university at Grenoble, and found that he really is Timothy Matz. He and his brother worked all summer in France and then went on to study. The authorities at Grenoble met the parents on a visit. They come from Kansas. The mother is a teacher, and the father does some sort of work for the blind. They were very thorough, the French police."

"The pictures," Claudia murmured. "I was so sure."

"It happens. Don't they say everybody has his double somewhere in the world? Makes sense. Let me tell you some more that's really amusing. Timothy Matz was suspicious of the Prescotts. He saw them photographing him, and he wondered why. It scared him. He thought they were criminal types."

"I guess it would scare you to have strangers staring at you like that. They said he looked suspicious. It all fits, doesn't it?" She sighed again. "So, where do we go from here?"

"To the FBI. Our department has already been in touch with them. We're all, the parents of the girls, too, naturally, and all of us in the department, in a hurry to get this solved."

"This" being Ted, Claudia thought. And the parents of the girls are in a hurry. Wouldn't I be, though, if I were in their shoes? Or in Bill's, or in Charlotte's?

And mustering all her resolve, she said quietly, "I'll do what I can to cooperate. You can tell everyone that no matter what my personal grief may be, I understand that the law comes first. Ted belongs back here to face it. I will not cover up for him. If I should hear from him in any way, you will know it."

Casper nodded. "These are hard times for you, and I'm sorry. Sorry that you people, that a man like Mr. Dawes, has to go through all this. He is one of our most respected citizens, he and his father before him. It's tough."

Yes, tough indeed. You can't imagine how tough.

"Well, I'll be going along, Mrs. Dawes. You'll be having your next visit from the FBI."

"And many more afterward, I suppose," she said wryly.

Casper agreed. "Unless they break the case fast. With Interpol in the act they may very well do it."

"So that's where it is," Bill concluded when they were taking their evening walk, "in the hands of the FBI."

It was the first time in many months that there had been any mention of Ted's name between Charlotte and her father.

"I know it's a horror for you to be reminded of him, and I certainly don't intend to harp on the subject, but it will be mentioned in the newspapers and by people you meet, so you might as well be realistic about it. Those two other girls must feel the same horror you do."

Not exactly, Charlotte thought. He didn't get them pregnant and sick. At the same time she was aware of an element almost childish in her comparison. It was like saying: *You* may have a broken leg, too, but *my* break is a compound fracture.

"I met Claudia yesterday afternoon," she said. "She stopped the car when she saw me."

"And what then?"

"She asked me to go home with her, but I wouldn't. I can't go to that house, Dad."

"I'm sure she would come to ours if you asked her."

"She said she would."

"So, did you ask her?"

"I didn't say yes or no."

"Charlotte, I think you should have said yes."

Sometimes she was sure that she could read his mind. Now he was thinking that she was in need of a mother. Everyone knew that a fifteen-year-old girl needed a mother, she thought ironically.

"I just think you need a woman to talk to."

Because Elena went away, he meant but had not said, because hers was another name that they, in their mutual hurt, rarely spoke these days. And he was right. For the whole year past while away at school, she had known only kids and kids' talk. It left her often with a sense of floating unanchored. Sometimes, although you were too proud to admit it, you felt the lack of a person who would tell you what to do, even though you might not want to do it. A father, no matter how wonderful, was different.

"I'm thinking besides that it's rather awkward for you not to be on speaking terms with my brother's wife. Try to forget whose mother she is, Charlotte. She can't help that, and she is suffering because of it. You even said once that you were sorry for her."

Yes, it was in the car coming home from Boston, and Elena's mocking laugh had scoffed.

She was silent. Her father was asking a favor of her now. For the whole year past he had asked nothing of her; he had cared for her as if she were a basket of eggs that with the slightest jar would smash. He must be very, very weary of all this. The whole year had been a year to remember — or rather, if it were possible, a year to forget.

"All right. Tomorrow I will ask Claudia to come," she told him.

They had walked as far as the river. On the other side between the road and the marsh the Dawes mill loomed like a soiled gray ship run aground. Bill stood there gazing at it. The wind was strong. Charlotte, shivering, crossed her arms over her chest and waited for him to speak; she still felt the worry and weariness within him.

Presently he said, "I'm afraid we're going to have trouble with our tenants before we're through. I don't feel comfortable with them. It's not the kind of operation we expected. Do you notice anything different? Look out over the marsh."

"Well, there are no ducks. Is that what you mean?"

"Precisely." He stood there frowning. "I don't know. Perhaps I'm imagining things. I don't know."

"Well, there are butterflies, anyway. Look, Dad."

Crossing the river, heading south, there appeared a flying army, a broad band of monarch butterflies.

"Starting toward Mexico for the winter. Look at them speed. Hundreds of them, with more to follow. They know summer's almost over."

He meant: *The butterflies know where they are going, and you had better make up your mind too.*

She was uncertain whether to stay or go. She had been sure that she hated Kingsley, but she was not so sure now. For why did she often weep at night in Margate Hall? Yet when she was there, she was rid of certain haunting ghosts. The mournful emptiness of Elena's room at home; the terror of rounding a corner to find that Ted had reappeared.

Her father was looking at her, hoping for an answer to his unspoken question, but she had none to give, and now, grown suddenly silent, they started home.

* * *

It seemed to Bill that he had long known he would eventually confide in Claudia. The more he knew her, the more he liked her. She was a lovely woman, calm and courageous. Slowly and tentatively during these last weeks of summer, Charlotte and she, the one fifteen, the other more than twice that age, each needy, each separated from the other and the same time connected by a common disaster, had begun to come together.

A subtle change was visible in Charlotte. She had gone back to swimming every morning and was losing weight. Instead of spending solitary days at home reading, she was cautiously venturing out with her old neighborhood friends. Bill had no doubt that Claudia was responsible for these changes. One afternoon he went to tell her so.

"And I've come with a question. What do you think I should do about school? Charlotte doesn't seem to know what she wants. You see," he explained, "her fears conflict with each other. She hasn't told me so, but I feel it."

"For one thing, she must be afraid that Ted will be brought back."

Respecting Claudia's honesty, he returned it in kind. "That's true."

"You don't conquer your terrors over-night, Bill. It's taken me almost a year to conquer my particular terrors, even to walk into the supermarket with my head up. I couldn't bear knowing that I was being pointed out or whispered about, even sym-pathetically. It was awful." As she spoke, the color on her pink face grew deeper. "Awful," she repeated.

"But if you have done nothing wrong," Bill said, "if you can live with yourself, that's really all that matters in the end, isn't it? And God knows, Charlotte has done noth-ing wrong."

Who would believe, he thought, that we two would be able to talk like this? And yet, how civilized it is that we should do so.

"Tell me, then, what we should do about her, Claudia."

"Keep her home. Strangers in boarding school can't restore her strength the way you can."

"Or you," Bill said steadily.

"Oh, I don't know. I hear myself talking like a ridiculous know-it-all, I, who don't even understand why my own child went wrong."

"You were and are a mother, not a miracle worker."

Claudia's hands made a gesture of helplessness. "I did the best I could."

"That's all any woman can do. Some, of course — well, that's past and gone," he said roughly, looking away for fear that his eyes would fill. "I'm afraid Charlotte will have to get used to that particular loss."

"She will weather it. She's going to be an exceptional human being. She's intelligent and sensitive, probably too sensitive. She's been wounded badly, and she needs to be healed. And she will be."

"So I will tell her that I want her to stay home." He looked directly at Claudia. "And will you help with the healing?"

"You know I will."

Still he persisted, "Will you be her mother?"

"Yes," said Claudia. "Yes, I will."

PART TWO

1994–1997

ONE

Neither of us has any real comprehension of the other; to her, life always looks so easy, Charlotte thought. And yet, there must be plenty of other people in New York's tower hotel suites, with a view of both rivers and the city below, with hush-foot carpets and potted azaleas in January, who do not find everything so easy. Elena's particular kind of ease was her own. Not only her words revealed it, but also her shrug and the way she wore her diamonds with her plain black dresses.

"Ten times in ten years," Elena wailed, "and I've always been the one to go to you. Every single summer, to say nothing of all the Christmases and other times in between, I've begged you to come to Italy."

Now that the first tearful embraces were past and they had come to the end of their vacation, she was repeating her customary complaint.

Although Charlotte had expected it, the need to respond to it yet again was tiresome. She was tired anyway, simply from five days of following Elena through the shops — "Things are so much cheaper here than in

Italy" — to theaters, and fashionable restaurants. A little of that sort of thing went a long way for her.

Nevertheless, she answered patiently, "I keep telling you, and you know, that I've worked every summer through college and graduate school — oh, what's the use! You don't understand that there just isn't enough money for travel."

"That's nonsense, Charlotte. Time and again I've offered to send you the fare."

"I can't afford to take the time off from work. I'm very lucky to have even a bottom-level job in an architect's office where I can see what's going on."

"How can things be all that bad? I don't understand it."

"There's no mystery. Nothing's changed. Dad lives on the rent money from the mill, the small salary he gets from the state commission, and on Uncle Cliff's repayments. It's a finite amount. He can't stretch it."

"Cliff should have sold that house. Two people rattling around in that huge barn! He should have gotten a good job for himself, anyway, instead of writing books that nobody reads."

"People do read them, Elena. His book on textiles got a lot of praise, even though it didn't make a fortune. And he has a contract for two more, on Third World industry."

Elena was not so easily defeated. "Well, each to his own. I still say that Bill, with his brains, should go back into business, too, instead of working for the government for peanuts."

"Dad is doing something important, something he loves to do. And he wants Cliff to stay in the house. It's the kind of place that should be preserved, it's a treasure in itself, it's a bird sanctuary and the trees are a century old," Charlotte said, rather hotly.

When Elena laughed, her curls shook and her bracelets tinkled.

"Aren't you a Dawes, though! You're just like them, with your head in the clouds. But you're very, very sweet, all the same. And so pretty. I never dreamed you'd turn out to be so pretty. You were such a *large* kid, weren't you? Here, let me show you something."

She got up and crossed the room to the table where she had placed the photographs that always traveled with her. One was of the husband whom Charlotte had never seen; a dark man with elegant features, he looked both intelligent and sardonic.

"Mario hates traveling," Elena had always

explained, "so that's why I have to come here alone. Besides, he is such a busy doctor. He has a tremendous practice. We never go very far from Rome."

She said now, "Look at our new apartment. It's in the seventeenth-century palazzo near the Piazza Navona. Those are our windows on the second floor."

Here, indeed, was something worth seeing. The wonderfully balanced, serene facade was ornamented with simplicity and grace, as if to temper the truth that the structure was strong as a fortress, built for protection in a bloody time.

"Beautiful," Charlotte murmured, adding, "It's only a few hundred years, not long as history goes, when people lived behind those walls in fear of being attacked."

"It's not too different from New York today, my dear. Each year when I come here, I think it's the same, only more so. Do you get here often?"

"No, very seldom."

"You should. There's so much going on here in spite of everything. And it's practically next door to Philadelphia."

Charlotte smiled. "There's plenty going on in Philadelphia too."

"I do hope you're not burying your nose in work, Charlotte. Of course, it's marvelous and I'm proud you're doing what you always wanted to do. I only mean that architecture, a career, isn't everything for a woman. There's more to life than work."

She sees me as a grind, hopelessly dull and hopelessly unlike herself, thought Charlotte. But maybe I like being what she calls a "grind." I probably could have squeezed out a few days and a few dollars to visit her and her Mario; the fact is that I haven't wanted to. She makes me uncomfortable.

Her gaze wandered out to the somber, wintry sky. And suddenly, without forethought, she asked, "Are you happy, Mama?" using the name she had not used in years, ever since her mother had asked to be addressed as Elena.

"What a question! Life's a great bag, Charlotte. You stick your hand in and see what you pull out. You unwrap it, and if you don't like it, you try again, that's all. You go from happiness to unhappiness and back, if you're smart. Anyway, let's not be so deep. Tell me the news. What's going on at home? How's my friend Claudia, who doesn't approve of me?"

"She never says a word about you, Elena."

"Okay, don't be indignant. I meant nothing. I know you love her."

Love. How many kinds are there, anyway?

Charlotte wondered. The kind I feel for you, Mama, is mingled with an old, old ache. I try not to let it be judgmental, but I don't always succeed. My love for Dad is total trust, companionship, and gratitude; he has always been there for me and always will be. As for Claudia, she is my friend, my teacher, and my therapist. At fifteen I had turned away from the world, and she led me back into it.

You can do anything with your life that you want to do, Charlotte. You can be beautiful. You can be unafraid.

All this she did for me when she herself was beset. . . .

"Life must be very hard for her."

"They've had their troubles. Nuisance troubles, magazine writers wanting interviews, and even TV interviews, which they won't give. And there was even a letter from Ted, but of course it was a hoax. The police told Claudia right away that it was, but she didn't want to believe them. It was typewritten, sent from England. Somebody reported the kids who had sent it. It was cruel. They thought it was funny."

"She ought to give up and accept the inevitable."

"Nothing is inevitable. After fifteen years they found a man who had murdered his whole family. He'd been living in the United States all the time. And it's even easier to hide abroad. The Interpol people aren't going to make it any priority to find Ted. They're looking for big-time crooks. Oh, he's out there someplace, that's sure."

Curiously, Elena asked, "Does it — does he not haunt you anymore? I mean, you've never said so much to me about him in all these years."

"You have to come to terms with reality."

"I see. It's good that you have. It means that you're gradually forgetting. Or am I wrong, being terribly tactless, as I can sometimes be?"

"I don't think much about what happened anymore, not consciously, anyway."

Ah, but it was continuously with her! It was the albatross around her neck, hidden under her clothes and her smiles.

"Well, I'm glad. I do sense a new kind of lightness in you that I never saw before. And I repeat, you look lovely. I can't get over your hair. I never thought you'd color it."

"That was Claudia's idea. She thought I should lighten it."

"Well, it was a good idea. But I'm surprised. I wouldn't have expected her to care about such things."

"You don't know her at all, Mama."

"I know that she's been good to you, and I accept that."

Please let us not end with any strain or bitterness, however masked, thought Charlotte.

Apparently Elena was having the same thought, for she brightened her expression and, brightening her voice as well, said briskly, "I'd like an enormous late-afternoon tea right now, so I won't have to tackle dinner on the plane. Let's go down to eat. Then I'll catch the plane, you take your train, and we'll say good-bye till next time."

The parting was to be, as it always was, a moving ceremony, symbol of this strange relationship woven out of dream and memory, hopeless opposites, and its own steady love.

In a way, Charlotte would have liked to tell Elena about Peter. Perhaps she had been too wary of possible comments, for Elena had once made a remark that had seemed cutting — although again, maybe it had not been cutting at all, but merely Elena's singular brand of humor.

"I can see you married to a professor with leather patches on his elbows. You'd be snowed in somewhere in a town like Kingsley, except that there'd be a college on the outskirts. And you'd have parties on winter nights, with everyone sitting around earnestly discussing the world's problems from *a* to *z*."

On the other hand there was as yet not very much to tell about Peter. He was not a professor, but a young associate, one of the best she had ever had as a graduate student. In her first year she had taken his course on the History and Evolution of Architecture; she had been fascinated by Viollet-le-Duc, who had restored Notre Dame, by Le Corbusier's pioneer "modern" cities, but most of all by Peter Frank himself.

He was red haired and expectedly, though only slightly, freckled. He was very tall, with a fresh, outdoor look, as if he had just come in from very cold weather. He had wit, used vivid adjectives, and moved his hands expressively, so that as he spoke, art and stone took shape in the air before him.

And he had not ever noticed Charlotte Dawes, who sat in the second row and worshiped him all through Architecture and Construction in the Modern World.

Then, six weeks ago, they had met in the cafeteria during that dead time between three and four in the afternoon when there is hardly anyone there. Charlotte had been holding a coffee cup in one hand, while in the other she turned the pages of a text. He came over and sat across from her.

"So you're going to be an architect," he said abruptly.

Finding the remark rather odd, she answered lightly, in a tone that revealed her surprise, "Why, yes, yes, I hope so."

"I've been giving you A's, and if there had been anything higher than A, I'd have given you that."

As if she were standing outside observing herself, she knew she was hiding her feelings very well. "Oh, I have been designing houses in my head ever since I was in junior high school," she said, laughing.

"Did you have that braid halfway down your back when you were in junior high school?"

"No, I had a ponytail."

Then he laughed too. "I must tell you, whenever you turn your back as you leave the room, I have the worst temptation to pull your braid. It's a Chinese man's old-time queue, except that it's blond."

Quite astonished, she replied, "I had no idea you even knew I was in the room."

"Oh, I knew very much that you were. But I make it a policy not to be involved with my female students. It's a prudent policy. In fact, I'm surprised at myself right now."

She said nothing. It seemed to her that she was hearing her own heartbeat.

"Where do you live?" he asked.

"I have an apartment with two friends, five blocks up the avenue."

"I'm out that way too. If you're going home now, we can walk together."

That was the start of it. So far "it" had meant a few art exhibits, movies, long dinners, and long walks, all of these curtailed by heavy snows and Christmas vacation. They had had no privacy because of Charlotte's roommates and the other tenants in Peter's house. Nevertheless, there had been between them a quivering excitement with promise of more.

This was Charlotte's first experience of hot emotion. Her social life all through college and up to the present had been just that: social. She went out in groups. Men and women both liked her, for she was likable, a good dancer and tennis player, interesting, a thoughtful friend, and, as she could scarcely help knowing, more than averagely attractive. . . .

The train went rattling toward Philadelphia through the night. Along the track, the little suburban towns and the little houses scattered in developments bare of trees were buttoned up against the cold. By turning her head in their direction she could avoid the intermittent glances of a man across the aisle. His interest was unmistakable. The new crimson coat, bought this week with Elena's money and at her insistence, was attention-getting. And her long, thick braid, she thought, chuckling at the memory of Peter and the braid, was even more so.

Charlotte was accustomed to men's glances, accustomed to their expectations and their propositions. Yet, she was still a virgin. (The thing that had happened to her did not count, and must not count.) Virginity in the last decade of this century was an astonishment to virtually everyone she knew. She explained to herself that she was fastidious, perhaps overly so. A friend had told her once that some of the men in their group, intending no malice because they were fond of Charlotte, had labeled her "the untouchable" and made joking bets as to who might be the first to touch her. Some said that she was obviously frigid. She did not think she was.

She thought sometimes about Claudia and Cliff. Despite all their trouble there was such an aura of sensuality, a thrilling tenderness, between them! Once when she was still in school, she had come upon them embracing in the kitchen and been astonished. She had never witnessed much affection, let alone desire. . . . That was how it should be, and with Peter, it would be. Even though they had not yet touched upon the physical, she knew that it would be.

Without a break, without a moment's hesitation, they had come together. Their conversations were long and deep, so that by now, in these few weeks, they had reached the point at which two people are almost able to read each other's thoughts.

She had told him everything about herself except the one thing that was never to be told to anybody. Now and then, as time passed and in certain moods, she asked herself why not. The answer always came with a shudder: What if you had a hideous wound in a hidden part of your body? Would you want to display it, even to someone you loved? No, a thousand times no. You would not.

He knew how she felt about each of her parents. He knew that it was Claudia who had urged her to go away for graduate study; Dad's hope, which he tried to conceal, was that she would stay near home. He knew that she was a virgin, and he knew about her ambition.

"I want to build. I want to see something that began in my head and was roughed out on paper by my hand turn into steel and stone, or brick, or wood, that you can touch, walk through, and see in its outline against the sky. And one day — please don't laugh — I'd like to build something in my hometown, sort of a monument, to take the place of the mill that used to be the heart of it. I don't know what it would be or whether I'll ever do it, but it's kind of fun to think about. I can even see the bronze plaque with my name on it: Architect, Charlotte Dawes. I'm aiming high, Peter. I hope I don't sound pompous to you."

"You are far from pompous. The fact is," Peter had said, becoming abruptly serious, "you are going to be a great success. I feel it in my bones, as both my grandmothers used to say about a thunderstorm coming on a sunny day. Don't laugh, it always did. As for me," he went on, "I'm a teacher, that's all. I like to talk about the history of buildings and what they've meant within their cultures. I don't think I'm capable of putting up a building and keeping it from falling down. I'll never get rich. I'm not much interested in money, anyway. I shall be very pleased to remain just where I am now."

There had never been any money in Peter's family. He was one of eight children, and his mother was expecting a ninth. He had slept three in a bed on a farm in Oklahoma, and via a scholarship to the university there had worked the rest of the way to where he was now.

Opposites attract, Charlotte thought, and was very happy.

The train slowed down and entered the station. In a sudden rush to get home she ran down the platform and up the steps to find a taxi. There would be telephone messages; the one that left no name but only a promise to call again would be Peter's. They had both agreed that it was just as well to keep their affair — could you call it that yet? she wondered — private.

"Next weekend," Peter said, "the house will empty out. There are five of us faculty there. All of them except me belong to the same fraternity that's having a convention out of town, so we can have the place to ourselves for two days."

In class now Charlotte moved to the back row. There was such a sensual, such a tense, expectancy between them, all the more voluptuous for not yet having been defined in words, that it would have been impossible there in public to meet each other's eyes. When alone, she thought, with a touch of amusement, that this state of her mind was surely what an old-fashioned virgin bride must have felt just before her wedding.

Amused or not, like such a bride, she made preparations. On leaving home after her last visit she had hesitated to take back with her some of Elena's more frivolous presents, such as chiffon nightgowns, a silver-fitted dressing case, or a quilted satin bed jacket. Elena's extravagant choices had never suited Charlotte's way of life, and yet it was against the frugal streak in her nature to ignore them entirely.

"Take the bed jacket," Claudia, who was helping her pack, had advised. "Some freezing night when you're still studying for a test at two A.M., it'll come in handy. And while you're at it, take a couple of the nightgowns too." She had laughed. "You never know."

Now Charlotte was glad she had brought them. The white with the black lace would be the right one; it was innocent or it was seductive, depending upon how you looked at it. Her scuffed bedroom slippers would never do, so she went out and bought slippers with heels and marabou. She packed perfume and a new lipstick. At bedtime, when she undid her braid, she lingered before the mirror to appraise her face in its frame of long, loose hair. On Tuesday it seemed unbearable to have to wait until Friday.

And yet, on Wednesday, a troubling cloud, a nasty memory, a quiver of fear, passed over the glow. What if something were to go wrong? But what possibly could "go wrong"? And she fought the memory, despising it for its absurdity. What did that old horror have to do with this joy, this splendor? Nothing.

"We're going to break the bank on Friday night," Peter said. "We're going to have the fanciest dinner in the city. Believe it or not, I'll be wearing a jacket and tie."

When they met at the entrance to the restaurant, they startled each other. She had never seen him wearing other than campus clothes, and he had never seen her in the urban dignity of fitted crimson coat and slender dark blue dress. For an instant they stared as if each had seen a solemn metamorphosis.

At dinner this mood lingered. Here their eyes could frankly meet, and hold without concealment. There was no need for them to speak aloud what they were feeling, and indeed, they, whose talk was always vivacious, spoke very little. Now and then their hands reached out for a quick clasp across the table.

In this same state of gravity they rode in a taxi to Peter's house, one of a long, monotonous, dark-brown row. He fumbled with the key, fumbled to find the light in the hall, and broke abruptly into fumbling speech.

"I'm afraid you'll find it pretty dreary. No feminine refinements here, just a masculine hodgepodge. I'm sure it was different in the 1890s when some rich merchant gave plush parties under the gas lamps."

He was nervous. Perhaps, she thought, it is because it is my first time and he thinks I'm nervous. Or it's because he has never had an inexperienced woman before me. And on impulse she flung her arms around him.

"I'm not at all scared," she whispered, "in case you're thinking that I might be. Not scared and not shy."

He kissed her. Their lips and their cheeks were cold. Still wrapped in their coats, they stood in the center of the room, fastened together, swaying a little, unable to let go.

Presently, his fingers undid the buttons on her coat. They moved to the sofa and rested, lying back in a prolonged kiss. She felt his heartbeat. Naturally she had read everything about foreplay, tenderness without hurry, prolonging the sweetness. For an instant she thought how unnecessary all this talk was. As if you needed instruction books. . . . Maybe some people did. . . . But not I, not now.

"All these clothes," he murmured.

"Yes. Where shall I —"

"If you want to go in the other room —"

They were speaking in broken sentences, as if they were barely able to speak at all.

It occurred to her as she stood in the bedroom, an ugly room of the sort called Spartan, with its narrow bed and chair and chest, that he might have wanted her to undress while he watched. You really are inexperienced, aren't you, Charlotte? Well, not altogether. . . . But for God's sake, that was something else. Stop recalling it. Stop.

In the semidarkness her shoulders gleamed out of the mirror over the chest. He would smell the rich scent of gardenias upon them. Her hands, trembling with excitement, almost ripped her clothes off and slid the white chiffon over her head. Let him first see her in its transparent folds; let him be the one to remove it himself.

In the kitchen, an alcove about as large as an oversized closet, he was standing, still only half undressed, doing something at the counter.

"I'll be with you in a minute," he called.

Waiting, she was conscious of an incredible joy. That they were really alone together, behind a locked door, undisturbed! And but for the tray that he was carrying, she would have run again into his arms.

On the table in front of the sofa, he set it down and looked at her.

She watched his eyes travel from her face to her breasts and along the fall of the sheer white cloth to her feet in their feathered slippers.

"How beautiful you are!" he cried.

She watched his eyes travel back upward again and smile and gleam.

"Sit here. I've made a rum punch, just right for a winter night. We won't need to warm the sheets."

On the tray there were a pitcher, two glasses, and a plate of English biscuits. He filled the glasses, touching his to hers, and gave a toast. "To all things beautiful. To you. To us."

The liquid heat went quivering toward some hollow, some deeply hidden pit inside Charlotte that she had never even known she possessed. She heard a sigh, a long intake of breath — her own and his; she heard an inarticulate murmuring — her own and his; avid lips met hers, a determined hand moved beneath her skirt —

Something incredible happened. Through Charlotte's head, and all around her, a fiery illumination flared. Sofa, table, glasses, plate, man, were all there in full color; the winter night was the summer afternoon, the biscuits were a slab of leftover chocolate cake, the unkempt brown room was flowery and green, the man was a lunging weight upon her; his lips smothered her and his hands tore at her.

She was in total, crazy panic. What was she doing here? She knew nothing about the man who was so tightly holding her, knew only that this could all end in terror and pain. The delicious throb and surge in her blood, all that tremendous pulsing of desire, were gone, simply flooded away.

Closely pressed as they were, Peter felt her powerful shiver and, mistaking it for passion, pressed closer.

Calm. Calm yourself, she said without making a sound, while her eyes filled with uncontrollable tears. This is Peter. You wanted to be here. You wanted to do this. For God's sake, you've been wanting it for the last two years.

"What is it?" he cried out as she pulled away.

"I don't know. I don't think I feel well."

He stared. "Are you feeling pain somewhere? What is it?" he cried again.

She understood that he must be totally shocked and afraid of what he was seeing. "Maybe it's the rum," she whispered foolishly.

"Of course it isn't. What hurts you? Show me. Do you need a doctor?"

"No, no. Please," for he had started across the room as if to reach the telephone. "No, don't!"

"But why the tears? What can I do for you?"

"Nothing. It's nothing."

Bewildered, he came back and stood over her, still staring while a large tear slid down her cheek into her mouth.

"It can't be 'nothing.' Why won't you speak? Can I do anything for you? Do you want to lie down?"

"No, no, I'll be all right. I'm sorry." And she set the glass back on the tray.

"That's strange. Are you sure you don't want to lie down?"

"I don't know. No. I'll be all right. I'm sorry."

Theater of the absurd, she thought. A woman in a fancy nightgown and a man in his underwear shorts, she wishing herself to be out of this place and not sure how to get out, while he stood helplessly and surely deflated. All passion spent, as in Sackville-West's famous novel.

She must hold on to some dignity. She sat quite still. Even her face muscles went still, and her tears stopped.

She looked up at him, trying to smile, saying once more, "I'm sorry. It came over me. . . . My stomach . . . I'm sorry."

"Please, will you stop saying you're sorry?"

"Sometimes my stomach does queer things. . . . Nothing serious. . . . Such a nuisance."

For a few moments Peter studied her thoughtfully. Then, as if he had reached a conclusion, he said quietly, "I don't believe you're physically sick, Charlotte."

There was a long pause, by the end of which she, too, had reached a conclusion.

"It's true, I'm not. I guess the least I can do is to be truthful with you. The truth is in my head. Everything just suddenly — it just suddenly went away."

"I see," he said. "Just went away." His tone that had been so concerned and kindly turned cold. She understood that he saw this disaster as a rejection of his manhood.

"Oh," she cried then, "I'm so ashamed! I came here wanting the same thing you wanted, you know I did. You do know it. I never meant to give you the wrong idea. I'm not a tease. I have only contempt for women like that. You are the most wonderful man, so bright, so handsome —" She began to sob.

At that he laid his hand on her shoulder and comforted. "Don't, don't. Do you want to tell me your trouble? Let me help you."

She shook her head, whispering so low that she did not know whether he heard or not, "It's impossible. You must be so furious with me, Peter, because I can't tell you the whole truth, after all."

At any rate, he kept standing there, stroking her back, while within Charlotte the same imploring question kept repeating itself: Am I to keep this incubus with me forever? At long, long intervals, so long that she was sometimes sure it had left for good, it always returned. That it should have returned at this crucial moment tonight, was cruel. Cruel!

After a long while she grew quiet inside and raised her head. "You must be so furious with me, Peter."

"I'm not angry, Charlotte," he answered gently.

Well, maybe not that, but baffled, frustrated, and in a hurry to be rid of her. So she struggled up from the sofa, aware, too, of the humiliating picture they must be making in their state of undress, a pair of lovers who had not loved.

"It's cold," Peter said. "The heat goes down after eleven. You'd better get your clothes on."

I'm wretched, she thought as she replaced the dress, the pumps, and the festive pearls that in a state of joyous excitement she had first put on.

When she reappeared in the outer room, the tray was gone, and there were two cups of coffee on the table.

"Decaffeinated," Peter said. "I remembered. No, don't protest. We'll have a half cup and then I'll take you home."

He was back in his suit with his tie done properly. The picture had changed. Had things turned out as expected, Charlotte would have found humor — Peter had often remarked her sense of humor — in reflecting how so much depends on clothing. This distraught pair had changed ten minutes after the debacle into a decorous couple having their decorous after-dinner coffee.

"You're so kind," she said, "considering what I've done. So kind."

"You don't have to apologize. You don't have to make all the right noises. Take it easy. You're miserable. You're in some sort of trouble, and all I can do is to offer again to help you."

"I don't want to be secretive, Peter. But there are some things that a person can't talk about."

"I suppose not. I suppose there's not one of us who doesn't have something hidden."

"Only believe that this had nothing at all to do with you. Nothing at all."

"I believe you," he answered gravely.

When they arrived at her door, he simply kissed her cheek and walked fast away. She went inside, lay down on her bed, and wept.

She did not hear from him. On the first day after the disaster, she thought that he had not telephoned because he did not want to disturb her. When two more days passed, it was clear that he was not going to call. The brutality of this first stunned and then crushed her. Had she been so worthless to him that he could simply dispense with her as one returns a defective article to the store?

She took her seat in the back row of the classroom, from where she was only able to glimpse him between heads. At the end of the hour he did not linger. And she knew that he was avoiding her. How dare he treat her like that? A violent hatred rose into her throat and clenched her teeth.

After all, there was no reason why he should burden himself with her mysterious sorrow, was there? Had she not told him that she would not talk about it? He had decided, undoubtedly, that she was profoundly, pathetically neurotic. There were plenty of women who could come to him without bringing such baggage. . . . So gradually, the hatred seeped away, leaving behind it a dull resentment toward what had been her fate, along with a sickening sense of humiliation.

He continued to mark her papers with A's, which she knew she deserved, for she was working harder than ever; work was now her distraction, escape from the loneliness of loss. Had she really been in love with him? Perhaps no one ever could know the difference between love and infatuation until a long time had passed; if it endured, then one would know it had been love. And yet she was certain that it had been love.

She began again to have more frequent nightmares, in which Ted came back and terrified her. He followed her through the streets into her house, and was there beside her bed when she awoke, so that when she actually did wake up in the apartment here, he was present, just as he had been that night in Peter's room.

She knew, of course, that Ted was the barrier to sex and love and everything except her work. Had he not been the barrier between Peter and her? What she did not know was how to get past him. Go for "help" again? More than once, after much inner resistance, she had done just that, but "help," however professional, did not infallibly help.

"Get out among people," Elena would say, that being her remedy for virtually every ailment. Charlotte, however, was not Elena. Time alone would either cure her, or it would not.

Shortly before graduation on one of those late spring days that are so blue and green and blossom-filled, so sheerly perfect as to seem unreal, she met him crossing the campus. And wanting to test herself before taking leave of this place and of him forever, she stopped to speak.

"I hear that you're getting a promotion," she said boldly, and smiled. "I hope you'll be very happy, Peter."

He thanked her, and they stood for a moment, uncertainly, under the trees. There he was with the same fresh, outdoor look and the same lambent eyes that had so enchanted her, yet now there was a terrible embarrassment between them. All passion spent, she thought again. And she wondered whether, sometime or somewhere, it might ever be rekindled. No doubt it was foolish to have such a thought. Or was it?

"And what are you planning after graduation?" he asked.

"I have a job in Boston. It's with a fairly young firm, but they're up and coming, and they've taken me on," she said with some pride.

He told her that he was glad for her and that he wished her well.

"You are going to be a great success, as I told you," he said sincerely. "Mark my words."

Like formal strangers they shook hands and went in opposite directions.

TWO

The Lauriers were an interesting couple, he from French Canada and she with an ancestry going back to the first settlers of Boston in 1600-and-something. Both in their early forties, they had migrated first from a firm that concentrated solely on restorations and strict reproductions — "broken arches, dental moldings, and Palladian windows," said Rudy — to one that had bestrewed America's cities with office towers — "faceless concrete slabs," said Pauline — and had finally decided to start out for themselves.

Their office filled three floors of an old brick building. They had started with two draftsmen and already needed one more.

Pauline told Charlotte, "I think we will get along very well."

She reminded Charlotte of Claudia. There certainly was no physical resemblance between them, since Pauline was dark haired and thin as a stick, nor did she have Claudia's calm gestures and thoughtful way of speaking, but her cheerful, commonsense approach was Claudia's. Charlotte suspected, too, that underneath the surface lay a softness that Rudy would monitor and, when necessary, curb much as Cliff did with Claudia.

"You have an impressive record. What parts of the training had most appeal for you?" Pauline had asked.

"I guess I'd say design and land regulation, how to make buildings fit the environment and people's lives."

"Then you speak my language, Charlotte. Rudy can worry over structural engineering all by himself." Pauline laughed. "He's a whiz at it, too, which I'm not."

There was a friendly, an almost homelike, atmosphere in the busy little firm. The two others in the drafting room were Mike, newly married, and Rosalyn, newly widowed. Mike found a small apartment for Charlotte in the building where he lived, for which she was grateful, having had enough of communal living. Rosalyn invited her home to lunch on her first Sunday, with a standing invitation for any Sunday.

Neither of these two, Rosalyn still locked in mourning and Mike locked with his bride in a world of their own, was apt to introduce Charlotte to a wider circle. She thought about that but, deciding that time would eventually take care of such things, decided that she would devote herself entirely to her very promising job.

The drafting room was on the top floor. Sitting tall on her drafting stool, Charlotte looked out into the clear white northern light where clustered skyscrapers made dark serrations against the rim of the sky. Below lay the old, meandering streets of this colonial city at the water's edge. Now and then she looked up from the plan of a vacation house to consider the life that was surging now through these streets and structures, in all of which she was a stranger.

From early childhood her free hours had consisted of whatever minutes might be salvaged from school hours; now, whenever the office was closed, she was totally free, without required reading or need to study for examinations or any obligations at all. After a few months this freedom, which had at first been so welcome, began to trouble her. It was lonely. It was unnatural. Her thoughts sank deeply and dangerously into the past.

Absurd as it seemed when she reflected upon it later, it was that fat blond braid of hers that finally brought about a change. Because of it she was noticed, identified in the apartment house as "the girl with the braid." Thus she gradually became acquainted with a young crowd, and her weekends began to take on more color.

Yet she found none of the compatible joy

that she had found with Peter, none of the good talk, the wit and laughter. These men took her to bars, watched the inevitable television in the corner, and drank. When, on bringing thcm home, she did not allow them into her bed, some tried once more before dropping her, and some did not even try a second time.

Then it happened that she met a man who showed promise. He was a cousin of Rosalyn's, well spoken and quiet, like her.

"I had a hunch you'd enjoy a concert," he said, so they went, and indeed she did enjoy the evening, especially because when he took her home, he left her at the door without grabbing or fumbling. The next time, they went to a play, using Charlotte's tickets, since he was, like herself, a working person who had to watch his dollars. They had some dinners with a group of his friends, compatible all, so that she began to feel involved and accepted as she had been in Philadelphia in the days before Peter.

One night when they were having a drink in her apartment after seeing a movie, he broke abruptly into their conversation with a complaint.

"Don't you think it's about time, Charlotte? I've been waiting for a signal from you, but it hasn't come."

She felt her eyebrows rise as if to convey a surprised and total incomprehension, although she did comprehend, very well. "Signal?" she repeated.

"Oh, come on! Can't you see that I'm being — have been — a gentleman? I've been very, very patient, waiting for the ice to melt, to show a few drops of warmth, but I haven't seen one yet. You even shrink from a good-night kiss."

A trap was closing down on her. And she replied, knowing how inept was her reply, "But I like you! I thought we could be good friends."

"Does that mean we can't have some normal mutual pleasure? This is 1994. Unless you find me, me in particular, repulsive."

He paused. Of course he was waiting for her to say that he was not. It was true that she had been attracted to him by nothing more than his intelligence and congenial ways, but he was certainly far from being physically repulsive.

"Please. It's nothing personal," she said gently. "It's just that I don't want to go to bed with a man to prove that I like him, even if it is 1994."

He persisted. "You mislead a man. Everything about you is misleading, the way you look, your laughter, your gestures, everything, and you turn out to be made of ice."

Plainly, he was feeling a sense of injury, and she was sorry about that; yet underlying his accusation, she recognized anger. And this in turn aroused some anger in her.

"I never tried to mislead you or anyone," she said. "It's your fault if you read something in me that wasn't there. And I've never thought I was icy. In fact, I know I'm not."

There was a silence during which he seemed to be studying her as they stood, for they had both risen, confronting each other.

"Perhaps not," he said then, "but you're certainly wound up tight. I don't mean to insult you, I mean this as a friend, but you ought to look into yourself, Charlotte. Even now you're standing with your arms folded over your chest as if you were afraid I might rape you."

He might have meant very well; nevertheless, the blood was already racing to her head.

"You'd better get out," she said.

Disbelieving, he cried, "You're not serious? Get out? You're actually putting me out?"

"Yes. Please go."

He picked up the jacket that he had flung over a chair. In a daze she heard his last furious words from the outer hall: "Go back to 1884 with a fan and a bottle of smelling salts. It's where you belong."

The closing door left a thundering silence. She sat down on the sofa with her head in her hands. It was all so ugly, so shaming, a replay, in spite of the major difference, of the scene with Peter. Benumbed, she sat for minutes without moving. Only her blood still moved and pounded.

After a while the blood quieted, and logical thought resumed. He had been rash, not what she had thought he was, true. But it had been absurd to put him out like that as if he had harmed her or threatened harm. There had been no reason to humiliate him so and goad him into fury.

For he had seen her plain. Was she not "wound up tight"? She had acted a role in a melodrama. She had gone out of control because he had used a word: *rape.*

"Look into yourself," he had said. My God! As if she had never looked!

She went to bed, and only in the exhausted hours before morning, fell asleep.

The rain, driven by the wind to an acute angle, struck hard at the tall north-facing windows. It was darkest February. Charlotte looked out into the blast and back at her work, a final watercolor drawing, ready for the client's approval, of a tropical pastel house.

Looking over her shoulder, Mike remarked, "Nice. What about a tall, cold glass on the terrace after a swim, with the breeze blowing through the palms? I could be very comfortable in a house like that."

Charlotte studied the picture. "Actually, Mike, it's pretty awful, isn't it? Two-story Corinthian columns on a plot in Florida? It should stand back on a sweep of lawn among copper beech trees a century old, not in a dinky suburban yard. And the columns are too heavy, anyway."

Mike shrugged. "If the client wants it, you have to give it to him. At least until you're an independent, big-name firm, you have to."

"Do you ever dream of having an independent, big-name firm of your own?" she asked.

"Dream! That's about what it is, like winning the lottery, so I don't bother dreaming."

When Charlotte did not comment, he looked at her with curiosity. "Why? Is that what you're aiming at?"

"Yes," she said simply.

His expression changed to amusement. "Have you any idea what the competition is? You must have. Take my advice, do the best work you can, as you are doing, marry a great guy, have a baby, and be satisfied. Susie's pregnant, she'll take a year off from her job, and we'll get by nicely even if I don't reach the top of the ladder, which I won't."

He didn't know, nor could he know, that she had entered a new phase of life in which she would rely on no one but herself: a rigorous, proud life of labor and achievement.

So she smiled, saying only, "Mike, we're all different."

This, then, was the change. The search for a social life, for men or for a man, no longer absorbed her spirit. She began a regimen that, like a diet, would energize her in body and mind.

She walked for miles, all over the city. She watched the swan boats and saw the first leaves appear on the weeping willows in the Public Gardens. In the mornings she jogged. After work she swam at a businesswomen's club. On weekends she went alone to concerts, bookstores, museums, and foreign films; it pleased her to be making independent choices, deferring to no one's tastes but her own.

Sometimes she asked herself a sharp question: Was this simply a case of sour grapes? Was it because she was unable to be what she wanted to be that she must now turn away in defiance? Yes, possibly so. But if that is how it is, she said sternly, I must accept it.

Besides, her head was filled with designs. She was only a beginner in the drafting room, yet she had lordly views of fabulous projects: opera houses, civic centers, and monuments so grand that she could almost laugh at herself — almost, but never entirely.

One afternoon Pauline summoned her into her private office.

"It must be hard to come to a strange city without knowing a soul," she began. "I can't imagine it. Rudy and I were thinking that you're too smart and pretty to go to waste, which is my way of inviting you to a party. You don't have to accept, though. We won't be insulted if you say no."

Charlotte was certainly not about to say no to the boss.

"We do this every spring," Pauline explained. "You might call it a block party. All of our neighbors and other friends come together to celebrate the end of the winter. It's kind of dressed up," she added, and then, as if fearing she might be giving the wrong impression, corrected herself with a laugh. "Oh, not really dressed up. I mean — anything goes. You may see everything from diamond earrings to — well, not quite to jeans."

She was being considerate. No doubt she thought that Charlotte, on her limited salary, had probably a very limited wardrobe as well.

Charlotte had to smile to herself. It was really funny. In her dingy little flat there was a closetful of expensive clothes, all bearing Italian labels. She owned diamond earrings, too, good-sized studs that had been Elena's present on her twenty-first birthday. It had been quite a long while since she had worn them or had wanted to. But she would wear them to this party, along with a strand of pearls, a lime-green dress the color of April, and a pair of cream-colored shoes.

Actually, it was the Lauriers' house that allured her. It was one of those old, red-brick, Beacon Hill residences where the brasswork on the front door glistens and the window boxes drip cascades of fuchsias. Inside, Charlotte was pretty sure, behind the lavender-paned windows, there would be cog moldings and original mantels. Pauline said frankly that they could never have afforded to live there if the house had not been left to her.

Apt to act motherly, she also said, "I have

at least two men coming whom you might like."

"I'll be happy to come," Charlotte told her, "and thank you for asking me."

The house had all the charm that she had expected. Wandering through the rooms, she lingered before an eighteenth-century portrait of a woman in a mobcap and stood fascinated by an ancient map of the New World on which this continent was joined to Asia.

There seemed to be few people present with whom Charlotte had much in common. Many of the guests were elderly householders who, having known each other forever, naturally gathered together. Young people seemed to have come in pairs; they were either married or might as well have been for all the attention, once past the first politenesses, that they paid to an unattached woman.

A white-haired woman gave her an approving smile and a kindly compliment. "You look lovely, dear. What a pleasure it is to see a young girl not wearing jeans."

"Young girl" indeed! But I suppose, Charlotte thought, twenty-five and fourteen must look very much the same to her.

A pair of quite attractive young men struck

up an enthusiastic conversation, but it turned out that they were college sophomores who could have no more interest in Charlotte than she could have in them. As tactfully as possible, then, the three drifted, sophomores to the bar, and she in the direction of a corner where a group of women had collected.

Pauline, intercepting her, was distressed. "This is perfectly awful, your standing here alone. I'm absolutely furious. Those men I mentioned made last-minute excuses just this morning. I could kill them. No manners. I wouldn't have believed they could be so rude. Now we have at least four extra women. It's awful."

"It's not awful at all," Charlotte said. "I can manage beautifully without men, so don't worry. Really, Pauline."

It surprised her that a woman as competent as Pauline, one who was making her way in the world, should still be thinking in terms of Noah's ark: a male for every female, with a few extra males for good measure.

The women in the corner group were quite possibly the most interesting people in the room. They were a lawyer, a psychologist, a buyer of imported fashions, and a bright young mother of three. The conversation, quickly started up, began to bounce like a ball and was carried right through to supper, where the five sat together at the end of a long table. The talk sped from clothes to child care, from divorce law to historical preservation, and slid into gossip. The fashion expert, who went by the name of Birdie, had too sharp and flippant a tongue but was at the same time hilarious.

"Take a look at the round table over there," she whispered, "at the guy with the yellow tie. Doesn't he look like a whiskey ad where the butler brings it in on a silver tray? Or else an ad for a BMW? It's all there, graying hair, ruddy smirk, big stone house with a circular driveway, elderly wife, and, you can bet your Armani suit, a darling little secretary on the side."

"I don't have an Armani suit," Charlotte said, laughing.

"Why haven't you got one? You're wearing a European dress. Italian, isn't it?"

"Yes. A present from my mother. She lives in Italy. I can't afford things like this myself."

Now, why had she said that? She had said it because her eye, trained by Elena, saw that the others, with the exception of Birdie, were very inexpensively dressed.

It's your sensitivity, Claudia had always said, and would say now if she had been here. *You always sense what other people must be feeling. It's a fine trait if you don't carry it too far.*

"Now, there's a dress for you," said Birdie. Like conspirators they all leaned toward her to hear her whisper. "Look at the white that's coming now."

A tall couple were sitting down at the far end of the table, he a dark, impeccable young man and she a flashing person with regal posture. They were immediately greeted and noisily welcomed by all the other couples at the table.

"Late again," said Birdie. "She is one big nuisance. She comes in an hour late for her fittings and nothing's ever right the first time, or maybe the second time either. Well, I suppose when you pay what she pays, you feel you have to throw your weight around. It must be kind of thrilling."

Charlotte was seeing, or rather trying not to see, the dark young man. Actually, she was seeing Peter, which was absurd, because they were so different. Red-haired Peter in his baggy shirts . . .

Yet there must have been something else that her first glance had caught, something to cause this quick agitation. The couple had made a difference in the atmosphere. But perhaps it was only the woman by herself who, with her striking dress, had made the difference?

"What do you think? Are they real or not?"

Someone had directed a question toward Charlotte, who had not been paying attention.

"Are what real?"

"The earrings."

Like tassels, they dangled, glittering, almost touching the white spaghetti straps.

"I don't know. Probably not."

Birdie contradicted her. "Probably yes. Almost certainly yes. That's brand-new money. With brand-new money you don't wear imitation stuff, dear. You want the world to know you can afford the real thing."

Birdie was angry. Underneath the vivacious wit she was bitter and angry. What was her story? Charlotte wondered. For everybody had a story. Everybody.

Ringing laughter came from the far end of the table, and she raised her eyes toward it. The dark young man was the only one not laughing. Whatever it was that had appealed so heartily to the rest of his group had not appealed to him. *He was not one of them.*

He was pushing his cuff back to see his wristwatch. When he looked up again over the long room toward the windows, she had a full view of his face, which was aquiline and not like Peter's at all; yet the slight smile, as private as the thought that had caused it, was Peter's; sometimes, at a pause in his lectures, he had looked toward the window with just such a smile, close lipped but soft.

Damn! Damn memories.

"The trouble with good-looking guys like him," said Birdie, who, to no one's objection, did all the talking among the women, "is, first, that they're hard to catch, and second, that if you do catch one, it's worth all your wits and energy to keep holding him."

"He's very attractive," remarked the psychologist, sounding wistful.

The lawyer asked Birdie, "Who is he?"

"I've no idea. She's always got new ones on the string."

It would have been totally eccentric to say, or else Charlotte would have said: *He's not on her string! He doesn't even want to be here, can't you see?*

"Don't look now," Birdie said to Charlotte. "He's looking at you."

"That's ridiculous."

Birdie shook her head. "I have a hawk's eyes, dear, and it's not ridiculous. He noticed you about three minutes after he got here."

All this talk was inane. Girls in junior high

school, giggling at the lunch table, nudging each other when a boy came near, behaved like Birdie, who was supposedly a sophisticated woman. Nevertheless, when Charlotte raised her eyes above the wineglass, they met unmistakably the full, thoughtful gaze of the man who sat beside the tasseled earrings.

"You see?" said Birdie, who missed nothing.

"No, I don't, because there's nothing to see," Charlotte replied shortly.

"If I were you, when we get up from the table, I'd meet him halfway. In spite of her it can be done."

"I know it can be done, but I don't want to."

"Well, that's your problem," Birdie said with a shrug that dismissed Charlotte for the rest of the evening.

She went home, having been one of the first to leave, in a queer mood, irritable and flat. She who was such an orderly person kicked off her shoes, dropped her dress into a heap on the floor, and went to bed.

Dreams interrupted her sleep all night, bizarre flashes of people in places where they did not belong. She was having a tooth pulled without Novocain; the dentist was Peter. Rudy and Pauline balanced on a steel beam one hundred floors aboveground and stopped her heart; she went to a party at her own house in Kingsley, where Dad was offering a drink to the dark young man with the aquiline face who had been staring at her in Pauline's house.

She woke late with a headache. For the first time in months the solitary Sunday loomed empty and bleak. Undoubtedly, she had been working too hard, nose to the grindstone. She needed a rest. It was four months since she had been home. Tomorrow, she decided, I will ask for a week off without pay, and go.

THREE

The pleasant dining room in the European-style inn near the Thailand-Myanmar border was almost vacant, the last tourist group having departed after an early breakfast. Only one man remained alone at the far end of the room, so that Cliff and Claudia had the quiet space to themselves. She looked outward to the surrounding grove, where vines such as she had never seen and could not name twisted their purple flowers through dense shrubbery. An enormous banyan tree, whose trunk had the girth of six stout men, stood in a heap of its own snake-twisted roots. It must be at least a hundred years old, she thought, or maybe even two hundred. From somewhere came the bronze clang of a gong, so mysteriously different from the sound of ringing bells at home.

Everything was strange here, the fat Buddhas with their placid gaze, the fruits in the markets, the dusty villages, the slender women with their rich, long hair, the curious sound of a cry in an unintelligible language, a tiny monkey sitting in a tree, the gold and scarlet of the temples — all were marvelous and strange.

She knew quite well that Cliff had wanted this trip for her sake. Travel no longer had the allure for him when, in his twenties, he had gone wandering.

"We can't afford it," she had objected.

He had argued her down. "The advance for the next volume of my *History of Industry* will pay for it, and people do owe themselves something nice once in a while."

Careful as she was to conceal those periods of deepest sadness he must be aware that she had them. For, someplace on this globe, her son, too, was wandering, not as the youthful adventurer that Cliff had been, but as a guilty, wary fugitive.

And Claudia shook her head as if to shake off an insect that was buzzing at her cheek. This was the last day here, and she must not waste the smallest scrap of it.

"One more temple today," said Cliff, "and then we'd better get back here right after lunch to pack, or we'll miss the plane. You hate to leave, don't you?"

"Yes, I could do another week, or more," she added, "but I know you're thinking about what's happening at home."

Things had been going rapidly downhill. The mill's tenants, Premier Recycling, were a bad lot. And she remembered how Bill had been doubtful about them from the start.

Perhaps she ought to have said something then, while the deal was taking shape. . . . But she had been a newcomer to the family, she had run a bookstore; so what could she know about a business of such magnitude? The old Dawes Textile Mill, for goodness' sake! Nobody would have listened to her maunderings, especially when an esteemed firm of lawyers was advising the brothers. Now they were caught in a trap, caught by a long lease that no longer paid enough to cover the property taxes, which had more than doubled during these intervening years.

"Everything's heating up," Cliff said. "I spoke to Bill last night while you were having your bath."

She was all attention. "What's happening?"

"There was a town meeting. Bill said it was a shocker, an attack. We have come from being the chief employers and main benefactors of Kingsley to being villains. Well, sad to say, we've known that for quite a while, and yet Bill said he hadn't realized how high the feeling was running. It was like running a gauntlet, he said, and you know how sparingly he uses words."

"True. And yet sometimes he can be so emotional, so excitable. Of course I can't possibly know his ways as you know them,

277

but — hasn't he changed awfully since everything happened, since Elena left?"

Cliff sighed. "Yes, yes, he has. He's hard to talk to some days. Changeable. Supersensitive. And now there's this business on top of the rest. He told me that people got up and spoke, people he'd never have expected to turn against the Dawes family. They said it was a disgrace to have this filthy eyesore practically at the town's front door, that the stench was hideous — which is true — and that we're breeding disease — which may or may not be true — and that we, Cliff and Bill, should be ashamed of ourselves. We're hypocrites, with Bill going around the state talking about the environment —"

Indignantly, Claudia broke in. "Just what do they think you can do about it?"

"Cease and desist, naturally. But we've tried to work it out with the tenants, haven't we? You know that, and you know it's been like talking to a stone wall. They deny that there is any hazardous waste. Why, they're disposing of industrial waste, that's all they're doing. We signed a lease, didn't we? It has nine years to go, hasn't it? That's their answer, flat out. Take it to court if you don't like it."

"Well, can't you?"

"Have you any idea what that would cost,

with appeals and the countersuits they would undoubtedly trump up? That's to say nothing of the time it would take, with half Kingsley up in arms over it."

Claudia was silent. Even here on the other side of the world, your troubles found you. And her mind made a quick connection: My trouble too. Not that Cliff's isn't also mine, and God knows, mine is his. They, and we, are entwined.

Cliff reached over and touched her hand. "I hope I haven't spoiled the day with this tale of woe," he said ruefully.

"No, I'm fine. It's going to be a good day."

"You looked sad for a moment. Or were you perhaps in one of your philosophic trances?" he teased, wanting, she understood, to restore her early-morning enthusiasm.

"Yes, philosophic," she said, smiling back at him.

"I forgot to mention something nice that Bill told me. Charlotte's taking a week off. She'll be getting home just about when we do."

"Oh, great! I've missed her."

"We all do. Okay, shall we start out? Where's the camera?"

"It's in the room with my sun hat. I'll run

up for them and meet you on the veranda."

On the veranda when Claudia returned, Cliff was talking to the man from the dining room.

"We've got a car coming to take us to our final temple. Can we give you a lift anywhere?" he was asking.

"Thanks, but I'm going to sit here in the shade and go over these papers," the man answered, indicating his briefcase.

"They told me the car's going to be fifteen minutes late," Claudia reported.

"Oh? We might as well sit here in the shade too." Cliff said politely, "Cliff Dawes, and my wife, Claudia."

"Monte Webster. Glad to meet you."

Hands were shaken, and the pleasantries requisite when compatriots meet at a distant place were begun.

"This temple we're seeing is supposed to be especially grand," Cliff said, "noteworthy for — what was it, Claudia?"

The stranger provided the answer. "Some fine carvings. In fact, an entire wall of dancers in bas relief. You shouldn't miss it. Go around to the north side."

Webster was a lean, tanned man, no more than thirty. He had an intelligent face, an easy manner, and nothing that would identify him as a tourist, no painful sunburn, no camera, and no jeans. In his pressed slacks and in spite of his casual shirt, he looked actually a trifle formal.

"Interesting countries here in southern Asia," he said. "This your first trip?"

"Not mine. I went through here twenty-five years ago. Bangkok was thrilling to me then. Now it's an imitation of New York, traffic jams and all. But it's my wife's first time. And I must say Myanmar — Burma — was a thrill for both of us. Twenty-five years ago you couldn't even go in there."

"Right. No traffic jams. Not yet, anyway."

"To me it felt dangerous," Claudia said, "and that was part of the thrill, I guess. Probably silly of me, though."

Webster shook his head. "I wouldn't call it silly. I go there all the time on business, and I can tell you there's a lot happening that isn't very pretty, quite aside from what we all know about the government."

"What's your business?" inquired Cliff.

"Farm implements. Tractors."

Claudia, growing restless, wished that the car would hurry up. They were wasting time, standing here making useless conversation.

But Cliff, sociable Cliff, was very good at making conversation. He said now, "I had an idea how nice it would be to surprise my wife with a fine Burmese ruby while we were there. The only problem was, I couldn't afford one."

"There aren't that many around, anyway. The big business nowadays is drugs. The place is loaded with drugs, producers, smugglers, and foreign kids. It's a pity to see so many American kids hiding out in these countries."

Claudia asked quickly, "Hiding out? How is that possible? You need visas, passports —"

"Anything's possible," Webster said, "especially things you would think are impossible."

"So a boy, a young man, could really spend his life there. . . ."

"That depends. But probably he could, yes, unless somebody's looking very, very hard for him."

"We loved the landscape," Cliff said quickly. "So colorful. Dramatic. A great James Bond setting."

"James Bond? Oh, you're right. Yes, of course —"

"But if you wanted to find someone," Claudia persisted, "how would one go about it? I mean, are there special places where these young people gather, certain towns, you know, where maybe they can find a job or —"

Without touching him she felt Cliff stiffen. A darting reprimand came from his eyes. She did not understand it, but it silenced her.

The car stopped at the veranda, and Cliff said, "We've got to make time. Thanks for the tip about the sculptures. North side, I'll remember."

When they got into the car, Claudia inquired, "Why are you annoyed? Why were you looking at me like that?"

"Didn't you know you were asking stupid questions? 'How long could a young man safely' — for God's sake, Claudia!"

"Well, I stopped, didn't I? Although I do believe it's paranoid to suspect everybody."

At this Cliff laid a not-so-gentle hand on her knee. Angry at being so absurdly chastised, as though she were a child or an idiot, she subsided, and they rode for the rest of the way not speaking.

Out of the car on the temple grounds he began to scold again.

"You really are naive, Claudia. You behaved like a sap, if you want to know. Didn't you see how that man pricked up his ears? Didn't you realize how interested he was? Didn't you sense anything?"

"You freak me out, Cliff. You really do. You are thousands of miles from home, you meet a friendly American man, a tractor salesman, and —"

"To begin with, he's not a tractor salesman. Huh! Water buffalo salesman is more like it. He's either in drugs himself or, ten times more likely, he works for the United States government intercepting drugs."

"I wish we were that lucky, that he did work for the government. If Ted's anywhere around here, he might find him for us. I'd like to ask him right straight out to help us."

"Oh, sure. You dropped your needle in a haystack, and you're going to ask, 'Please, friendly man, find my needle for me? Please?'"

They were standing in a blaze of heat without having taken one look at the facade of the famous temple.

Claudia's jaws were hard set. "Cliff Dawes, you don't want to find my son. No, you don't want him to come back."

"That's a rotten thing to say to me."

"Life's more comfortable without him. That's true, isn't it?"

"Ask yourself whether you're eager to have him come back and go to prison."

Pain, the forerunner of tears, began to press against the back of her eyes.

"When one of those girls he raped is now married to a political lawyer who'd love nothing better than a fat juicy case on behalf of his own wife — can you imagine the trial, the media, the melodrama?"

"I can't say I'm a hundred percent eager, but still . . ." And closing her eyes, clenching her fists, Claudia fought tears yet again. "But I do want, how I do want, to see him once more. I need to ask . . . I need to understand, if it's possible, why — Oh, never mind, you never had a child, so you don't know. Your brother would. He knows, even in spite of all that happened, still he knows I remember when Ted was a baby, how he laughed, a laughing baby boy. . . ."

She stopped to take a long breath. That was how you brought yourself under control. You took deep, long breaths and exhaled.

Cliff put out his hand and took hers, not speaking. They began to walk. A boy came up to them holding a caged bird, a little brown bird, common as a sparrow, in a cage too small to let it even spread its wings.

"Ten cents?"

The appeal, accompanied by ten raised fingers, was probably the only English the boy knew. Countless times before, they had seen this appeal. The dime was handed over and the bird, released, sped off into the trees.

"I can't stand seeing anything in cages," Cliff muttered.

"I know."

He pressed her hand. "We're in all these troubles together. Let's forgive each other for the dumb things we just said."

"Of course, my darling."

There was a fragrance in the air, and a sense of peace. Could it be emanating from the Buddha? That, after all, was the general purpose of his life and teaching. Peace, in a latticed framework of scarlet and gold. They walked toward it. Perhaps it will touch us, she thought. Peace.

FOUR

The week at home had not given Charlotte any relief from her tired, restless mood. To the contrary she was in a hurry to go back to work.

At the table on the last night, while eating the good food that Emmabrown had prepared, she was impatient with herself. What on earth had she expected, some sort of comfortable, warm return to the womb, or at least to childhood? As if, she thought ironically, my childhood had ever been all that warm.

Bill broke a silence that had lasted for at least five minutes. "Do you hear anything special from your — from Elena?"

"Just the usual. She plans to be in New York next fall and expects to see me there. I wish she'd fly to Boston sometimes. It's not easy for me to take as much time off as she wants me to take."

"Still, it's nice for you to be together."

This ordinary, even trite, remark lingered in the air, heavy with sad connotations, like a final note in a minor key.

"I had a birthday card from her with a nice message. She was always punctilious about birthdays and Christmas."

Bill's vocabulary had never been imaginative. *Nice* was usually his most descriptive adjective. Charlotte wondered about the "nice message" and wondered what it could possibly mean to him, if anything. She wondered about things she would never know.

So much had changed in this place that had been her home!

"It hurts me to see what's happened to the Dawses," Emmabrown had told her. "Years ago if anybody had predicted things like this, I couldn't have believed it. Your father's so depressed, so run down, I don't know what to make of him. Even this house going to rack and ruin."

The house was hardly "going to rack and ruin," but it was unmistakably shabby. The dining-room curtains were brittle and yellow. Paint on the ceiling was peeling. Elena would be appalled if she could see it now.

And Emmabrown had continued, "No, no. He's not himself. I only come once a week to clean the house and cook enough for a few meals. I guess he does for himself the rest of the time, eats out and goes to his brother's. I could come more often, but he says he can't afford it, not that I mind. I can always get jobs if I want them. But it hurts me, Charlotte. He's not himself, your father isn't."

If to "be himself" meant to be without burdens, or at the very least to carry them totally concealed, then it had been a long time since Bill had "been himself." Still, there had been nothing she could do about it, and there was nothing now.

Her impulse was to touch his hand, to show him that she was aware and cared so much. But she knew that neither male pride nor parental pride would accept that from her. He would hate it.

Briskly, as if with a sharp instrument, Bill's voice cut through the thick atmosphere.

"Tell me about your job, about your life. I never hear enough."

"It's wonderful," she said, responding in kind. "I love the work and I'm lucky to be working. Jobs are scarce, what with the end of the eighties real-estate boom."

"So I read. There've been articles about big firms laying off half their staffs, and articles about architects leaving for jobs in the Far East. That's where things really are booming, as I should know."

There could be no denial of that, so she said only, "I'm glad I'm in a small firm. We do things that don't involve big millions, so somehow we keep busy. We do a lot of historical preservation on country houses. Of course, Rudy likes to play around with modern design whenever he can find a client who can afford some brand-new dazzle."

Charlotte smiled. There was an artificial quality about this conversation, an avoidance of reality.

"What do you like?"

"Either, or a combination when one can properly be made. I'm eclectic."

"I'm proud of you. I still can see you lugging those big coffee-table books on architecture. You were — how old? Fourteen, maybe?"

As if abruptly aware that "fourteen" was an unfortunate choice of year, he stopped and, quickly recovering, went on, "How about your private life? Still no serious love, or shouldn't I ask?"

"You may ask. The answer is no."

"Just as well. You're young yet. Don't make any sorry mistakes."

Now his voice, which, unlike his vocabulary, was always expressive, told her that his own mistake still pained him. And in Charlotte's mind the contrast between him and Elena, who seldom expressed regret about anything, was a keen one.

Bill poured a second cup of coffee. She saw that he wanted to prolong this last evening. "I miss you," he said abruptly. "We all do. Cliff and Claudia too. They've been having a hard time this past year on account of that fellow. That's why Cliff took her away. Has she told you?"

"No. Our phone conversations are short." And we never mention "that fellow," Charlotte thought, discomfited that he was being mentioned now.

"Well, it's all come back to life after lying dormant for the last few years. All of a sudden two different families, perfectly well-meaning people, one family in Tennessee and another in Connecticut, sent letters claiming that they're sure they've seen him. Then come the newspapers, naturally, one of them with a TV crew, at the front door. It was all a false alarm, as you might expect."

"Why 'as you might expect'? Somebody's going to find him somewhere. I've thought . . . God knows, I've thought . . . of coming face to face with him on a street, and how it would be. . . ."

"The chances of that happening are one in a billion. I wouldn't give it another thought if I were you. Don't make yourself sick over this thing, dear. Poor Claudia was almost turning inside out. Some people in town are saying that the Dawses really know where Ted's hiding and are protecting him.

Can you imagine anything so cruel?"

A dreadful thought shot through Charlotte's mind: could it be possible that Claudia did know? Ted was her child, after all. Then, instantly, she was ashamed of the ugly, disloyal suspicion.

"Well," Bill said, rising from the table, "enough of that. How about an evening walk? We haven't had one since last fall."

They stepped out onto the road, which now, at April's end, was covered by an arch of maples so barely greening that the sun, which still had an hour's worth of light to give, was able to flicker brightly through the arch. To the right lay the way to the lake, a familiar route still quaintly, peacefully countrified, while to the left lay the downhill way from the plateau to the river, the town, and unavoidably, to the mill. Or to what remains of it, thought Charlotte.

She hoped Bill would choose the direction of the lake, but he chose the opposite. So they walked, making inconsequential conversation about the houses they passed, so-and-so's eighty-fifth birthday, or so-and-so's lavish display of crocuses. Bill's mind, as Charlotte did not need to be told, was elsewhere, drawn toward the river's edge, where, finally, they stopped.

There it lay, the proud old mill that she

had used to compare with a huge, menacing prison. But now, in this state of decay, it looked more like a beetle whose innards bulged from its outer shell.

"Crammed," Bill said. "There's hardly room to set foot inside. It's crammed with rubbish. They've even put up more sheds for more stuff! You know, don't you, that the commission, over my signature, has given Premier two warnings this past year, and then got a court order for them to clean up. They've ignored the order, just submitted a worthless clean-up plan that fools nobody. Now the state is suing them, but it'll probably take half a century to get through the courts. And in the meantime Cliff and I have to take the heat. Look there!" he cried impatiently when Charlotte failed to respond. "And the windows are all gone. The pressure's done it."

Charlotte asked gently, "Why do you come here to torture yourself?"

"How can you ask? Here, see these." From his jacket pocket Bill pulled a packet of folded newspaper clippings. "Letters to the editor, even a couple of editorials by my friend Howard Haynes. My friend! Listen. 'In spite of his eloquence at the recent city council meeting, Bill Dawes failed to convince anyone that he and his brother are doing enough to curb their tenant. They are the owners, and it is their responsibility to correct conditions at their property. For too many years now the community has been subjected to an unbearable, windblown stench.' Et cetera, et cetera. Now hear this letter by a science teacher at the high school. 'What was supposed to be a recycling operation has become a dumping ground for hazardous trash. The acres behind the building have become a viscous, noisome swamp. Ducks and wildfowl that used to live there are long gone. Soon there will be no more fish in the river because the waste that's been mixed in with the so-called construction-site waste is bound to leach into the river. Eventually it will enter the neighboring groundwater and the food chain. We are faced with disaster, and nobody is doing anything about it. Mr. Dawes should be ashamed to keep his job on the state environmental commission. He should know enough to resign.' Well, there's more," Bill concluded, tucking the papers back into his pocket, "but I guess that's enough. You get the idea."

The sun was fading away into a pool of foggy pink clouds, against which the ruination below became all the more depressing. And involuntarily, Charlotte turned toward the greening landscape at her back.

"Our good name is mud in Kingsley," Bill said bitterly. "Between this mess and that other business of Claudia's — and Cliff's — we've been marked as liars, or fools, or both."

When she stared down again at the mill, it seemed to her that it had always been the pivot around which her life revolved. She remembered standing here and hearing her father's prediction, remembered it as clearly as if he were giving it right now: *We're going to have trouble here yet.*

"If we had moved the whole thing away to Central America or someplace, we'd be rich and respected now. But we made a fine product in a thriving town, and we wanted to save them both, wanted to save the good jobs. No one gives us credit for that. We tried our damnedest to make a go of it here, but the cheap competition hurt us, and the town died with us. That's the whole story."

The town died with us. The dying was slow; one by one the good shops that had thrived on the grid of old streets that led to the river's edge closed down. In the gray, dilapidated town there was no park, no recreation, no inviting place to sit with friends over a cup of coffee, no entertainment since the theater had been shut, except for the multiplex movie in a row of gimcrack chain stores and strip malls out on the highway. Life had moved out to the cheerless highway.

Of course it was not only the death of the mill that had caused this; it was happening all over America.

And suddenly Charlotte was seized by an idea. Afterward, she could not have told how it came to flash into her head any more, she supposed, than a musician might explain how a melody had been born to him. But as it flashed, she saw what ought to lie below in the broad curve of the river, under the lovely rise of the pine-covered bluff where she was standing now. What should be there was a beautiful public space.

"Yes," she said aloud, "a public space."

"A what?"

"Oh, you know. Something like a square, a place to attract people, with things for them to do. The sort of thing," she said with a vague wave of her arm, "that they've done on the Baltimore waterfront, or at Faneuil Hall in Boston."

"This isn't Baltimore or Boston. There's no comparison."

"But why can't there be, on a smaller scale? A town square like the ones in Europe, a lively marketplace with new businesses and new jobs —"

"I'm afraid that's a pipe dream, daughter." When Bill was jovial or, as now, was trying to humor her, he called her "daughter." "But you mean well." He patted her shoulder. "Thanks for trying. Even if it were possible to carry out your idea, there's that small matter of the tenants. They're a tough crew, Charlotte. We can't possibly outwit them. And if we could — if we even could manage to find lawyers who'd take a chance on suing them — the case would cost God knows what. Then, if we were to win in court and get rid of them, which I don't think we have one chance in ten of doing, how would we manage without their lease money? Who else would want to lease this ruin? And who would buy a property in this town?"

"I just gave you my thoughts, Dad."

Again, Bill gave her his proud-father smile, a mixture this time of amusement and affection.

"Come away," he said. "Let's go home. This place haunts me."

Whether the visit home had done Charlotte any good was a moot question. Maybe everything one does is moot, she reflected. At home, it was true, the virtually rural quiet without responsibilities or schedules had been temporarily soothing, but then the parlous state of affairs there, the sight of Bill so beaten, had caused a deep anxiety. It was with her even while she was at her work, the work she so loved. It was with her now, a vague, dim presence as she sat on the Common having her late sandwich lunch.

Most of the benches were being vacated as, reluctantly on so perfect a June day as this one, people returned to their offices. Charlotte, having almost three quarters of her free hour remaining, sat back and made an effort to absorb, to *feel,* the perfect day. Uninhibited couples lay on the warm grass. Important-looking men in dark suits, carrying their attaché cases, took a hurried short-cut across the Common. Around the old folk who daily came to feed them, pigeons collected, cooing mournfully even as they were being fed. All was color: the comical strut of pigeons on their shocking-pink feet, the extraordinary charm of a tiny boy in red shorts pulling a toy car on a string, the creamy clouds that swam over the city — all moved, all were vibrant with life. It was impossible to close one's eyes on so much life.

So her eyes, moving everywhere, came suddenly to rest upon a row of red brick houses. At this distance they formed a wall. . . . And something clicked into her vision. Of course! A wall! A broad, river wall with a walk on top, and below, paved in red brick, the square that she had almost carelessly suggested to her father and he had called a "pipe dream." She had put it out of her mind because he had called it that. But it need not be! He was wrong! Surely something might be worked out.

The whole picture rose and glowed in the air before her. Excited now, she reached into her tote bag, unfolded a large square of tissue paper in which the repairman had wrapped her old shoes, spread it out, flimsy as it was, upon the bench, and began to sketch.

The four acres where the building now stood would be the center, a huge square with shops, and at the rear an open-air market to be glassed in during the winter. Wings would be attached to the square, two stories of condominiums, housing for the retired or for the young, with a view of the river; an inn might go there, too, for businesspeople coming to the region and for tourists who loved New England. Then a fine restaurant, and a skating rink in winter. . . . Imagination, with all its delicate, small gears, clicked into place. A rapid, fluid sketch took form.

Then she was conscious of someone standing behind her. Startled, she turned and saw a young man, one of those who used the Common as a shortcut, a young man in the typical dark suit with the typical briefcase in hand.

"I was going to go past you," he said, "when I saw the braid. I thought at once it must be you." He smiled, showing fine teeth. "The Lauriers' party. You don't remember me. Why should you?"

Indeed she remembered him, if only because that silly woman had urged her to pursue him.

"I'm Roger Heywood."

"Charlotte Dawes."

"That looks interesting. What is it?"

"A development, a town improvement," she answered, wishing he would go away.

"Then you're an architect?"

"Yes. I work for the Lauriers."

"What's that curve? A river, or a road?"

"A river, with a road beside it."

"The road to go between the river and the project, I assume."

"That's right."

"But then, where you've written 'walks,' do you mean two walks?"

He puzzled her. Why was he so interested? If he was merely flirting, this was an odd way of doing it.

"There will be a second walk on top of a wide, thick wall," she explained.

"Ouch!" he said. "That'll cost a fortune."

"I daresay it will. But like most plans it will probably have to be modified. To my sorrow, naturally," she added.

"Yes, it always costs more than you expect, doesn't it? I'm a builder, you see. Or I should say, I work for a builder, so I know."

Now she was curious. "What sort of things do you build?"

"Commercial buildings. Nothing that would fascinate anybody. I studied city planning, all very idealistic, but I found that the ideals seldom came to fruition." He looked at his watch. "I'm afraid I'm late."

Charlotte, looking at hers, shoved the sketch quickly back into her bag. "I am too. I've got to run."

"Before you run, will you give me your phone number? You can ask the Lauriers about me. They know me, or I should say, they know my family."

That's rather nice of him, she thought as she scribbled the number. Nice. And somehow old fashioned. These days people didn't bother to consider whether you might like to know more about the man than his name. Besides, he had such an appealing smile.

"If you build it, they will come," Charlotte

301

said. "I always forget who said that first, but I do believe it."

Pauline frowned. "I don't know how you can believe it when you look around at all the half-empty buildings, the for-sale and for-rent signs."

"That's because they weren't much good in the first place."

It was late afternoon, and everyone except the two had gone home. Charlotte had stayed to discuss a draft on which Rudy had asked for changes. When that problem had been solved, she had ventured, a little shyly, to show her personal project to Pauline.

"It's only a preliminary sketch," she had explained, that being patently untrue. Far from being a sketch it was already in its second stage, a preliminary drawing, done to scale and fine enough to be framed, the standard drawing for which clients paid handsomely.

Pauline, having scrutinized it for several silent minutes, expressed some astonishment.

"For heaven's sake! What is this meant to be? When did you do this?"

Charlotte smiled. "When? Not on the firm's time."

"I know you didn't," Pauline said impatiently. "I mean that it's beautiful. Really beautiful. The drawing is a gem."

"The drawing workshop was one of my favorite classes. Wait till I do the final watercolor. You'll see."

Pauline, tilting her chair back and propping her feet on the desk, regarded Charlotte with a serious, puzzled expression.

"Tell me what this is all about," she said.

So Charlotte gave a brief account of how the Daweses' business had fallen away and of her own inspiration.

"I suppose you could call it an inspiration," she concluded, "because it really did come to me in one breath. And I have been breathing it in ever since. Every day. Oh," she said earnestly, "I want so much to see it built, Pauline."

During the telling Pauline had put her feet down and had leaned forward over the desk with her chin in her hands, attending, as the story progressed, to every word. At the end she went back to studying the design, turning it this way and that.

"Of course, there's nothing original anymore about the idea of the festival marketplace," she said slowly. "Goodness, when you think of Quincy Market — now, that was original! And those first riverfront developments — I was in Minneapolis when they began theirs along the Mississippi."

Raising the paper, she examined the work from another angle. "Still, this does have a new feel, curiously new. It's a housing development with a difference, a recreation center that doesn't advertise itself. It's a wall without being a wall."

Charlotte interrupted. "No chain stores allowed. People can go out on the highway for those. No, this is to be a village, a place for independence, for individuals who can display their wares and their work, from handwoven cloth to naturally grown vegetables to —"

"Yes, yes, I understand. What you've made here is a complete neighborhood." Pauline mused. "You might live in it without ever needing to leave it for anything, couldn't you? And all of this not in a major city, but in an ordinary town like thousands of others. You must have studied your town very thoughtfully."

"I grew up there. Also," and Charlotte gave a laugh that was both a little proud and a little shy, "also, I had a good course, called 'Economics and Society.' That helped, I'm sure."

Pauline, still engrossed with the design, had further comments. "I suppose what you've done here could be labeled 'neomodern' or 'neoclassical,' but not, thank goodness, 'neomishmash,' like those sixty-story glass towers topped with some reminiscences of Chinese Chippendale." She nodded. "Yes, yes, it's correct and yet relaxed, and seems to fit the landscape like a traditional New England village. I can't wait to show it to Rudy. Congratulations, Charlotte, and my deep respect."

The eager thrill that ran through Charlotte at this serious approval reached her eyes, which glistened, and her mouth, which trembled.

"However, I really do advise you to put it mentally on hold. Put it neatly away until the right time comes."

"The right time is now, Pauline."

Pauline shook her head. "A lovely idea is one thing, but you don't know anything about financing, do you? I hate to throw cold water, but it sounds as if your father is in deep trouble. That's why I'm telling you not to waste too much hope and energy on this project right now."

For a few moments Charlotte did not reply. There was nothing in Pauline's words that she could gainsay. And as a light is blacked out, her high mood died. Gathering her papers, she prepared to go home.

Pauline said kindly, "Don't be too down-cast. Good heavens, look out there at that landmark. Do you know how many years the Heywood people had to wait before they could get it started? The land belonged to an estate, the brothers were warring, and the litigation went through three courts before it could be sold."

Charlotte followed Pauline's waving hand to the spiring steel giant, the looming "landmark" that pointed to the sky above the neighborhood. Then something echoed in her ears.

"Heywood? Is there anyone named Roger in the family?"

"Oh, yes. He was at our party in April. Didn't you see him?"

"I saw him, but I didn't talk to him. Then I saw him again on the Common a few days ago."

"And?"

"Nothing much. He just recognized me and said hello."

"That's all?"

Curiosity almost bubbled out of Pauline's upturned voice. Charlotte had heard it so many times whenever a man was mentioned, a man who might be a match for the widow Rosalyn, or for one of the young typists, or certainly for Charlotte herself, that she actually expected it and would have been surprised if it had not happened.

Amused now, she bantered with Pauline, adding, "He wanted my telephone number."

"I hope you gave it to him."

Charlotte laughed. "It would have been pretty rude to refuse, especially after he gave you as a reference."

"You don't look a bit pleased. I don't understand you. You look bored, as if it was nothing."

Charlotte shrugged lightly. "It's simply that I haven't been very lucky with men, that's all."

"Ridiculous. With the qualities you have, it's ridiculous."

Charlotte knew this refrain word for word. She knew, too, that Pauline, for no reason other than her usual frustrated or misplaced motherliness, would have liked to know more about her, more about the "lost" mother in Italy, for instance, and surely more about Charlotte's own supposed bad luck with men. But having no intention of satisfying anybody's curiosity or maternal instincts, she stood up and moved toward the door.

"Roger Heywood," Pauline began, thus forcing Charlotte to stand and listen, "is a very worthy young man. And not because of these skyscrapers that they build all over the world, in Shanghai and Kuala Lumpur, and

— don't you think he's really good looking, I mean, really?"

Charlotte said, teasing again, "I've never been less than five thousand miles from Kuala Lumpur, so I wouldn't know."

"I'm talking about Roger. You're joking, and I'm serious. You can surely imagine how many women run after him. Didn't you notice at the party?"

"I only noticed the one who was with him."

"Oh, that one! She's some sort of third cousin. She manages now and then to hook him for a dinner or a benefit. They tell me he can't stand her."

"Well," said Charlotte, "I always prefer red-haired men with freckles, anyway."

"Don't be a fool, Charlotte. Go home and hope the phone will ring. And don't be too downhearted about your design," Pauline called after her. "Some client may know of some project in Oklahoma or Idaho — you never know."

Pauline, being Pauline, had meant well, Charlotte knew, as she walked home slowly, heavily, through the fine summer evening, but the likelihood of such a client's appearing was no better than her chance of winning the lottery. Besides, the design had been intended for Kingsley, for Dad, and for nothing else.

No doubt it was foolish to fixate upon a wisp of an idea without any practical way of turning it into fact. No doubt it was. But now that the idea had lodged itself so firmly in her head, how was she to forget it?

FIVE

"At that party I wanted to talk to you," said Roger Heywood over the telephone. "I even looked for you later in the evening, looked all over for a beautiful green dress with a tall girl in it, but you had gone."

"I left early."

"Well, I would have if I could have." He laughed. "There was too much gabble at my table, all about what things cost and who had bought what."

This, she knew, was an oblique way of telling her that he had no ties to the bejeweled person who had been making a fuss over him. It did not really matter to Charlotte whether he had any ties or not. Nevertheless, she was somewhat pleased that he had phoned, since the summer days and nights ahead looked very long.

"I have an idea you must love concerts," he said surprisingly.

"As a matter of fact I do, but what makes you think so?"

"Because music goes with mathematics, and architects have to — oh well, you know what I mean. Let's say you just looked as if you knew something about music. So I thought maybe you'd like to go with me tomorrow night. Will you?"

"I'd love it," she said promptly.

So they came to be sitting together on a blanket in a crowd under a sultry sky and the distant threat of thunder, listening to *Tales from the Vienna Woods.*

This was not the kind of music that leads to deep feelings or thoughts, and Charlotte's mind wandered. It was odd how clearly you remembered the first time you met somebody, and also the final time. Time in between, whether long or short, faded into a motley blur. There was that promising man who had, a few months ago, started out with a first concert and ended by being ordered out of her apartment, an event that still brought to her the hot sting of shame. There was Peter, quite another story. And now this one. She had a feeling that tonight was not going to be the last she would see of him, which, again, pleased her, although it would be no great disappointment if it should turn out otherwise.

"Good summer-night music," Roger observed during the intermission. "Beethoven, for instance, belongs to winter nights, or maybe to a dark afternoon when you're closed in with your thoughts. Not necessarily somber ones," he added. "They can be full of energy, like Beethoven himself."

Charlotte liked that.

They went out afterward for a hamburger. Walking beside him, she became aware of his height. She had wrongly remembered him as a small man, perhaps because he was narrow, but now she saw that although he was certainly no rugged outdoor man like Big Bill, her father — was it not generally agreed that women unconsciously admire young men who resemble their fathers? — he was sturdy. His body moved firmly, with agility.

Once confined to the space of a booth, with music no longer the obvious easy subject, there came a sense of constraint. They began conversation with the usual background remarks, as if to identify themselves. She learned that he had grown up in Boston until his high school years, which he had spent in Chicago after his father's job transfer. He had returned to Boston because he loved the city and because his uncle, who had no children, had offered him a position in his business. He had graduated with a degree in engineering. He learned that she had grown up in a New England town, that her parents were divorced and her mother lived in Italy. Yes, she had wanted ever since junior high to be an architect. Yes, she liked Boston very much and had been exploring it from one end to the other.

After all this the dialogue began to lose momentum, much as those ancient phonograph records in the family attic began to die down halfway to the end. They both felt this, and struggling to reenergize it only made things worse.

Then, when two men stopped to hail Roger, there came rescue. Introductions were made. The two were invited to sit down, but they were in a hurry, on their way out. One hesitated for a moment, asking Roger whether he "had heard anything from Larry?"

"A postcard," Roger replied. "He's on vacation in Maine with his family, improving his golf score."

"What you did for that guy! If it hadn't been for you —"

"Oh, well," said Roger with a wave of dismissal.

"Oh, well, nothing," said the other, turning toward Charlotte. "I don't know how long you've known this man here, but you probably haven't heard this because he never talks about it."

"Cut it out," said Roger.

"I absolutely won't. Listen, Miss —"

"Charlotte," said Charlotte, who was becoming interested.

"Here's the story. We were undergraduates, a bunch of friends in senior year, the three of us here and two or three more — one of them was Larry — all hung out together. Larry had the greatest personality, the most wit and life in him. Am I right, Roger?"

"You are," Roger said soberly.

"And you were the silent one who saw everything and kept your mouth shut. Oh, yes, that's a fact. Well, Charlotte, we were out celebrating the end of exam week, all of us except Larry. He said he had a cold and fever. About the middle of the night Roger here just suddenly got up and said he was going back to see how Larry was. He was worried about him."

"I wish you wouldn't," Roger said.

"Okay, I'll make it short. We argued with him, but he went anyway, and — well, Larry had swallowed a bottle of aspirins. No need to draw pictures. If Roger hadn't been worried about him, enough to care — and Roger was the only one of us who ever guessed there was anything wrong."

"Tim, will you quit?"

"All right, I know you hate to talk about it. At least now your young lady will know she's out with quite a guy. So long. See you around."

"He had too many beers," Roger said when the pair had gone.

They had embarrassed him, Charlotte saw. Yet the story was extraordinary, and she could not help but ask a question.

"Excuse me, I don't want to probe, but was it some sort of ESP? Do you believe in that? I don't, and still —"

"No, I don't either. It was only that, although he never confided in me, I sensed through things Larry said and didn't say that he was profoundly troubled. It doesn't matter now what the troubles were, but he had them. The wit, the humor, were a cover-up. They often are. And that's the sad story."

They faced each other across the table. He raised his eyebrows in an unspoken question, which she answered.

"It was a very moving story. And you are an unusual person. That's why I'm staring at you."

"Come on," he said, laughing. "Try some dessert. They have homemade pies."

The episode had changed the atmosphere between them. It had become intimate. They began to talk about everything under the sun. If I had a brother, Charlotte thought suddenly, this is what I would want him to be like.

Roger met her at lunch on the Common the next day. "Whenever I can avoid a business lunch, I do," he explained, "and I have a sandwich in the office. But today I thought I'd join you, unless you're going to work on your sketch again?"

"No, it's finished." Propped up as it was on a table in her apartment, it would have been better laid away where it was not visible. And yet, she kept it there.

"It was nice last night. At least for me it was," he began.

"It was for me too." And she felt comfortable, felt free enough to say honestly, "I'd like to do it again."

"We will. It was a little hard getting started, though, wasn't it? At first I couldn't think of anything to say. And you couldn't either."

For a moment, until Roger spoke again, it seemed as if the previous night's first awkwardness was about to recur. He looked out across the grass in the direction of the Public Garden.

"This is the heart of the city, Charlotte. When I was a kid, I used to play at the frog pond. When I was old enough to have a crush on a girl, we went out in a swan boat

316

along with the tourists. I'll bet that's one thing you haven't done yet in Boston. And seeing the *Constitution*. Am I right?"

"You are."

"I can take you through the Athenaeum. My uncle's a member. You'd like that, wouldn't you?"

"That I'd love," she said, thinking that he was moving too fast. He walked quickly, spoke quickly, and now he was leaping from one plan to the next in too much of a hurry. Soon she would have to fend him off, and that would be nasty again.

But then, remembering last evening's episode in the restaurant as well as other things he had said, things that revealed sensitivity, she decided that he was a man with whom you could have a friendship. Once Elena had scoffed: *One doesn't have friendships with men. It comes down either to sex or nothing.* But Elena was not a modern American woman. . . . And if friendship should turn out not to be what Roger Heywood wanted, no great harm would have been done after all.

That summer he made no move toward Charlotte other than a good-night kiss on the cheek. They were wonderfully compatible; they played tennis as guests at Uncle Heywood's club in the suburbs, they went

317

to the beach, had dinner in famous restaurants, and, at her little flat, dinners that Charlotte cooked, for Claudia had taught her well. By now they talked easily together. Roger told her about his experiences in Shanghai, where the firm was building a skyscraper. He told about his father's experiences with Mafia kickbacks in Chicago. He could talk about a Vermeer exhibit and the Boston Hockey Club equally well.

Through it all their talk was seldom personal. The nearest they came to anything personal was once, when discussing a movie, Charlotte heard herself asking whether he thought it was odd for the character in her twenties to be still a virgin. He had looked at her for a few moments. When he himself was not speaking in his fast, urgent way, he was a thoughtful listener, giving the other person his full attention. His eyes then were tranquil, and his speech slow.

"It's not all that long since, as history goes, a woman was expected to be a virgin." He smiled. "So, no, I wouldn't say it was odd. It is certainly unusual today. But then, the woman must have her reasons."

They never came near the subject again.

They moved casually about the city. Sometimes on a Sunday they went to the market together; this was an errand on which she had formerly gone with Rosalyn, who forgave her for the desertion with a friendly, knowing smile, as if she assumed that Roger was living with Charlotte. Now and then he took her out to a building site; one was a vast new library in a wealthy suburb; it was an oblong concrete box, stark and dull, and when he asked what she thought of it, she told him the truth. He agreed, and they both laughed. They agreed on many things.

She wondered whether he was even a little bit in love with her. Sometimes she thought he was, and more often that he must not be. They saw each other, after all, only once or twice a week, which left plenty of time for other women. Then she wondered why she was not in love with him. She loved being with him and she admired him, but there was nothing of that almost breathless adoration that she had felt for Peter. It was simply not there.

One day Pauline saw them together on the street. "You never even told me he called you. You never said a word," she cried accusingly the next morning.

"It didn't seem worth mentioning," Charlotte replied, which was a foolish fib and not kind to Pauline, who meant so well.

"I can't believe you!" Pauline shook her head in disapproval. "Or can it be so serious that you won't talk about it?"

"We're friends, that's all," Charlotte said emphatically. "Just friends."

"That doesn't make much sense to me."

This was not the first time that Pauline had sounded like Elena. Pauline, the busy architect, to sound like Elena!

"You mean that there's nothing between you, that you never —" Pauline began, and stopped, having no doubt seen Charlotte's expression. And she apologized volubly. "Oh, sorry, sorry! Rudy always tells me I say things I shouldn't. It's just that when I care about a person, I tend to pry before I realize I'm prying."

"It's all right," Charlotte said, meaning it.

"I'll never open my mouth about it again, Charlotte. I'll just say one thing more now: Nothing would make me happier for both of you."

There came a week when she did not hear from Roger, and she was very much troubled that he might be ill or might have been in an accident. But when she called his office, her message was accepted without comment, so neither misfortune could have been the case. She considered telephoning him at home, but decided not to; if she was to be dropped, there was nothing to be done about it. It happened all the time. Anyway, at the very start, had she not foreseen it?

Nevertheless, she was saddened. And the week had been depressing for other reasons. Affairs at home had apparently reached a crisis. Emmabrown had said that things were bad, that her father was terribly worried; he tried to deny it, but Emmabrown was not to be fooled. Bill, when Charlotte called him, said that Emmabrown had always exaggerated, and Charlotte should know that by now.

So she was sitting, disconsolate and unsure of everything at this moment in her life, when the doorbell rang.

"I'm dripping wet," Roger said. "Let me put my raincoat in the kitchen. I had a devil of a time finding a cab."

He had just flown in from Chicago. "I should have called you, but I didn't. A car struck my kid brother, who was riding his bike. I went right out, of course. My parents were half out of their minds, you can imagine. I stayed through the operation and until they brought him home. He's going to be okay. Thank God. How are you?"

She was so glad, so glad to see him! He had brought light into the room. And before she was able to answer, he answered his own question.

"You're not yourself. What is it?"

So she told him about affairs in Kingsley, and about her ambitious plan that was so beautiful — had Pauline and Rudy themselves not said so?

"Is that the sketch you were doing in the park? Let's see it."

He spread it out on a table under the light and turned it from angle to angle as Pauline had done, asked a few questions, and nodded from time to time as Charlotte explained it.

"Over here, I was thinking, there could be a huge community swimming pool, indoors because of our long winters. It could be our gift to the town. Then we could give the ground floor of this building in back of the inn to the little theater group. They meet now in a former bus garage that's absolutely horrible. Naturally, they'd pay rent. With attractions like these there'd be no trouble leasing stores, a fancy baker, a music store — what do you think, Roger?"

"I think you've got a good head for business and for daily life, besides for architecture."

"They go together. They should, or else architecture is meaningless. Oh," she said, "you've no idea how much I want this to succeed!"

Curiously, he asked her why.

"Because I want to do something good for my father and for the town, and — well, honestly, I want to prove myself."

"That's a very honest answer."

"It's such a pretty town, between the river and the hills. My mother hated it." Now, why had she told such an intimate thing? "But the rest of us love it. We've been there for five generations or more, I believe." She broke off. "Am I being a bore with all this stuff? Tell me."

He was gazing at her. Perhaps she really was being a bore. She had no idea what he was thinking.

"Would you like me to go and look at Kingsley with you?" he asked. "As soon as we can get a couple of days off?"

She was astonished. She also had a feeling, against which she fought simply because it was a feeling without any reason behind it, that from Roger would come a solution.

SIX

From the bluff above the river they looked down upon the ruination of the Dawes mill. They had been standing there studying it for a quarter of an hour. And the vague idea that had once flashed through Charlotte's head began to form a shape: Would the Heywood Company perhaps be interested in the project, or was her idea just too ridiculous?

"I wanted you to see this first so you'll know what they're talking about at home, because that's all they talk about these days," she said.

"It's a nice, level piece of land, worth a good deal, I should think, if you can find the right buyer."

"Oho! As if that hasn't been the problem!"

At the moment the scene offered nothing tempting to a buyer. The size of the dump had tripled, so it seemed, since Charlotte had last seen it several months before. It was all discouraging: the debris and decay, with the damp wind presaging an early fall — shades of Elena, who in July had always felt the onrush of winter — blowing through her cotton shirt.

"Let's go," she said. "Dad moved lunch

to Cliff and Claudia's house because Emma-brown, who comes in sometimes to cook for him, is sick today. You'll like their house. It's got that soft, worn feel of old things, furniture and books and wonderful trees around it. And I think you'll like them all too. Cliff's writing a series of textbooks. My dad is a conservationist. And Claudia's interesting. She gardens and cooks and volunteers in the library. Beside all that, she saw me through my awful adolescence."

"I can't imagine your being awful."

"Well, I wasn't easy, and I know it. Oh, and one more thing," Charlotte added, "just so we won't get on the subject of sons or daughters. Claudia has a son. He ran away. Nobody knows where he is or why he ran."

Roger winced. "Ran away! How terrible! How old is he?"

"Not quite thirty." And as she spoke, the face in the nightmare appeared on the windshield as clearly as if it had been drawn there, the narrow-jawed, narrow-eyed, watchful, gleeful, terrifying face. . . .

For years, she had trained herself, steeled herself, not to see that face or to think of anything but normal things when she entered that house. Now, suddenly, as they went up the driveway under the maples and stopped at the familiar green door with the brass pineapple knocker, she was overcome with that first fear as if it were happening all over again.

Claudia had prepared a lavish lunch, actually a midday dinner.

"You people must be starved after driving since six this morning," she had explained.

Claudia's well-intentioned hospitality embarrassed Charlotte. Probably it had been a mistake to have Roger come here. The overstocked table and the heartiness of Claudia's welcome must seem to him that he was being accepted as a lover, suitor, or whatever you wanted to call it.

On the other hand, Bill and Cliff were airing their catalog of worries almost as if they, too, were alone at the table. And that, too, was embarrassing.

Often Bill sighed. She had started to notice that. He was visibly aging. Pity moved in her throat.

Roger, taking quick advantage of a breach in the dialogue, inquired, "Has Charlotte ever shown you a sketch of her plan for your property?"

"No," Bill said, "but she's described it. It's a pretty idea."

"It's much more than that. I'm an engineer in the construction business, and while

I'm neither an architect nor an artist, I've seen enough to be a fairly sound critic, I think. Believe me, Charlotte has something superb in mind. It's very impressive. Distinctive."

"I understand. I'm proud of her, and I wish to God we could go ahead with it. It would be a blood transfusion for the town and for us if we could do it. But we can't."

Roger interposed. "Perhaps if you showed it around, you might get up a syndicate to finance it."

"It's too late for that. Charlotte knows our situation. We owe back taxes, and the only reason Kingsley hasn't foreclosed on us is that they would be left with Premier Recycling — they're the tenants — and that crowd is something to cope with, let me tell you. Kingsley would be in the courts for years. It already has been.

"Justice Niles has ordered Premier three times to clean up, and three times has granted them delays," Bill said.

"Why on earth," demanded Charlotte, "don't they just clean up and avoid all the trouble?"

This time it was Roger who replied. "Because it's cheaper to play along with the delays. They'll go as far as they want to, then quit, declare bankruptcy, and move on to the next venture, leaving you without a lease or a tenant. That's how it works. They've got nothing to lose; the real money is with the parent company."

"If I had money, I'd fight them all tooth and claw," Bill cried, gritting his teeth.

Claudia, who had been silent, remarked quietly, "They also have teeth and claws, strong ones."

"Have you ever looked at those ancestor companies?" Roger asked. "They're mostly mob operations, these carters and waste removers, interlocking pyramids of companies." And when Bill raised his eyebrows, he continued, "My father is in business in Chicago, and once in a great while he's had to come into contact with this sort of thing. A damned nasty contact it is too."

"Yes," Claudia said, "I lived in Chicago once. Not," she added hastily, "that Chicago is any worse than any other place."

"There's a rumor," Cliff said, "that the top man in the group that owns Premier is from Chicago and that he's in town this week, going over the books."

"Because of the court orders?" asked Claudia.

Cliff shrugged. "I have no idea. I only heard it through the grapevine, anyway. It may not even be true."

"If he is here, somebody should go to see him," she said.

"Not without a lawyer and a couple of armed guards," Roger said with a wry laugh. "These people, if that's who they are, are smart and tough. And I mean smart and tough."

There was a long pause. A feeling of weariness was in the air. Charlotte saw that the three who sat opposite Roger and herself were approaching the limit of their endurance. And in a way that she could not explain, she also sensed that they were concealing something, that there was something they were not telling.

Claudia got up to serve the dessert, her famous orange mousse. She had lost too much weight too suddenly; her usually full pink cheeks were sallow. Charlotte was wondering whether it was her heart again, when the doorbell rang.

"Now, who can that be?" Cliff said, going to the door.

Men's voices were heard in the hall. A moment later Cliff came back.

"Now, take it easy," he said, laying his hand on his wife's shoulder. "There are two men here from the FBI."

Bill started up from the table. "What the devil — "

329

"Wait a minute," Cliff ordered. "They showed their badges, they have a search warrant, and there's nothing we can do but behave well. Let them go through the house. We have nothing to hide."

Claudia sat down, clutching her chest. As she implored, her voice quavered, "It's about Ted, isn't it?"

"Of course it is. What else could it be about?"

Oh, God, Charlotte said silently. Of all days . . .

"I will take them through," Cliff said. "They are orderly gentlemen. Sit here and have your coffee."

"Nobody wants coffee or anything else," Bill said. "We will sit on the porch. Go the back way, Claudia. You won't have to see them. If you people want to leave," he told Charlotte and Roger, "go ahead. You're spending the night at my house, anyway, so maybe you'd better go there now."

But Charlotte had to know. Her heart was spinning. She had to stay there, to find out, to know. . . .

"It's about the son," she whispered to Roger, drawing him out onto the lawn. "I didn't tell you. He raped two girls, and that's why he ran away. He was out on bail."

"They really know that he did it?"

When she nodded, he asked how they could be sure.

"They have evidence. The girls," she said, thinking: Oh, God, he's coming back.

"Still," Roger persisted, "the girls may not be telling the truth. They may have wanted it and afterward gotten scared, and saved themselves by putting the blame on him. I don't say it happened like that, but it could have. He was foolish to run away without defending himself."

I am the witness who can prove that he rapes, Charlotte thought. I am the one who can see justice done, if it should ever come to that.

They stepped up to the porch. Charlotte's eyes met Claudia's, and turned away. After all these years of avoidance they were back to Ted. The time had come.

As if strength had even left her voice, Claudia was whispering, "He's coming home. They'll be bringing him home soon. That's what this is."

"That makes no sense," Bill chided, though not unkindly. "If they knew where he was, why would they be searching your house? They're looking for any letters you may have hidden, that's what it is."

"I didn't say they know exactly. But he's somewhere in that area where we were. That man we met in Thailand is the clue. Cliff was sure he was some kind of government agent. He got our name from the hotel registry, Cliff said. We even had a quarrel about it that morning."

Voices came through the open windows on the second floor. They were in the bedrooms now, searching closets and drawers, just as in the movies. Probably even opening pocketbooks. On the porch no one spoke. The utter strangeness of what was happening in the house had silenced them all.

After a while Claudia resumed her half-hysterical whispering. "Casper. You remember Casper, Bill. He's been so nice. Decent. Almost a friend. He's been telling me that the FBI would probably be coming here. Funny, I didn't think he knew what he was talking about. But he said things were heating up. The families of those girls, especially of that one who's married, want action, and they've got influence."

Charlotte, glancing toward her father, knew what he was thinking. Influence, the kind the Daweses used to have. Not that they had ever misused it. No, never.

"Casper told me people are even saying that's why we went on the trip to Southeast Asia, to meet Ted. They're saying our mail should be watched. I daresay it's been under watch for years. Oh, what this does to people! It's so ugly. I've even had suspicious thoughts myself and then been disgusted over having them, for thinking that maybe Casper is a plant with his stories about those girls and how they need to have this over with so that they can get on with their lives. As if I've not felt for those girls! As if —"

"These gentlemen would like to see this box," Cliff said, coming onto the porch.

The pair, in their proper business suits, were neutral, neither old nor young, and bland, neither affable nor hostile. The large wooden box toward which they moved was the only piece of furniture beside chairs and plain tables.

"There's nothing in it but gardening tools," said Claudia, her face so flushed with what must have been a blend of anger and humiliation that Charlotte had to look away.

No one acknowledged the remark. The men put the contents of the box on the floor, where they made a pile of trowels, green string, gardening gloves, and packaged rose food. After looking inside the latter they replaced everything more or less as they had found it.

"Well, that's it. Thank you," said one of the pair, addressing nobody in particular.

Cliff went with them to the front door.

"No doubt they're disappointed," he said bitterly when he returned.

No one answered.

"They were decent," he said. He took a paper napkin, the nearest thing at hand, to wipe his sweating face. "They hardly spoke more than to ask directions to the attic. It was systematic. One did a cabinet, the other a highboy. I just stood in the doorway of each room. They took everything from every drawer and shelf, but they were considerate. They didn't toss things around the way you might imagine they would. There's not much of a mess."

Charlotte understood that he was trying to calm Claudia, who was obviously fighting tears. Why don't you just go ahead and cry? she thought. But Claudia would never do that. And an aberrant image came to her, something almost comical: it was Elena in a situation like this one, screaming her fury and smashing to the floor every object within reach.

"An outrage," Claudia moaned. "An outrage to a family like this one."

"This family is not what it was," Bill reminded her.

He should not have said that. Claudia would take it to mean that it was her son who had changed the family's image. But then, as if he had become aware of the same thing, Bill went on to console her.

"All they did was to find nothing and prove themselves wrong. They wasted two hours of effort. Now they're gone, so don't exhaust your emotions. We have too much else to think about, anyway."

Claudia stood up. "You're right, Bill. If you'll all excuse me, I'd like to go tidy things. I hate the idea of those strangers upsetting everything I own." And she went out.

"It'll be a terrible shock to her if Ted is brought back from wherever he is," Cliff said, shaking his head in dismay.

Bill was looking at Charlotte. Even if he and Charlotte had been alone, there would have been no need for words between them. It was the terrible shock to Charlotte that they foresaw.

"Why don't you two go on over to our house and make yourselves comfortable?" he suggested. "There's plenty in the refrigerator for some supper tonight. You've had a long day."

Charlotte was nervous. Her whole chest quivered. "Would it be awful," she asked Roger, "if we went back to Boston today? If you don't think it's a crazy idea, I'd like to. I'll drive this time so you can rest."

"There's no problem with that," he said,

so promptly that she knew he, too, wanted to leave, "neither with going nor driving."

"You don't mind, Dad? I'll be back again soon, I promise."

"No," Bill said, "go ahead. We've got more business to discuss today, anyway."

Her father understood that quivering in her chest. He always did.

"It was an awful day. I'm sorry," she said when they were in the car.

"Charlotte, I know you're thinking that we've only known each other since June, and here you've had me witness all these private troubles. You're embarrassed, but you shouldn't be. You really shouldn't," he said gently.

"I can't help it. The whole thing was wretched."

"Yes, it was an ordeal. I have to admit I was a little shaken up myself when right in the middle of dessert, your uncle announced the FBI. It was terrible for your aunt. You know, even before it happened and she was being a smiling hostess, I saw the sadness in her eyes. It made me think of my mother and my brother's accident."

Charlotte's hands tightened on the steering wheel. And words totally unexpected came out of her mouth. "That's different.

336

Claudia's son was not lovable. He was careless, conceited, and cruel. A rapist."

"Can you be sure?"

"Yes," Charlotte said, "sure."

She ought not to be talking like this. She was walking close to a ledge above a precipice; a few more words, and she might topple over.

"Then it is a real tragedy. I liked Claudia — liked them all. Anyone would look at her and never guess her story."

"That's true."

"You never know what people have hidden inside, do you? The most average-seeming people on the street can tell you some amazing things about themselves if they want to."

God knows that was true! And again there came an ugly, traitorous surmise: If the authorities were going to so much trouble to find Ted, must there not be a very strong reason, and was it possible that Claudia was helping him to hide out there beyond the Pacific?

Please God, she thought then, let her help him to stay there. Don't bring him home. Don't make me live it all over again.

They were crossing the bridge above the river's curve. Downstream lay the mill, at this distance mercifully indistinct.

"Last look," she said.

"Try not to be too dejected, Charlotte. I know you had your heart set on this, but you'll have plenty more opportunities in your life. You'll just have to face the truth. I hate foolish optimism. Your father's right. From all they were saying at lunch today, there are just too many obstacles."

Suddenly she saw herself as a little girl dressed to Elena's fastidious taste, being taken to visit Daddy at the office. A flag flew on the pole in the center of the lawn. Along the walkway toward the long white building, there were flowers; you could see that this was an important place. In Daddy's room he sat at an enormous desk, and you could see that he was an important man.

"It's not just me," she said now, "it's my father. He's so changed. He's defeated, and trying hard not to show it. The last ten years or more have been nothing but a downhill slide."

"I'm sorry," Roger said.

"Well, I'm sorry you've come all this way on a wild-goose chase."

"Charlotte, I wanted to come. It was my idea, not yours. And I'm glad I came."

She looked at him. "You really are a friend," she said gratefully.

"I want you to think so. Now, do you

know what you're going to do? You're going to pull over and let me take the wheel. You're exhausted."

"I'm not," she protested, but the protest itself sounded weak, and after a little more urging from Roger they changed places.

The car hummed down the highway. She laid her head back on the seat. After a while, as air rushing through the half-opened window cooled her face and whirred in her ears, she began to feel drowsy.

"Close your eyes," Roger said. "Don't fight it."

When a few minutes had gone by, she sensed that he was looking at her, and opened her eyes.

"That braid's in your way," he said. "Don't you undo it at night?"

"Of course."

"Then undo it now and be comfortable."

"Good idea. I will." For some unknown reason it amused her to play the part of the obedient child before him.

They were in the outskirts of Boston when she awoke. It was already dark. But when they stopped at a lighted intersection, Roger's face was clearly visible. Lean, perhaps too lean, the nose aquiline and perhaps too prominent, the expression very serious, it had a singular masculine grace.

And for a moment, before she was entirely awake, before anxieties came flooding back, she had a curious revelation, there in the snug shelter of the car, that the world could be, in spite of all, a serene and solid place.

SEVEN

In Kingsley some days later a critical discussion was in its final hour.

"So," Bill said, "our lawyer is as sure as you can ever be that Justice Niles is about to make us, the owners, the chief responsible party. That's where we stand. The town fathers are sick of getting nowhere with the tenant, but if they go directly to us under the federal Clean Water Act, they can obtain an order for us to cease any more waste deposits. And the only way we can force our tenants to cease is to sue them. Simple, isn't it? Makes a lot of sense, doesn't it? Oh, the law!" he cried. "The logic of the law!"

Evening had entered into the somber room where they sat, unheeding the growing darkness. Claudia rose and, turning on the lamps, scattered brilliant circles on the floor. The three were talked out and tired.

"Simple," Cliff repeated. "A fine of twenty-five thousand dollars a day for every day we fail to comply."

"We're dead," Bill said, throwing up his hands. "Dead, that's all."

"Didn't you say that the top man is in town?" Claudia asked timidly.

Cliff answered, "So I heard. But nobody knows for sure. And you couldn't get to him, anyway, if you did know. And if you did get to him, what would you say? Appeal to his sense of honor, for God's sake? So what's the difference?"

And again, silence fell. From outdoors the monotonous stream of summer sounds, the chirp and rattle of crickets and locusts, merged into the silence.

Bill spoke again. "It all ties in with another thing I heard. I'm putting jigsaw pieces together. We'll be pushed into bankruptcy and Premier will buy the property for pennies. They'll clean it up — what's a couple of million to them? — and be more careful about keeping it clean afterward."

"Do you think they'd want it that badly?" asked Cliff.

"Why not? Where, at that rate, could they buy any cheaper?"

Claudia's voice came unexpectedly out of the shadowed corner where she sat. "They'll never buy it. Those people never do. They leave when their lease is up and move on because, as you are seeing, tenants are not ultimately liable for violating environmental laws. Owners are."

Both men looked at her with surprise.

"I've read about it."

Bill got up and went to the window, stood there for a minute, then, walking to a pair of photographs on the library table, stood there looking at them.

"My parents left so much for me to build on," he said without turning his back, so that it seemed as if he were talking to the photographs. "And I have nothing for Charlotte. I'm not talking just about money either."

Cliff, obviously moved, spoke gently. "Charlotte will have a good life, Bill. She has her work, and if I'm not mistaken, she has a very fine young man in love with her too."

Claudia smiled. "You saw that, Cliff?"

"Of course. It was obvious."

"She hasn't said a word to me," Bill said, facing them, "but if that's true, it can only deepen my grief. Now, in her time of joy, that — after everything — she so deserves, all I can give her is my ruination. And on that note I'm going home to bed."

Big Bill, thought Claudia, the strong one. It was like watching a great tree axed and falling.

Claudia stared into the bathroom mirror. She was thinking that she had been prettier when her face was pink and rounder. Then, she had had the wholesome, very feminine appearance of a mature, healthy country-woman, not much concerned with fashion. This morning, quite perversely, she seemed younger than before, almost girlish; her cheeks had grown paler and thinner than she had realized, so that her blue eyes had become darker and larger. There was a certain greater interest and fashionable glamour in her sharpened features.

She had to laugh at herself. Glamorous Claudia! An oxymoron if ever there was one! Especially of late she had these fleeting, odd sensations of precarious balance that caused her to grasp banisters or suddenly sit down for a minute while weeding the flower beds.

Today, however, she was energized. It was while lying awake last night after that miserable session in the library with Cliff and Bill that she had made up her mind. She knew exactly what she was going to do, and now she must dress the part, must look smart and confident. Those people had no respect for weakness.

In early fall black-and-white was the way to go. She had learned such things from Charlotte, who had unmistakably been taught them by her mother — poor Elena, as Claudia always mentally referred to her. The dress was simple. Her hair, still bright and fair, was pulled back to display the handsome gold earrings that Cliff had bought on their trip to Asia — best not think of *that* right now! They, her wristwatch, and the diamond ring that had belonged to Cliff's mother were enough. Less was always more.

As she drove downhill toward the riverfront, her heart began to do startling leaps; pulses seemed to beat in her ears and weaken her wrists. But these things, given the circumstances, were only to be expected.

She parked the car and, moving carefully in her high heels over the potholes in the broken walkway, entered the wide front door above which the letters DAW S ND CO P NY were still barely discernible. In the lobby a young man wearing a business suit was talking to a man in work clothes.

For only an instant Claudia hesitated. Then, addressing the man in the business suit, she took her gamble, or perhaps as she thought about it later, she was obeying a strong hunch.

"I've come to see Joey V.," she said.

Both men looked her up and down. Indeed, she was not the usual visitor to that place. The one in the business suit took his time to reply.

"Who are you and what do you want?"

His hesitation and his surliness told her that Joey V. was in the building.

"Tell him that I'm Claudia Marple, and I need to talk to him. That's all," she said firmly.

"Wait here."

She watched him climb what had once been a graceful flight of steps to the second-floor offices. The ceiling was high; it would be easy to push someone down from the head of the stairs, and he would never survive to tell about it. Such things have happened. . . . She was thinking this when the surly fellow came back and directed her.

"You can go up. It's on the left."

She was almost out of breath when she reached the top. But straightening her posture, she walked in to where, in what must have been either Bill's or Cliff's private office, Joey V. was seated behind a large, finely carved desk, chipped raw in spots and covered with a disorderly pile of papers.

"Well, well," he said, not rising. "Claudia Marple. Long time no see."

"And no doubt you never expected to see me again."

"I wondered where you went."

His twisted, humorless smile hid his teeth; incongruously in that dour face a dimple formed in each cheek.

"Well, I went as far as I could without ending in the Atlantic Ocean. You could have found me easily enough."

"Who needed you? It wasn't worth the effort."

Although she had not been invited to sit down, she sat. After more than twenty-five years since their last brief encounter, it was natural for these two people to appraise each other. What Claudia saw was a man still easily recognizable. He was thicker, and his hairline had receded halfway across his skull; his diamond cuff links indicated that he had risen in life, but his almond-shaped eyes were unforgettable, without luster, alert, and cold.

No, he — or rather, they — had definitely not needed her. After Marple's death — ever since then she had come to think of her husband as "Marple" — when, to her unspeakable horror, she learned for the first time what his business had really been and who his associates really were, the only thing these people had most needed from her was her silence. Oh, wouldn't it have been highly inconvenient for them, to say the least, if she had stood up in the courtroom and testified that she, walking down the back street on her way to Marple's office that late afternoon, had seen who it was who had come running out of the building and fled down the alley!

She believed that she really would have stood up in that courtroom and spoken the truth if there had been no child to care for. She would have taken her very slim chance, yes, she would, not because she was so extraordinarily brave — she was not — or because she was suicidal. She was not that either. She had just been so outraged at having been deceived, as a wife, by Marple, and as a citizen, by men like Joey V., that she would have been prepared to take any risk that would bring them to punishment. But she had been the mother of Ted, her rascally, bright little boy, her Ted. And they, who had been well aware of what she knew — although she had been careful not to reveal to them that knowledge — had also been aware that she would keep silent.

"There was a thing in some rag I read at the barber's about a kid named Marple that they're looking for. I kind of wondered whether he might be yours."

"He is."

"Tough," said Joey V. He nodded, contemplating Claudia with an expression almost sympathetic. "Yeah. Very tough. Just took a powder. Left the country?"

"They think — they're pretty sure   he's

someplace in Southeast Asia."

He took a cigar, bit the end, and frowned. He was interested. "Who's 'they'?" he demanded.

"The FBI."

"FBI, for Chrissake! There are people — say, you want me to see what I can do?"

"How? Have you gotten as big as all that?"

"Yeah, I'm big. I run a lot of things, and the world's a small place. Haven't you heard?" He made a little flourish with his cigar.

She had read, had felt a compulsion to read, and learned a good deal over the years about Marple's "business." You had only to read the newspapers. It was quite clear to her that the rescue of Ted must come from legitimate agencies.

"Thanks," she said. "I'll let things stay as they are. But there is something else you can do for me, if you will."

"Yeah? What?" he said, glancing at a letter in front of him. He had lost interest. "What do you want?"

"It's not exactly for me. It's my husband, Cliff Dawes."

"Dawes? That's you? You married Dawes? You did pretty well for yourself," he said, regaining interest.

"Not at all, if it's money that you mean.

But if you mean the man, yes, I couldn't have done better. I'd go on my knees from here to Timbuktu for him. I love him." And feeling a sharp catch in her throat, or perhaps it was in her chest, she stopped.

"I was talking about when you married him. They're on the skids, now. I know that."

Hesitating until the catch should go, she replied, "Yes, and they don't deserve to be."

" 'Deserve,' " he mocked. "Who deserves? You get what you can grab."

"People don't always grab what's available to them," she said.

His quick eyes shot toward Claudia's. The astonishing computer inside his head had read another sense, a possibility, in her words. It was never too late, after all, to reopen a murder case.

"Hey, Claudia, are you threatening me maybe?"

Meeting his eyes without blinking, she replied with a question. "Do I look that stupid?"

She had a chilling thought: Possibly he thinks that because we so desperately need money, I plan to make some bumbling threat, some inept attempt at blackmail. It is never *too late to reopen a criminal case.* If that is what he is thinking, he will make his prompt response right here, right now. . . .

And so, with an appealing smile, she repeated her question. "Do I look that stupid?"

Joey V. considered. His hard scrutiny went slowly from her patent leather pumps to the top of her head. "Nah," he said. "What you look like is a Sunday school teacher. Yeah, Marple always went for broads like you."

"I still am a Sunday school teacher."

"Marple used to show off about you. You two were a queer pair, a crazy match, only you never knew it."

"Not until I went through his papers after he — died. But that's over with. I don't know anything, and if I ever did, I don't remember it."

"That's good, that's very good."

The room was stuffy, her hands were sweating, and it seemed hard to breathe. So she took a deep breath and raised her voice.

"I never expected to be asking you for anything. Could I have dreamed that we would ever come in contact? But here we are, and I don't need to tell you what's going on in this town because you know it better than I do."

"What do you want? Get to the point. I don't have time for gabble."

"I want you to stop any more dumping on

this property. They're going to charge this family twenty-five thousand dollars a day until it stops."

Joey V. tipped back in his chair, removed the cigar from his mouth, and smiled his sardonic smile.

"Stop the dumping! Ain't you got the nerve!"

"I suppose I have, but I'm fighting. It's called 'fighting for your life.' "

"Is that so? Why don't the Dawes brothers stand on their feet and ask me, instead of sending a woman to do the job?"

"Come on, you know the answer to that. They've been asking, they've been in court, and they have given up. They didn't send me here either. They don't even know I'm here, and I might not even tell them I was here."

Joey V. did not reply. When he stood up and went to the slimy window looking out, she was surprised to see that he was a short man, half a head shorter than she. He was strong, all muscle. It had been foolhardy to come here. Not that he would touch her himself, not personally. Once in the top ranks you didn't dirty your hands.

"You've got nerve!" he said, turning suddenly to her. "What makes you think I should do any favors for you? Why you?

What are you to me?"

"Nothing at all. I simply took my chances. People like you respect a fighter, and I thought — although maybe it was a crazy thought — you might feel like doing some charity. You people do a lot of charity."

"Yeah, we do. We like charity. It's good for the ego." He laughed. "It's respectable."

I am so tired, she thought. It's easier to scrub the kitchen floor or to weed three rows of carrots than to do this. Nevertheless, she pressed on.

"Your lease doesn't have all that long to go. What if you were to cut down a little sooner? You must own dozens of these carting companies all over the country. It would hardly make a dent in your pocketbook, while to us" — she took another long breath — "to us, to my husband and to my son, who will need money for his defense when he comes back, it is . . . it is life."

"And you thought I would care about his life or yours?"

"I didn't think you would care — no, although you did know him when he was a little boy." She stopped, and went on. "And you have sons. . . . I thought you might see, after what happened with Marple, how in my ignorance I was tricked when I married him, and was left with nothing but a hundred dollars and a child. That in all fairness I was owed something."

"By me? Owed something by me?"

"Why not by you, since you right now are the only one in a position to do it?" She paused, and gambled. "You said charity was respectable. So here's an opportunity to be respectable."

"I've gotta laugh. Mrs. Respectable herself comes here telling me — me! You sure have guts."

He went back to the window and stood there drumming on the pane with his fingers. Minutes passed.

I tried, she thought. It was a naive hope. Well, I guess I am naive. That's my type. I even look it, so they tell me. Always trying to find the best in people. Always trusting in a miracle.

And suddenly Joey V. cried out, "Oh, what the hell!" He turned, examined his soiled fingers with disgust, and exclaimed, "Hell, why not? This always was a penny-ante operation, anyway. Came out here to look over these books" — he swept his arm toward the desk — "hardly worth the trouble. You're right, we wouldn't miss it. So what the hell, okay. No more dumping after tomorrow. And after that, wait out the lease. Or break it, whatever you want."

Claudia got up and put her hand out. She must thank him with dignity, not showing the faintest sign of tears, her tears of utmost, merciful, unbelievable relief.

"Oh, I thank you," she said. "I thank you. You see, I was right about you. I knew you would be charitable and fair. And you have been."

Joey V., accepting the compliment with grace, even paid one in return. "You've aged well, not that I ever saw you enough to remember much. But you're okay, a good-looking woman for your age. And you are a fighter. I like a fighter."

So he accompanied Claudia to the office door; she went safely down the stairs and out.

She had odd sensations. First there was the physical release into the cool, pure air. Then came the lessening of tension, bringing the awareness that her shoulders had been rigid and every muscle tight; she had been frightened almost to death. A fighter, she thought ruefully. If he could have X-rayed my insides, he wouldn't have said that.

Then, as she drove slowly home, she began to doubt. The victory was too good to be true. Those people were hardly famous for their compassion! That promise of Joey V.'s might well be a cruel, macabre joke;

after her departure he might have summoned the saturnine young man from the lobby, and the two might even now be laughing their heads off at her expense.

On the other hand — so one often read or saw in a movie — men like Joey V. sometimes had whims, giving a thousand-dollar tip to a headwaiter, or, having read in the newspapers about some stranger's tragedy, starting an educational fund for his children.

But if it should turn out well, what a gift, a gift of gratitude, she would have made to Cliff, and to his brother, too, who had stood by her in her trouble and, in spite of their own burdens, were standing by her still! And, as she imagined their astonishment at the news, which, if it was to come, would surely come within the next few days, a proud, excited little smile appeared on Claudia's lips.

The morning's great undertaking had been accomplished. And now she was left with the remainder of the day, with the afternoon hours to be filled until Cliff should come home. Still too stimulated to answer mail at her desk or to do any household chore, she decided to walk to the lake. The far end was often deserted; nothing except the ripple of water would break the silence or disturb the perfection of dark green leafage against the sky.

She changed her shoes and called Roy. Rob, at fifteen, was too lame to walk the two miles, while Roy was still able. He plodded, but he was eager, and she would walk slowly enough to accommodate him.

On a large rock conveniently shaped like a love seat, she sat down while Roy stretched out beside her on the warm grass. His nose was low between his paws, and his eyes were fixed on the unmoving indigo circle of the lake. A small white butterfly hovered on a weed not more than a foot away from his nose, but he did not stir.

Not worth his while, she supposed, or else it's the walk that's tired him. It was a long two miles, she conceded, aware that it had never seemed quite so long before.

But the day itself had been a hundred times longer than an ordinary day. And still so much lay ahead. There were great hills yet to be climbed. It made her tired just to think of them.

Even with the tenants gone a fearsome problem remained. They would be back to square one, the time when Premier Recycling had been a godsend. There was irony for you! It was a blessing that people couldn't read the future. And she recalled her wedding day, when the future had been so assured, there in that old peaceful house with its lovely gardens, there with her wonderful Cliff, who would be such a good father to her wonderful son. . . .

There were pains in her fingers. And stretching them out before her, she saw no explanation, saw only the rainbow radiance of the diamond. Since they had dropped the insurance on the ring, she almost never wore it; she had indeed asked Cliff to sell it, but he had refused to because, he said, it had belonged to his mother. She suspected that it was also because of pride, a resistance to the admission of final defeat. Her heart ached, thinking of him.

And as so often during their time together, she told herself that she must stop postponing the truth. Tonight she would tell him about Marple. She should have done so at the start. It would have made no difference to Cliff. Always, though, she had wanted to protect Ted, to shield him from that knowledge, to do nothing that might affect his self-esteem if somehow the information should slip out.

Doesn't every one of us have something, she asked herself, something that he hides even from those he loves?

But now, Ted must come back and face

the facts. He was out there, slipping through every net, afraid all this time to write home because he knew the family was being watched. There had been enough cases in the news for him to be aware of that.

Casper reported fresh clues that Interpol had finally sighted him. The hunt had taken on new life. They were close to the quarry. Deadly serious now, they were about to close in. Let them bring him to justice, Casper had told her kindly. It was possible, after all, that the girls were lying.

No, they were not lying. Charlotte could tell them that. . . .

And once again, she mourned. Whatever his fate, I hope he will regret and do better. I hope he will live at last a decent life, harming no one, and will be safe himself. When he comes back, I will tell him all this, and he will listen to me. He knows how I love him, so he will listen. It is never too late.

She felt a great hope, a great love. It seemed to her that the love and hope were all around her, in the sun on her back and in the September hum of insects, and in the flare of fire lilies along the road. Every day the sun rose, every year the wild lilies bloomed again.

Then her heart began throbbing as it had

that morning. "You're too emotional," she said aloud, so that Roy, thinking she was speaking to him, turned his solemn brown eyes toward her. "Too emotional. That's what's the matter with you."

A shadow swept over the lake, and automatically she looked up into the sky; it was bright, without clouds; far and high, too high to distinguish what kind they were, a long stream of birds was moving in a spiral formation toward the south. It made her dizzy to watch them.

And her heart, accelerating, raced through her chest. Her heart flew to her throat and stuck there in a surge of nausea. It grew darker here under the trees. She slid down from the rock onto the grass beside Roy.

I had too much excitement today, and then that long walk in the heat. I should really start home, she thought. But there's no need for alarm. This has happened before. I must just get home and lie down. It will be all right. I'll just lie down here for a little, she thought again, and was thinking it when, in one instant, the world began to swim. All went swimming in a dark red fog. The most extraordinary pain attacked her, and she grasped her chest, tearing frantically at her shirt. Night fell over her. The lake's glitter, the leaves that roofed her blind gaze as she fell backward, all went whirling, whirled into that sudden night, and ended.

EIGHT

On the morning after the funeral the rain came down. Streams of it splashed on the windowpanes. The air was gray with it. And Charlotte, at early breakfast in Claudia's immaculate kitchen — copper pans, eighteenth-century spice cupboard, potted ivy — was thankful that yesterday had been so bright. The crowd at the services had been enormous. Even people who had been denouncing the family in the editorial pages and at public meetings had come. And there were all the special friends of Claudia, those many women who had worked with her at community affairs, and teenagers who knew her from the young people's reading room at the library, and all the neighbors up and down the road, and more.

"She loved this house," Cliff said. "And she was happy here. Yes, in spite of Ted and all the troubles, thank God we knew a lot of happiness together."

Roger, with a quick glance at his wristwatch, made his meaning clear: *It's a long ride back to Boston.* Charlotte replied with an almost imperceptible nod. She was still astonished that he had accompanied her

362

here. They had been at her apartment when Bill had telephoned with the news, and Roger had at once insisted upon going home with her. It was not, after all, as if he were a longtime friend who would rightly feel an obligation.

"She was the best thing that ever happened to me," Cliff was saying.

Almost every word that had been spoken since yesterday had been a reminder for Charlotte. She thought now of the times Claudia had worried that Cliff must secretly regret the marriage that had brought him so much trouble.

Cliff gazed out into the dreary day and, for the third or fourth time, repeated his story; it was as if he had to prove that it was true, not a nightmare.

"I waited and waited. It was almost suppertime. And then Roy came home alone. I thought she would be coming along behind him, although usually it was Roy who fell behind. He's getting old. . . . So I went to meet her. Then I thought, but I didn't want to think, that something might have happened. And when I got there — where she was — there were people already there, cars and people. It's all a mystery," he finished, in a voice so low that it was hardly audible.

"No mystery," Bill said gently. "It was her heart."

"I mean the other stuff. The stuff that came — was it yesterday or the day before? I've lost track of time."

"Ah, yes," murmured Charlotte, as if to herself. It was all so strange. The big brown envelope had been hand delivered. Inside it, torn in half, was the lease for the Dawes property, with a signature scribbled out and a note: *Sorry about Claudia. She had guts. You can put that on her tombstone. She had heart, she was smart, and she had guts.*

"What was it all about?" cried Cliff.

"There's no use speculating," Bill said. "We'll never know. Yesterday, after this came, I went down to talk to 'the boss.' Nobody was there except a couple of young pups who pretended not to know as much as his name." Bill gave a short laugh. "Anyway, he wasn't there. All I learned was that they're closing down."

"Cleaning it before they leave?" asked Charlotte.

"Don't be silly. Of course not."

"I have a feeling that it has something to do with her first husband," Cliff said. "If there were things on her mind, why didn't she tell me? I could have helped her. But then I suppose it's natural for a woman not to talk to her second husband about her first."

"You're only guessing," Bill said.

Charlotte was feeling a great sorrow. Obviously, Claudia had had a secret, something too painful to disclose. And she remembered how often Claudia had warned her not to "let anger eat you up." She must have suffered some terrible injustice, some betrayal, some —

"I don't want to pull you away," Roger said as he rose from the kitchen table. "But this rain doesn't seem to be slowing, and we'd better start."

The two men stood in the doorway to watch the departure. They looked forlorn, as if they had no idea what was coming next, and indeed, they had no idea.

At the river's curve Roger stopped the car. It was Saturday, and there was no sign of life at the mill.

Looking down at a scene of abandonment, Charlotte said only, "It's amazing."

"Surely is."

He got out of the car and stood as if in thought, unmindful of the rain. Then he walked around to the back of the car and observed the far view. She wondered what he might be seeing, and when he returned, she asked him.

"It's a good level piece of property," he told her. "And the river frontage is nice."

"It'll be nice when somebody buys it. If no one does, it will go to foreclosure."

"Whoever builds on it will have to build back from the river," Roger said, as if he had not heard her. "Of course, it would take a pile of money. You'd need a tremendous group to get behind it." Still talking, he released the brake and turned toward the highway. "That cryptic note about Claudia's 'guts,' the whole business, is an enigma, isn't it? A riddle inside a puzzle."

Charlotte did not want to talk about it. And deftly, she changed the subject. Later she could not have said what it was that they talked about all the way to Boston, for her head had been filled with pictures, pictures of lavender chrysanthemums on Claudia's grave, and of the two anxious men in the doorway, waving good-bye.

One day Roger telephoned her at work. He had never done so before, and she was startled by the summons from the drafting room to the telephone.

"I've been thinking," he said, "although I haven't mentioned anything about what your father calls your 'pipe dream.' Frankly, I've had to agree with him. But somehow or other my thinking's changed a bit. Maybe it isn't a pipe dream. Maybe it's worth looking into."

Charlotte was stunned. She herself had given up the idea, or at least, in following Pauline's and Rudy's always judicious advice, had resigned herself to putting it away until some unknown distant time and place. Now she did not welcome the resurrection of hopes that must only end again in disappointment.

"You yourself said that the cost would take one's breath away," she argued. "So there's the chief obstacle right at the start. After that there'd be a hundred fights over zoning and the environment and God knows what else."

"Am I hearing right? Is this really you, disclaiming your own baby? Listen, meet me tonight at the hamburger place down the street from your house. We need to talk about this."

Talk would be futile. What was there left to say? The thing already had been talked to death. Nevertheless, when she arrived at the restaurant, she brought with her a rolled-up copy of her precious drawing.

"You know," Roger began, "as we drove through Kingsley on the way to the cemetery and back, I got a pretty clear bird's-eye view of the place. And it seemed to me that it's ready, ripe and ready for just the sort of thing you originally had in mind. Of course, I personally — if you'll forgive me, because I'm not an architect — would make a couple of changes. I would move the inn away from the activity, putting it back here with access to the main road." His finger moved across the paper. "And here, where you want the open-air market, I would move it —"

"Aren't you getting way ahead of yourself?" Charlotte interrupted. "You haven't even mentioned obstacle number one. Money. Number one."

"Dear architect, I'm way ahead of you. I talked to Uncle Heywood on Monday. Nothing ventured, nothing gained, I thought."

She laughed. "You actually pestered your uncle about Kingsley? A man who builds skyscrapers in Shanghai, for heaven's sake?"

"That's exactly the reason why I could talk to him, because the cost of your project wouldn't make him blink an eye. It's peanuts compared with the sums he sees."

"Are you telling me you asked him to build it?"

"Well, not exactly. I —"

"Why would a firm like his be bothered with peanuts?"

"It wouldn't. I asked him to help me build it. Me. Only me."

Charlotte marveled, "Crazier and crazier, my friend."

"Not crazy. Listen. Uncle Heywood — we call him that because there's another uncle named James, and that gets confusing — had two sons who were killed in a car accident. They were his only children. Now all he has left are me, a nephew, and my sister and brother, who are younger. That's why I work for him and why he helps me. What I'm asking him for now is guidance, advice, and contacts, but not money. Not a cent. I want to arrange my own loans and get everything moving. But naturally, I need to have something to show him before he'll give me any advice." Roger paused.

"Naturally," she said, wondering whether there could possibly be any sense in all these words. He was such a level-headed person! But this sudden enthusiasm made her doubt. It was almost alarming. And yet . . .

"I told him that you worked for the Laurier firm. He knows their reputation, of course."

"And I suppose you led him to think, without actually lying, that I was a full partner?"

Roger grinned. "No, although I didn't say you were just graduated the day before yesterday either. But when he sees you and hears you, he'll be impressed. No doubt of it."

"Sees me? What are you talking about?"

"I'm getting to the point. My idea is, if you're willing, and I think you should be, that you and I take this drawing to him so you can explain it all in your own words."

"You're actually serious about this?"

"No, I only love to hear myself talk. So what about it? They have a summer house on Cape Cod. We could drive up on Saturday and get back here late Sunday."

"I just don't know what to say."

Roger grinned at her again. "That's odd. You generally have plenty to say."

"Okay, I'll say yes."

"Bring a bathing suit, Uncle said."

"He sounds like a nice guy."

"He is. Sharp as steel, but nice. And so is my aunt Flo."

At the office Charlotte asked Pauline what she thought of it all.

"I think the man is in love with you, that's what."

"I don't know. What if he is? What's that got to do with this?"

Pauline sighed. "You are the strangest —

I can't even find a word for you. But you're right. It doesn't have anything to do with this. No man would be stupid enough to suggest a worthless project to James Heywood, no matter whose project it was. So who knows? This may be the miracle you dreamed about. You'll soon see. If nothing comes of it, you will have had a nice weekend, anyway."

The original house, standing among locusts and pitch pines, was a hundred years old, with new wings so perfectly matched to it that only a person familiar with history would know that they had not always been there. A sandbank, plunging to a narrow beach below, lay between it and the bay, which on that late afternoon was smooth as a pond.

The two men had been working for the last hour with pencil and paper at a long table on the terrace, while the two women worked at friendly, polite conversation.

Charlotte strained to hear what the men were saying. Immersed now in the mathematics of finance and banking, they had passed beyond her ken. The business of raising capital was in other hands. But she had presented her part of the case to her own satisfaction. James Heywood had been attentive and even complimentary, which, she saw at once, was not the usual manner of this obviously laconic man.

"Roger tells me you know a good deal about land regeneration," Heywood remarked to her.

"Trying to learn," she said. "It's one of the things they're certainly stressing these days."

He nodded. "Well, you do have a vision here. Frankly, I like it. Your people at Laurier's firm must think they have a find in you," he added with a smile. "However, I don't want to give any false encouragement. This, if it's to come about, will be my nephew's first venture entirely on his own, and before I advise him to take on any risk, I am certainly going to have a team of experts go over every single possibility. I'll send our chief engineer, Cooper, up before the end of the month to look over the property. If he and a few others give the okay, then the rest will be up to Roger. I don't know where the devil you're going to find the money, Roger, but if you can do it, I'll take my hat off to you."

"I believe I can do it," Roger said quietly.

"I understand that the owners — what is your father's name, Charlotte? Dawes? Yes. Well, with these troubles they're having, you

372

could be walking into a minefield, you know."

"I'm aware of that," Roger said.

"Not that I want to discourage you either. I'm just pointing out the facts. You'd need good lawyers right from the start. I suppose you'd be going to our old reliable Buckley?"

"No, Uncle. Since I'm on my own, I want to be on my own all the way. I've a couple of friends who've started their own firm. I have confidence in them."

Charlotte saw a secret satisfaction in the older man's smile. Plainly, he was pleased with Roger's independence. And it seemed to her that this was a fine omen.

"Well, good luck to the venture," Heywood concluded. "Now shall we go in to dinner?"

"There's no reason why you people should hurry back to the city at the crack of dawn tomorrow, is there?" Roger's aunt had inquired. "It's Sunday, and you might as well enjoy the beach. This is probably the last warm weather of the year."

So it was that they found themselves in midafternoon lying on warm sand after the second cold swim of the day.

"I had no idea you would show me up like that, or I wouldn't have raced you. I thought

I was a pretty good swimmer too," said Roger, completely unself-conscious and generous in his praise.

It occurred to Charlotte that not many men would be. But then, she and Roger were always so much at ease with each other.

She was feeling a luxurious physical pleasure, the first in all the weeks since Claudia's death. The awful grief had started to merge into the inevitable acceptance. Time was bound to do it, as everyone knew.

From the terrace above, where a few neighbors had gathered, came the friendly hum of voices. In front of and around them were the ripple of wavelets and the distant steady sound of wind. Low dark hills at either side of the cove lay curved like a whale's back, and under the sun the bay was streaked with silver. It was almost hard to stay awake. In all that peace, speech died away into a drowsy silence.

Suddenly, after what seemed like many hours, a wind rose out of some distant, arctic corner of the sky. And without warning the water began to darken beneath a mass of rushing clouds.

"Look at the water," Charlotte said. "It's the color of purple grapes."

"That's the reflection of the hill. You're shivering. Let me wrap you in a towel. I always bring extras. The weather changes here from one minute to the next. And can you believe it? We've been here almost three hours."

They stood up, and he wrapped her in turkish toweling from neck to feet, raising the towel into a protective collar, adjusting and smoothing, as you dress a child. She was acutely conscious of his touch; it was tender and possessive. And she gazed over his shoulder toward the bay. He loves me, she thought. But then, how can I know that? And I? And I? We have been friends, that's all. It has been three months, it has been only yesterday, and it has been forever. Friends. How can you tell when that ends and something else begins? And do I dare? I have never known myself. . . .

Involuntary, unwelcome tears rose into the corner of each eye. Wiping them quickly with the back of her hand before he should be aware of them, she said, "The wind — it makes my eyes water."

He stood still with a hand on each of her shoulders. "What are you keeping from me?" he asked.

"Nothing. Nothing." And her eyes kept filling, so that two tears stood trembling, overflowed, and rolled down her cheeks.

"But of course you are. And I've been

aware of it from the beginning, Charlotte."

"Aware of what?"

"Only that you have a trouble that keeps you from living fully. Oh, you have your work, and that's a marvelous thing, but there's more to living than that."

"So you have analyzed me," she said harshly, "the way you did when your poor friend tried to kill himself."

"Yes. Don't be angry. It's all right if you don't want to tell me. But you can't expect me to stand here seeing your tears without saying something."

Ashamed then, almost whispering, she answered, "I'm sorry. And I'm not angry at you. How could I be angry at you?"

They looked at each other. It was the first time they had ever looked fully into each other's eyes. What a startling instrument was an eye! The curved lid with its delicate lashes, the lustrous color, and the little round black camera in the center, the X ray, the penetrating beam with which, it seemed to Charlotte, he was reading her mind, seeing thoughts that she perhaps had not even known were there.

Something overwhelming happened. Something willed itself. Perhaps it was akin to that young man's will to take his own life — except that there would be no rescue this time, no doctor to reverse the deed before it should be final.

They had moved toward the water's edge. She looked down at the sand, where a tiny crab struggled toward the water. I shall remember this crab for the rest of my life, she thought, this frail, determined mottled thing now disappearing into a wave. I shall remember the gray, wet sand, the black pebbles, and the wind in my face. . . .

"That boy," she said. "Claudia's son. Do you know?"

"What? That he attacked two girls, do you mean?"

"Three girls," she said.

She must keep her voice flat, without drama, or else the telling would be impossible for her.

"Three?"

"Yes. Now do you understand?"

She felt his hand tighten on hers, so hard that her own nails dug into her palms. There was a long silence.

"How old were you?" he asked, very low.

"Fourteen."

There was another silence before he spoke again. "My God, my kid sister is fourteen."

When he put his arms around her, she clung, murmuring into his shoulder, "I've never talked about it with anybody. I always said I never would. I never thought I would be able to."

He was stroking her hair, holding her so close that she tasted the salt on his damp shoulder. She felt his lips on her forehead; the rest of her face was buried. She was at the living center of a storm. Her words could never be taken back. She could hardly believe what she had done. And now, pounding in her brain, dismay and relief contended.

"Oh, Charlotte, I love you so awfully," she heard him say.

Yes, they loved each other. . . . The thing that had been slowly growing had just been born. In one long look between two pairs of eyes it had blazed into life. But now, with the revelation that she had just made, how differently would he see her? As a woman in some way weakened and in need of care? That she would never be able to bear. False pride, maybe, but there it was.

Presently he spoke. "Let's get out of here. We need to be away from all those eyes up on the terrace. I don't give a damn about anything or anybody but you and me. Let's go back to Boston. I'll make an excuse."

"Talk to me," Roger said when they were in the car.

"Where shall I begin?"

"At the beginning. Or, no, where you want. Just as things come to you."

She smiled wanly. "You sound like an analyst or a detective."

"Pretend that I am one or the other. I want to hear it all."

And so she told him. With eyes half shut as the car sped over the Cape Cod Canal and onto the highway, she talked. In no particular order came shreds and pieces, tumbling as if out of a box that overturns and scatters its contents on the floor. Groping among them, she picked up, one by one, the contents of her life.

"I grew up overhearing, as children do, all the things they're not supposed to know. After it happened to me, I understood that Bill thought it wouldn't have happened if Elena had been different. Maybe that's true. I hated the things she did, and yet I loved her. I was so afraid she would go away and never come back, which is exactly what she did do.

"He was a savage. I still have nightmares. It's incredible that he was thought to be handsome. His eyes sneered. No, eyes can't sneer, can they? But I see them that way. Or sometimes they are just cold and flat, like a lizard's.

"In the hospital I was sure I would die. It wasn't the pain. They took care of that. But I was just so disgusted, so ashamed. I wanted to die. I was also afraid I would die and would be in a box as my grandmother had been.

"When it comes back to me, as it sometimes does, I am still ashamed and disgusted. And so angry that anyone dared to do that to me, as if he owned me, as if I were a *thing*. Not me, but a thing to be used.

"I owe everything to Dad and Claudia. That's why it breaks my heart to see him now, and why I have to help him. I have to. And Claudia. She taught me so much, from cooking to working hard at becoming an architect. We used to talk about bravery and pride, about everything together."

"How strange," Roger said, "that it should be his mother to whom you turned. How strange and wonderful. But is this helping you?" he asked. "I know I wanted you to tell me everything, but not if it's too hard."

"I've begun, and I might as well finish with it. That is, if it's possible ever to be finished with it."

"It's possible, and you will be. But you can't hide anything. Keep nothing back. Free yourself."

And so she talked on. Once having begun, there was no way she could have stopped. Having told some, she told all, even to the fiasco of her affair with Peter.

"Was it my fault?" she cried. "Was it my terrible fault? Is that who I really am?"

"No, and he should have known it was not who you really are. I would have gone after you the very next day when you were most in need."

It seemed to Charlotte that Roger saw her far more clearly than she had been seeing herself.

"You've been depressed all these years. You're very proud on the outside, but inside you feel soiled, as if the thing that was done to you had left a permanent mark."

"Yes, it's in all the articles and all the magazines. I know. The nightmares and bad feelings, they're the same for everyone."

"Eventually they will go too."

"How do you know all these things?"

He laughed. "I'm a very amateur psychologist, and my opinion is probably worthless. But I'll give it to you anyway. I do believe that the cure is love. Loving and being unconditionally loved, without any secrets. Tell me, what were you thinking while we were standing on the beach?"

"Oh, many things."

"I think you were hoping I would put my arms around you."

"But you had never done it, so how could I —"

"I had never done it because you didn't want to be touched. You weren't ready. But today, suddenly you were. Three months! No, three months and a half, it's been."

They stopped before Charlotte's apartment house, went running up the steps, and came together. The room was filled with evening light. On the table were roses, her occasional extravagance; still freshly scented, they were a celebration. This was only their second embrace, and yet to her it felt like coming home.

But then she thought, What if at the very last moment it should go badly? If, after all, I am not what a woman ought to be? How will we survive? And a cold thrill of fear ran through her.

"We'll go inside and lie down," he said.

She followed him into the bedroom. He pulled the shades and darkened the corner where the bed stood. He took her clothes off. All his movements were unhurried, gentle, and yet commanding.

"That other time, when you slept while I drove," he told her, "I kept turning to look at you. I wanted to run my fingers through your hair. Let me undo your braid now."

His fingers moving on the braid, and even his voice, were casual. "How do you ever do this thing up in the morning?" He laughed. "It's too complicated."

"It's a French braid, three strands, and then some extra you pull in at the sides."

"It's warm," he said, smoothing it. "Warm, honey-colored hair."

Then he tilted her head back to examine it as if it were a portrait. "Fine arched eyebrows, heavy eyelids, very fourteenth century. Did you know you have a sensual mouth?"

He was teasing her very lightly because she was afraid of herself. When he switched the lamp off, the room was quite dark. He lay down beside her and took her hand. Neither moved.

"Go to sleep, if you want to," he said after a minute. "We will just go to sleep together, my love."

A radiant peace filled the evening there in the warmth where they lay. And she began to tremble as she had done on the beach when, with caring hands, he had wrapped and shielded her from the wind. . . .

Suddenly, in the very core of Charlotte, things broke apart. Everything that had been wound up tight, all stiff, dry, fearful, and withheld, now burst into a flood of the most marvelous joy. She cried out, calling his name, and he came to her.

NINE

Last night I saw the full moon in the center of the window, wrote Charlotte in her new diary. She had never kept one, but when she saw the glossy green leather book in a shop, it seemed to her that since her life had now entered a new phase, she ought to make a record of it. And so, on the second day of November, she began.

November 2

Suddenly I felt as if I had never seen it before, this astonishing, white, silent globe, suspended in the sky so near to us that surely we must collide with it. But then, everything else is so astonishing to me these days. Everything is new! I never noticed until this morning that Rudy's baritone voice is beautiful, that there is a pumpkin patch in the yard on the corner, or that the people across the hall have one blue-eyed and one brown-eyed twin.

Pauline laughs. She says this is only to be expected, that it simply happens to you when you are in love. Perhaps so, but I rather think that in my case, it is very much because of Roger's example. He sees the world acutely, missing nothing. And he has so much pleasure in the smallest things. He likes shop windows, even a toy-store window with a huge stuffed gorilla in it. He loves food, New England food or Italian or Chinese. He likes comedies in the theater and organ concerts in churches, any church. Above all he likes people. They fascinate him with their differences and what is hidden in them. Didn't I learn that the first time we went out together?

I am very, very happy.

November 12

It is official. The Heywood engineers have approved the site. They were up in Kingsley for almost a week, part of the time with Roger there, too, making surveys and talking to the zoning authorities in town. Dad can hardly believe this is happening. He's been a skeptic for a long time now, and I can't blame him, considering the downhill slide that he's been on. He keeps telling me, though, that Roger is "a fine young man." I know he's fishing about us. But it's all so new that I don't feel quite ready to talk about us yet. Soon I will.

November 23

Roger understands how I worry about Dad. He saw right away how soft "Big Bill" is under his sometimes forbidding silences. He understands everything. We lie in bed and talk. Last night there was the worst terrifying storm, with fiery lightning and thunder that sounded like what I imagine a bombardment to be. It felt so good, so secure, to be there together.

He was still asleep when I woke up this morning. He has such a handsome profile, an aristocrat's profile. He thinks that's funny. His great-grandfather was the most aristocratic hog farmer in the entire United States, he says.

November 29

It has been an exciting, exhausting week. R. has been meeting with bankers and making progress. He is the first to admit that it is the parent company that has opened these doors for him. Still, once the doors are opened for you, you have to produce some goods! I went along on one of these conferences, feeling very tense. Here were these strangers, all of them strict and cautious as if they were actually holding big canvas bags filled with gold pieces and must guard them against people who've come to seize them. But in a sense we did come exactly for that, because without the gold, you're helpless. When we left, I had a sense that we had done very well.

Pauline says that if anybody had told her we could get so far with an idea that just jumped into my head that day last summer, she wouldn't have believed it.

December 6

I saw a painting in a gallery window this afternoon, a watercolor of a woman sitting on a rock with a collie lying on the grass beside her. It almost took my breath away. It was Claudia's death scene! It was also Claudia's life. No one who has known her can ever forget her.

December 25

Christmas at home. Naturally, the snow was already deep here, and now it is snowing again. The house feels cheerful, and Dad and Roger get along so well. Emmabrown came to make a wonderful dinner. Friends dropped in. Amazing how people flock to success, or even to a rumor of it! The project is now being talked about all over town. It's been a lovely day.

December 27

Cliff came over this morning before we left. He has more news about Ted. (I used to be unable to write that name.) The latest is that he's definitely been identified among a group of young Americans in the drug network, I don't know whether as a user or dealer or both. He's been eluding the authorities for almost two years now, which is no wonder, given the size of the drug network. Still, there is no doubt in anybody's mind, and certainly not in mine, that they'll get him and bring him back.

When Cliff said that, I saw his worried glance toward me. I'm sure he was immediately sorry he had said it in front of me. So I told him I was fine and wasn't at all afraid of looking straight into Ted's face if I ever should have to.

Roger said quickly, "You won't have to. I shall see to it."

January 10

R. laughs. "Now I'll tell you something," he said. "The first time you mentioned this scheme you'd hatched, showed me your sketch and told me about the property, remember how I said of course I was interested and wanted to go see it? Well, the truth is I was no more interested in getting mixed up with legal squabbles in some godforsaken town than in becoming an astronaut. But it was a good way to keep you interested in me."

February 5

Progress in the money department! One of R.'s former classmates who has inherited a pile, or maybe a few piles, will take shares in the company, and also may interest some more friends. So it grows.

February 27

I am wearing the ring that R. bought this afternoon. It is a plain gold band with a small round diamond on it all by itself. I will never take it off as long as I live. I called Dad with my news. He sounded sort of teary in his happiness. We are so alike, he and I. Then I called Elena, and she was happy, too, all delight and effervescence, with a hundred questions and demands: I must send a photograph of Roger, when and where is the wedding — we haven't decided anything like that yet — have I got a gorgeous ring, we must come to Italy as soon as possible. . . .

"So, Miss Hard-to-Please! Somebody finally broke you down after all," Pauline said.

I told her it hadn't been that hard to do. I was simply a prudent, old-fashioned woman who took my time.

" 'Old-fashioned woman'!" she said. "She conceives a multimillion-dollar plan, works on it all winter like a team of horses, and calls herself an old-fashioned woman!"

Naturally, I loved hearing that. God, I am so lucky!

March 16

I don't believe it. Rudy wrote an article about the project, sent it, along with drawings, to *Design Engineering* magazine, and it's going to be published. Of course it's great publicity for the firm, I know that, but full credit is given to me, so I'm on cloud nine. R. and Dad were both practically speechless when I told them.

April 4

I have new business. It seems that Dad, who is beautifully reinstated in the Kingsley city hall's good graces, has worked out a deal whereby we give the city a piece of the land for a new library in return for a nice tax abatement. So here I am feverishly studying libraries. They're a whole lot different from what they used to be before computers were invented.

Roger was furious today — not at me, thank goodness. It seems that a supervisor on the current Heywood job, which is a school addition, failed to notify him that a supplier of brass fittings was going to be delivering two weeks late. And did R. dress him down! I was in his apartment and heard the phone call. R.'s face was so red that afterward I told him that his blood pressure must have been 300.

"I cannot stand concealment," he said. "I cannot. The man knew it all along. If he had come right out, said there'd been a mistake and told the truth, I wouldn't have minded. But he covered up, he hid, he concealed, and I find that unforgivable."

He looked quite fierce. I never want to be the object of his anger, justified or not.

May 18

We have to make one change in the master plan. R. says it may drive up the cost a little, but not to worry, it's not going to break the bank. The town doesn't want the library, which naturally has to be on the main road, to have a marsh at its back.

I really don't agree; the marsh is not a manicured park, that's true, but it's natural and has a casual beauty with its tall grasses and clear, open space. Anyway, they want it to be drained, and, as R. says, it's a reasonable request and in our best interest to do it.

We should be able to break ground and start construction of the central square by midsummer. Three cheers.

June 16

We had dinner at the Heywoods'. By now, of course, they know about Roger and me, so this was a quiet, personal celebration for us alone.

Aunt Flo admired my little ring and smiled when R. asked, "Isn't Charlotte beautiful?" They had a decorated cake, toasted us in more champagne, and gave us an engagement present, a pair of antique candlesticks.

We came home feeling contented and very fortunate. The full moon was hanging in its usual place at the center of my window when we went to bed.

June 17

I'm scribbling this while I swallow some breakfast. We were just getting dressed to go to work, when the phone rang. Dad sounded really agitated. What's this business with the library? He said he won't sign it. What do they mean by draining the marsh? It's a wildlife sanctuary, a wetland, to be protected, not ruined! Are we all out of our minds?

R. says I should take his car and go right up to talk to Dad. He has a million things to do today, and can't leave town, so I'll have to go alone and find out what's in Dad's head.

TEN

Weary now, Bill repeated, "I've told you my reasons. This thing was sprung on us at the last minute, and I don't like it, that's all."

Charlotte rested her eyes on the blue-green hills that had been the background of her deepest thoughts, even when, as a child, she had sat at her bedroom window gazing out at them. From behind the terrace where they were sitting came the roar of the vacuum cleaner, this being Emmabrown's day to clean the house. There were no answers in either of those directions.

At the very moment of arrival she had inquired of Emmabrown whether there was anything wrong with Dad and had learned only that, "Mr. Bill is awfully cranky, not like himself."

"Are you feeling sick, Dad, and keeping it from us?" she asked gently, appealing at the same time with a look toward Cliff, whom, in her frustration, she had summoned to the house.

"No, I'm fine."

"I'd feel better hearing that from a doctor. Cliff, will you take him to one?"

"Anytime. Tomorrow morning," Cliff

said, who as the session entered its third hour was beginning to look uncomfortable.

"Does a man have to be ill to have second thoughts about something?" demanded Bill. Large and towering, he stood up and walked to the edge of the terrace to face them. "I will go over my reasons again, and for the last time. I don't mean to be impatient, but I'm tired and you both must be tired too. So listen. For almost twenty years I've worked on the Environmental Commission. It was and still is the most significant thing I've ever done with my life, except for being your father, Charlotte. I don't need to remind you what hell I've gone through in this town — you have, too, Cliff — on account of that property, of those crooks with their filthy, decaying trash leaching mercury, arsenic, lead, and God knows what more, while I, the owner, go around the state talking out of the other side of my mouth. Now, thank God, and thanks to a miracle that we'll never understand, the crooks have cleared out and we're getting our good reputation back. I'm not going to destroy that reputation again by destroying that wetland. And I can't understand why you can't understand that."

The ball is back in our court again, Charlotte thought. There was a long, tired pause before Cliff answered tentatively, "As a matter of fact, Bill, it could be a healthy thing. That swamp is not so many acres removed from those poisons you just mentioned. Who knows whether —"

Bill interrupted him. "It is not a swamp. It's a marsh, a natural marsh, and you know better than to talk such nonsense."

"Well, suppose you're right about that, Dad," Charlotte began, trying another tack.

"No supposing," Bill said. "I am right."

He spoke gently to her with the reproving little smile of correction that she had always called his "fatherly" smile. It was devastating to be here quarreling with him!

"Okay," she responded. "You're right, it's a lovely, natural wetland. But the town doesn't want it. The library doesn't want it. And the library is the twenty-carat diamond in our crown. What do we do? Throw the diamond away?" Her own smile pleaded.

"Yes," Bill answered quietly.

"But we have a tremendously advantageous tax deal that makes the difference between day and night for the whole undertaking."

"We can lower our expectations. The project doesn't need to be all that big and all that grand."

"I don't understand you, Dad. It's big, but it's not grand. And anyway, that isn't the point. The point is that we've been working for almost a year, all of us, although seventy percent of the work has been Roger's. It's he who went to banks and combed the city for investors, won them with his energy and his enthusiasm." Her voice rose with the anger of frustration; she was on the verge of furious tears. "You'll ruin him! You're humiliating him and making fools of us all."

Bill threw up his hands. "My God! Do you think I want to harm you? Or for that matter, harm anyone? Do I want to harm my brother? I'm not asking much, only that you don't accede to this last condition. Talk of humiliation! This would humiliate me and all I've stood for. Can't you see that, Charlotte? Can't you, Cliff?"

"No," Cliff said, "I can't."

"Talk to the library board," Bill urged. "We'll go together, you and I. We know everyone on the board."

"Will you do it, Cliff," asked Charlotte, "even though I'm sure it will be a useless errand? They've made their wishes perfectly clear."

"They have. We're down at the finish line, final contracts being drawn, people coming up from Boston for the closing, only a month away. Great timing, I must say."

"Well, try it, anyway," Bill said, with a long, tired sigh.

"All right, but it won't work, I tell you."

"I won't sign if it doesn't work, Cliff."

"I think you're crazy," Cliff muttered. "It's one thing to have convictions, and I've always respected yours, but now I think you're a stubborn damn fool and I'm fed up."

"Think it over, Dad," Charlotte urged. "You've always been able to see all around a problem. So do it, and we'll talk again in a few days."

"You're not staying? Going back to Boston now? You just got here."

"Yes, I have things to do."

She could not get out of there fast enough. What an unspeakable, unheard-of mess! A disaster, unless Dad — but Big Bill had never been known for easily changing his mind.

In the following week Charlotte's mood went from exasperation to fear and worry.

"Is it possible that something is happening to my father?" she asked Roger when he returned from a hasty, unsuccessful trip to Kingsley. "I don't understand it. Is he getting sick, or what? He's always been so involved in the world, so reasonable."

"You don't mean Alzheimer's or something, I hope. No, he's as *involved* as anybody can be. He was actually quite reasonable as he sees it. A lot of people might agree with him. Lovers of nature, of wildlife, migrating waterfowl —"

"Don't tell me you agree with him."

"Of course I don't. If this were an estuary under a flight path, or a tidal basin of any size or importance, I would. I'd be among the first to say, 'Hands off.' Your dad's just got his proportions wrong, that's all."

"And so you got nowhere with him."

"Well, not very far."

"That means nowhere. Please don't spare my feelings. Tell me the whole story."

"I've told it to you," Roger said patiently. "There's nothing to add. We went over all the stuff about the toxic muck around the mill, the contaminated water, dioxins, all the reasons for which the town, including him, had been fighting the disposal company. He insists that this area is too far away to be affected, so we argued back and forth and finally I left."

It was embarrassing that her father should appear so stubborn, so stupidly stubborn, before Roger, and she said so.

"Let's not call it stupidity. Let's call it just a blind spot."

She knew that while Roger was giving comfort, he himself could be feeling none. He had to be deeply distressed, or maybe close to frantic. The interest he had aroused and the monies raised among his family's and his own connections — what was he to do about them now? And she felt, although it was not her responsibility, deeply and miserably responsible.

"Well," Roger said, "let's give it a rest for a week or two. How about a picnic basket on the Fourth? We could go hear the Boston Pops, if you want. It'll be our thirteen-month anniversary. Come on, cheer up, we're not beaten yet."

"Charlotte, I wish you didn't look so distressed," Pauline said gently. "It's not your fault."

"It's my father's fault, though, and that concerns me."

She had just gotten off the telephone with Bill. A new idea having occurred to her, she had rushed to convey it as a solution: reforestation, creating a bird and wildlife sanctuary. But he had turned it down as a "disturbance of nature's balance." And she had spoken to him in dreadful anger as she had never done in all her life, or had any reason to do. Now, at the drawing board, unable to concentrate, she sat staring into space.

Pauline put her hand on Charlotte's shoulder and reasoned with her. "Listen to me. I know you plan to be married in late summer. But you're in no shape to organize even the simple little wedding you want. You know what I think you should do right now? Postpone it by a month. Roger's told you that he can't, and it's obvious that he can't, go anywhere now. To marry and stay here, wrangling and wrestling with this project, is no way to start life together. A few weeks will make all the difference. I'm sure they'll straighten this out somehow."

"You really do believe it?"

"Yes. With all that money at stake and the Heywood prestige, something's got to give." Pauline attempted a cheerful laugh. "Even Bill Dawes."

Maybe. Maybe so. And Charlotte was exhausted. . . .

"Go to Italy. You can honeymoon someplace else this fall. Go to Italy, see your mother, and — I've got a splendid thought. There's a week's lecture course in Florence on Renaissance building. You'd love it. I've got the announcement in my desk down-stairs."

"Yes," Roger said, "Pauline's right. This has upset you far too much. Just leave it to me and Cliff. We'll work it out."

Sadly, she acknowledged, "Yes, Cliff's al-ways approachable."

Her father was, too, except for those sad, silent spells that she had always attributed to Elena's leaving him.

In any case, now was no time to go delving into what was not fathomable. How can you see inside another human being if he doesn't want to let you see?

"Go, darling," Roger said again. "It'll do you good. In the fall we'll go back to Italy together, or anywhere else you'd like."

ELEVEN

"Once you get on that plane and head out over the Atlantic, your spirits will rise with it. You'll see," Roger had promised.

Charlotte had doubted that a mere change of scene could make much difference. Nevertheless, from the moment the plane had lifted off and she had settled in for the long flight, she had begun to feel a faint enthusiasm. His parting kiss was still fresh on her lips; in her tidy carry-on were two new books, the camera that he had given her for her birthday, and a small box of her favorite chocolates.

By the time she entered Rome, her spirits had definitely lightened. The charm and strangeness of the foreign place produced a sense of adventure, so that slowly she felt a return of confidence and optimism seeping back into her veins. She would find on coming home that order had been restored. Roger would have solved the problem.

Now relaxed, she drove through sun and wind, with the top down, from Rome toward Venice. The back roads wandered through Umbria's vivid summer, past vineyards, hills, and the ancient stones of hilltop villages. All history was here. It was enchanting, and she began to sing.

Then, suddenly, she had to laugh. Her mother had not changed! Had she ever really expected Elena to change? Here I've come all this way, Charlotte thought, and when I telephone her house in Rome to say I've arrived, what do I hear? A servant tells me that she isn't there. Where is she? I'm given a telephone number; I call and I find that she's at a villa near Verona. She will join me in Venice. Why in Venice? That's not important, Elena says. She's taken hotel rooms for us. It's an absolutely magnificent place, right on the Grand Canal, and I will adore it. She can't wait to see me, it's been so long.

Indeed it has, Charlotte agreed. And as suddenly as she had begun to laugh, was sober.

The bed had a brocaded pink silk canopy to match the walls. Two chairs were covered in rose-colored velvet. On a table stood a bouquet of crimson gladioli and a bottle of champagne in a bucket of ice. Now if Roger were here, she thought, we would really enjoy this champagne and this bed, this sumptuous, extraordinary, this positively royal, bed!

Her posture belied this attempt at good

cheer. Actually, she was standing stiffly in the center of the room, both welcoming and dreading the meeting. There was too much emotion in these meetings with Elena, a summoning back of things that her mind had stored away and wanted to forget.

We meet in passing, in temporary places, she reflected, whether here, or in New York, or all the way back to those rooms in Florida so long ago. We meet in expensive places, always with suitcases ready for departure. Even at home during the years in Kingsley, where now, with after-knowledge, she was able to see so much more clearly, Elena had been in some vague way a temporary presence, unsettled, discontented, poised to leave. Always she had been looking for something. . . . For what?

And Charlotte, parted from Roger for no more than three days and already longing for him, felt a rush of thankfulness for steadfast love. In every way he had supported her; he was healing her.

But enough of this. She must unpack, hang up some clothes, and take out Elena's gift. A final watercolor rendering of Dawes Square in a delicately gilded frame — Elena had a penchant for gleaming objects — it was certain to please her.

Presently she looked at her watch. It was

time to go down to the lobby. The concierge smiled. They, like waiters in expensive restaurants, knew whom they were looking at and did not waste their smiles. Shrewd eyed and courteous, they were expert at intimidation, so that the unsure — the girl Charlotte had once been — would think immediately that her clothes were unsuitable or that something else was wrong with her.

Now, in her hard-won strength, she sat down, crossed her legs — good legs in smart shoes — held her polished handbag on her white linen lap, and was sitting so when Elena came rushing through the front entrance.

They embraced, the daughter looming half a head above the mother. Then, following Elena's custom, they separated to observe each other. There were lines around Elena's eyes, the faintest threads. Surely those too-luxuriant eyelashes were false. And Charlotte was shocked by the stab of passing time. People like Elena were not supposed to grow old.

"My God, Charlotte, you're positively fashionable! You look stunning. But where's the famous Roger?"

"Business. He can't get away right now."

"Oh? Everything else all right?"

"Of course. Couldn't be better."

Elena's keen eyes examined her daughter, missing no nuance of expression. Apparently satisfied, she bubbled over, "Look, I'm tearing, you're making me smear my eyes. Oh, this is wonderful! Do you like your room? I suppose you're wondering why I had you stay at a hotel. It's quite a story. I'll tell you when we sit down. Let's go outside. You've never been in Venice. Don't waste a minute. You must start at San Marco. It's a marvelous day, so let's go. We'll sit there and have a drink and talk."

This stream of words flowed until they reached the great square with the church, the cafés, and the pigeons that, Charlotte reflected as she gazed, would be familiar to anyone in the world who had ever received a postcard picture of Venice.

"So," Elena commented, "now tell me about yourself. You never say anything in your letters."

"Nor do you," Charlotte said gently. "Maybe you should begin by telling me what you're doing in Verona."

"Not Verona. I'm in a villa near Verona. Well, I might as well put my cards on the table." Elena sighed. "I left my husband last week. There wasn't enough time to inform you because everything happened so fast."

"But I thought you were so happy with Mario."

"I was and I wasn't. I suppose at bottom it was a question of boredom, getting fed up, I with him and probably he with me, although he never said so. But he never wanted to do anything except practice medicine. I've always told you how he hates to travel, how I could never get him to come with me to America. Goodness, it would have been a miracle to get him to your wedding. Thank heaven, I don't have to worry about that now. It's not that we had a bad life, you know. The apartment was perfect, and — well, you've seen his picture. He's as good looking as your father, but in a different way, much more sophisticated. However, it's all been quite amiable. Possibly — even probably — he was relieved. We should have done it sooner. We had no little children, nothing to keep us, after all, so I just left."

"You just left."

It was astonishing to Charlotte. As you trade in your car or reupholster your furniture, you end it.

Her astonishment must have been very visible, for Elena resumed quickly, "It's a hard subject for you and me, considering our past, isn't it? You could write books about those things. People do write them, don't they? But books never really explain things properly. Sometimes you can hardly explain them to yourself while they're happening."

Elena's delicate wrists, each embellished by two or three gold bangle bracelets, rested on the table. Her face, circled with glossy black curls in her timeless style, was bent as though she were examining the rings on her fingers. Then abruptly, she raised it and looked straight at Charlotte.

"The truth is that I met someone," she said. "His villa is where I'm staying. That's why I thought you might prefer a hotel, you see. Things get complicated. You do see, don't you?" she asked anxiously.

Sad, thought Charlotte. Sad.

"Yes," she said, it being simpler to agree.

"You'll meet him sometime. He's Swiss-Italian. In the winter he goes to his house in Gstaad. He's an investor, some sort of banker — I don't know much about those things. You'd like him. He's cultured and charming, a little younger than I am, but . . ." Elena threw out her hands palms up.

That most probably was the reason why a twenty-five-year-old daughter was to be kept out of sight. With a soft pity Charlotte saw again, in the afternoon light that had no pity, the tiny lines that were around her mother's eyes and the parentheses around her mouth.

Elena caught her glance. "You're looking at my smile lines? I'm having them taken care of next month. I'm going to a first-rate clinic in Switzerland." She gave Charlotte a rueful, apologetic smile. "You don't know yet how terrible it is to see fifty approaching. Five more years, and my cheeks will start that little drooping, those little pockets that squirrels have when they're holding a nut in their mouths."

"You know you're being silly, don't you? At eighty-five, after a few more face-lifts, you'll still be young," Charlotte said, thinking almost tenderly, A careless, foolish child. And nobody, least of all I, can really know what made her that way, any more than you can explain why Claudia should have had the son she had.

"White becomes you," Elena observed. "There's nothing like white linen in the summer. Yes, you do look wonderful. Glowing, the way people do when they're in love. I always say the glow is unmistakable. But you never give me any details. You were a secretive child. You still are. All you write about is your job and that project in Kingsley."

"Well, all right, I'll tell you. I am very much in love. Here's his picture." Charlotte was amused to hear herself saying what people always say: "It's only wallet size and doesn't do him justice."

Elena examined it critically before giving her opinion. "He looks as if he's probably tall. A nice, strong face. Yes, a very nice face. Serious, I think, like you. You were such a serious child. Is he like that too?"

"Yes and no," Charlotte replied, seeing them walking through Boston without umbrellas in an April downpour, soaked and loving the rain, laughing like a pair of teenagers.

Elena's musings interrupted these bright images. "Love. Sometimes, Charlotte, I find myself wondering whether I ever really knew it. Maybe I didn't and only thought I did. Is that possible, do you think? Oh, well! What does your father say about Roger?"

"Dad likes him."

Perhaps, though, he didn't like him as much as he had at the start, not after reaching this impasse. It was a case, the last time the two had talked, of an irresistible force meeting an immovable object.

"Then Roger must be very much okay," Elena said, laughing. "I see Bill as the typical father who never thinks any man is good enough for his daughter." She jumped up and, drawing a bracelet from her arm, said impulsively, "Here, you must have this to remember the day you sat on the Piazza San Marco and told me about Roger. Here, put it on."

"No, no, I don't want to take your bracelet," Charlotte protested.

"The occasion calls for a present. Besides, it's not emeralds, for heaven's sake. Take it. Now let's walk back and dress for dinner. We'll have a gala celebration, and afterward you'll telephone to Roger and tell him about it."

Very much touched, Charlotte put on the bracelet. Life with Elena, she thought. Generous gifts, generous galas, generous, foolish heart.

They sat long and late over dinner, from fish soup to chocolate bombe, to the final cheese and fruit. On the table, candles bent in the wind. Far below the dining room the lights of gondolas and vaporetti splashed wakes onto the flat, black water. Elena chattered like a nervous young girl, rushing from one topic to another, from place to place: the film festival here in Venice, the music festival in Salzburg, and the Highland Games in Scotland. Nevertheless, she was still interesting; between visits, Charlotte thought, you could forget how she sparkled.

Indeed, she was as sparkling as she had ever been. It was almost comical to think of her in Kingsley, hiking out to the lake or discussing the budget at the Board of Education meeting.

"I took a room next to yours," Elena said, "so we can talk. Let's go up now, if you're finished. You must tell me more about Bill. How is he, really?"

"Dad's pretty well," Charlotte began when they were sitting in her room on the rose velvet chairs. "Of course it was a great relief to get rid of those awful tenants without having to fight a court battle that we'd most likely lose."

"I can imagine. Oh, your marvelous project! Kingsley won't recognize itself. I'm so proud of you, I could burst. I'm going to hang this beautiful picture you brought me in my bedroom, right across from the bed, so I can see it when I wake up. When do you expect to be finished? It should take at least a year or two, shouldn't it?"

"I don't know." She heard her own words ring in a minor key. "We haven't even started it yet."

"Haven't started? Why not?"

She was about to give an evasive reply. And yet, why not admit the troubling truth? So she told it, while Elena listened with sharp attention to the detailed, plaintive account.

"So that's where we're stuck, you see," Charlotte concluded in that same minor key. "I can't understand Dad's thinking, especially since he's in such bad shape financially — even worse than Cliff is, who at least earns a little from his book."

"I would gladly help Bill out, although I suppose he wouldn't accept anything from me," Elena said.

Charlotte had to smile at that piece of truth. "No, I'm afraid he wouldn't."

Elena got up and poured two glasses of wine. "Let's not spoil our first evening with troubles. Let's drink to better luck," she said briskly.

"If a drink could bring it, I'd drink a whole bottle," Charlotte replied.

"Yes, you've had a hard year with all this going on. And Claudia's death too. That was sad. She was too young to die."

"It's especially sad that she didn't live to see her son come home again, even though it's the FBI that will be bringing him."

"My God! The FBI?"

"Yes, the native police are well on his track. The FBI were at the house searching through everything, every paper in Cliff's and Claudia's desks. It was awful."

"Yes. Awful. You didn't tell me. . . . But how will it be for you when he comes back?"

"Mama, you know that I've put that past me. I'm over it," Charlotte said steadily.

"Oh, I'm so glad to hear you say that." Elena shook her head, her face gone grim with recollection. "You went through pure hell back then. We all did. It almost killed your father. You didn't know that. How could you have known, at your age? He's such a loving man. I have always admired him, Charlotte."

A loving man. As if I, of all people, didn't know.

"That's why I'm so upset about what's happened," Charlotte lamented. "I was very angry at him the last time we talked. It hurts to think about it."

Remembering that telephone conversation, she felt chilled. And she sat there silent for a minute or two, crumpled in the chair, hugging her knees.

"Cliff has been trying to reason with him, although to no avail," she said at last. "Maybe I'll phone Cliff tonight and ask him to get hold of Dad again. If Cliff were to be furious, really furious, about this craziness of Dad's, I believe he could force him to change his mind."

Elena, who was still standing with glass in

hand, now replaced it on the table. She opened her mouth to speak, was hesitant, and said, "I wouldn't do that. I wouldn't try to force Bill. No. Leave him alone. Don't call Cliff."

Surprised, Charlotte asked, "Why? But why?"

"Oh, I don't know." Elena made a vague gesture. "He's had a bad time, that's all. So many troubles." She straightened a tilted gladiolus in the vase. "I remember how Bill used to fuss over these, taking them out of the ground in the fall, storing them, and replanting them in the spring. So much work, I always thought. But they are lovely, really lovely." And she went on, murmuring, "Such striking colors, so intricately made, folded and folded."

She made a picture, standing over the flowers in her robe, lemon colored and sumptuous as an evening gown. Yet her features had contracted into a troubled frown that had no connection with her words or with the folded petals. The flowers were irrelevant. In an instant Charlotte sensed that they were a diversion, an artificial gesture. And were those tears that had glistened in her eyes before she turned away from the lamplight? If so, they were extraordinary; Elena had never easily shed tears.

"I don't understand," Charlotte said. "Don't I know Dad's had troubles?" She was thinking that she knew it far more intimately than Elena possibly could. "But why must I not call Cliff?"

Elena hesitated. "I meant — I meant only that Cliff — that he's had a bad time too. Why bother him? I'd let the whole matter drop if I were you."

Charlotte pressed for an explanation of these queer, mysterious remarks. "Let what matter drop? You can't mean the whole building project?"

"Why, yes, if you must. Or at least the part of it that's causing the problem."

What on earth could Elena know about it? She had never been interested in business to begin with. And feeling both puzzled and somewhat impatient with such interference, Charlotte replied, "Excuse me, Mama, but you don't know the first thing about it."

"I suppose I don't." Elena sat down, twisting her rings and staring at her fingers for a long minute while Charlotte waited.

In a swift yet subtle way the atmosphere had changed. Elena the self-possessed had entirely lost her self-possession. Several times she seemed to be on the verge of speaking, but unable to speak. She trembled. Her agitated movement trembled in the Venetian mirror on the opposite wall.

Presently she said, "You're a responsible woman. You can be trusted. Can you be trusted, Charlotte? If I were to ask you never, never to repeat a thing, would you never repeat it?"

"Well, I should think you know you can count on that," Charlotte said.

"Yes, you're Bill's child and he's the straightest, most responsible person I ever met. Look at me."

And Charlotte, now reflecting the other's almost hysterical condition, obeyed. The two pairs of eyes, solemn and scared, looked into each other.

"Charlotte . . . I have something to tell you. I'm trusting you. You promised. God forgive me if I'm making a mistake."

"Please!" Charlotte cried out. "What are you saying? Please!"

"Listen to me," Elena whispered. "Listen. That Ted, that monster, is never coming home. They can stop waiting for him."

How on earth did Ted fit into this subject? An aberrant thought struck Charlotte: She is ill. She's having a breakdown. Unconsciously, she put her hand on her mother's, as if to calm her. And humoring Elena, as she had read somewhere that you are supposed to do when a person is distressed, she said quietly, "I'm listening, Mama. What makes you say that?"

"Because he's dead," Elena said, still whispering. "He died a long time ago."

"But they have found him. People have seen him."

"Ridiculous, I tell you."

"How do you know that?"

"Because I was there. God forgive me if I'm making a mistake," she repeated, "but I don't think so. Not with you."

Another chill passed, shuddering through Charlotte's body. And she said, "You're not making a mistake. Tell me the truth."

"I saw it. I was there when it happened. It was an accident. Or maybe it wasn't. I don't know. Sometimes I don't think it was."

"Somebody killed him?"

"Yes."

"Who was it?"

"It was your father."

There was no sound in the room or in the corridor or in the night outside, where a few lights shone upon the Grand Canal. Here, all was safe and sheltered, cushioned in silk velvet. In such a setting this raw, terrible sentence was an act of vandalism and of madness. Charlotte closed her eyes.

"Yes. And I, too, I was part of it."

Is this real? Charlotte thought. I don't know, I don't —

"Are you all right?" Elena asked.

"Go on with the rest. All of it."

"It was the day I left for Italy. Bill insisted on driving me to the airport. We started at dawn, to beat the traffic. It was still quite dark." Now that Elena had begun to speak, her words rushed. "We were passing the mill when we saw him, Ted — I hate to say his name — walking fast with a backpack and a suitcase.

" 'The bastard,' Bill said. 'Where's he going? What's he doing? Is he jumping bail too?'

"He leapt from the car. I heard him call, 'Stop! Where the hell do you think you're going?' Ted kept walking. He began to run, Bill after him. Then I got out of the car. I saw Bill grab him by the shoulders. They were shouting, tussling, furious. I was so scared! Oh, God, I was scared! I didn't know what to do. There wasn't a soul in sight. At that hour the world is dead. Then suddenly Ted — he — broke free and, still holding the suitcase, rushed past the building, through the marsh, into all that mess, with Bill after him. I remember calling to Bill to come back. It's quicksand there in spots. I called and called, but they kept racing. They grappled again and I saw Bill start to fall, so I ran toward them. I don't know what I thought I could do, but I pulled on Ted's coat. Maybe I pushed him too. I'm not sure of anything. Or I guess I am, in a way. Bill fought him. It was so dark. . . . There was a scream." Elena stopped.

Charlotte stared at her. She still had a queer sense of unreality, as if Elena were relating not facts, but some fantastic horror story.

"And then," Elena resumed, "I heard Bill's cry. Stumbling, he turned to me. 'My God,' he said. I remember — how could anyone ever forget? — the words: 'My God, did you see, he's gone down. Drowned in the sump. I almost fell in myself. It's got to be twenty feet deep.'

"I remember us standing there, absolutely terrified, in that lonely, black place. I asked Bill what he was going to do.

" 'Do'? he said. 'There's nothing to do. He's already dead. A fitting death for a bad lot. Let him rot there. Come on. We have to get out of here before we're seen.' "

"I didn't know how we could continue on to the airport, how I myself could possibly get on a plane, or how I could leave him that way. I thought I'd go back home and stay until we had settled ourselves somehow.

But he insisted that I leave. We had, after long reflection, made a decision, he said, and there was no sense postponing it, since we were both agreed that it was the best decision. He promised me he would be all right. He couldn't afford not to be. He had to take care of you.

"We left. In the struggle he had lost his shoes. They'd been sucked into the swamp, along with his money clip. Of course I had to drive until we could get to a shoe store. To this day I don't know how I ever kept the car on the road. I was sure we were being followed and would be caught at the airport. I was half crazy with fear. I bought some sneakers for him and gave him some money so he could get back from Boston. After a while he was able to talk. Actually, he wasn't able to stop talking. For an hour or more he raged. Then he began to admit that a death like that was horrendous for any human being, even for the most evil. He had tried to prevent it, had tried to pull both of them back. No doubt in his fury he had not tried hard enough. But given the circumstances, no one would believe that he had not pushed Ted in. That's true, isn't it? Of course it's true."

And would anyone believe that you hadn't been part of it too? Charlotte thought. Frozen, with her hands clasped on the chair's arms as if for support, she sat.

"So we parted at the airport," Elena said. "And that's the story."

Charlotte's mind was split in two. During Elena's narration she had become part of the scene, of the dark, still morning, and the agony; at the same time she was herself, observing herself as a recipient of these facts and this devastation. What was she to make of them, now that they had been given to her?

Yet experience had forced her to face realities. And so, after a few minutes had passed, she was able to ask a blunt question: "What is to be done?"

Weakly, Elena replied, "Why, nothing. The body, or what's left of it, is still lying there. Poor Bill, it must give him nightmares. I'm pretty much able to put it out of my mind, but he's not like me."

Poor Bill. Poor Dad, who has had this weight on him. All the time, whether he was at the high school play, hiking into the hills with her, or reading her college papers, this weight had been on him.

"And that, of course, is the reason why that particular section of the property must not be disturbed. That's what you meant," Charlotte said.

"Exactly. Now you see, don't you, why you cannot do that?"

Charlotte's hands were wet. I'm sick, she thought. I'm sick.

Trying to reason, to pull facts together, and recalling Elena's phrase *given the circumstances,* she asked, "What circumstances did you mean? Since nobody knows about what happened to me, why would Dad come under suspicion?"

"The money. Ted was jumping bail, which Bill and Cliff had raised."

Charlotte mused. "Then Cliff, too, would be a suspect, or more so, because Claudia was his wife."

"Ah, no. You're forgetting the money clip and the shoes. I'm sure the shoes had his name. I always wrote his name in his shoes when I took them to the shoemaker. And the bill clip was a good one, gold, with initials."

Indeed, every possible article in that house, from towels, sheets, and shirts to silverware, had borne initials or a monogram. Still those articles of Bill's must be past recognition by now, she thought, and said so.

"No, not at all. Look at the things, shoes and suitcases in very fair condition, that they've brought up from the *Titanic*. And it's been lying on the ocean floor since 1912."

That was true.

"So you see what you must do. Or, rather, not do."

"Yes, I see."

"Are you feeling all right? I keep asking because I know I've shocked you awfully, and probably I shouldn't have done it. Are you sure you're all right?"

"I am, I am, and you had to do it."

"For God's sake, you'll never let this go any farther, will you, Charlotte? Of course, you can tell Bill. Yes, you should tell him that you know. But no one else. Not your — not Roger. God, no. Promise me."

"We're going to be married!" Charlotte cried.

"Yes, yes. And what if you should be divorced? All divorces aren't like your father's and mine. They can be horribly revengeful, my dear."

"Roger and I will never be divorced. That's one thing you can be sure of."

Elena's smooth, arched brows rose with her skeptical smile. "Come on, Charlotte. This is 1996, and we don't live in never-never land."

Charlotte made no effort to hide her resentment of that smile. "Not everyone has your attitude. Look at Cliff and Claudia, for example."

And suddenly she thought, What if Claudia had known about this? It was appalling. Claudia had been really fond of Bill. The two of them had surmounted the unmentionable subject of Ted's crime. . . . And she thought of her father, looking down at the wreckage of the mill on the very day she had had her "inspiration."

"This place haunts me," he had said.

Elena persisted. "So you won't be divorced. Okay. Guaranteed. That still has nothing to do with your promise."

Miserably, Charlotte argued, "You don't know the kind of man Roger is."

"He can be a prince, but even so, things have been known to slip out accidentally or innocently. And this is not your dangerous secret, anyway. It's Bill's."

And yours, Charlotte thought. I have heard too much. I don't want to hear any more.

As if she had read Charlotte's mind, Elena continued. "You want me to be still. But I need your promise again. Bill's peace and safety are at stake."

She was protecting Bill, not asking on her own behalf. And Charlotte's heart was moved.

"This is serious business, Charlotte."

"As if I didn't know!"

"Then give me your promise never to tell this to Roger."

Peace and safety . . . "I promise never to tell Roger — or anyone," Charlotte said.

She was overcome with the need for silence. Yet words burst out of her mouth. "I can't bear it anymore. My father —" And then her voice broke. "I can't believe —"

"If there's any thought in your mind that he could willfully have caused that monster's death, put it out of your mind. I could have done it very easily," Elena said, laughing a little, "but Bill never could."

She was right, of course. Having passed through this last terrible half hour, she was already putting it behind her, and was able to laugh.

"Go to sleep. You've heard enough." Silk rustled as Elena rose and placed a kiss on Charlotte's forehead. "Do you want something to help you sleep?"

"No, thanks. I'll sleep."

"Get a good night's rest so we can make an early start in the morning. We'll put this behind us. Venice is a fairyland. I wish we had a month to walk around in it."

She did not sleep. Her mind raged; it

428

raged backward and forward, round and round. And the next two days, while following her mother into museums and churches, over arched bridges, down narrow alleys, her mind, in mourning, was scarcely able to believe itself.

Elena, though, had always been able to dispose of burdens at will. "I told you Venice was a fairyland! An idyll," she exclaimed. Having said everything that needed to be said about the burden, she had no need to say more.

Yet there was so much remaining. . . . It was only beginning. Bill's unimaginable anxiety, the public resentment when the project should be abandoned — and it would have to be — the untangling of investors' accounts, all these went whirling and churning within Charlotte while Elena played guide.

"There's the most enchanting little square I must show you. After lunch we'll go and watch the children coming out of school. We haven't crossed the Rialto Bridge yet either. . . ."

It was as if the conversation on that first night had never happened. And still, along with this apparent unconcerned frivolity, there was that loyal, deep concern for Bill whom Elena did not even love and had, very likely, never loved.

As so often in the past but more acutely now, Charlotte asked herself what had made Elena the person she was. There was no answer. Or if there was one, it was not divulged to her. She had often wondered at and, growing older, had been astonished at, but was now in one shocking instant aghast at, how little she knew about her mother. Who was she? An orphan, abandoned to the vague relatives who had reared her? She had always had more money than anyone could ever really need. So much had been glossed over, and so many questions evaded! After a while one lost interest and ceased to ask.

Poor Mama, Charlotte thought now. You have been afflicted. You must have been.

"The next time you come, you and Roger, I'll have my situation all straightened out. You'll stay with us in Verona." The chatter flowed. "Now, when you get to Florence, don't make it all study. It's a goldsmith's heaven. I'll give you some money to buy something nice for yourself."

"No, thanks, Mama. I don't want anything."

The original plan to rent a car again and visit Palladio's villas on the way to Florence had lost its zest. She would go by train. So, on the morning of the fourth day, she stood at the station with Elena, saying good-bye.

They embraced, made cheerful commitments for future celebrations, and embraced again as if everything were perfect in the most perfect of worlds. Charlotte's last glimpse of her mother as the train rolled away was of a gay, scarlet figure under a flowery, wide straw hat.

In Florence, in another hotel room, she set down her suitcase and took out the folder in which the lectures on Renaissance architecture were listed. But these, too, had lost their zest. So, gathering her few possessions once again, she left the room and, with less than an hour to spare, caught the next flight for home.

TWELVE

A few nights ago, on the edge of the Grand Canal in Venice, the story had begun. Now, a world away on the familiar back porch, it continued as her father's voice merged with the ceaseless music of katydids and crickets.

"My hatred became so hot that I could have killed him. Yes, yes, I could. And maybe I did kill him. I knew how dangerous it was there in the muck, in the dark. And I myself knew where the boundary was and where to stop. So I could have warned him, although he was in such a rage that he might not have listened. But up against his body, a football player's body, young and powerful, all I saw was him with my little girl."

The voice faded. Darkness was thick, and no one had turned on a lamp, so that Charlotte was able to see only the outline of Bill's shape, his forehead leaning on his hand. She wondered whether the conversation was a total agony for him or whether, since this was the first time that he had ever spoken these words, it might not in a way be a catharsis.

On the long drive from the airport she had labored over the best way to broach the subject to him, and at the end, after all her labor, had virtually blurted it out. Through the long evening they had been sitting here in a state of shock, each of them more or less thinking aloud.

"And you," Bill said, "you being wheeled on the gurney into the operating room. I saw that too. I saw your little pigtail. . . . And in a flash they came, those pictures. He was a savage, a brute. Those girls, the one whose nose he broke — he threatened them both if they should ever tell. The fool! How did he think she could hide her nose?"

The old wicker chair creaked when he stood up and switched on a light. He handed Charlotte a magazine.

"Here, look at this tabloid trash. Big article about Ted Marple: ACCUSED RAPIST TRAILED TO SOUTHEAST ASIA. Et cetera, et cetera. Damned idiots! Nothing better to do with their time than to fabricate sensational yarns. Want to read it?"

"No. I can imagine it."

Bill sat down again, choosing this time a rocker that creaked even more loudly as he moved and mourned.

"Claudia used to say to me sometimes, 'I'm so ashamed of what my son did. How can I look you in the face?' Poor woman. She used to tell me how 'large minded,' how forgiving, I was. And all the while I knew what I had done. It was locked up in here." He held his fist to his chest. "A big, hard knot of conscience. Whenever Cliff told me how she longed to see her son again and how she hoped to 'reform' him, and whenever another foolish, mistaken report of sightings was heard, the knot grew bigger."

He knew, too, Charlotte thought, how I dreaded Ted's return, how terrified I was. "Don't worry, you'll never need see him," he used to tell me, wishing only, I'm sure, he could tell me the truth instead.

Abruptly, Bill stood again. Plainly unable to be still, he walked to the edge of the porch and, with his back to Charlotte, spoke into the air.

"I've often thought I should just report the whole thing. And then I never did it. Cowardly, I suppose. And still I hadn't thought of myself as a coward. In the army . . ." The words drifted away.

"You're not a coward, Dad. You're also not a murderer. But they would not have believed you."

"I know that. But what I really feared was the fallout, the damage to Claudia and to your mother. I tried to protect them. . . . I tried to protect you."

"I know."

In the lamplight his smile now turned to her. "You understand that?"

"Elena told me you said you would be all right because you had to take care of me."

"How is she? I should have asked you before."

"Very well, lively as ever." There was no point in reporting Elena's current situation.

"No, liveliness was never her problem."

Her father's expression puzzled her. Was it bitterness or ruefulness that she was seeing and hearing?

"Did you mean that literally? Does Mama have a problem?"

Indeed, Mama had very obvious problems. But those were not the ones Charlotte meant.

"I would think so. Whatever it was, she kept it to herself, as people do. We hardly knew each other when we were married, and when she left us, I still didn't know her."

The sadness, thought Charlotte, Elena's, and Bill's, and mine. It hung heavily upon the air. She felt the chill of it on her skin.

"I hope," she said, "that you aren't angry at her for telling me all this."

"No, in a way it has even clarified things. You can see now, I hope, that I am not simply an unreasonable fool about this property."

"Yes, I see."

"If they dredge, they will find him."

"With your money clip and your shoes."

"There's more. My shirt was almost ripped off when we fought. When I got back from the airport late that afternoon, I had to stop for gas in town. 'You've had a long day,' Eddie said. 'I was opening up this morning when I saw you driving down the mill road, out to the highway. You got up ahead of the chickens.' I said, yes, I'd gone to Boston and back. I remember being worried about my ripped shirt and hoping he hadn't noticed it. But of course, he must have. He's a nosy type, notices everything."

It appeared in Charlotte's mind to be a tenuous case. But she was no lawyer, and it might not be so tenuous after all. A skillful prosecutor, or an unscrupulous one — depending upon your point of view — might use those scraps of information to turn Bill Dawes into a vengeful murderer. And Elena had been with him. That man might have seen her. There could be no predicting the outcome. In any event the connection with the rape cases would fill headlines and talk shows to infinity.

Her gentle father. He, a country dweller

who had never shot and could never shoot a deer. The thought of him exposed to the criminal courts, to that inevitable cruel glare, was unbearable. And sitting there in the suddenly fallen silence she had a quick vision of Bill's years; moving pictures fled past her; she saw his disappointing marriage, his failing business and lost esteem, his devoted fatherhood, and last, the lonely years since her own departure from their home. One would expect him to have found a woman to love; but then, with this threat hanging over him, he must have been hardly in the mood.

His voice cut into the silence. "Cliff and your Roger have been after me to change my mind. Roger even brought a lawyer and one of the investors from Boston. Heavy artillery."

"I know. They think you're being a damn fool."

"I can't blame them."

"Dad, I thought so too. But now I'm sorry I was so nasty on the telephone before I went to Italy."

"You were entitled to be angry. My arguments don't make any sense. They sound fanatical."

He paused. Seeing him there in such distress, it was hard to believe that a man of his strength and bulk could actually seem frail.

"This means so much to you. And Roger. He'll be so terribly disappointed. You've both put your hearts into this."

Hearts, thought Charlotte, my own is thudding in my ears. Regardless of what he says, Dad can't understand what this truly means to Roger and to me. A whole year's work gone down the drain! *Disappointment* was hardly the right word.

It was late. The night air carried a first faint harbinger of summer's nearing end. Bill said, "It's late and you must have jet lag. Let's go in."

"Yes, I want to leave early tomorrow. Good night, Dad. I hope you won't worry too much."

And wasn't that an impossible hope! After the abandonment of the project, the wreck of the mill would still stand with its dreary acres around it, and ruination would return.

In the morning as Charlotte approached the site, she slowed the car for a last look. Surveyors' stakes were planted where Dawes Square was to rise beside the river-walk. They looked jaunty there, like a little troop of marchers on their determined way. And with a sinking spirit she thought of Roger.

But the body that lay beneath the ground behind Dawes Square was the determinant. Nothing mattered but to keep that body's silence. No happy inspiration, no ambition, no money, pride, or satisfaction could possibly be measured against the value of that silence.

"When I got your message, at first I didn't know what to think," Roger said. "Then I thought something must have happened over in Italy, and that's why you came back and went rushing up to Kingsley."

He himself had come rushing in to "their" hamburger place down the street and was out of breath.

"No, Italy was lovely. But I was lonesome, and I wanted to be home with you." All day she had been mulling over what to say and how to begin it. The absolute necessity of lying to Roger was terribly painful; it frightened her, increasing her heartbeat and muddling her speech. "Then there were things — personal affairs of my father's — he had telephoned me — I felt I had to go see him."

"What is it? Is he sick?"

"Well, not exactly, not physically. It's — it's things on his mind."

"I should think so," said Roger with a

grimace. "We were up there while you were away. We laid everything flat out on the table. Old man Jessup, who'd brought in three more investors, a total of over three million dollars, was burnt up. He didn't spare any language, I'll tell you that. Even Cliff didn't know what to make of his brother. All we got out of him was the same totally inane and inaccurate argument about the wetland."

Charlotte took her time eating food that her stomach did not want to accept. Using up more time, she took a long drink of water. A reply of some sort was expected, and trying to think of one, she floundered.

"Yes. Yes, it's very hard."

Curiously, with an edge of impatience, Roger regarded her. "What's hard? If you mean trying to deal with the man, it sure as hell is. What's his trouble? And what has it got to do with the project, anyway?"

"It's hard," she repeated. "Hard to say. It's a very personal matter, and I can't talk about it. I wish I could, but I can't."

Roger nodded. "Confidential."

And Charlotte nodded. "Yes, very. Darling, I'm sorry I can't say any more. I'm so sorry."

"But what can be confidential that's connected with the project?"

440

It occurred to her that she had clumsily confused the issue, and she answered, "I didn't say it was connected."

He considered that for a moment, and said then, "In that case the existence of a private problem need not affect Kingsley Village. I'm sorry that your dad's having troubles, because as you know, I like him. But that's no reason why I can't straighten him out about our project. I'm arranging to bring a group of ecological scientists from the universities, maybe three or four people, to straighten out his thinking so we can stop this foolishness. I'm sure it'll do the trick."

A committee to face her father! Again she saw him as she had never seen him before, propped against the porch railing, bewildered and frail — frail, at six feet four! Alarm made her cry almost piteously, "Oh, don't do that! Please don't, Roger. He mustn't have to handle anything like that right now."

"When, then? We can't wait forever. Everything's ready to go — money, lawyers, corporate papers, filings, zoning, you name it. Do I have to describe it to you, of all people?"

There was such a lump in her throat that she could not possibly pretend to be eating a normal meal or to be under full control of her voice.

"I'm in a very difficult position," she said, "and I hate it. Can't you see how I am?"

"Yes," he replied as he studied her face. "I do see, and it scares me. What is it? Is it about yourself? Is it that you're sick and you don't want to tell me?"

"Darling, no, I'm perfectly well and I would tell you in a second if I were not. This concerns my father and not me."

Reaching across the table, he laid his hand over hers and gently urged, "You saw your mother in Italy and she told you something. Isn't that so?"

My God, he is clairvoyant, Charlotte thought, replying only with a shake of the head and a whispered "No."

"I don't understand why you can't speak freely to me," he urged, still gently.

"I could," she replied with emphasis on the *I,* "but I'm not speaking for myself."

"Don't tell me your father's robbed a bank and he's in hiding," Roger said as if some jocularity would ease her.

But far from easing, it tightened every nerve instead, so that she clapped her hands to her face, crying, "Please, please. Do we have to?"

"Well, I suppose we don't have to do anything," Roger said, turning instantly serious, "since you have no doubt worked out in your

442

mind just how we are going to retreat from what's been started without leaving a bunch of bleeding bodies on the field."

For a moment she saw the boardrooms, the long tables, and the long, dour faces of the moneymen; and she saw whiskered old gentlemen in carved gold frames, walls of tan books, and stacks of smooth white papers to be signed and witnessed in the halls of the law. She knew exactly what Roger meant.

"So you must have it all worked out," he repeated.

His tone had become ever so slightly sharp. He was sparring with her. A mutual frustration was growing. They were, for the first time, on the verge of annoyance with each other.

"No," she said. "I see that it will be very hard, and I wish I could prevent it."

"Your beautiful idea going to smash! How can you accept that so easily?"

"I'm not accepting it so easily, but I am accepting it, since neither I nor anyone else can change my father's mind."

The silence between them was eerie, a silence that comes while people await portentous news. It did not last very long, probably because it was too painful for both of them.

"May we talk about this tomorrow?" she asked.

He stood at once. "Of course. You will have time overnight to relax and give it more thought. Anyway, you must be feeling jet lag. I'll sleep at my place."

A sketch of the most recent ground plan for Kingsley Village was propped against a pile of books next to the telephone. There was no way when using the telephone that Charlotte could avoid being stabbed by the sight of it. Yet she still had not put it away.

She was staring at it while her father's anxious voice rang into her left ear.

"So you got back all right, Charlotte? Did you have a chance to see Roger today? I'm so worried about you. . . . The situation's impossible. How did you explain it?"

The barrage of questions was exhausting. A five-mile jog or a complete housecleaning would be nothing compared with this total drain of energy.

She said calmly, "I saw Roger for only a few minutes. He wants to bring some experts to convince you that you're wrong about the wetlands. I asked him please not to do it because you have these personal problems and shouldn't be troubled right now."

"Problems like what, for heaven's sake?

444

Not terminal cancer, or a clinical depression?"

"No illness at all. Of course not. Just something personal."

"It was a big mistake to bring up any 'personal problem' business, Charlotte."

"I had to explain why I went to see you the minute I got back from Europe, didn't I?"

"You needn't have told him you had been here."

"I don't want to lie to Roger."

"Well, all right, let it go. But why object to his bringing some experts to change my mind? Let them come."

"But I wanted to spare you."

"I understand, and it was thoughtful of you, but I think you must let them come. I can listen and still not change my mind."

"Then you'll look like a fool. You'll look irrational."

"Huh! Cliff already thinks I am. He hardly talks to me, just stares at me and shakes his head. Actually, I know he's furious, but being Cliff, won't show it."

"Roger is furious, too, although he hasn't shown it either."

"Why wouldn't they all be furious?" Bill asked bitterly. "Oh, I'm sick with guilt, Charlotte! Sick with it! Not over that . . .

other business, but about what's happening now, the destruction, the senseless destruction. If only those library people, the town council, all those people hadn't thrown a monkey wrench into everything with their idea!"

"I know."

Charlotte's eyes moved around her small apartment. With plants, books, and pillows, at small expense she had filled it with color and comfort. Now suddenly it had become meager and cold. Beyond the open door the bed, too large for the space, was forlorn. And she thought that it would have helped her so much if Roger had stayed here tonight. They had been apart for ten days.

"I've decided," Bill said. "There's only one decent, logical thing to do, only one way out of the wilderness: Tell the truth."

"What truth?"

"*The* truth. To the appropriate parties."

"You can't mean what I think you mean."

"I can mean it."

"That's masochism, Dad, or martyrdom."

"It's neither. It's practical, a common-sense solution for the benefit of the majority. I can't go on this way, Charlotte, can't sit back and watch things disintegrate. So I want you all to go ahead as planned. I'll say Elena had nothing to do with it, or she wasn't even there. I'll manage something. And I'll take my medicine, whatever it may be."

Whatever? Oh, maybe they wouldn't find the shoes or the initialed money clip. And maybe Eddie at the gas station would not remember seeing Bill at dawn. But they would and he would. . . . And would her father be able to survive?

She thought of the headlines: PROMINENT CITIZEN INDICTED IN DEATH OF YOUTH. And so on, and so on. Toward what? Toward murder, or certainly toward manslaughter at the very least. Then prison and total despair.

She said quickly, "Dad, this is no subject for the telephone. We've said enough for tonight. But promise me you won't do anything until we talk again."

"I'll have to use my own judgment about that, Charlotte."

"Please promise me." And she brought out her most potent weapon, a plea on her own behalf. "You're making me sick, Dad. I don't feel well and I need to sleep tonight."

"All right, I promise. I want you to sleep. I'll hang up."

Trapped between two huge rocks, she trembled. Wherever she turned, she would have to batter her head against the rock that

447

was Roger and the one that was her father. And wishing that Elena had never drawn her into this secret, she at once regretted the selfish wish. At once she felt an overwhelming need to talk to Elena about it. But, no, you never could be sure about crosswires, thousands of conversations, skimming through the air. So instead, in the midnight chill, she wrote out the story of her predicament to be sent by express mail to Italy.

With the disconnected sentences and hasty running script that was so appropriate to her, Elena replied: *Don't let him do it! I am mailing a letter to him today. That monster is not worth his suffering. It would be damnation, and what sense would it make? The whole thing would be too complicated for a stupid jury to know whether he meant to or didn't. And what difference is it now, anyway? As for your man, let me tell you, they're none of them worth a father. You've known him one year, for God's sake! How can you put Bill's fate into his hands?*

On the telephone, but cautiously, Charlotte tried to convince Elena. "You don't understand. You don't know Roger. I can vouch for him, I swear it."

"You already have sworn it, and I've already told you that the secret does not belong to you. Good God, I should never have revealed it. My mistake!"

"If you hadn't, I would still be very angry at Dad, so it's better that you did reveal it."

"You gave me your word, you know."

"I know. And I'll keep it, Mama."

Charlotte sighed. And the great intake and expulsion stirred her with a wretched, deep foreboding.

If Roger was not completely frantic after so many days of frustration, she realized, it was only because he was keeping extraordinary control of himself.

"I've been on the telephone all day," he said. "It's been ringing off the hook. Everybody wants to know what's happening, and I have no answer to give except that we've run up against a barrier in the road, a stop sign. And then they all want to know why I can't remove it."

His pause contained a question. The only answer that came to Charlotte was a weak apology.

"You can't know how I feel because it's I who got you into this."

"You didn't get me into anything, and I won't have you feeling guilty. I did it myself. It was, and still is, a great idea."

They were having a late supper in her

kitchen. They had not been there together for more than a week, since Roger had been keeping late hours, trying to fend off all the various parties concerned with the project.

"Uncle Heywood calls twice a day. Kingsley is on the calendar for early fall groundbreaking, ahead of the snow. We're wrecking his schedule."

While she was listening with total comprehension, she was also wondering whether he would stay all night. It was not desire that she felt. How true it was that anxiety kills desire! First you must have relief from anxiety. First you must have consolation.

"I hate to see what this is doing to you," Roger said.

"Why? Do I look so awful?"

"You look worried and tired, that's all. Go on to bed."

"I wish you would stay. If you want to," she added quickly.

He glanced at her and, replying as quickly, said, "Of course I want to. Charlotte, this is a crazy time, abnormal, critical — it has nothing to do with us, with you and me. But it's bound to affect our moods and our energy." He stood up and put his arms around her. "Come on, Charlotte. Leave the blasted dishes and let's get some sleep."

They lay close in a silent, perfect intimacy,

and she was wishing for a magic carpet on which they might fly away and leave everything behind forever, when he spoke.

"I can't make any sense out of your father. When those men — one of them is an expert on wetlands, he's worked all up and down the East Coast — when we were up there, they got nowhere with him. I hate to say this, but he made a fool of himself. His brother even told him so. With all the background experience he's had, his ignorance astounded them. Maybe you should go back home and plead with him. Let him really see what harm he's doing. Maybe he'll finally listen to you."

"I've already tried," she said.

"Well, try again. It's our only hope."

She had no choice but to concede. Still, she made a slight demurral. "I'm in the middle of a job at the Lauriers'. They may not like my asking for time off."

"What's more important right now, your job or all these debts that are piling up? My credit record, my good name! Talk of respect and reputation! What's going to be left of mine? And speaking of debts, I imagine that the Lauriers, too, would like to be paid for all their work on this damn job."

"I'll go next week and see what I can do," Charlotte said.

The peace was shattered.

"There's even talk in the town council of a lawsuit," Bill reported. "Nonperformance. Something the lawyers dreamed up. It seems that the town, because of the deal with us, missed out on another desirable property for the library. I don't know how far they would get with a suit, but in any case it means trouble and money that we haven't got."

In the white light of the kitchen's fluorescent bulbs, he looked haggard. And Charlotte was remembering the walkway, bordered with flowers, up to the door of the Dawes mill. It was queer, what trivial things you remembered. She thought that, sad as it must be never to have achieved anything, it was sadder still to have achieved everything and to lose it all.

"I've a letter here from your mother. Do you want to read it?"

"No, just tell me what it says."

Her head was full. It was as though the single subject that had for weeks now been whirling there as in a centrifuge was now hardening into a solid mass, prepared to burst.

"She reminds me that if I do reveal myself, there'll be an army of investigative reporters on the case. Somebody will remember the name, and somebody will talk, maybe the nurse at that doctor's office where you went first. Or people at the hospital in Boston. Yours wasn't a case they see every day. Your age, the family name, et cetera. It was barely eleven years ago, after all, not very long as memories go, especially memories for scandal. Elena's right, you know. She's very clever and always was. . . ."

So it never ends, Charlotte thought. She took a drink of water, paused for a long minute, and spoke. "I could bear it. If that were all that's at stake, I could. I committed no crime. I was only a victim, and at my age I should have learned enough to know there's no shame in being a victim. I do worry about you, though, and about Mama. You can't be absolutely sure you can keep her out of it."

"True enough. But you are still the chief reason why I haven't done what I want to do."

"I could bear it, I said. What I could not bear is your going to prison. What do you think that would do to me?"

"You would bear that, too, Charlotte."

"No, not that."

She was silent. Then after a minute she asked, "By the way, what is the latest news from Southeast Asia? Are they still hot on his trail?"

"Nothing lately, unless Cliff knows something. I don't know. We haven't talked in over a week." Bill reached for one of the cigarettes that Emmabrown kept near the table, remembered that he had given up smoking more than three years before, and put it back. "I blame myself. I should have confessed the whole business to Cliff long ago."

"Why didn't you?"

"I've told you. It was because of you, and your mother also. Beside that, the thought of telling Claudia how her son had died was appalling to me. And then after she herself died, it seemed no less appalling to admit to Cliff that I had allowed his wife to keep on hoping, while all the time I knew her hope was useless. I wanted to protect you all, and now look at the mess."

Lonely night-sounds jarred the recurring silence; a dog gave a short warning bark nearby, the furnace rumbled, and wood creaked as the house settled.

"Roger," Bill said abruptly, "I suppose he's still unforgiving? But that's a stupid question. Of course he is. Why wouldn't he be?"

There was such a cold, hollow place between her heart and her stomach!

"I don't know what he's going to do," she said.

"He's a very fine young man. . . . I hope this fiasco won't cause any upset between you."

He was asking a question and waiting for her to assure him that no sorrow would touch her.

"We'll be all right," she said. "Don't worry."

Of course they would be. Admittedly, the atmosphere during these long weeks had not been bright with the gaiety and celebration of lovers on the way to their wedding. But that was only a sorry, temporary hitch. They would survive it and get back to normal. Of course they would.

"The costs must be pretty large."

Did he want her to say they wouldn't be?

"I wish I had the money to settle everything myself, but as it is . . ." Bill's voice faded.

As it is, she thought, he is one step away from the end of the long downhill slide that began when the Dawes mill closed. This house would surely go; it had been mortgaged to the hilt. More importantly, Cliff's house, the old family home of the generations, would go, too, and that would really hurt. It would hurt them all deeply, even those who did not live in it.

Still, millions of people had lost everything they owned and gone on living. It wasn't the end of the world. Yet what good did it do a terminal cancer patient to tell him how many other patients beside him were suffering too?

They had reached the end of the discussion. Another word would only be repetition. And so once again, Charlotte went upstairs to sleep in her old room, now grown so strange. Early in the morning she would return to Boston.

"So nothing was accomplished," Roger said.

She had been back for three days, and on each of them their conversations had been held in mounting tension, ending with the same hopeless refrain.

"No, nothing," she repeated.

They were sitting in a coffee bar. It was Saturday afternoon on a graying fall day of warm, intermittent drizzle, a day, Charlotte thought as she gazed out through the steamy window, completely suited to their dismal mood.

He was staring with a most puzzled expression into her face. "What is it? What are you hiding?" he demanded.

"Nothing," she said. "I have told you a thousand times, nothing that you don't already know. You've talked to my father yourself."

"Yes, and all I've heard is a cock-and-bull story about the destruction of ecological balance, a story that he doesn't believe and you don't either."

"But could he perhaps be right? I have lately been thinking that. He really might be, after all."

Roger shook his head. "No. There's something missing here. And I — we — are victims of some deception. You can't convince me otherwise."

"I know you are desperate," she said. "Don't you see that I'm desperate for you? Is this what I want for you whom I love? I want to help you. At least I can pay the Lauriers' fee. They've already said I can pay it off gradually."

"What, live on cornflakes and canned soup while you're doing it? Don't be absurd."

The wedding, she thought. Did he mean that they would both be "living on cornflakes" together, or did he mean something else? And she felt her eyes begin to fill with tears, bitter ones made out of sorrow, humiliation, and anger.

The anger was surely not directed at her father. Nor could it be directed at Roger, who, from his point of view and from anyone's who did not know the situation, was justified in *his* anger. It was only fate, life, or whatever you wanted to call it, that enraged her — that and the fact that she was unable to do anything at all about it.

"Let's get out of here," Roger said.

They stood uncertainly on the street. Their afternoon, those precious hours away from work, was, for the first time, unplanned. They were in no mood now to fill it with love back in the apartment. All they really wanted to do was to get over this insurmountable hurdle, and they were baffled.

In their frustration they began to walk. Now and then they stopped to look at a store window, one filled with models of sailing ships and another filled by a huge aquarium. For a while they watched fish dart or idly glide among green grottoes and underwater caves.

"The colors. They look like jewels," Charlotte said, not caring about the fish, feeling only the growing distance between Roger and herself that was producing these inane comments.

They walked on past thinning trees and browning chrysanthemums, crossed a wide avenue, and stopped with a sudden jolt as Roger turned to her.

"You told me once that your father had a personal problem."

Ah, yes, her clumsy mistake! He remembered everything, even the most minute.

"It was completely unimportant. Nothing."

"It was enough to make you come tearing back from Europe."

"I didn't 'come tearing'! Why won't you drop the subject?"

"Because I think it has something to do with what's happened. Because you are not telling me the truth."

"I am!" Her voice rose, and a man passing by turned about to stare. "Oh, please, Roger, can't you drop it?" she pleaded.

"I may go bankrupt," he told her, "and you ask me why I don't drop it?"

He looked so grim! And they stood there on the street corner, just staring at each other.

Suddenly the drizzle turned into a downpour, and people ran for shelter.

"I want to go home," Charlotte said.

"No. We have to talk this out first. We'll go in there. It's the Isabella Gardner Museum."

A museum, she thought, when I just want to go home and shut the door.

They went in out of the weather to a courtyard. She was aware of sculptured stone, shrubbery, and Grecian heads. Wet and frightened, she trembled. And again for the sake of saying something, anything, to cut through this incredible hostility, she exclaimed, "The Grand Canal in Venice is lined with palazzos like this."

"What are we going to do?" he asked, ignoring the inappropriate remark.

"I don't know what you mean."

"I mean . . . how can we marry each other when we can't trust each other?"

"Oh, my God," she whispered.

He was telling her here in the hushed elegance of this place, this place that she would never forget, that they were losing each other. She knew that surely.

Once more she met his eyes, which were pleading and tense. Don't you know I would die for you? she thought.

But there are blood ties, and no one can possibly feel how strong they are until they are tested. Her father's life . . . Even Elena — even Elena! — all these years had guarded it. For with that recent letter to Bill she had meant to protect her daughter. Blood ties . . .

"If I allowed myself to think it," he said, "I'd think there must be another man."

"Am I really hearing you say that, Roger?"

"I haven't actually said it, have I? But if you cared about — us — you would let nothing keep you from being open with me. You insult my intelligence, you and your father, with an excuse that even a child might see through. No one believes it. The lawyers, Uncle Heywood, the Lauriers, too, no doubt. No one. But here you are, watching the ship head toward the rocks, and still you will not speak. What am I to make of you?"

"Make of me? I love you." Her lips quivered and she stopped.

"There's more to love than just making love," he said quietly. "No, I cannot continue like this, Charlotte. That shouldn't be hard to understand."

"Take me home," she said, "I need to get home."

"Then wait in the doorway while I find a cab."

Neither of them spoke in the taxi. The only sound was the rushing of traffic and rain.

That evening he telephoned. By his voice alone she knew that he was desolate, though his words were only a repetition of what he had so many times already said.

He wrote: *We have loved each other. Need I tell you what you have meant to me? Yet now I feel that I don't know you.* And he explained again how impossible it was for a relationship to exist alongside of such enormous, damaging secrecy, to which she gave the lame reply that was the only one she had to give.

After a week or two she heard no more. So she returned his little ring that she had not once removed from her finger. Now it was back in its velvet box, wrapped and addressed to the man who had given it. Then all contact came to an end in silence.

Often Charlotte wondered about herself. Remembering that first-love episode with Peter, her wounds and spasms of weeping, it seemed strange that she could be dry eyed and quiet now. Perhaps she was simply too shocked to accept the fact and finality. Perhaps she was like those stone-faced parents at the funeral of a child who has met some kind of violent death.

Indeed, Pauline thought it was like that. "A heart can be too broken to show itself," she said. She was being very kind and asked no questions, which was the greatest kindness of all.

She also said, "People heal, and work is the best healer."

Well, Charlotte knew that. She passed her days at the drawing board, thankful for having work. She often stayed there late, and was thankful again for being tired when she went home. She had no desire for company, and had no contacts, anyway, since Roger and she had been too busy and too engrossed with each other during the past year to keep any.

As for her father, she could but wonder. There was a sore and heavy ache in her chest when she thought of him, alone now in the neglected house in these dark, short days of fall.

Most painful of all for him, she knew, was his sense of responsibility for her break with Roger. Again and again she had to assure him that his own conviction for murder would be far worse for her.

She was filled with a vast loneliness. The city, too, seemed to hold a loneliness that she had never observed before. In its parks she looked at the statues of its great, of John Adams with the troubled face, and Garrison, solemn in his stone chair, with wet yellow leaves on his long coat. She stood there thinking, Well, he had his troubles too. And turning, she beheld an old man, not stone, but alive, sitting on a bench with his arm around his dog. Lonely. Lonely.

"Do come for Christmas dinner with us," Pauline urged. Since Charlotte was no longer "attached," she had again assumed her motherly role.

The prospect of a lively dinner with interesting people had been cheering, but there was no doubt that Charlotte must go home instead.

There were just the two of them in Kingsley. Cliff was dining with friends. Bill had made reservations for dinner at a country inn, one of those Revolutionary saltbox houses with a spinning wheel in the corner and pewter tankards on the mantel over the original fireplace. The moment they walked in, Charlotte recognized it as the place where they had stopped for lunch on their journey back from the hospital in Boston so long ago. No doubt her father had forgotten.

The tables were filled with elderly people who were probably there because they had no other place to go. Here, also, there was too much loneliness. . . .

They tried to talk of neutral subjects: Charlotte's work, the election, and Bill's neighbor, who was being transferred to Texas. But the talk was false and finally died away. Back home again, they watched carol singers on television and then, both admitting to being tired, went to bed.

In her old room Charlotte sat on the window seat looking out at the empty night. It came to life when she turned off the lamp; lights glittered from scattered houses on the nearest hill, and above the farthest darkness shone the stars. And she wondered where Roger was tonight. Last year at this time — yes, just around ten o'clock — they had taken a walk together, crunching through the snow.

She turned the lamp back on and readied the bed. Elena, knowing that Charlotte would be spending Christmas here, had sent her usual bounty in a glossy box. It lay now on the bed, spilling its contents in crackling tissue paper: a powder-blue cashmere sweater, an alligator handbag, and a silver picture frame with a note attached.

Darling, save this for the photo of your next lover. He's out there. He always is. Brighten up, and go find him.

All the agony that she had so determinedly controlled until now exploded and tore her apart. She burst into tears, lay facedown, and sobbed into the pillow, beating it with desperate fists. Nothing mattered anymore. If she could only lie there and die there! If only her heart would stop before morning!

After a while, a very long while, there were no more tears left. Her exhausted chest heaved in its final spasm, and she became aware of the cold. She got up, undressed, and crawled under the quilt.

In the morning she was calm again, but this calm was different from the contrived calm that she had had before. The outburst, the total collapse, had in some strange way cleared her head.

Some days later she went to Rudy and Pauline with a proposal. The firm had been commissioned to draw plans for a semisuburban housing project, where low-income families might purchase their own homes. She asked them now to let her work on it.

"I've been thinking and drawing pictures in my head. It seems to me that there should be a variety of facades, maybe four or five, all in harmony, but differing enough to be interesting. Maybe a few Victorian touches here and there?" She paused as if to wait for a reaction, but none came, and she continued. "Each front yard should have shrubs and flowers. I've seen pictures of English towns where even the most modest houses have a front garden. It makes a greenbelt up and down the street, makes it all seem larger.

What do you think?"

Pauline and Rudy looked at each other. They were smiling, and Rudy said gently, "We have, as a matter of fact, been wondering when you'd be ready to tackle another big job like that."

And Charlotte smiled back. "I'm ready now," she said.

THIRTEEN

Late in January, Charlotte had to return to Kingsley. Each of the brothers had been served with notice of foreclosure. The news, although long expected, came to her abruptly one morning when Bill telephoned, and for all the rest of that day she was filled with a melancholy nostalgia. With sad irony she thought how true, after all, were the trite icons of childhood and family life, the Halloween pumpkin at the door and the backyard barbecue on the Fourth of July.

Of the two homes Cliff's was the one with the more valid treasures, things not all of them worth as much in money as in remembrances of three generations. He was asking Charlotte to come and take whatever she wanted before the rest was sold.

"I really don't want to take anything," she told Pauline. "It's all too sad."

"Nevertheless, you should take whatever you can, those early American antiques you described, and the paintings —"

"There's no place for them in my life," Charlotte objected.

"There will be. You won't always live in a tight little flat. When you're married —"

"No," she objected again.

Pauline smiled. "All right. When you're a prominent architect living in a house of your own design —"

Charlotte threw up her hands. "Okay, you win. I'll go next week."

Snow was melting on the roadsides. Thick and grainy, it slid into puddles on Kingsley streets, where people walked with open collars, as if this were April instead of a January thaw. Over the landscape there lay an air of weariness, which was certainly not dissipated, when she arrived home, by the sight of cartons in the back hall, filled with discards.

"Amazing how much junk you can collect in twenty-five years," Bill said. "Thought I might as well get to work on it gradually. Emmabrown's taking all your toys for her grandchildren, unless of course there's anything you want."

"Only a few books, *Charlotte's Web*, *Little Women*, stuff like that. I'll sort them."

"Don't bother. I'll sort them for you. I'll know what you want to keep." Bill smiled. "I ought to know."

Yes, he ought. He was the one who had bought the books, had read them to her before she had learned to read, and even long afterward; summer afternoons and winter evenings had been good times for reading aloud.

Heavyhearted, she inquired about Cliff. "Do you still not speak to each other?"

"As little as possible. What is there to say?"

Indeed, there was not much to say anymore between these brothers, or between Bill and herself, so their little supper was eaten in the kitchen, while *Tosca*, playing on the stereo, removed the need for a conversation that could only be depressing.

After a while Charlotte got up and went outside to look again at her old familiar hills. The sky was filled with whorls and shreds of dark clouds, deep gray-blue over glints of a cold silver sun about to disappear in the west. The evening felt ominous to her, although that was, of course, only her mood, the mood of the place and the circumstances. And she went back inside.

That night the rain began. It might have come on slowly, but by the time it woke her, it had the force of an open faucet splashing into a half-filled tub. Peering out, she could see water streaming down the roof of the porch and could hear it gurgling in the leaders. An eerie wind, roaring and shrieking, wrenched the apple tree near her window. It seemed to Charlotte that something extraordinary was happening.

She went back to bed, but the noise outside kept her awake and, in a sense, watchful, as though at any moment that noise would attack the house, which was surely absurd. Yet, dark and early as it was, she got up again and dressed.

It was just past five o'clock by the kitchen clock. She was putting a pot of coffee on the stove when Bill, also fully dressed, came downstairs.

"A real northeaster," he said. "Wind must be thirty miles an hour. This'll take down a lot of trees, I'm afraid."

He sounded almost cheerful, and she thought she understood why. Just as during a war people forget their personal problems, so a great storm unites people against the common menace. And they waited for daylight while Charlotte made pancakes and Bill fiddled with the radio.

When full morning came, they looked out. The ground, now almost bare of snow, was covered with the debris of broken branches. Few cars passed, and only one neighbor had emerged as yet to struggle on the walk with his chow, who cringed against the rain that drenched his orange hair. Down the sloping street a stream fled toward the river.

Later, Emmabrown telephoned. "It looks bad out, Charlotte. Your dad won't mind if I don't come today? There's plenty of food in the freezer. Take out the chicken pie. Put a spoon of vanilla ice cream on the apple pudding, your dad likes that. I'll get to see you before you go back, maybe even tonight, when it lets up. It can't keep on like this all day. Never does."

Charlotte thought, I'll miss Emmabrown. I'll miss many things. There's altogether too much parting and giving up in life. However, there's no use being philosophical, is there? Better to go to work.

She had brought a briefcase full of notes and sketches for the low-cost housing project. And now, laying these out on the dining-room table, she began to resume where she had left off the day before. But concentration did not come easily today. There was, to start with, a pervasive sense of uneasy change in the house. Added to that was the drone of the radio, to which Bill seemed to be fastened in the kitchen.

Above all, there was the rain; eventually, by the fourth or fifth hour, she was used to the monotonous background splatter, although intermittently a violent gust of wind would send it drumming against the win-

472

dow, demanding attention. She could not remember when or whether she had ever seen such rain.

Once Bill came wandering in and, looking over her shoulder at her work, asked a few suitable questions, telling her yet again how proud of her he was. Yet she knew that his heart was not in his words, and his thoughts were elsewhere.

"I wonder how Cliff is doing," she said.

"The same as we are," he replied, and wandered back into the kitchen.

He had infected her with his restlessness. She got up and, going to the window, looked out upon the water-soaked afternoon. The wind that had so furiously been whipping the trees was now visibly dying down, while the rain, impossible as it might have seemed that morning, was actually increasing. Like a screen or curtain it was almost opaque, so that, before Charlotte's eyes, the landscape was dimmed like a faded photograph.

As if mesmerized, she was still standing there when Bill came back with a cup of coffee for her and a grim report.

"All hell's broken loose upriver. The Smithtown Bridge is submerged, and the highways are closed. The Bradley Road collapsed, and two cars went into the river. Five dead. Eleven inches so far." They stood silently at the window until he resumed, worrying, "The river will be rising over flood level here, too, if it doesn't let up soon. Last time it flooded was about fifty years ago, wasn't it? I don't remember."

Emmabrown phoned again from Kingsley, talking fast. "It's a mess here. You wouldn't believe it. They've got firefighters running extra buses to take people to shelters in the schools and churches. But no shelter for me! I'm loading the car, overloading it, with grandkids, three dogs, and a hamster, going to my relatives uphill toward Walker. If we don't leave this minute, we won't be able to get out. Other side of Main Street, cars are already sunk up to the windows. Take care. I'll keep in touch."

"I'm calling Cliff," Charlotte said.

"What for? He's all right. He's as high up as we are."

"I'm calling him all the same."

She had barely spoken when a terrific crash blasted in the backyard; the windows rattled, and in the front hall Elena's fancy crystal chandelier jangled frantically.

"A tree's down," Bill cried. "Look! The ash tree's gone."

There it lay. Over a century old, taller than the house that it shaded, it was stricken and fallen. Its roots, ripped out of the soil, were a soldier's torn, bleeding wound, and the topmost branches, reaching as far as the fence line, were his pitiful, broken arms.

"Thank God," Bill said in awe, "it fell away from the house. Imagine, the ground's too sodden to hold it up." Then, squinting through the rain, he reported, "The telephone line went with it too. Look."

A moment later the lights went out and the room turned dark blue. The furnace, which had been humming, went silent. All up and down the street the lights were out.

"Power lines must be down all over," Bill said with some lessening of his first exhilarating sense of adventure. "Let's get the candles and flashlights out right now before night."

They ate cold chicken pie by candlelight. The house grew gradually colder. Charlotte, trying to read by candlelight in sweater and outer jacket, gave up and, having anyway been awake since before five that morning, decided to go to bed.

"Well, at least they promised that it would stop by tomorrow morning," Bill said cheerfully.

It did not. At seven o'clock the rain was still coming in cascades and cataracts. The sky was drowned. The ground was a waste of barren brown grass spotted with islands of mushy snow.

News came from the little transistor radio in the kitchen. People were being rescued from rooftops, this was the worst calamity in they weren't able to hear how many years, and the governor had declared a state of emergency.

"Thirty-six hours now, and no letup," Bill said. "No letup in sight either."

Again, Charlotte spread out her work on the dining-room table. For a few minutes Bill watched her, considerately refraining from interruption, then walked away and went down again to the radio in the car. After a while she heard him come up, rummaging for some cold food in the kitchen. He did not know what to do with himself. And she went to him, saying gently, "Why don't you just give up worrying? There's nothing you can do about this, so you might as well accept it."

"I wish I had work to do as you do."

"Get a book. Sit down and pass the time with a book."

"No," he said suddenly, "I can't sit still. I'm going out."

"Out! For heaven's sake, where to?"

"Just out. I need to move around."

"In this torrent, this — this tempest? This

476

all-time record? Are you crazy?"

"I'm not crazy. I just need to go."

She stood there while he pulled on his boots and fastened his raincoat.

"You don't know what you're doing," she burst out. "There are fallen wires all over. You'll be electrocuted, if you aren't drowned first."

"I'll watch where I'm going. I know what I'm doing."

"Then I'm going with you," she said.

"No, no, not you!"

"I'm as determined as you are, Dad."

Yes, she thought, I know what you're thinking. And following him, she did not have to question what direction he would take. She knew that too.

From the door he turned left toward the river. Except for a huddle of sodden, pathetic sparrows in some naked shrubs, there was no life on the street. There was no one, either, at the top of the bluff, where they halted to look down on the darkened river. Tons of earth, and the Dawes mill with it, had toppled and washed into the torrent. The dirty mountain of trash had been swept away, to be carried along with the devastation from the north. A crate of drowned chickens, a dead cow, a live dog struggling to swim, branches, broken lumber, a lone tire — all whirled downstream. Behind the place where the mill had stood, the land stretched flat and spongy under a shallow film of muddy brown water.

"Scraped almost clean," Bill said, as if to himself.

Rivulets ran down their yellow slickers as they stood. Their boots slid dangerously, and the rain beat into their faces. Here was nature gone wild, and fear gone wild within them both.

Charlotte was looking at Bill's woolen scarf, the same brown-and-yellow plaid scarf he had been winding around his throat for as long as she remembered. Now it was inside out with the name tag showing clearly. Elena's meticulous name tags and monograms . . .

A helicopter clattered overhead. "Rescue work," Bill said. "I ought to help."

"You can't fly a helicopter."

"There's other work. The radio said that the deputy sheriffs have called for volunteers. I'll drive the car as far as it can go and get into a rowboat. They have boats ready."

"If you go, I will too."

"No, you go home."

"I told you I'm as determined as you are, Dad."

She was thinking that she would not let

him out of her sight, for who knew how long — ?

That field behind the mill was almost bare.

In separate boats they went downriver through Kingsley and beyond. In Charlotte's boat, along with a brawny male, there was another female, her former swimming coach, still young and strong. Together, they hauled in a stranded mother and child, reached for a terrified cat in a carrying case, and rescued two exhausted boys who had themselves been rescuing others all day. They worked their mission, going six miles downstream, until it was nearly dark. Only then, with the rain still beating down, did they return.

Bill was waiting at the car with Cliff, Charlotte was pleased to see, beside him. Perhaps this experience today had softened them.

"Cliff has nothing in the house but crackers," Bill said, "so I invited him to go back with us."

She smiled. "Good. I'll make sandwiches. Without hot coffee you'll have to make do with beer. Or whiskey might be more like it in this weather."

At home they sat in their coats. Candlelight that in other situations could cast so lovely a glow was now merely melancholy.

There was no pleasure in the simple meal. They were only hungry and very tired.

Suddenly Bill spoke to Cliff. "You saw our place, I suppose."

"Yes. Nothing much left of it."

"That acreage in back," Bill began, and stopped.

Charlotte's heart began to pound. It was uncanny that she could be so absolutely sure of what he was about to say! And she looked at her father, asking a question with her eyes.

"All right, Charlotte," he said. "The time has come. And, Cliff, I have something to tell you. Listen."

The candles were almost burned down, and Charlotte got up to replace them. In the fresh flare of light the men's faces came clear, with all their fear and sadness and disbelief revealed.

The muscles in Cliff's cheeks were taut. At last he said, "If you had told me this while Claudia was alive, I would have been — I would have wanted —"

"You would have wanted to kill me," Bill said.

Cliff struggled for words. "I can't imagine what it would have done to her. She lived to the very last for his return."

"I knew that. And each time her hope

turned out to be false, I felt her agony."

Cliff interrupted. "How she suffered because of him! He was a devil."

"A devil? No, it's more complicated. I'm no psychologist, so I can't explain why people do the evil things they do. I only know that it's more complicated than that."

Charlotte, feeling a deep compassion, looked from one face to the other. "So now you understand," she told Cliff, "why all the plans fell through."

"I understand." Cliff rose, went to his brother, embraced him, and spoke softly. "Whatever happens, we're here for you. We'll do —" Then he choked on the words.

On the third morning the rain began to slacken. Faint light seemed about to break through the sky, so that looking upward one no longer felt as if one were at the bottom of an aquarium.

Cliff went to the car phone to call a man he knew at the newspaper office. When he came back upstairs, he was very sober.

"They found a body on the edge of the property. It got washed up near the road. That's all I know."

The three sat down. I'm going to be sick, Charlotte thought, and dared not meet her father's eyes; he was studying the carpet at his feet.

Cliff's preliminary cough was false, a sound made to fill a blank space in time and to cover his emotion. "This was no ordinary northeaster. They say that twenty-five billion gallons flowed into the river. Not million; *billion*," he repeated.

No one answered because no one cared. The rain had ceased, making them aware of another kind of silence, for they had become accustomed to the rush and spatter. Now past the window lay waste and quiet water, while beyond the wintry trees, down the hill and in the stunned town, lay terror, a great beast waiting.

"I guess I'll go home," Cliff said. "If I can find a way to get into town and find out more, I will. The river won't be rising now, and with my wading boots I might get down Main Street to the paper's office."

"Thanks," Bill said.

Charlotte, too, had to fill the emptiness, even with trivia. "They'll be out working on the power lines, I'm sure. They do that right away in a disaster area, don't they? So maybe we'll be able to use the stove soon. I'll make some coffee."

"Thanks," Bill said again, there being nothing else to say.

He took a book and sat at the window in the brightening light, pretending to read. Charlotte went back to the dining-room table, on which her work was still spread, and tried to fix her mind on it. Toward noon, when the lamps turned on, she went to the kitchen and made coffee and cereal, which she carried in to Bill.

"Dad," she said gently, "you need to eat, or you won't be able to — to do anything for yourself. Besides, we don't know anything yet about that body, whose it was or —"

"I'm only thinking about you. You have a career, I know, I know. But you will be alone."

"Look!" she cried. "The telephone people are in the yard already. Isn't it amazing how promptly they get to work on repairs?"

"You don't have to exert yourself with all this cheerful talk to divert me. We're not fooling each other." And he gave her the old "fatherly" smile.

"Okay, Dad. I'll let you be. Maybe I'll go to the kitchen and do something about dinner, something hot for a change."

Bless Emmabrown, she thought, as she searched the freezer and found a beef stew. There were enough greens in the refrigerator for a salad. They would eat in the kitchen.

The dining room was too big and dreary for the two of them in their despair. Nevertheless, in spite of the despair, she moved efficiently about the kitchen, mixing a salad dressing according to Claudia's recipe. Biscuits would go well with the stew. These, too, she would make as she had learned from Claudia. Bill needed sustenance. . . .

She had just tied on an apron when the doorbell rang. Cliff, she thought, going weak inside, Cliff with the rest of the news, God help us. And she opened the door.

"Hello," said Roger.

For an instant she thought she might be mistaken, that this man only resembled Roger, and she would be making a fool of herself if —

"Are you going to let me in?" he asked.

She began to cry. He stepped inside, closed the door behind him, and took her into his arms. She felt his hands on her shoulder blades, under her braid, stroking and stroking; he was kissing her tears, whispering her name, and talking in broken sentences.

". . . drove fifteen miles north . . . couldn't get through the town, all swamped . . . came south, back way . . . disaster on television . . . tried Pauline . . . knew how much I loved you . . . what a damn fool I am."

When Bill came into the hall, they broke apart, and Roger held out his hand, saying frankly, "You're shocked to see me."

"Well," began Bill.

"All these months I kept thinking of her. I was so angry. . . . She wouldn't tell me. . . . She saw what was happening and wouldn't tell me. . . . I couldn't stand it, so we fought. . . ." Breathless, he raised his hand to prevent interruption. "But when this happened here, people homeless, people dead, I had to come. All of a sudden I was frantic. If something happened to her . . . I got a speeding ticket on the way. Oh, God, Charlotte, can we be all right again? Can we?"

"It certainly looks as if you can," Bill said. "But you find us here at a strange time. There are things happening —"

Somebody was coming up the walk again. Bill opened the door.

"Bill," Cliff said, not even seeing Roger, "it is. There's no mistake. The wristwatch has *Cliff to Ted* on it. My birthday present."

So here it was, here after all these dread-filled years. Charlotte, searching her father's face, saw no expression. It was as if he were under anesthesia. Perhaps that was nature's mercy for the wounded.

A moment later Bill recovered. "If you can just keep in touch for me, Cliff. It seems to be the day of reckoning."

"Tomorrow, more likely. They'll need some time to reach any conclusions."

Suddenly the men became aware of Roger. Cliff was the first to speak.

"We're all glad to see you, Roger. It's been too long."

And Bill added, "Yes, very glad. Very. You'll stay overnight, I hope? I'll stay at Cliff's."

Conservative as he was, Charlotte knew, he wouldn't want to be in the house while his daughter slept with Roger. Nevertheless, and typically, he wished his daughter joy.

"So we'll be going. Give him a good dinner, and, Charlotte, you may tell him the whole story."

When the two men had gone, Charlotte and Roger sat down on a sofa. With his arms around her and her head resting on his shoulder, she began.

"When I was in Italy, my mother told me . . ."

"If they find anything," she concluded, "he will be under suspicion of murder."

"And if he really had done it, he would have had good reason," Roger said darkly.

"Ah, yes! But it doesn't work that way. You're the only one to know this beside Cliff, and he found out just yesterday. Don't you know that I would have told you long ago, except that it wasn't my secret?"

"I'm ashamed. I talk so much about 'understanding,' and then, when I should have understood, I didn't. I was afraid to walk in the Common, because I might see you and you would not talk to me. Still, in another way, I hoped I would see you."

"I was so ashamed that you had all these debts because of me. And you still have them."

"My firm — Uncle Heywood — finally paid them to save the firm's name, and mine. So now I owe him. But that's not so bad," Roger said quickly. "I pay back a little every week."

No wonder, thought Charlotte, his aunt Flo pretended not to recognize me on Newbury Street. And if there had not been a flood, she thought, he would not be here! Again the pain of loss swept through her, as she turned her head now to look at him. He asked her what was wrong, what she was thinking, and she told him.

"No, no," he said, "I would have been here anyway. You can ask Pauline. I met her accidentally last week, and I — well, you can ask her. She told me you were about to go home for a few days. I wanted to see you and beg you to come back, to wear the ring again. Look, I've even brought it with me. Give me your hand."

So they talked all through what remained of the day, had a small supper, and talked some more until it grew late.

"There's only a single bed again," Charlotte told him.

"I rather like that. Perhaps we should even have one when we're married." He laughed. And then, turning serious, asked quietly, "What time can you get the newspaper here in the morning?"

"It's delivered early, only now on account of the flood, there's no telling."

"If it doesn't come, you'll give me your father's boots, and I'll go into town for it."

But Cliff got there first. Waving the paper in hand, he cried out the news.

"Safe! Safe! We're home free! Here, take a look."

All bent over the newspaper to read the lead column: "ACCUSED RAPIST FOUND DEAD. . . . Ted Marple, long sought overseas, drowned. . . . Positively identified. . . . Fleeing with passport and large sum. . . . Apparently taking a shortcut to avoid roads.

. . . Suitcase, backpack, and some extra shoes."

Charlotte asked, "No name?"

"No name. And nothing on the bill clip."

They must have been the only things in the house except the stove that weren't labeled. Elena was probably rattled because she was leaving just then.

"You're sure?" Charlotte asked.

Cliff nodded. "I've been downtown half the night, been everywhere from my friend at the paper to the medical examiner's office, asking a hundred questions. It's only natural, isn't it? I'm so distraught that they had to tolerate me. He was my wife's son, after all, and I loved the boy."

Charlotte felt the tears that come with a wide, wide grin. "And Dad?" she asked.

"You can imagine. I made him go to bed. He hadn't slept for two nights."

"A whole lot more than two nights, I'm thinking."

"I don't know how he's stood up under this. Now I'm beginning to remember things, times I wondered about his moods, silence, avoidance — things like that."

"The terror he must have felt!"

"Yes. Well, I'll be getting back home. They're sending reporters. I'm going to tell them as little as I can. It's all past and it needs to be forgotten, so people can get on with ordinary life."

Then Roger spoke. "You realize, don't you, that we can get on with our project now?"

Cliff smiled as he left. "I've already thought of that," he said.

Sunshine out of a pure sky, with not a drop of rain in sight, lay over the breakfast table. Roger began reading aloud from the paper, but Charlotte barely heard. She was filled with a vast thankfulness, unburdened by secrets.

"I feel light," she said, "as if I had wings, as if I could fly."

He looked over at her. "You can," he said. "We'll fly together."

EPILOGUE: 1997

A wooden fence enclosed the vast area in which, seen from the hilltop, tiny toy men were raising toy structures. Lumber trucks and cement mixers were moving in and out. Along the riverfront a brick wall, high enough to keep the next flood away, was being completed.

Despite all this activity the final plan was clearly visible: the village square at one end, and the library, already partly finished, at the other. Between these lay an expanse of greenery, sprouting now in the spring sunshine. Where once a gloomy swamp had stretched lay a large, clear pond, fringed with willows.

"Kingsley never had a real park," Bill said, "so I thought this would be my personal present to the town. I've got people coming this week to design it, with a rose plot and walks and benches, places to relax and watch the ducks." And shading his eyes, he looked out toward the place where once the textile mill had stood. "The march of time," he said. "Well, you two have to get back to Boston, and I've got things to do. See you soon."

They watched him walk away and get into his car.

"Even his voice has a jaunty lilt these days. Have you noticed?" Roger remarked.

"Of course. He's Big Bill again. Emmabrown says he has a girlfriend, a very nice woman, she says. I'm glad. It's about time too."

"That secret was too heavy for him to be thinking of anything else, poor man. Hey, it's late, Charlotte. We'd better start." And as she still stood unmoving, he teased, "Can't you tear yourself away from your brainchild?"

It was not that. She was thinking there, or seeing, rather, the whole long ribbon of her life unrolling to this place and moment.

"What are you thinking?" Roger asked, as he always did.

"I don't know. Just maundering, I guess, about how lucky I am."

"I'll say. Being a name already at your age, with a feature in *Design and Engineering*! Besides all this." And he waved his arm toward the activity below.

"Not that. I'm glad about it, of course I am, but really more for the rest of you than for myself. It's true I wanted the glory, but suddenly it's not all that important to me."

"What is, then?"

"Do you need to ask?"

"No," he said with that lovely smile of his, that illumination that said everything. "Sweet Charlotte, let's go home."

We hope you have enjoyed this Large Print book. Other Thorndike Press or Chivers Press Large Print books are available at your library or directly from the publishers.

For more information about current and upcoming titles, please call or write, without obligation, to:

Thorndike Press
P.O. Box 159
Thorndike, Maine 04986 USA
Tel. (800) 257-5157

OR

Chivers Press Limited
Windsor Bridge Road
Bath BA2 3AX
England
Tel. (0225) 335336

All our Large Print titles are designed for easy reading, and all our books are made to last.